The Melded Child

Jane Routley

Bernarra Press

Also by Jane Routley

The Dion Chronicles

Mage Heart

Fire Angels

Aramaya

The Three Sisters

DEDICATION

To Terry

The Melded Child

is published by Bernarra Press

Melbourne Australia

Published as an ebook by Clan Destine Press

Copyright © 2017 by Jane Routley

www.janeroutley.com

Edited by Terry Cooper and Seán O Séaghdha

Cover by Willsin Rowe

ISBN: 978-0646-97136-0

ACKNOWLEDGMENTS
Thanks to my partner Terry Cooper.
Thanks also to Lindy Cameron of Clan Destine Press for her help
and patience, to Sean O Seaghdha for his help in proofing and to
Russell B. Farr and Liz Grzby of Ticonderoga and Liz Kemp for
their advice and imput.

.

Three children born of life force,

A bridge from death to life,

From imbalance to harmony.

The warbird flies at their command

To rein in the people of the dragon.

A demon fire that burns toward Ermora

Yields to their quenching.

A melded child of their making

Is born to rule the dragon,

To bring harmony in clasped hands.

Prologue

Pels - a small island in the Archipelago

Alyx Verdey sat in cover on the cliff top watching the Mirayan mercenaries disembarking from the three ships on the beach below.

"Alyx. What are you doing here?" hissed a voice. "Your mother will kill me. Where's Didier?"

Yani Tari, Alyx's aunt, slid into the bushes beside her. Alyx nodded toward the troops on the beach below.

"Look at them. Two hundred soldiers and two whole phalanxes of mages. And all to fight a community with less than 50 warriors. Mirayan bullies! What makes them think they have the right to do this? They're not even Archipelagans."

Yani shrugged. "You know it's all about might. If we Tari weren't here to keep the peace, all the other tribes in the Archipelago would be acting like this too. Look at the Seagani and the Mori. Or the Dani and the Ishtakis."

"At the least the rest of us wouldn't have the cheek to call it civilisation. And think we're somehow superior."

Yani laughed. "Come on. Most of them aren't like that

anymore. Since the Tari have returned to their Guardian role, most of the Mirayans have settled down to live quietly beside us natives.

Alyx scowled. "This lot haven't."

"Every barrel has bad apples. And the Pels islanders did make a treaty with the Mirayans."

"Stupid fools. They should have known this is how the Mirayans operate. First it's a treaty and then suddenly the Mirayans announce that they're in control. Why didn't you kick them all out of the Archipelago ten years ago when you came back?"

"And where else would they go? It's not the Tari way to put people in the way of harm. Anyway the Mirayans have been here over forty years, even over a hundred if you count the merchant families. Some of them count themselves as Archipelagan now."

"They mess up their own country so now they come here and mess up ours. Great."

Yani grinned wryly, shaking her head. "So a few Mirayans are bad. That doesn't make them all bad. And well you know it, Alyx Verdey-Tari. And well I know that if I sat here and argued with you till the sea froze over, I'd never get you to admit it. So why don't we just get back to the others? Didier will be fretting and the fun's about to start. The Mirayans are forming up for the attack."

Alyx was aware of a stab of anger, but somehow, by the time her aunt had finished speaking, the anger had flowed away and she was grinning too. Yani was impossible to get into a fight with. Strange that the world's only Tari warrior should be so peaceable and easy-going.

"Are Tari allowed to see this kind of thing as fun?" she needled her aunt. "I mean it's to do with warfare, isn't it?"

"My, my, we are in a prickly mood today, aren't we?" said Yani cheerfully. "You forget. I'm the Raven. My business is warfare. And the quicker it starts, the quicker it's over. Come on."

Crouching low, she crept away through the seagrass tussocks. Alyx took a last look at the view. Beyond the beach the placid sea shone with a smooth, silky sheen and along the horizon a couple of nearby islands showed as dark blue smudges against the lighter blue of the sky. This was a beautiful island and a lovely day.

Too lovely for warfare.

Following Yani, Alyx crept through the heath on the cliff top, into the forest beyond. Here the trees, gnarled and stunted by the sea wind, smelt spicy and salty. In the clearing where everyone was gathered, Didier, Alyx's mentor and bodyguard, was standing, hands on his hips. He scowled at Alyx for giving him the slip, but all he said was, "You are too clever for your own good, Forest Child."

His forbearance made Alyx feel guilty. She knew it was irresponsible of her to put herself in danger. She was half-Mori and, as the Forest Child, heir to the Mori chieftainship. If the Mirayans had taken her prisoner, Didier would have sacrificed his life to rescue her. He'd already risked himself often enough for her. To change the subject Alyx asked him if her other aunt, Marigoth, had arrived.

"Not yet," he said grimly. He turned to Yani. "Raven, without her we are undermanned. It could be dangerous for the Forest Child."

"Undermanned? How?"

"Two Tari mages against so many Mirayans."

"We've taken more with less," shrugged Yani. "Don't worry Didier. Mari always makes it. She just likes to make a big entrance."

Didier grunted. He had little time for frivolous people like Marigoth.

"We could stay to the back if you're not happy," Alyx suggested.

"True. But if we do that, you will not be able to lead the parley."

"I don't mind," said Alyx hopefully. She had horrible visions of making a fool of herself in front of the Mirayans. Could it be that she was a little afraid of them? Never!

"Your mother wishes you to have this experience," said Didier firmly.

"I can't see how I am going to benefit from talking to a pack of stupid Mirayans."

Yani grinned at her.

"You'll be glad once you've done it. Who knows? Maybe you'll talk some sense into them."

"Pigs might fly," muttered Didier

They had come to the edge of the forest. Beyond was the place where the end of a ravine widened out to become a field. An excellent place for the meeting of two armies.

"I hate Mirayans," protested Alyx.

She should have held her tongue.

Two Tari mages, Syndal and Mathaman, were sitting on horseback just in the shadow of the forest, looking very otherworldly with their high-cheek-boned Tari faces and their long fair hair moving slightly in the breeze. They turned and looked reproachfully at Alyx. Oh no! Now she was in for a lecture.

Sure enough, the male mage, Mathaman said, "Hatred does no honour to the life spirit. Especially if you hate people you don't know, just because they happen to be of a certain group."

Inwardly, Alyx protested that they were only here because this group of Mirayans were acting like thugs, attacking the peaceful island of Pels in order to extract taxes from them. Why shouldn't you hate such people? The life spirit could be so unreasonable.

But as she was about to protest, someone came up behind her.

"How can you hate Mirayans, my darling?" said Aunt Marigoth. She tweaked Alyx's cheek. "You don't know any."

Marigoth had the same high-cheek-boned beauty and fair hair as the other Tari mages but there was nothing otherworldly about her. She was just too cheerful. Without waiting for Alyx's answer, she breezed over to the horses and leapt up onto one with an ease that indicated the assistance of magic.

"Finally!" sighed Yani. "Where have you been, Mari?"

"Watching the funny men on the beach," said Marigoth

lightly. She smiled reminiscently. "Such nasty words they use when they trip over. Shouldn't we be getting into place? The mages are coming up the ravine. Come on. We won't make a splendid impression if we look hurried. We want to look calm and eternal." She urged her horse into motion and the other Tari mages followed her.

"Brat!" said Yani, shaking her head, which was the only thing anyone could do about Marigoth. She turned to Alyx.

"Come on. Onto your horse."

"Do I have to do this?" muttered Alyx. "I don't like Mirayans. I've got *reason* not to like Mirayans."

"You are heir to the chieftainship of the Mori," said Didier tartly. "Nobody cares what you like. If Mirayans must be spoken to, you must do it."

"I know, I know." Alyx had heard this argument before. Endlessly.

"You don't have to like them to speak with them," said Yani, giving Alyx a quick hug before she helped her up onto the horse. She might be a warleader, but she was an excellent aunt too. "In fact, it might work better if you don't."

Waiting between the mages at the head of ravine, Alyx was struck by how normal everything seemed. Gulls still circled in the blue sky. The breeze still smelt deliciously of salt and dry seagrass.

She had never actually seen the Tari guardians in action and, wouldn't you know it, now that she finally had the chance, she was too worried about making a fool of herself in front of the Mirayans to enjoy it. Thank you very much, Mother! Once, just once she'd like to do something that wasn't training for her future.

She heard the clattering of the troop's armour well before she saw the Mirayans. Time seemed to have slowed down. *Will these men never reach us?*

Then the leading troop, a shield wall of men surrounding the ten mages that always acted together as a phalanx, came out of the ravine to find Alyx's group arrayed across their path: the mages, Marigoth, Mathaman and Syndal in Tari green, the warrior, Yani Tari in her Raven's black and Alyx herself, a dark-haired girl with Tari features and a Mori warrior at her side.

The Mirayans faltered for only a moment before they came marching onwards. The mage at the head of the phalanx lifted his magic crystal.

"Oh lovely! They want to fight. Can I go first?" cried Marigoth.

"Hurry up then," said Syndal tartly, as a blast of magic shrieked out of the Mirayan's crystal.

Alyx wanted to duck but held firm. The blue fire hit something with a thud and the air all round them wavered.

A defensive shield! *When did the Tari set that up?*

Marigoth made a wide gesture with her arms.

The soldiers surrounding the mages collapsed, falling to the ground like scattered logs and lying there.

That's scared them! thought Alyx with ferocious satisfaction.

"Concentrate!" shouted their leader, pointing the crystal at Marigoth.

Marigoth gestured again and the crystal shattered. The Mirayans recoiled but recovered, lifting their arms to send out individual blasts of magic.

"You have to admit they're a brave lot," muttered Yani.

"Lady, there's another troop coming up," cried Didier.

He was right. Another phalanx of mages surrounded by more troops was just appearing at the top of the ravine.

"Mari, finish them off, will you?" cried Yani irritably. "There are more coming."

"As you wish!" Marigoth gestured a third time and the whole phalanx of mages fell down.

"You really shouldn't play with them like that," said Mathaman. He too made a wide, sweeping gesture and the front three rows of the next troop fell down.

"You two have no sense of style," grumbled Marigoth.

Syndal humphed and gestured at the crystal bearer of the following phalanx, shattering his crystal. With a second gesture she made another three lines of troops, including the first five mages in the second phalanx, fall down and lie still.

The rest of the soldiers took one look at the still bodies that littered the ground ahead and took to their heels.

"Over a bit quickly, don't you think?" said Marigoth.

Syndal looked at her and, for the first time, grinned.

"You're such a big, bad sorceress!"

Marigoth stuck her tongue out at her.

"I'll just go make sure no one's hurt," said Mathaman. "Is one of you going to cover me?"

"Yep!" said Marigoth.

That was impressive! Alyx looked at the field below them. She knew that the Tari were much stronger than other mages, but she'd never seen it so clearly demonstrated before. If you didn't know that all the soldiers were only sleeping, you'd think something terrible had happened.

"That was quick!" muttered Yani. "Mathaman, get back here! Get ready, Alyx. Here comes the leader."

"Oh look, it's that Guilius Appius," Marigoth grinned impishly. "How red his face is! If he's not careful he'll be carried off by apoplexy."

The Mirayan leader was striding up the ravine towards them at an impressive pace for such a heavily armoured man. His two armoured companions trailed behind, staring with wide, scared eyes at the bodies on either side.

"The Guardians! What an honour!" sneered Appius. "To what do I owe the pleasure of your company?"

Yani nodded at Alyx.

"This island is now under our protection," said Alyx.

Appius glared at her.

"What? Are you going to add insult to injury by letting some little girl lord it over me? A half-breed no less."

Alyx felt herself flushing.

"Have a care, Appius!" snapped Marigoth.

"You Guardians never hurt anyone. Just humiliate them and take away their livelihood."

"A livelihood based on violence," said Mathaman.

"How do you justify that?"

"Mathaman!" said Yani sternly. "Alyx, proceed."

"Oh, Alyx, is it?" snarled the Mirayan. "I've heard of you. Alyx Verdey, brat of the great whore of the Mori. Was Eldene Verdey really your father?"

"Shut up!" shouted Alyx, reaching for her sword. Didier grabbed her wrist.

Suddenly Appius rose into the air as if an invisible hand had grabbed the front of his armour. He swiped furiously at the air in front of him.

"I told you to have a care," said Marigoth. "I never kill anyone but I can give pain."

Appius fell sprawling to the ground. His two companions rushed to his side, but Appius was back up on his feet with impressive speed.

"That was not an action of the life spirit," muttered Syndal, under her breath.

"No, but I really enjoyed doing it," replied Marigoth

"We are here on a legal mission," shouted Appius. "This island has a treaty with Prince Ipius of Ishtak. Yet it refuses to pay the taxes it promised!"

"The elders wish to void the treaty," said Yani. "They say they do not see any sign of Prince Ipius' protection from one year to the next, except for tax time. He has done nothing about the pirates, so they've decided to deal with them themselves. If the prince wishes to send an envoy to sort out his differences with the islanders, we will not seek to stop him. But the Guardians will not countenance any fighting on Pels. It's an offence to the life spirit."

"How is the Prince supposed to assert his authority without force of arms?"

Yani shrugged. "Is authority that needs force truly authority? If the Prince wants help in his negotiations, I'm quite happy to give it. Otherwise this is not our problem. In an hour or so your men will wake up but if you try another attack on the island it will end just the same way. Save yourselves the trouble."

She turned her horse around with obvious contempt. Alyx followed her lead.

"Fuck you!" screamed Appius. "Fuck you and all your accursed kind!"

"Temper, temper!" said Marigoth derisively. "If you want to fight so much, why don't you go back to Miraya and fight in that civil war of yours? Nobody wants you here."

As Appius stormed off, Alyx drew her horse close to Yani's.

"I'm sorry. I didn't do very well, did I?"

"Nonsense," said Yani. "You didn't hit him. That's a good start. Who could have foreseen that Appius would be so unreasonable? I guess he's dealt with the Tari often enough not to be awed by us any more."

"I wonder where he'll go now," chuckled Marigoth.

***

As he stormed back down the ravine, Guilius Appius was wondering the same thing. This was the third time he'd been confronted by the Guardians and he hadn't liked it any more than the previous times.

"How did they do that?" wondered Kindrus, Appius's second in command, fresh out from Miraya, who had never seen Tari before. "Three mages putting twenty mages to sleep. Even death mages can't do that."

"They hardly seem human, do they?" said the other lieutenant, who had seen Tari before but never seen them in action. "Those strange eyes. If the Inquisition were here they'd make roast meat out of them, I'd bet." He raised his voice to speak to Appius. "I thought the Guardians were from that central island, you know, Yarmar. What are they doing out here on Pels island?"

"Ten years ago there were no Tari anywhere," Appius snarled back at him. "Then those bloody witches appeared out of nowhere like some kind of filthy disease, calling themselves 'Guardians', and bring down Olbia. Then they prevented the subduing of the rest of the islands and now it looks like they've decided to run the whole Archipelago. They claim to love peace but they just encourage the

13

natives in ignorance and paganism. Damned whores!"

He turned to a waiting Sergeant at Arms and said, "When the men are back from their nap, get them to form up on the beach."

"Do I start loading up the ships?" asked Kindrus.

"Shut up! I need to think." Appius strode over to the tent which had been set up for him in the lee of the headland, flung in through the canvas door, dashed his gauntlets on the ground and, with a growl of fury, swept everything off the table.

Ten years ago he had been heir to the greatest estate in the newly colonised Principality of Olbia in Southern Seagan, before the Tari had fomented a slave rebellion, driven his family off their hard won land and replaced them with native chieftains. Now he was nothing more than a landless mercenary and, after this day's work, an unemployed mercenary at that.

"Curse them!" he muttered.

"Tedious, aren't they?" purred a voice.

Appius jumped, his hand leaping to his sword. Then he recognised the speaker. "What the hell are you doing here?"

"I came to help you."

"What? Against the Guardians?" He snorted derisively. "I know you're a great mage but..."

"If you know their weaknesses, they're not such a problem."

The mage was sitting in Appius's chair. He crossed his elegantly booted legs at the ankle. "Do you know that there are only eight of them?"

"What? I'd heard there were thousands up in the hills."

"Those ones have turned their back on the outside world. No, there are only eight of the creatures out here in the real world. Ten if you count Yani and Elena Tari, but they're not mages. The half-breed daughter doesn't count at all. If a person could get rid of those eight creatures, only eight..."

"No one can defeat a Tari mage. They're superhuman."

"Not with magic, it's true. But with cunning, there are

14

ways. I already hold one Tari prisoner and soon will have more."

"You have a Tari prisoner? How?"

The mage smiled silkily. "If you can get witch manacles on them, iron disrupts their magic just as it does with any other mage." He leaned forward. "Now, my dear friend, I have a plan for reasserting civilisation in this Archipelago and I need some well-trained mercenary troops to do it. Soon I could be in a position to offer you back your family's lands in Olbia. Maybe even a Dukedom. Does that appeal?"

"You know it does." Appius looked at him speculatively. "But I need money before that. Otherwise this company of dogs will scatter."

"I understand entirely. I want you to set sail for the pirate haven on the island of Baracau. Any ally of mine will find good welcome there - food, lodgings and entertainment provided. In the meantime, here's a little something to tide you over." The mage threw a leather pouch on the table. "In return, when I order you out, you will come immediately. Understood?"

"Done!" said Appius, offering his hand.

The mage shook it.

"Good. Someone needs to stand up to these Tari bitches before they destroy every Mirayan colony in these islands!"

Chapter 1

3 months later.

Warm torch light shone on polished wood panels, rich red and gold tapestries and tables set with silver plates loaded with succulent looking fruits and nuts. Ezratah Karanus, the Guardian's representative at the court of Lamartaine allowed himself to feel a glow of satisfaction as he surveyed the room. Beside each Seagani sat a Mirayan and all were chatting together very civilly - the two dominant racial groups of the Duchy of Lamartaine forming bonds of friendship over a pleasant evening's feasting.

For the last ten years Ezratah and the rest of the Guardians had worked hard to smooth relations between the recently arrived Mirayan colonists and the native tribes. This feast celebrated the fruition of these efforts, for earlier that day nuptial agreements had been signed between Duke Wolf Madraga of Lamartaine's oldest son and the heiress of a leading Southern Seagani Chieftain, strengthening Madraga power into the next generation, and ensuring that the Seaganis would continue to have a stake in it.

The engaged couple – tall, fair-haired Paulus Madraga

and delicate-boned, dark-haired Dianou Seagani - sat at the centre of the high table, drinking from the same cup and smiling into each other's eyes. The fact that the marriage had been at their own suggestion made Ezratah feel all the happier about the alliance.

Ezratah's gaze moved to where Duke Wolf Madraga sat beside his son's betrothed. The Duke was laughing easily with Dianou's father Geran Seagani. Duke Wolf, a small neat man whose easy manner disguised an iron will, might have gone the traditional Mirayan way of refusing to countenance a mixed race match, but Duke Wolf had always been too practical to be a traditional Mirayan. That was what had made him so popular with his Seagani subjects and was probably why, after the collapse of the Mirayan domination of Yarmar ten years ago, Geran had put the Mirayan Duke forward for the elected Chieftainship of the Seaganis of Lamartaine.

The door of the great hall swung open and steaming bowls of soup were carried into the room by a procession of well-disciplined servants in the red dragon livery of the Madragas. Ezratah cast another glance around the room and was alarmed to see an empty place. A source of potential insult? He scanned the tables again and was relieved to see that the only one absent was Serge Madraga, the Duke's scamp of a youngest son. No one was going to be offended by the absence of that popular but notoriously unreliable young roisterer.

The Duke's second son, Gideon, was up at the high table being, as usual, handsome, gracious and a credit to his father and the Duke's youngest child, his five-year-old daughter Olga was sitting very solemnly at the table opposite. Remembering how excited she had been at her first grown-up feast, Ezratah winked at her. Olga giggled and wriggled in her chair. She was a sweet little girl, a melded child, with the pale skin and fair-hair of her Mirayan father and the green eyes and high cheekbones of her Tari mother. In some ways she was a symbol of what Ezratah and the Guardians were trying to achieve here on Yarmar and on the rest of the islands of the Archipelago.

"... an outrageous pollution of pure Mirayan blood with the foul native taint," muttered a voice beside him. Ezratah's glow of satisfaction flickered out. Damn Lev Madraga and his stupid friend! Every time Ezratah came to Lamartaine, the Duke's brother seemed to be making snide remarks to someone about the shortcomings of the Archipelago. If he hated the Archipelago and the natives so much why hadn't he stayed home in his "infinitely preferable" Miraya? These days Ezratah found it hard to believe that he had once been close friends with the haughty mage. At least it was he, their fellow Mirayan, who was listening to this tripe, not one of the locals. That was why he'd seated himself next to Lev in the first place.

"I can understand the charm of these native women," said Lev's friend Neevus, a skinny little man with a fluffy quiff of hair. "She is quite lovely and of course, there is a shortage of pure-blood women. What I don't understand is why your brother married her? And why make her Duchess?"

Sweet Life! They were running down the Duchess. Again!

"Oh Neevus," sneered Lev. "These natives are so superstitious and they regard the Tari with such slavish admiration. My brother's rule has benefited immeasurably from his marriage to the creature. I feel for him, but these are the lengths we Mirayans are forced to go to, now those Tari witches have seized power. It's the only reason he married the creature, I assure you. And he has to trot her out at these kind of gatherings and let her show herself unveiled to all these vulgar people. It makes these knuckle-headed barbarians feel comfortable."

Ezratah clenched his fists to stop himself from interjecting. The talk of the Duke marrying the Duchess for political reasons was gross slander. It had been a love match from the start and the Duke and Duchess still seemed to be devoted to each other. Ezratah had told Lev this many times and he always got an infuriating reply and wound up losing his temper. He wasn't going to risk such a scene on this important night, even to put that stupid Neevus straight. With stern concentration, he fell to spooning soup into his mouth.

After a few minutes his eyes strayed to where the Duchess Jindabyne was talking politely to the bride's mother. She caught his eye and smiled, almost as if she knew what was going on at his side of the table and she didn't mind and didn't think he should either. Ezratah always found Taris' smiles calming and he felt his annoyance fade to be replaced by the tolerant glow of the life spirit.

He'd always regarded the Duchess as, in part at least, his creation, for he had been instrumental in changing her from the wild, mindblasted creature in witch manacles who had been dumped at Lamartaine ten years before, into the elegant woman well in command of the little magical power she still retained. He had not been able to tutor her in magic for the workings of Tari magic were still a mystery to him. However he had been able to teach her to control the distracting whisperings of the life spirit - whisperings which always filled a Tari mind and which could drive them mad if uncontrolled. Ezratah understood those whisperings, for they filled his mind too, even though he was not a Tari.

The soup had just been removed when a breathless figure rushed through the door, almost knocking over a servant, and came hurrying to the table. The Duke's youngest son, Serge Madraga, had arrived at last.

"Finally," muttered Lev Madraga. "No doubt he's been off dabbling in some native cesspit!"

"Hawking," replied Ezratah, certain now that he was being baited and determined not to rise to it.

"With his native friends!" Lev gave his nephew a stern look. "No wonder the boy has no polish."

Ezratah didn't think anyone else cared about Serge's lateness. There was nothing wrong with his manners; he was already bowing to the guests and begging them to excuse his tardiness. The Seaganis smiled indulgently as, with a minimum of fuss, he settled down beside the bride-to-be's brother and fell quickly into talk of hunting. The first course was brought in - roast taldra in honour of their Seagani guests, roast chickens for those like Lev who refused to eat native meats, and a pottage of seasoned vegetables and nuts for those who, like the Duchess and Ezratah, followed the Tari way.

The food laid on the table, the servants began to process out of the room again, but as the door was opened, one of them yelped with surprise and tripped, stumbling into the servant behind him so that both men fell to the ground with a clatter of plates. Two small shapes came racing across the floor.

"Oh no!" cried Serge. "Lexie, Gallant. Heel!"

"Serge!" protested Paulus, while Gideon, burst out laughing. The smaller dog, who had a large piece of meat in its mouth, darted under the table and took cover between its master's legs. Serge scooped him up, and, with his arms full, struggled out of his chair, while the other dog, an elegant greyhound, jumped around him barking deafeningly. Fortunately, the Seagani, who were not a formal people, were highly entertained.

"Serge!" cried Duke Wolf. "Will you keep your dogs under control!"

"I beg pardon, Sir." Red-faced, Serge carried the smaller dog to the door, trailed by the noisy greyhound. "My lords and ladies I apologise for this unmannerly intrusion." He bowed low.

This brought the dog in Serge's arms closer to the floor, giving the greyhound the opportunity to seize hold of the piece of meat. But the smaller dog, growling furiously, was not about to let go of its prize. A ferocious tug-of-war ensued with Serge desperately exhorting both dogs to let go and behave.

The Seaganis roared with delight, Duke Wolf shouted furiously as he strode towards the chaos, and a sneer settled on Lord Lev's face.

Lady Jindabyne stood up.

"Heel, Gallant!" she said, in the commanding voice of a mage.

Instantly Gallant let go of the meat and sat neatly down

at Serge's feet.

The Duchess looked at the other dog.

"Drop it, Lexie!"

The meat fell to the ground with a soggy splat.

The Duchess spoke again, this time in Tari. Both animals put back their ears, assuming the shamefaced attitudes of dogs who have offended the pack leader.

"Thank you, my dear!" said Duke Wolf. He reached down and helped up one of the fallen servants.

"Serge, take your dogs away and this time tie them up! Ah, Lord Alain..."

This last remark was addressed to a flustered young man, who had come bursting in at the door, carrying a hawk on his wrist. The tattoo of Nezrhus on his cheek and the torc at his neck, showed him to be a native Seagani of chiefly rank.

"Your Grace, I'm very sorry about the dogs."

"Lord Alain, you are most welcome in my house," said Duke Wolf formally. "I'm sure you are not at fault." He glared at Serge.

Ezratah was conscious that the Seaganis were now watching intently to see how the Duke dealt with Alain. He himself did not feel worried. The Duke always treated all his vassals politely, regardless of their race.

"Perhaps you would be kind enough join us for dinner now you are here," the Duke continued.

"Thank my lord. I'll... I'll just help Lord Serge... um..."

Alain was so flustered that he had forgotten to hood the hawk on his wrist or to hang onto its jesses. Unfortunately, Lev Madraga chose that moment to take a chicken leg from the plate in front of him. The hawk caught sight of the movement and swooped across the room, whisking the chicken leg out of Lev's hand.

Lev squawked in surprise. The rest of the company burst into laughter again and one of the Seaganis cried out, "Hooray! Splendid flying!"

Livid with fury, Lev leapt to his feet. "You stupid native cur!" he shouted at Alain. "Why in Mir's name did you bring that *thing* in here?"

Instantly the room fell silent, but for intakes of breath on every side. Ezratah resisted the impulse to put his head in his hands in despair. Alain, who understood the importance of this meeting, managed to look scared and angry at the same time, while the Duke scowled at Lev. Serge, of course, made everything worse by shouting, "How dare you! Take that back immediately."

Then Paulus jumped up and said, "My lords and ladies! I propose a toast. To this beautiful hawk and the fine young chieftain who trained her, Alain Seagani."

Thank Mir! A masterly move. No one was angry enough to refuse such a toast and to Ezratah's relief, after a moments scowling, Lev joined in as if he were a good sport and his dim friend Neevus played along. Ezratah was even more relieved when a servant appeared just then with a message for Lev, forcing the mage to excuse himself. The man was a diplomatic incident on two legs.

But Ezratah couldn't relax yet. Lev's friend Neevus, lacking anyone else to talk to in Mirayan now Lev had been called away, turned, introduced himself, and said,

"So I believe you are the Mirayan they call the native's friend, Lord Ezratah."

To my face, thought Ezratah. I bet they call me something much worse behind my back.

Aloud he said, "I am he. Delighted to make your acquaintance, Lord Neevus."

"So tell me, how many islands are there exactly in this lovely little archipelago? Have you visited them all?"

"Hardly. Some of them are only very small. But there are 204 islands. One of our own scientists counted up their total area as being almost as great as that of Miraya."

"Really. So whoever controls the Archipelago would be as powerful as our dear Emperor."

Ezratah shrugged. "Except that islands don't really lend themselves to being one kingdom. Each island has quite a distinct culture. Even the Mirayan colonies on them have become quite distinct."

Neevus gave Ezratah a long stare, his eyes curiously expressionless. Then he said,

"And here we are on Yarmar, which is so big. I had never thought of islands as being so big, but it must take days to cross. And with not one but six different tribes on it."

"Well yes, although four of them have the same language - Seagani. And the Seagani speakers are very alike in religion and beliefs too. But they do tend to fight among themselves, which is why the ones on this part of Yarmar have been happy to recognise a Mirayan as their ruler. Of course, they fight much more with the Mori."

Neevus stared again, before speaking.

"Ah the Mori, they are the forest dwellers, right? They have the whole of the western side of this island, don't they? Which they insist of keeping as forest. And I hear they're lead by this wonderfully, sinister-sounding woman, what do they call her - The Hooded Queen. But of course the most sinister of all are the Tari. Lord Lev says they are mighty mages, mightier even than he. I hadn't thought to meet one and yet I gather the lovely Duchess is a Tari. And hasn't she produced a lovely little girl. Hello darling." He waved at Olga, who looked shy and stared at her plate. "Has she inherited her mother's powers I wonder?"

He gave Ezratah another long stare.

"So is the Duchess really able manipulate actual matter and change it permanently. I can't imagine how it is possible."

"Yes, Tari <u>can</u> actually change the nature of matter," replied Ezratah, finding it hard to meet Neevus' eyes. "But the Duchess was the victim of a mindblast spell, so she is only a shadow of what a Tari mage should be."

"I would love to study that. Do you think the Duke would let me speak with her about it?"

"I don't think so," snapped Ezratah, insulted on Jindabyne's behalf. The man would never even consider making such a request of a Mirayan woman. "She may be a native woman, but the Duke is a true Mirayan."

Neevus gave him another long stare. He didn't seem offended. Indeed it was hard to tell if he had any emotions at all.

"And you yourself, I believe you have adopted their religion, Lord Ezratah," he continued evenly. "Has it enhanced your powers? Oh!"

A servant lent over Neevus' shoulder and whispered in his ear.

"Lord Ezratah, pray forgive me. I must leave our delightful conversation," he said, as he got up and followed the servant away. Ezratah was disconcerted to find he wasn't sure if Neevus' "delightful conversation" remark was sarcasm or not. Usually he could read people better than that.

He was just beginning to relax again, when he felt a hand on his thigh and a voice whispered softly in his ear, "Darling Ezratah, won't you meet me privately tomorrow morning?"

Since the wife of a Seagani Chieftain was sitting to that side of him, Ezratah froze in alarm. Then he turned, only to find that the She-Chief was deep in conversation with someone else.

The voice laughed, tickling his ear. "Oh 'Tah, did you think you'd made a conquest? How disappointing for you!"

He caught the scent of orange blossom. He knew that scent.

"Marigoth!" he hissed under his breath, slapping the hand off his thigh. "What are you doing here?"

The voice laughed in his ear again. He felt the pressure of a hand on his shoulder, but kept his eyes firmly on his plate. Looking would have done no good anyway. He knew she had made herself invisible. If only he could persuade her to leave before she unfolded whatever dreadful practical joke had brought her here.

"Don't look so terrified," Marigoth cooed, pressing her hand onto his shoulder. "I'm here to give a blessing to the betrothed couple. And as it happens I do need you to meet me at *our* beach tomorrow morning. I've got an important mission for you in Ishtak."

"How can I? I'm in the middle of this!" he hissed out of the side of his mouth, hoping no one would notice that he was talking to thin air.

"Oh 'Tah. Fooling aside now. It's really important that you come to Ishtak. If you won't do it for me, do it for Yani."

There was a note of something like worry in her voice.

"What do you mean Yani?" he hissed.

But the pressure of her hand on his shoulder was gone.

A few moments later a servant announced, "The Lady Marigoth Tari attends to congratulate the happy couple!" and the door opened.

Visible now, Marigoth swept in, looking wonderful as always, and bowed deeply to the betrothed couple and the delighted Seaganis. She'd grown up into a beautiful golden-haired woman, though small and delicate-boned for her race, and was magnificently dressed in Tari green. She glowed with power, and a hint of unearthly music filled the air. *A nice touch - not as overdone as some of her illusions.*

The Duke welcomed her formally. He had a personal grudge against Marigoth, but few people apart from Ezratah knew of it, and watching now, no one would have ever guessed it.

With charming courtesy, Marigoth declined the offer to join them at the feast. Instead, calling Paulus and Dianou out to stand before her, she blessed them in the name of the life spirit and wished them a long and prosperous marriage. As she spoke, a green vine appeared to grow out of the sleeves of the each of the betrothed couple. The vines bound their hands together before meeting in the middle and twining up and up till both stems joined as one and burst into a beautiful thornless red rose.

At this everyone clapped and cheered.

"How charming!" sneered a malicious voice, reminding listeners that Lord Lev had returned to the table.

"Yes," Ezratah replied absently, as he watched Marigoth glide gracefully backward from the room so as not to insult the company by turning her back on them. She was *very* charming. He always forgot how diplomatic she could be. Then he shook himself and turned to Lev.

"What's charming?" he asked carefully.

"Why, the little play with the vine and the rose,"

smiled Lev, with an unpleasantly knowing look on his face. "Though the lady herself is also quite beautiful, of course."

He looked very smug about something.

"No doubt she's told you about the kidnapping of Yani Tari."

Despite himself Ezratah's jaw dropped.

"Yani...? Yani's been kidnapped?"

He was surprised rather than alarmed. Yani was stronger than most men, she was a brilliant warrior and, unlike other Tari, she was able to kill. There were very few situations that she couldn't get herself out of.

"Oh dear, didn't she tell you?" purred Lev. "I just received a message from good friends in Ishtak, who always let me know everything. And, I, in turn, tell my brother, who finds it useful to know when the balance of power changes. Do you think Yani Tari's disappearance will weaken the Tari?"

"No!" snapped Ezratah. "She is not our leader in the Mirayan way, only the first among equals. Not only that, but even if her kidnappers manage to keep her, which I doubt, the Tari are the most powerful mages in the Archipelago. Possibly the world. Only a fool would try to harm her."

"Yes, yes, I agree with you," said Lev, in a humouring tone. "A very ill-advised attempt. And, of course, I wish you all the best in recovering her safely. But my informant can't help being hopeful that it might bring some relief from the endless Tari interference in other people's affairs."

"The Tari seek only to bring balance," said Ezratah. How was it that Lev always managed to get under his skin!

"Too much power in the hands of any one group is hardly a recipe for balance." Lev lifted up a wine jug and poured some into Ezratah's goblet. "Let us not talk of it, my friend. We never agree on these matters and this is no place for disagreement."

Ezratah could do nothing but accept his toast and seethe silently.

The beach Marigoth had called "our beach" was in a secluded cove some distance away on the other side of a wooded headland. As he rode through the forest toward it the following morning, Ezratah's heart both rose and sank at the thought of a mission with Marigoth. This uncomfortable contradictory feeling had become normal whenever he thought of her.

He shouldn't even like her. He'd first met her when she was masquerading as a child and she'd put him under an enchantment and exploited him ruthlessly. Because of her, he'd found himself in Ermora, the Tari homeland, and in the Tari spirit cave. Because of her, he was now this strange half-Mirayan, half-Tari person, whose countrymen looked to him for help even as they called him traitor.

Yet at the same time he now knew a peace and joy he had never thought possible, because he could hear the whispering of the life spirit that bound the world together. Forests like the one he rode through now filled him with sparkling joy, making him feel that all was in balance - that perfect peace was possible. Marigoth had changed his life even if it had been accidental.

He'd seen her many times in the past ten years and several times he'd found himself in difficult situations of her making. She was as powerful as only a Tari mage could be and as frivolous as only the most powerful dare to be, and when it came to magic, she could have wiped the floor with him. The problem was, he'd be happy to be her floor cleaning rag any time it gave her pleasure. The moment he'd realised this, he'd put all his energies into hiding it from her. She loved a joke and damn the consequences to anyone else.

For instance, there was the time she'd first shown him her secret beach near Lamartaine. He'd been living in the fortress then, invited there by the anxious Duke Wolf to train a mindblasted Jindabyne Tari. He'd been riding along this very path when he'd heard the sound of beautiful singing and, fascinated by it, had followed it into the trees. The singer had teased him, stopping as soon as he got close and starting again every time he seemed likely to turn back to the path. An unwary moment caused him to be knocked off his horse by a branch. He'd come to with an aching head and Marigoth leaning over him half laughing, half contrite - full of sympathy but telling him not to be so stuffy when he'd protested at what she'd done. He'd felt stuffy too, because it had been a very elegant joke and the singing had been truly beautiful. Oh Mir! A mission with Marigoth. He was done for! And eager to be so, poor fool that he was!

At the bottom of a path which led steeply down to a narrow beach, a small boat was drawn up above the level of the waves. *Thank Mir! A real boat.* Sometimes Marigoth travelled using a magical boat created out of a stick of wood and a handkerchief, but even though it never sank, somehow you always got soaking wet.

As his horse crunched across the beach toward it, two figures rose up from under the boat's shadow. Marigoth was one. The other was a singularly beautiful young man. *Trust Marigoth, the shameless flirt!*

"'Tah! You came!" Marigoth rushed over to hug him. The young man slouching up behind her looked darkly at Ezratah. He had the tattered clothes and bare feet of a fisherman. Ezratah disliked him on sight.

"Oh Gasparr. This is my uncle. By marriage," lied Marigoth in a 'you don't have to be jealous of him' voice. "Gasparr's been kind enough to keep me company while I was waiting for you, Uncle."

Ezratah didn't protest. He'd masqueraded as Marigoth's uncle by marriage before and as her cousin, too. It was always simpler to go along with what she said. He just hoped this Gasparr was not going to be a permanent figure in their lives.

He thought not. Marigoth hadn't revealed her real self to him. She was wearing a glamour so that she looked like a pretty, fair-haired, half-Mirayan girl.

She and the young man were whispering together now and the young idiot's arm was around her shoulders. Marigoth didn't look like she minded at all.

"What about my horse?" said Ezratah loudly. "I'm not

sure he can find his way home without me."

"Oh!" Marigoth looked at Gasparr. "I'd be so grateful if you'd take my uncle's horse back to the Duke's castle. Could you do that?"

The young idiot murmured something. From the adoring, puppy-dog look in his eyes, probably, "Anything for you, my Lady." He leaned down and kissed Marigoth's hand.

"Thank you, Gasparr. You're so sweet." She kissed him on the cheek. The young man looked as if he was going to faint with delight.

Nauseated, Ezratah turned his back on them and busied himself taking off his saddle bags and putting everything into the boat. Over the years he'd seen plenty of men look at Marigoth like that. *Poor saps!*

"Do you think we could leave sometime before dark?" he said.

"Of course, Uncle." Marigoth came to his side and looked up at him, eyes twinkling. "No need to get grumpy."

A short time later, the boat was moving out to sea, its sails filled with a magical breeze. Marigoth stood at the back waving goodbye to Gasparr.

"So who was he?" asked Ezratah.

"I met him yesterday when I was asking after you in Lamartaine. Beautiful, isn't he? Such a dear, too. It's nice to have some company in a strange place."

"Put an enchantment on him, did you?"

"Of course not!" said Marigoth crossly. "I'm not that ugly."

"Typical Marigoth! A boy in every port."

"I don't hear the boys complaining!"

"You realise you've probably ruined him for normal life now." Ezratah knew he should shut up, but he couldn't seem to help himself.

"Well, what a compliment!" retorted Marigoth. "First, I'm so ugly I need to put an enchantment on him and now I'm so wonderful I've ruined him for normal life. I wish you'd make up your mind."

She smiled at Ezratah's scowl.

"Admit it. You Mirayans just hate people having any fun. Actually," she confessed, "I did put a little enchantment on him just before we left. If he takes your horse back by tomorrow, the Duke's steward will decide he's a fine young man and offer him a job in the Duke's service. Much nicer work than fishing!"

Ezratah laughed and shook his head. What could you say in the face of such cheerful shamelessness?

"You win! So tell me what's happening with Yani. Surely she doesn't really need rescuing?"

Had it not been for the flicker of emotion crossing Marigoth's face, he would have thought she hadn't heard him. She turned away and seemed to be coiling a piece of rope in the prow of the boat. Ezratah could tell from the set of her shoulders that the subject upset her. For the first time alarm bells went off in his mind.

"Mari? What is it?" He moved forward and gripped Marigoth's wrist. "Is Yani really in danger?"

"Yes I think she is," said Marigoth huskily, sounding for all the world as if she was going to burst into tears. "As far as I can tell someone's taken her off to Miraya."

"Miraya! I thought she was supposed to be meeting the Prince of Ishtak. How did Miraya come into this?"

"Oh 'Tah! You're so dim. Miraya comes into everything." Marigoth laughed shakily and drew her free hand across her eyes. Ezratah ignored the insult and pulled her down onto a seat opposite him. If Marigoth was upset, Yani must really be in danger. He should have considered it earlier instead of dismissing the whole thing as one of Marigoth's jokes.

"Tell me what happened," he said.

"Yani met with the Prince, she and Diyar, who was doing the protection on her, and that was the last anyone heard from either of them. Except our agents in Ishtak found witnesses who saw an unconscious Tari woman being loaded onto a Mirayan ship called the Open Eye. No sign of Diyar. The Prince says he has no idea where she is. I bet it would be a different matter if we mindsearched him."

31

Nightmarish visions of diplomatic disaster filled Ezratah's head.

"You can't..."

"I know! You can't mindsearch someone that important without his permission! But we can follow this Mirayan ship. I only hope it's not a false lead."

"Right!" agreed Ezratah. So they were going to Miraya! He'd never thought to see his homeland again and he was surprised to realise he didn't much care.

He was much more worried about Yani. Yani might be special but she was only human and Miraya had been in a state of civil war for the last forty years. It was swarming with the kind of people who flourished in civil wars - pirates, mercenaries, assassins. Worst of all, there were death mages everywhere. Pray that Yani hadn't fallen into the hands of such people. A Tari, with their strong connection to the life spirit, would be of great value to one of the Dark Brotherhood. He shook off the evil thought. No. Probably one of the Mirayan settlers, maybe even the Duke of Ishtak himself had paid for her to be taken out to sea and ...

An even worse thought occurred to him.

"Are you sure she's still alive?" he said gently.

"No!" snapped Marigoth. "I'm not sure of anything. We just have to find the Open Eye."

Chapter 2

For the last thirty days Yani had sat in the darkness, chained to the wall behind her by the iron witch manacles round her neck and wrists. Every time the light in the corridor outside her room lightened to grey she'd made a mark in the spongy wood of the wall as a way of keeping time. Her little prison room stank of rotting wood and the sour stinking water in the bilges beneath, but the worst of it was the rats that lived in this hold. When she fell asleep they would come creeping up to bite her and even though she had caught and killed many, there seemed a never ending army of them.

For thirty days she had listened to the bilge water sloshing back and forward as the ship creaked and rolled across the waves, but today the waves had smoothed and the rhythm of the ships creaking had slowed. Yani had a cold feeling in the pit of her stomach that they had arrived. She was not sure what their destination was, though she had a strong suspicion it was somewhere in Miraya because the old man who was her warden spoke Mirayan. Evil bastard!

She had not been physically mistreated and every day bread and water had been brought to her and the slops bucket taken away. She had no physical reason to fear the old man but every night he would come to the door of the cell, light a candle and leer at her through the small barred window.

He had the face of a skull - greying parchment skin stretched tight over his bones - yet he had the most amazingly white and perfect teeth that he said came from eating human flesh. Sometimes he just stood there shining the light in her face so that she could not sleep. Other times he talked, telling her long stories of rape, torture and cannibalism. The sensual pleasure with which the old death mage spoke of these things - the way he rolled each story round in his mouth as if he were savouring the flavour of some delicious food- was more frightening than the stories themselves. He seemed quite sane - he simply revelled in other people's pain. The very existence of such a being, defiling the life spirit, made her physically ill.

She had offered him gold. She had threatened him with Marigoth and the others. She had even tried to make him curious about her, to lure him into mindsearching her, hoping thus to touch him with the power of the life spirit and perhaps change him. But he did not listen to her. She suspected that he did not regard her as sufficiently human.

Sometimes when he came she prayed the Morning Chant to herself so that those beautiful words could drown out his speech. Sometimes she did not respond at all, but withdrew into the Raven and let it deal with the stories. Sometimes she made herself weep and screamed at him in the hope that that would satisfy him and make him go away quicker. None of these strategies seemed to make his visits shorter. He stayed talking and staring at her until it pleased him to go away and leave her to the rats.

"You are bait," he would say every day. "Those who love you will come after you. Your loved ones will fall into our hands and we shall feed them to our servants. Or worse still, we will suck them dry to use their power. Those people you love. Then I shall have you for myself and we shall see how long you can last my pleasure. Meditate on that."

He must be speaking some truth. The Mirayans in the Archipelago hated her and wanted her gone so there was no reason why they should keep her alive unless they wanted bigger prey. Death mages could always put a Tari to good use. But did her captors actually know this? Was this why they had not touched her?

Marigoth would come after her. They must know that that was certain. And Marigoth was a much bigger prize.

Yani prayed that her younger sister would come prepared, yet in the end what was the power of a great mage? What good had it done her bodyguard, Diyar? When Yani had realised that she had been drugged, she had staggered to the door of the room and pushed it open. And seen Diyar there, her guardian mage, slumped on floor bleeding from the head, a man with a cudgel standing over him. You might be a great mage able to make whole armies fall asleep, but you were still only human when they hit you on the head. Where was Diyar now? Was he on the ship? She'd asked the old man but he'd only laughed.

Sweet life, she regretted swapping the sword for diplomacy, especially when she thought of that bastard Prince Ipius. She never should have trusted him.

When his Chamberlain had called Yani to his house for a secret meeting, she had gone in good faith, assuming that the Prince had wanted to make a deal that his supporters would not approve. She'd thought the Prince smart enough to want to avoid offending the Tari, but even then she had taken care. The Chamberlain had offered her wine while they awaited the Prince and she had drunk only because the Chamberlain had poured his cup from the same jug and sipped before she did. Then the Chamberlain had passed out as they spoke together and the world has started to go round and she had realised she'd been fooled. Idiot that she was. She shouldn't have expected that bastard Prince to have had the decency to be war-weary after just a couple of failed tries taking Pels.

This had the hallmarks of a very well thought out plan and she did not think the old man was lying when he talked of others being involved. Marigoth might really be in danger.

She must get out of here, and do something. With the witch manacles around her neck she couldn't change into the Raven and fly away from the ship, but now they were still and possibly in some kind of port... For thirty days she had been working at the staple that affixed the chains to the rotten wall. Today she had finally pulled it out. Now sitting with it carefully behind her, she waited for the one of the guards to come with food. The grey light of the hold was darkening. The guard would be here soon and he would open the door to take out the slops bucket. Even weakened by the bread and water diet, she should be able to overpower the fellow. Then they would see what sort of a bait she was.

She tensed as footsteps came towards her. But they were the footsteps of someone new, not the old man or the guard. They moved confidently as if they were meant to be there. Was she going to meet her ultimate captor this time?

Yani pushed the staple back into the wall and tried to look helpless.

A mage light flared at the window. Though the glare Yani could make out the shape of a face with a shroud of hair on either side of it.

"Hmm," said a woman's voice.

"What are you doing here, bitch?" cried someone. Yani thought it was the old man.

The head was gone from the window.

"I came to see my brother's prize," cooed a voice. Definitely a woman's voice. "It's not much, is it? I'm starting to wonder if I even want it."

"Your brother's prize?" snarled the old man. "I'll have you know this is my..."

The woman laughed and then with a roar, magical fire flowered, filling the hold with blinding light, screams of agony and the smell of burning flesh.

Heavy blackness was fading to grey. *Danger!* whispered the Raven.

Yani fought the urge to open her eyes as reality seeped

slowly, reluctantly back to her. That woman. *Danger!*

She'd been unconscious and now she was somewhere new, propped up in a corner against some kind of wall that rocked back and forth. She could hear horses ahead. She must be in some kind of cart. Her hands and feet were unbound, but cold iron still chilled her wrists and neck. Damn.

She slid her eyes open just a crack. A woman was sitting opposite her looking away out the window. Dark hair laced with gold thread. Was this the woman from the ship?

Through half open eyelids, Yani examined her surroundings looking for an advantage. This was some kind of enclosed cart with a canvas covering like a tent stretched above them. Two benches covered in gold brocade were fixed to either side of it and luxurious red and gold cushions were strewn everywhere. It was full daylight outside. How long had she been unconscious?

She took another look at the mage. She was dressed as richly as a queen, her thick black cloak thrown back from a golden brocade gown. Long black hair. The face of a beautiful hawk. Blood red lips that couldn't be natural.

The mage turned suddenly to look at Yani. She feigned unconsciousness again.

"You can stop pretending. I know you are awake," said the mage.

Yani kept her eyes closed and forced her face to relax. Best to stay as she was - wakefulness seemed certain to bring unpleasantness.

But unpleasantness was determined to come to her. The woman's dress rustled and she felt her sit down beside her. She pulled open Yani's bodice.

"Hmm. What nice breasts. My men will be pleased. Still pretending to be asleep, are you?"

Caressing hands slide into Yani's bodice and ran over her breasts. She forced herself not to cringe from the touch. What was the creature at? Suddenly the mage pinched her hard on the nipple, digging her fingernails in and twisting. Despite herself Yani winced and pulled away.

"I'm awake," she said.

The woman smiled smugly.

"Now you're being a good girl."

"Who are you?" said Yani coolly.

"My name is Daria Symina," said the woman. "If you were from round here, you'd be afraid."

"What do you want with me?"

"That's for me to know and you to worry about," smiled Daria. "One is subject to whims and when one is as powerful as I, one can do what one likes. Perhaps I was curious to see one of the Archipelagan folk. Perhaps I just want to have some fun." She stroked Yani's thigh. "Perhaps I thought my men would like a change of diet."

Intimidation always made Yani combative. She returned Daria gaze calmly.

"I did not think Mirayans allowed women to be mages. I thought they killed you all at birth."

"Sometimes the great families marry us so that they can breed mages from us, but mostly they just send us to nunneries," said the woman conversationally. "We are taught healing and other white-souled lily-livery. Pah! Such would I have been if my brother had not killed our parents."

"Nice brother," said Yani.

"My brother, Malov Symina, is the most feared man in Miraya and he sent for you. Do not try that brave face on me. Fear should be gnawing at your vitals. Unless you are a *great* fool."

"And why has your brother brought me all this way?"

"Why indeed?" said Daria mockingly. "Think of pain, my dear little slave. Think of torture, rape and despair."

To hell with the woman! Yani wasn't going to be scared.

"You're death mages, aren't you?" sneered Yani. "Those sad creatures who can only achieve power by prostituting themselves to demons."

"Ooh hoo!" cried Daria. "Aren't we cheeky?" She seized Yani's hair and pulled her face close to her.

"I'll teach you manners."

Her long sharp nails came out and raked Yani's cheek, menacing her eyes. Yani lashed out and pushed her off. Daria hissed. There was a sudden flash of magic and Yani felt as if every bone in her body had been jolted out of its socket. She cried out despite herself and suddenly Daria was on top of her jolting her with that magic again and again until every joint was burning.

"Do you still doubt my power?" shouted Daria.

"Stop it, you bitch," cried Yani, trying to grit her chattering teeth.

Daria laughed, but the jolts of magic stopped. Through her pain, Yani could hear the mage panting heavily. She was astride Yani and her face was so close that Yani could feel her hot breath on her cheek.

"You're so brave, aren't you? I wonder if you will be so brave when my men shove their hard dicks into your soft little cunt," she hissed into Yani's ear.

She rolled the words sensually over her tongue and her body arched and moved with pleasure as she spoke. Then suddenly her weight was gone. She was over the other side of carriage, breathing hard, struggling with some strong feeling.

Daria wants you, whispered the Raven in her head.

The death mage pulled open a small chest that was bolted to the wall of the carriage, and snatching out a little bag, sniffed two pinches of a white powder up her nose.

Yani's joints were burning too much for her to worry about Daria for the moment. How easily she had cried out! Humiliated, she turned her face to the brocade. It smelt of dust and sweat.

"Now you see who is mistress here, girl!" panted Daria "You will treat me with respect."

Rage filled Yani. *Control yourself,* cried the Raven in her ear. *This is not the way through. There are other paths to freedom.* Its harsh voice brought sanity.

"Answer me, girl," snarled Daria.

Don't fight back, counselled the Raven. *You can't win. Try to get over rough ground as easily as possible. Submit for the moment and wait for an opportunity.*

"Yes," Yani whispered, not looking at Daria. Her voice was trembling with hatred. Hopefully Daria would read that as fear. Yani knew that she should beg for mercy but she was too angry to do it. She just lay there face down on the bench, hearing her own breath rasping in her throat while the Raven whispered soothingly in her head.

"Did I hurt you?" cooed Daria mockingly. "How naughty of me."

The bitch! thought Yani furiously.

Stop it! whispered the Raven. *You are only angry because you are afraid.* But warrior's recklessness had seized Yani.

So Daria wanted her, did she? Perhaps that made an opportunity.

"Please lady," she said softly, sweetly and deceitfully. "Please don't hurt me any more."

She rolled over slowly, letting her skirts ride up her legs. Her bodice was still open and she let it gape so that her breasts showed. She moved her chained hands with false grogginess from her forehead along down her body, brushing over her breasts with her fingers as she did so, arching her back sensuously.

For a moment she saw or thought she saw naked desire on Daria's face.

Then the mage let out a shrill shriek.

"Cover yourself, slut," she screamed and burning, juddering pain burst over Yani. Pain that went on and on until the rage was burned out of Yani, and then the strength. Pain until she began to weep and truly beg for mercy.

Suddenly it stopped.

"I will not kill you today, whore!" said Daria Symina with utter coldness. "But be warned. My brother wanted you alive. But he didn't say in one piece. Or sane."

Yani huddled on the floor of the carriage where she must have fallen. Cushions were scattered all around her and grit from the carriage floor dug into her cheek. Her every nerve was jangling. A wave of despair filled her and she wanted to cry. The mage on the ship had been evil but this Daria...

The carriage kept rocking beneath her as if nothing had changed. The Raven came into her mind. The rustling of its feathers was full of the whispering of the life force and it spoke the morning chant, comforting her.

The blessings of life enfold and encircle you always. Do not despair. We shall find another path.

Slowly cold, calculating calm returned.

Meanwhile the carriage charged on and on at a headlong pace. Every time they stopped to change horses, someone lead them past the carriage window and Daria performed some spell on them. But she never left the carriage, and there was no opportunity for Yani to escape.

The second time they stopped to change horses, Daria kicked Yani hard in the kidneys and ordered her to get up. By now Yani, immersed in the calm of the Raven, saw Daria from a long way away with an eye only for strategy. She was quite young this mage, no older than her early twenties. Remembering her previous need for deference, Yani showed as much fear as she could, which wasn't difficult as she would have wished.

"You're not so tough, are you?" sneered Daria. "They told me your people were great mages, but you're not. You're just some snivelling ordinary. Just meat. Tell me, why is my brother so hot to own you, *Meat?*"

"I don't know, Lady," said Yani.

"So what are you then, if you're not a mage? A servant? A kitchen maid perhaps? Or are you just some whore who kneels down and takes it in the arse like a bitch?"

Fighting spirit burned up in Yani's chest, but she pushed it down. Daria stroked her arm.

"How did you get such big muscles?"

"Among my people I am counted a warrior," snapped Yani, despite her best intentions.

Daria threw back her head and laughed contemptuously. "A warrior! A lying bitch, more like. A laundress more like. Yes, I bet you got those muscles heaving round sweaty sheets at some inn, didn't you? She leaned closer. "And I'll bet you learned to fight being gang raped on some smelly dung heap. A warrior! Ha! You're just a woman."

Daria seemed to lose interest. She leaned back against the brocade cushions and sighed. Perhaps she was growing tired. Unless they drew on the life force, even powerful mages had limited power and Daria was making heavy use of her magic. She kept peering through the blind at the window in a way that made Yani suspect they were moving through dangerous country. Were they expecting an attack? Sweet life if only!

Daria did not touch Yani again all that day, but every now and then she shot questions at her.

"Are you Tari really so full of life force? Tell me how these special links with the life force work? Are you some kind of nature mage?"

To all these questions Yani answered, as submissively as she could , "I'm not a mage. I don't really know." Daria was horribly well-informed. She knew of the Tari's connection with the life force and that demons desired Tari lives above all others. She sneered for a long time over the Tari's reverence for life. She even knew that Tari could not kill without experiencing the death of their victim. Very few people knew these things about the Tari even at home in the Archipelago. How had Daria learned so much?

From the wording of Daria's questions it seemed as if she and this brother of hers had been expecting Yani for some time. She even asked Yani how she had liked Cav Cannus, the horrible old mage who had tormented her on the ship. Yet she did not seem to know about any plot to capture those who might try to rescue her, which was odd considering what the mage on the ship had known. But she was no fool.

"I suppose one of these great mages will try and rescue you," she asked several times. "Answer me!"

"No!" cried Yani, as she had to the mage on the ship. "My people despise warriors. I am a person of violence. A killer. An outcast."

"You're lying. There is someone following us even now, isn't there?"

"No, they will not come for me. All my life I have fought to defend them. And yet they despise me."

"Lying bitch. Did I not teach you enough respect?" said Daria, hotly lunging at Yani.

Yani shrank back into the corner. "No, Lady. I swear I'm not lying."

Daria slapped her face several times, but physically she wasn't very strong and the slaps didn't hurt all that much. "You're lying." She seized Yani's hair. "Tell me the truth or I will hurt you as never before."

Yani reacted as if Daria had hurt her more than she had.

"No, Lady. I... I really don't know the answer. I am an outcast. I... maybe they will send someone."

"They would not want one of their own to be fed to demons, would they?" hissed Daria in her face. "They would not want death mages probing you to find out more about your people. If all these stories are true, the Tari would be like gold to us. If you were mine I'd come after you, if only to kill you to prevent you from being mindsearched by such as me."

"Yes, Lady. I'm sure you're right, Lady," cried Yani breathlessly, hoping to plant seeds of doubt into Daria's mind.

"Pah! Weakling. You are disgusting," said Daria. "I shall enjoy watching my men cut you about."

She pushed Yani down onto the floor of the carriage and turned away. This was bad. It was hardly worth the trouble of planting seeds of doubt in Daria's mind. If Daria even suspected Marigoth was coming for her, she'd be ready for her. And now she was talking of mindsearching Yani.

Mindsearch. Then she would know everything, even about their outcast status, about Elena, all about the Tari's weaknesses.

But the Raven in Yani's mind let out a satisfied caw and Yani remembered how Diyar had once let a curious

Mirayan priest mindsearch him.

"Don't do it," Yani had warned. "He'll tell the Mirayans our secrets and they'll use them against us."

Diyar had just smiled at her.

"Have faith in the life spirit," he had said. He had known a lot more about Tari magic than her. Diyar had not been surprised when, after the mindsearch, the Mirayan priest had gone into a religious trance in which he claimed to have seen the face of Mir. Nor was he surprised when the priest left his ambitious path upwards through the clerical hierarchy to live the life of a lone forest hermit.

"To touch a Tari's mind is to touch the life spirit," he had said simply. The Mirayans never sent anyone to mindsearch a Tari ever again.

Night came and still the carriage thundered onwards stopping only to change horses. Sometimes the road was very bad and they were thrown around. Daria must have been saving her strength for she did nothing to soften their ride and when the time came to light lamps in the carriage, she did not use her own power but lit the feeble little mage lights that you could buy in any market. They filled the carriage with a sickly white glow which made things even more nightmarish. Yani was exhausted. She had had no food and only a little water all the day. She feigned sleep, but tension kept her alert. Beneath her eyelids she watched Daria, hoping for an opportunity.

But even though she, too, must have been exhausted, the accursed mage did not sleep. Instead she took a vial from a chest beneath the seat and drank from it. For a few minutes afterward she shuddered. When she lifted her head again, her face was sharp and hard and her eyes glittered. With hands and face twitching wildly, she leapt feverishly upon Yani and laughing shrilly, pinched and poked and slapped her. It was not the beating itself, but Daria's malice and enjoyment of Yani's pain that made it horrible.

With breathless speed she asked Yani all the questions she had asked during the day but she did not wait for a reply before she hit her and shouted that she was lying. Then, as suddenly as she had pounced, Daria lost interest in

Yani. She took a little cage full of sleepy butterflies from under the seat and shook the cage until they awoke and fluttered around.

"So beautiful," she cooed before she took them out one by one and pulled them slowly apart, giggling the whole time. Then bored with that, she set upon Yani again.

The night seemed to go on for ever.

In the grey light of dawn the carriage slowed, changed direction and after a few moments stopped. Daria sprang up and flung aside the window curtain.

"We're here," she cried, as if they were two children returning home. "Safe at last." She turned on Yani.

"Now we shall see some fun."

Iron usually burned the skin of mages, but if it bothered Daria, she ignored it. She grabbed Yani by the neck manacle, hauled her out of the carriage and threw her on the ground so easily she must have used magical strength to do it.

Rough male laughter rang out. Yani estimated that there were about ten men in Daria's troop of guards and she tensed with dread, but no one touched her. The men were probably as exhausted as she was. She dragged herself up. The ground here was wet and muddy rather than hard and nothing was broken. Above them a stone building towered against the grey dawn sky and Daria was scampering up a huge flight of stone stairs towards a big brass door flanked by two smoking torches.

"Bring her!" she shouted.

The building was some kind of fortified manor house, built of crumbling grey stone. Inside was a great hall, lit by torches and a large log fire, where frightened looking servant girls, most of them little more than children, scurried here and there, passing out cups of hot wine. Yani tensed her spine, ready to be attacked by the seven or so men who had followed her up the stairs guffawing and making ribald remarks. But the two who flanked her simply dragged her through the hall and down a long corridor into a large private room, decorated with flags and shields and swords. If only she could get hold of one of those swords.

Daria was standing in front of another big fire. Oh shit! She was drinking from another vial. Did the creature never rest?

The men shoved her into the centre of the room and left with a speed that indicated fear. They obviously knew all about these vials. A table and a set of chairs dominated the room so Yani sat down on one of the chairs, forced her limbs to relax and rest and checked the room over for weak points.

Daria's brocade gown glistened in the fire light as she leant against the mantelpiece shuddering, but all too soon she was standing before Yani, swaying slightly, her eyes hard and glittering.

"Get up," she snarled.

As Yani stood nervously before her, there came a frisson of magic, and the torn and filthy gown that she had been wearing since Ishtak suddenly fell in heap around her, leaving her standing naked and barefoot in the centre of the room. Was it the ease of Daria's power or just the cold that made the goose flesh stand up on Yani's skin?

"My, my!" said Daria, looking her over intently. "What a lot of scars. You have led an adventurous... What the hell's this!" she said suddenly, for her pacing had taken her round behind Yani where she could see the black raven wings that were tattooed upon Yani's shoulders and back.

"Tribal marks," lied Yani.

"How barbaric," sneered Daria. Yani could feel her hot breath on her back as she smoothed her hands over the tattoos. Could Daria feel the power in them? No way of knowing.

"These shouldn't be too hard to cut out," said Daria, after a moment. "Or shall we flay them off? Ah! Choices, choices!" Her hands slid off Yani's back. She swung her round to face her.

"Tell me why my brother wants you!"

"I don't know," snapped Yani, without looking Daria in the eye. She needed Daria to mindsearch her, but she couldn't be too eager for it. She needed to convince Daria that no amount of torture would make her tell the truth and that was going to be hard going. Yani set her teeth.

"I think you do know," said Daria. "I think he's using you as bait. Who's coming for you, *Meat*?" She stroked Yani's face. "Who?"

Yani screamed as a powerful shot of magic lanced through her.

"You're going to tell me," hissed Daria, seizing her by the throat and squeezing. "Who is following? Your father? Your brother?"

"No! Nobody! Nobody! I swear."

Magic juddered through her again. Daria squeezed her throat as she pushed her face into Yani's.

"Or is it some big meaty lover who's going to ride you till you scream with pleasure, hey?"

Magic pain again.

"No," screamed Yani. "No one will come! I swear it! Please. Just kill me!"

"Pah! Useless lying bitch."

Daria seized Yani's head and pressed her fingers to her skull in mindsearch position. Yani squeezed her eyes shut so that her triumph would not show. Daria's mind came into hers like a blow from an iron bar, a painful violation. Yani forced herself relax, to reach out for the life spirit. It was there as it always was.

A great light burst forth in Yani's mind, momentarily blinding her. She heard Daria let out a terrible shriek and then excruciatingly, she felt Daria's presence rip out of her mind. As her vision cleared she saw that Daria was lying on the floor staring in horror. Seizing her chance Yani took a punch at her. To her surprise the dazed mage did not react and Yani knocked her unconscious, enjoying it more than a Tari should. That fixed Daria.

Pulling on her filthy gown and shoes, Yani quickly searched Daria's unconscious body. No sign of anything as useful as a manacle key. She could hear the men talking and laughing down the hall and dared not stay longer. Daria would wake up soon and since she was a mage, there was no point in wasting time tying her up. Yani made for one of the shuttered windows, pulling an axe and the best looking sword from the wall as she went. Pushing open a shutter she saw that she was only one floor up and, using a couple of banners from the wall knotted together to make a rope, she slid down to the ground below and found herself in a meadow covered in small white and yellow flowers. Dew was sparkling on the grass. At the sight of it, the beauty of the life spirit and its joy filled Yani, soothing away all the horror of the night before and filling her with strength and hope. The life spirit was always there even in the worst of places.

Beyond the meadow was a wall and beyond the wall there looked to be a forest. Yani made towards it.

Chapter 3

A cloud of songbirds, gulls and exuberant parrots swirled in the pale sky above the tower filling the air with a cacophony of shrieks, squawks and songs. Laughing, Duchess Jindabyne Madraga of Lamartaine placed a wide flat bowl of bread and seed upon the battlements.

"Come, come my little greedy ones! There is enough for all," she cried.

She made the soft twittering sounds that told each species of bird that they were safe - that here was plenty of food and no predators to fear - then stepped back to let them enjoy their feast. A couple of gulls seemed inclined to bully the smaller birds and she used magic to make them go to sleep. Otherwise she did not interfere with their squabbling. Birds were hierarchical creatures and to fight over the pecking order was simply their nature. If you supplied enough food, everyone got enough to eat.

A flock of small finches rose over the battlements and came swirling towards her like a whirlwind of multicoloured petals. One little bird got caught in her hair.

"Hush!" whispered Jindabyne. She willed a sleep spell onto the flurry of terrified feathers and suddenly it was still.

Gently she untangled it and held the fragile little creature in her hands, admiring the exquisite form and colour of this tiny piece of the life spirit as the terrified beating of its little heart calmed under her fingers.

"Awake and fly!" she whispered to it, tossing it up into the clear blue sky. The bird fluttered uncertainly for a moment before it joined its fellows clamouring at the bowl.

"Well done!" said her husband Wolf, who was leaning against the top of the battlements smiling at her.

One would think after seven years of marriage she would feel more cynical towards him, but it still turned Jindabyne's heart in her breast to see his blue eyes smiling. Every good thing in her life stemmed from this man. Ten years ago her memory had been destroyed by a mindblast spell and she had had to re-learn everything: reading, writing, magecraft, even how to tame to life spirit which was forever whispering in her mind. Wolf, the first person she could remember being kind to her, had cared for her during that time and brought the tutors who re-taught her the skills she had needed. She was certain that she had loved Wolf in that forgotten time before the mindblast, for she had loved him from the first moment she laid eyes on him.

"You're up early," she said, wishing she could find better words to express the strength of her feelings.

"I must ride out," he said. He came to her side and put the back of his hand against her cheek. "You're chilled, my love."

"Only on the surface," she said, leaning her head against his shoulder. "Why must you go out so early? Is there a problem?"

"No. No more than my brother arranging a hunting party this morning. That friend of his has just come out from Miraya and he wants him to see the countryside of Yarmar."

To Jindabyne's mind, hunting as the Mirayans did it, pursuing a living thing simply for the pleasure of chasing it, was an offence to the life spirit, but she was a good Mirayan wife and said nothing. Wolf already knew what she thought of hunting.

He continued, "I promise that whatever beast gives its life to us will be brought home for the pot so that its spirit will not be sacrificed for nothing."

She smiled up at him. "Mind reader!"

He squeezed her. "I am filled with regret."

"Why?"

"I'll be out hunting instead of waiting in our bed for you to come back from your birds. I could warm you up in some ... more efficient way."

"Mmm!" she said, nuzzling his neck. He was not much taller than her. "Perhaps there is time before you go."

He laughed ruefully. "They are bringing out the horses already. Ah well. There is always tomorrow."

There was a sadness about him.

"Is something amiss, my lord?"

"Nothing particularly. Last night Serge and Lev..."

"Another argument?"

"Why can't Serge be more controlled? Not that I can truly blame him. Why does Lev find fault with everything about Yarmar? He cannot expect it to be like Miraya. Why did he come back here?"

"Why indeed?" echoed Jindabyne, who heartily disliked her brother-in-law, but for Wolf's sake, tried to hide it. Lev had made his disapproval of her quite clear when she married Wolf seven years ago, and he had done nothing to heal the breech since he had come back from Miraya. Sometimes she wondered why Wolf, who was normally such a good judge of character, put up with this thorn tree in his flower garden. She sensed some past guilt toward Lev, but she did not like to inquire too closely into her husband's life before their meeting. Before they had married he had told her that there had been a woman who had hurt him very deeply, making it difficult for him to love again. Yet at moments like this, she was certain that he had come to truly love her.

"Anyway Lev told me he will return to Miraya before the year is out."

Thank life! thought Jindabyne. But aloud she said,

"You regret it?"

"Yes and no. This is obviously no place for him. I just wish it could be different. He's my only brother."

"I understand," said Jindabyne, squeezing him again.

"That's them calling me. I suppose I must go."

She caught his face in her hands and kissed him on the lips.

"Till tomorrow morning then," she whispered, making him laugh with delight.

"Till this evening," he countered, kissing her back. "I cannot possibly wait until tomorrow." He let her go and turned away, before hesitating and turning back.

"Oh, and when Serge finally shows his face don't go giving him healing. I know how kind hearted you are, but if he has to live with a hangover maybe he'll learn not to get so drunk and ill-tempered."

Serge was Jindabyne's favourite among Wolf's sons. The others were nice lads, but Serge had only been a child of eight when she had come to Lamartaine ten years ago. Since eight was still young enough for a boy to enter the women's quarters unchaperoned, she knew him better than the other two. He and his sister, Sasha, who was now married and living far away on another island, had been her first friends apart from Wolf and had helped her learn Mirayan.

When later that day, she did encounter a very green-faced looking Serge in the courtyard, Jindabyne felt sorry for him and would have healed him against Wolf's wishes. But Serge must have known of Wolf's wishes because he refused her offer of healing and would not even take a simple herbal potion. He might be a feckless lad, but he had a sense of pride and he was not about to go behind his father's back. Jindabyne left him to it and went back to her chores and the seemly endless preparations for Paulus' wedding to Dianou Seagani.

Though Jindabyne still lodged in the women's quarters, she no longer held to the stultifying seclusion typical of a well-bred Mirayan woman. She was not one after all. She was Tari, a native this island of Yarmar and revered by the other native tribes as a kind of holy person.

"Tari seek balance," her tutor Ezratah Karanus had told her. The life spirit that surrounded her and flowed through her had guided her into seeking her own balance between Mirayan and native-born womanhood, so she went about with her face uncovered, but made sure she was always modestly dressed and chaperoned. The more stuffy Mirayans such as brother-in-law Lev still disapproved, but those who had recovered from the shock of their lord marrying a native, had learned to live with her unconventional behaviour. The native Yarmarians, both Seagani and Mori, simply treated her with more adoration than she deserved.

There was too much to do to spend life skulking indoors. With the help of Bebeth, Wolf's children's old nurse and her housekeeper, Jindabyne ran Wolf's household more efficiently than any retainer had ever done. There were her beloved birds and her rose garden, and she had set up a healing hospice under the walls of the fortress. Here she spent hours helping Seagani healers to care for the poor and very sick, thus putting the astonishing power she had been gifted with to good use.

Ezratah had said that most Tari were stronger than her, that the mindblast spell that had robbed her of her memory had robbed her of much of her power as well. That was how she had discovered that he had known her before, in that blank time before she had been mindblasted. She had pestered him to tell her about it and eventually he had told her that she had been manipulated by an older relative into killing someone. The mindblast, a spell that destroyed memory and knowledge, had been her punishment for the murder she had committed.

She had been too shocked to sleep for days afterwards, tormented by the wrong she had done.

"It's past. You are a different finer person now," Wolf had comforted her. "You've paid for your actions. A good life is the true penance for such an act, a creative life that honours the life spirit."

After that she no longer sought to know about her

shameful past. She focussed on the present, on Wolf and their happiness.

Healing work usually refreshed Jindabyne, but that day she felt weighed down by a restless black mood. Several of her most difficult cases were making good progress, yet something was wrong. Had she forgotten to do something important? She wished Ezratah was here so that she could have talked this feeling over with him. But he had been gone for ten days now, on one of his mysterious missions for the Guardians.

She left the hospice with Bebeth and her guard earlier than usual and as they turned towards the fortress, a great cloud of ravens came out of the east and flew a full circle around the tower of the fortress. The harsh croak of their voices was like the sound of darkness breaking into the world and Jindabyne's presentiment of wrong suddenly became overwhelming.

"Something terrible has happened!" she cried, picking up her skirts to run.

When Jindabyne and her guards came bursting into the great hall they found a peaceful scene. Serge was sitting in the great hall listlessly rolling dice with his friends while around them the servants bustled about at their usual tasks. The moment Serge saw Jindabyne's face his hand went to his sword belt in alarm but Jindabyne did not stop to explain. Instead she rushed up the stairs, two at a time seeking her daughter, Olga. When she found her playing happily with her nurse, Jindabyne seized her in her arms almost crushing her, trying to make sure she was safe.

"What is it?" cried Serge, hovering in the doorway.

Jindabyne could not stop trembling.

"Something terrible has happened," she cried and suddenly she knew what it was. "Wolf! Oh no! Please! Life be merciful!"

"Serge, protect Olga!" she cried, thrusting her daughter into Serge's arms and racing headlong back down the stairs.

Thus it was that she met the messenger as he came

galloping into the courtyard to tell her of the Mori attack on the hunting party and thus it was that a short time later, breathless, and with her hair falling loose, she met the survivors of the hunting party at the town gate, bearing the dead body of Wolf Madraga, first Duke of Lamartaine, on a stretcher.

The men tried to stop her, but she brushed them easily aside with her magic. She pulled the covering from the corpse and faced the unthinkable, unbearable truth. There he lay covered in blood, wounds at his neck and chest, dead, her dearest, most beloved man. She could only scream and beg him to come back to her.

As the hunting party had ridden through the deep forest east of Lamartaine, a party of 30 Mori warriors had attacked them. Of the 15 men who went out that day, only four returned alive. Wolf, his two older sons, Paulus and Gideon, and five huntsmen were killed.

Lev Madraga and his friend Neevus had been separated from the main party, exploring another trail and, hearing the sounds of an attack, they had rushed to the party's aid. Being a very powerful mage, Lev had been able to chase the Mori raiders away, but it had been too late to save most of the party. Only two huntsmen had survived. From the way Lev wept as he told this story, no one could doubt that his brother's death left him heartbroken.

"We shall make them pay!" he cried, shaking his fist towards the Mori forest in the east.

As for Jindabyne, she let them use healing magic to make her reality hazy and lay on her bed, her hair over her face, too heavy with grief to move. Olga was brought to her, crying because they had told her she would not see her father again and Jindabyne found some comfort in soothing her and cuddling her while she slept. But when she woke, the little girl got bored with Jindabyne's stillness and Bebeth took her away to play. She was too young to truly understand that Wolf was gone for good.

The sky outside Jindabyne's window was full of birds. Sparrows chirruped. Finches twittered. Thrushes sang. They had come because they sensed her grief, but their beauty felt like a reproach because he was not here to share it with her. She hardly noticed when they fell silent.

Over the next three days, the castle became full as people came to pay their respects to Duke Wolf.

"I hope that Serge is up to the task," muttered Bebeth. "He's so young."

"What do you mean?" asked Jindabyne, who had given no thought to the world outside her room. Serge had come to see how she was every day, but she had barely noticed him through her dull curtain of grief.

"Serge is Duke of Lamartaine now," said Bebeth patiently. "It falls to him to keep the peace between the Seagani and the Mirayans."

Jindabyne knew what that meant. Lamartaine, which covered some of Western Seagan and all of Eastern Seagan up to the Mori forests, was a large territory. In many places Wolf had used the local Seagani tribal leaders to help him maintain it, absorbing them easily into the Mirayan system of vassalage. In others he had used other Mirayans, refugees from the war in Miraya, who had been part of the initial wave of colonisation. He was a good judge of men, taking only those who agreed with his light hand on the natives, but even so there was constant tension between his Seagani and his Mirayan vassals. Wolf had had to work hard to keep the peace between them.

"At least his uncle seems keen to help. Though if he really wanted to be useful, he would send that dog Guilius Appius packing."

"Is Guilius Appius here?" asked Jindabyne dully. She remembered how Wolf had distrusted the mercenary captain, describing him as a greedy young hound skulking around looking for territories to snatch up.

"Yes, apparently he's come to pay his respects. Appius is all confidence at a time when Serge is unsure. 'Let us attack the Mori', he says. 'You must avenge your father,' he says. I see only trouble in that one, worming himself into the empty space."

She came over to Jindabyne and squeezed her

shoulder.

"You must bestir yourself tomorrow, Your Grace. Tomorrow is the funeral and Mirayan widows have duties to perform."

On the morning of the Duke's funeral a great flock of silver thrushes, normally solitary birds, flew out of the forest and settled on the battlements and towers of the fortress singing their beautiful liquid songs. The sound woke Jindabyne from drugged sleep. Her heart was filled with joy and she reached out for Wolf before she remembered why she was alone.

Crawling from her bed, she allowed her maids to wash and dress her while she stood at the window in the grey morning listening to the birdsong and trying to draw strength from the life spirit in it. *Wolf has returned to the circle of life and one day you will to*, the song seemed to say.

"The funeral procession is ready for you, madam," said a maid servant. Bebeth and another maid arrayed her in the traditional mourning veil of a Mirayan woman, a huge piece of black cloth which covered her body completely. The only gaps were a latticework of embroidery through which she could see and slits in the front through which she could put her heavily gloved hands at necessary moments. She looked like a black ghost. Jindabyne had entered a calm, empty place where she was looking at herself as if from the outside. It was less painful place to be.

As she stepped out into the courtyard, Serge came over and drew her hand through his arm.

"How are you?" he asked. His face was pale and strained - all his joyful liveliness gone. Poor Serge, who had expected to lead the life of a loyal servant following Paulus' orders, now found himself master of a very unruly domain. She must try to remember to tell him that she had faith in him. He was very clever, perhaps the cleverest of all Wolf's sons.

She and Serge joined the funeral procession going into the darkness of the chapel. Only the women of the deceased's immediate family attended a Mirayan funeral. Wolf's mother and his daughter, Sasha, lived a long way away on other islands and could not attend, so aside from her, it was an all-male occasion as were so many of the rituals in Mirayan life.

Hierarch Taddeus wearing his finest vestments lead the procession, swinging the sun shaped incense burner. Jindabyne loved the dignified old priest, who had always nurtured her relationship with Wolf. A choir of acolytes followed him singing the funeral dirges of old Miraya and behind them came the mourners, Wolf's comrades and vassals, tall and splendidly dressed in shining armour, all walking in time to the rhythm of the dirges.

She did not shame the Madraga family by publicly breaking down, but several times during the service she wept secretly under her all-encompassing black veil, especially when they lowered her beloved's coffin on ropes through the floor of the darkened chapel into the crypt. So far down. She wanted to jump up and protest that he was not really dead and must be kept close until he awoke. But he was dead. She had felt the absence of life from the moment she had first seen his corpse.

At last the choir of acolytes began to the sing the final dirge in their deep bass voices and the service was over. Serge came over and took her arm to lead her from the chapel and as he did so, he pressed a piece of paper into her hand. Something about his face told her this was a secret. She pulled her gloved hand back though the arm hole of her veil, but it was too dark under this cloth to see what the note said. She put it inside her glove for safe keeping.

Next came the feast. This was also a man's occasion, but traditionally the ceremonies began with a ritual toast to the soul of the deceased by one of his female relatives. Bebeth had already told Jindabyne what to say. Now, whispering last instructions, Serge lead her up to the dais and helped her sit upon her usual stool at the foot of the Ducal throne. The throne itself would remain empty during the feast. The heir to the throne and the guests would all sit at the tables which lined the room and as the day went on they would make toasts to the throne and to the man who had once sat there.

Light streamed in through the huge arched windows on either side of the room, illuminating the rough stone walls from which the hangings had been stripped for the funeral, making the dais where she sat bright. Her huge veil made a little private world. Remembering the note, she slide it out of her glove and surreptitiously held it up so that she could read it by the sunlight coming in the latticework in her veil.

'You and Olga are in danger. Be prepared to flee the fortress tonight. Destroy this note.'

She stared at the note unable to comprehend it. Then her hand began to tremble and as quickly as she could she stuffed the note back inside her glove.

Olga in danger! She fought down panic. Life spirit protect us all!

At that moment Lev Madraga came up to the dais bearing a cup of wine.

He bowed before her.

"Honour to you, sister-in-law," he said.

Jindabyne took an iron grip on herself, determined not to appear weak in front of this horrible man. She took the wine from him and was immediately so shaken she could not help gasping.

The wine was deadly! It did not have the life giving nature of wine, but a dark absence that indicated poison.

"Now, now." Lev smiled at her. "Be brave! You must show us how strong a Tari can be."

He put his hands over hers pressing them around the cup. His smile seemed kind but his blue eyes were cold and in them she saw an enemy. He knew he was giving her poisoned wine.

For a moment she was paralysed with fear. Then she realised that he could not see her face through the veil and could not know she had realised.

Sweet life. She couldn't drink it and yet custom demanded that she drain the cup. Even though she must drink the wine under the veil everyone would notice if she spilled a whole cup. She scanned the room desperately looking for help. There were no Seaganis here! Only Mirayans. How could that be? To not invite Wolf's Seagani vassals to his funeral. Such an insult...

Lev was very much in control here. Now he was giving orders to the servants to fill the cups of the guests while Serge simply sat sadly at his place staring at the table. Jindabyne felt the jaws of a trap closing round her. Lev was popular with the Mirayans in Wolf's domain. She was not. If she accused him of giving her poisoned wine, would they believe her? A mere woman and a non-Mirayan at that. Or would they just say that she was a hysterical woman bringing shame on Wolf Madraga's funeral feast and have her locked away. Away from Olga.

The room fell silent with expectation as she stood. With a trembling voice, she said the toast and then she stood just there helplessly holding up the cup until the men below waiting with their glasses raised began to look uneasy.

Serge came to her side.

"Are you unwell?" he hissed. At that moment an escape plan came to her.

"No, no!" she screamed. "He's dead! He's dead!" and dropping the cup, she threw herself down on her knees, screaming and wailing, ignoring the murmur of anger from among the men.

"Just like a native," she heard one of them sneer quite loudly.

Serge, bless him, did not waste time disdaining.

"Call her women!" he cried, lifting her up.

"Step-mother!" he whispered. "Try to calm yourself. This does my father no honour."

She ignored the anguish in his pleas and clung to him still wailing so that without waiting, he helped her from the room. Outside, as her women gathered round her, she continued to cling to him, so that he was forced to help them carry her up to the women's quarters. Not knowing who among her servants to trust, she kept up the humiliating farce of hysteria all the way. Only when they were climbing the narrow staircase to her quarters, her women strung out on the stairs behind them, and only Serge and her trusted Bebeth level with her, did she stop screaming. She let herself go limp as if she had fainted so that Serge had to take even more of her weight and hold her closer.

"Do not drink the wine," she whispered to him then, "It's poisoned."

"Jin..." he stammered and then he looked over his shoulder and dropped his eyes.

"I hear you," he said softly. "Be ready. If something goes wrong, go to Hierarch Taddeus."

"I will," she murmured.

In her quarters she allowed Bebeth to pretend to revive her and then sent the rest of her women away. While Bebeth packed a small bundle of belongings, Jindabyne put on her favourite locket, which had a lock of Wolf's hair in it, and dressed Olga in her travelling clothes. That done, she and Bebeth set about sewing the rest of her jewels into the hem of her travelling cloak.

That fiend Lev Madraga! Had he had Wolf killed? Now she considered it, the story of an undetected Mori war party so deep in their territory was ridiculous. The Hooded Queen had never shown any interest in Seagani territory before.

Why would Lev do such a thing? A mage could not be ruler of any land. Did he simply want to start a war with the Mori? Was that the reason her dear Wolf had lost his life? Was that all? She cursed Lev and vowed vengeance. But some other time, when Olga was safely away from here.

Just before night fall there was a sudden outcry from the hall below and a clash of arms. One of the women came bursting into the room.

"Madam! There's fighting!"

Jindabyne grabbed Olga's hand and the bundle she had made for her.

"Where is Lord Serge?" she cried to the woman.

"Here! Let me in!" shouted a voice in the corridor. Jindabyne flung the door open and Serge came charging through, sword drawn and bloody, his two Seagani friends, Alain and Luc, at his heels.

"Quickly, they're right behind me!" he shouted.

Jindabyne slammed the door shut, bolted it and locked it with magic.

"My Uncle accused me of calling up the Mori to murder my father and many of the others supported him," Serge shouted. "We have to escape."

Jindabyne ran to the window and flung open the shutters. Outside the setting sun was casting blood red streaks across a sky heavy with cloud.

"You men there! Get up here. I will fly you down," she cried.

Nervously Serge's companions climbed onto the window sill and using her magic Jindabyne pushed them one by one out of the window and made them glide diagonally through the air so that they just cleared the curtain wall beyond the fortress yard and landed on the other side of the moat beyond. She waited till she felt the pressure of each body touch the ground before she reached for the next man.

Fists were pounding on the door of the women's quarters. Jindabyne's serving women huddled together in a corner. She thrust her bundle into Serge's arms and pushed him up onto the window sill.

"Come on Bebeth!" she shouted, as she climbed up beside him.

"No madam," cried Bebeth, passing Olga into her arms. "You go! I will be safe enough here."

There was no time to argue.

From the window sill the drop to the yard of the fortress beneath was dizzying. Men carrying torches were running around in the courtyard below. She could hear shouting and the clash of metal.

"Do not be afraid, my heart," she told Olga. "We are going to fly now. Hold tight!"

She flung herself out of the window, pulling Serge with her. Down they glided, first too fast, now too slow. She worried that the weight of all three of them might make her hit the curtain wall. The men below began shouting. Had they noticed them? She was almost at the wall.

Suddenly something caught her, jerking her back as she was being dragged by a net. She fell backwards on the top of the curtain wall with a thud, Serge and Olga sprawled on top of her, Olga kicking her painfully in the ribs.

She felt the hiss of power and a figure loomed over them.

"Where do you go with such guilty speed, sister-in-law?" cried Lev Madraga loudly.

Jindabyne had never pitted her power against Lev. She knew he was extremely powerful for a Mirayan mage and that she herself was just a faint shadow of what a Tari mage could be but at this moment, it didn't matter.

"Olga! Serge! Run!" she shouted, pushing them off her and trying to roll to her feet, her legs caught up in her dress.

Without waiting to stand, she threw a desperate bolt of power at Lev. He threw it off with a flick of his hand. It crashed into the battlement wall with boom and a shatter of stone fragments. Staggering to her feet, she threw another power bolt. As she did, she saw Serge lift his sword and run at Lev.

"No!" she shouted.

Lev flicked his hands again, deflecting power bolt she had aimed at him towards Serge. Using magic Jindabyne deflected the bolt away from Serge before it could smash him against the battlement wall. A shatter of stone rained over them as the bolt hit the wall without Serge.

She threw up a shield of defence just in time to stop a shattering blow from Lev.

Sweet life! He was so strong!

In the shadowy light from flickering torches, Olga huddled like a small bundle against the wall. Was she hurt? Jindabyne moved back to shield her better, fending off several blows from Lev. At last she could put her hand on

Olga's head and the child jumped up and put her arms around Jindabyne's waist, whimpering.

Hot red ferocity filled Jindabyne's mind. She would kill this bastard before she let him harm her baby. Teeth clenched, she began throwing bolts of power at him.

Blast! Blast! Blast! The speed of her attack disconcerted Lev, but he managed to speed up his own. Back and forth the magical blows went, each one showering stone fragments everywhere as they hit the battlement walls. Each one of Lev's blasts shook Jindabyne's defences and she could not see that her attacks were having any effect on him.

Suddenly something flew past them and thudded into Lev. He fell backwards, eyes widening in shock as he saw the arrow sticking out of his chest. Beside her Serge lowered his bow. All around him were Madraga troops, standing with weapons raised or hanging limply in their hands, obviously confused, under orders to attack Serge, but unable to bring themselves to do so.

"Men! I am your true Duke!" shouted Serge. "You knew my father! You know me! Lev Madraga is the only murderer here!"

But even as he spoke, more armed men began pouring out of the guard tower further along the wall. Appius' mercenaries. They would have no scruples about attacking Serge. Jindabyne could see mages among the soldiers their robes flapping as they ran to get into range. The guards surrounding them began skittering along the wall toward the other guard tower.

"Quickly! Go! Save Olga!" cried Serge to Jindabyne, as he ran after the fleeing guards.

Clutching Olga to her chest, Jindabyne launched herself off the wall, glided over the moat and the roofs of the closest houses of the town beyond and landed in a small street. The mages on the wall threw a few blasts of magic after her, but they fell far short and once she had landed, she was out of sight and range.

Down here, the town was in an uproar, the streets full of townsfolk alarmed by the magical blasts and sounds of fighting coming from the fortress. Jindabyne managed to land in a small street and few people noticed her. Still carrying a trembling Olga in her arms, she was hurrying towards the cathedral when a woman pushed past her screaming, "My house! Help me!" and Jindabyne, staggering under her impact, glanced backwards. The houses nearest the fortress were burning.

Those stupid mages! Their magical blasts must have set the wooden town on fire.

Jindabyne hesitated. More than anything she wanted to get Olga to safety and the church would be the best place for that. This was not woman's work. Surely the townsfolk were organised to deal with fire and surely they could manage it. Wolf had.... The thought of Wolf made her stop. This was his town. Another roof burst into flame.

"Hold on tight, sweet," she whispered to Olga and hoisting her further up onto her hip, she hurried back towards the fire.

The burning buildings did not take long to put out. It was just a matter of rebalancing the hungry element of fire by calling forth the element of water from a sky that was already close to rain. She simply made it do so earlier and all in one spot. As the rain quenched the burning houses, the townsfolk recognised her and gathered round, desperate for news. Anger filled her as well as a kind of triumph at using her magic. She found herself, all shyness gone shouting at them.

"Lev Madraga and Guilius Appius are trying to overthrow Lord Serge. Quickly! Go aid him! Spread the word!"

Most of the townsfolk were Seagani and hated Lev Madraga. People began to seize sticks and stones and rush towards the fortress gates and Jindabyne would have been swept along with them had not someone seized her arm.

She looked up into the kindly face of Hierarch Taddeus.

"Come! This is no place for you or Lady Olga. Lord Serge has mages enough on his side. Let us get you to safety," he said and gently drew her along the street to the cathedral.

Olga went to sleep, wrapped up in her cloak on a bench in the chapter house, her head on Jindabyne's knee.

"How has this happened?" wondered Jindabyne, listening to the sounds of shouting and explosions coming from the fortress. "Serge sent a note warning me to be ready to flee. He must have known something."

"He did," said Taddeus. "I discovered something strange about Duke Wolf's death and warned him."

Lev had insisted that his own servants lay out the bodies of those killed in the hunting party and Taddeus, all unsuspecting, had agreed. But one of the reasons Hierarch Taddeus was so well beloved in Lamartaine was that he allowed the Seaganis to practice their old religion in tandem with the new worship of Mir that he taught. When the Seagani grandmother of two of the huntsmen wanted to pray over her grandsons and anoint their bodies with the Holy Oil of Nezrhus, the earth goddess, he had allowed her to come secretly into the cathedral with a priestess and conduct her ritual. It was these two women who first noticed the rope marks round the wrists of the two huntsmen and brought Taddeus attention to the fact that both bodies showed no marks of violence except for the sword thrusts that had killed them. Strange that both men had been killed with sword thrusts, they told Taddeus, when the Mori preferred to kill with bow and arrow.

Alarmed, Taddeus sent an acolyte to distract the guards watching over the Duke's body and when they had gone, he and the priestess examined the Duke and the rest of the dead. None had arrow wounds and most bore the signs of having been tied up.

"At this point I sent secretly for Lord Serge and told him what had been found. We decided to get you and Olga away from here until he had sorted out what had happened. We suspected Lord Lev, but we did not think he would strike so soon. I don't know if he found out that we knew or if he had planned this all along..." Taddeus shook his head.

"Godless wretch. He could not even let his brother be peacefully buried. He must have been the one who had him..." he looked nervously at Jindabyne.

"Assassinated!" said Jindabyne firmly. "At least Serge has given Lev pause by wounding him so grievously."

"You do not think that he has killed him."

"Unlikely. Such is the instinct for survival that, in moments of extremity, a mage automatically throws all his magic into saving himself. But he will be too weak to use magic now and with any luck his followers will be cast into confusion." Jindabyne looked nervously at Olga, not wanting to let her out of her sight. "Perhaps I should go and aid Serge."

"No! Serge has mages with him and if he is defeated you will need to get Olga away from here. Lord Lev is a mage and cannot rule by himself. But he can still rule on Olga's behalf."

"But..." Even as she spoke Jindabyne wondered what she could do. From what she had heard of other Tari they could send whole armies to sleep with a wave of their hand but she no longer had that level of power.

"Holiness, men are coming," cried an acolyte, running into the chapter house.

Jindabyne scooped Olga up into her arms, but the group of thirty or so men who came trooping into the house had Serge at their head. They had been defeated and were seeking sanctuary.

"They were so prepared," said Serge. "They seemed to be everywhere."

One of the healers, who had gathered to help the wounded, came to Serge but he waved him away. Serge's face was spattered with blood but it did not seem to be his own.

"He must have been planning this for a long time," said Taddeus.

Cold horror gripped Jindabyne's heart.

"I should have seen it earlier," said Serge.

"My lord we must decide quickly what to do," urged Alain.

"We have to leave the town," said Serge. "Guilius Appius has said his mages will set it alight if the townsfolk do not hand us over by dawn."

"And some would do it too, the filthy curs," muttered Alain. "But most are behind you, Serge."

"I cannot let the town be burned for my sake," said Serge. "And I think you and Olga will be safer away from here, Lady. Some of the men have gone to gather horses. As soon as they return we will go north. Lord Petrus of Palffy will surely aid us. I think withdrawing to marshal our forces is the wisest plan at this point."

So it was that shortly before dawn, forty men rode out of Lamartaine with Serge at their head and Jindabyne and Olga at their centre, and took the road north-east toward the border estates of Lord Petrus.

Chapter 4

Around mid-morning the party stopped at a small farmstead to rest and water the horses. While Serge talked with his followers, Jindabyne left Olga in the care of the farm-wife and walked up a nearby hill, where hawks circled in the sky above. She called one close and it swooped down to her outstretched hand. Putting her hand on her forehead, she squeezed her eyes shut and sent her spirit into the hawk's mind asking to see through its eyes. When the sharp creature sped upward again, it bore Jindabyne's spirit within. High in the sky, savouring the speed and ease of the hawk's flight, Jindabyne could see Lamartaine and make out several blackened roofs near the fortress walls. Otherwise, the city looked peaceful. To her relief there was no sign of a pursuing force.

Suddenly something cannoned into Jindabyne's legs. Her spirit fell out of the hawk and plummeted to earth. The force of the fall toppled her over and she came back to herself sprawled in the grass, with Olga holding her tightly around the waist. Jindabyne opened her mouth to scold her for interrupting a mage, but then noticing that Olga was trembling, she held her tongue and hugged her instead.

Serge was standing nearby looking apologetic.

"She insisted on coming after you and when you didn't answer her call, there was no holding her back."

"I wanted you and you weren't there," cried Olga, her face muffled against Jindabyne's neck. Jindabyne squeezed her tighter.

"I'm sorry she took you away from your counsels," she said to Serge.

He shrugged. "We had finished all sensible talk. I have sent several men out to rouse those we think could be allies. I do not like to encourage racial tensions but most of our supporters will be Seagani Chiefs. Those Mirayans at the funeral who would have supported me were unconscious by the time my Uncle accused me - he may have poisoned them as he tried to poison us. And he had most of our own guards locked up. Everything so well planned." He sighed.

"You could not have foreseen it," said Jindabyne. "Your father trusted him after all."

"He accused me of killing Father," cried Serge. "I could not believe it. The things he said..." He flushed. "No matter what it takes, I will avenge my family's death."

Jindabyne squeezed his shoulder. "I do not doubt you and neither do the others."

"We should get going. Is he following us?"

"There's no sign of pursuit. I doubt he planned for you to injure him. It was a good shot."

Serge grinned. "One thing I can do is fight. Father always says..."

He stopped, misery writ large on his face. Jindabyne saw that he was remembering that his father no longer said anything.

"Sweet life!" whispered Jindabyne softly. "How will we bear such a loss?" At that moment she felt the loss more for Serge than for herself. She squeezed his hand and said, "I know it seems a disaster now, but you will rise again."

Flushing with embarrassment, Serge shrugged her hand off and turned away with a muttered "of course". She picked up Olga.

"Ah, you are heavy, child! Won't you let Serge carry

you?"

"No," muttered Olga, clinging tighter.

"We must find somewhere for you and Olga to hide," said Serge.

"Perhaps with Chieftain Jark," said Jindabyne, who remembered Alain's father fondly.

"Perhaps," said Serge. "Lev is a powerful mage. There is no chance of your own people... Up in the Gen Mountains? That country called Ermora?"

Jindabyne shivered. "I don't think so. All I remember of Ermora is that horrible woman, Kintora, telling me I had failed them all. I never knew why... Anyway, Ambassador Ezratah told me that Ermora has been closed to all outsiders for years. Even to the Tari who left."

"Yes," sighed Serge. "I thought that was the way of it." He looked beseechingly at Jindabyne. "I did think to leave you with Lord Petrus. At the moment this looks set to become a fight between the Mirayan Lords and Seagani Chiefs and we must avoid that. It might be diplomatic for me to show special trust in Petrus. He is the only Mirayan Lord I can still count on to support me."

Jindabyne's heart sank. Petrus was a good enough man, but a Mirayan of the old school who kept his wife and two daughters strictly secluded. But Serge was right to think he needed the support of more Mirayans. Strange that Lord Petrus had not been at the funeral. She opened her mouth to ask Serge this, but Alain came running toward them and the thought passed out of her head.

They rode on and on down endless dusty roads. Most of Jindabyne's attention was taken up with keeping Olga soothed. In the late afternoon she fell asleep in Jindabyne's arms. Olga's sleeping face reminded Jindabyne of Wolf and a bleakness fell over her. Olga was all she had left of Wolf now. Lev Madraga had taken him away. And for what? Mere power.

All through the day they met parties of Seagani farmers and Mirayan merchants on the road and enlisted them to their cause. Several times Serge sent men out to rouse neighbouring settlements to arms against Lev. They spent the night in the hall of a Seagani clan leader, a client of Alain's father who had been a good friend to Duke Wolf. The menfolk sat up all night discussing the situation. Jindabyne was exhausted by the long day's unaccustomed travel after a sleepless night, but there were still duties for her to perform. Seagani regarded the Tari as holy, and after she had bathed and eaten, she found that the private quarters were full of people who wished her to bless their children or to seek her healing touch. It was a long time before she could fall into bed.

They set out early the next morning and rode solidly onward with few breaks. Since Serge had been sending out messengers to potential allies, their party was now only twenty men and five hardy Seagani women. By mid-morning they reached the Eastern border of Wolf's lands. Beyond that border was the thick dark forest of the Mori kingdom - domain of the Hooded Queen. The Mori were a fierce people, traditional enemies of the plains dwelling Seagani, and relations between their sinister Hooded Queen and the Duchy of Lamartaine were uneasy. Even if Lev had lied about the Mori killing Wolf, there was still the danger of a Mori attack should their party go too close to the forest. Though the road was well out of arrow shot, a quiet watchfulness fell over the group and everyone's heads turned to constantly scan the nearby trees.

Shortly before noon, they crested a rise and saw a group of forty or so horsemen trotting up the road toward them. Jindabyne heard the woman beside her let out a soft hooray of relief, when they saw that the party was flying the Petrus flag.

A tall tanned man whose fair hair had become white with age was in the lead. Jindabyne recognised Petrus, the Mirayan Lord of this area. Serge urged his horse forward to meet Petrus, who clasped Serge's arm warmly, even though his face was troubled. The two men dismounted and Lord Petrus drew Serge away into a nearby field so that they could speak privately. But the conversation did not go well. Suddenly Serge recoiled from Lord Petrus in shock, and at that same moment Jindabyne felt a frisson of magic nearby.

Clutching Olga, she swung round in the saddle and with her mage's vision, saw the glow of magical power around the group of Mirayan men behind her. Something flashed in the hand of one of them. A magic crystal! Sweet life! An illegally disguised phalanx of mages.

A heavy blanket of magic came down on Jindabyne, making her limbs feel like lead and her breathing come in gasps.

She tried to resist, but she was no match for the combined power of ten mages working in phalanx.

"No!" she moaned, out of a mouth that could barely open. Olga screamed and Jindabyne felt her small hands pulling at her.

Then, with a high pitched shriek, a hawk plummeted out of the sky, straight into the face of the man with the crystal. He screamed as his face was blotted out by feathers, talons and ripping beak. The glistening stone fell out of his flailing hands. The magical pressure broke.

A couple of the mages went to their leader's aid, but others drew their hands back to throw magic at Jindabyne. All around, men were shouting, drawing swords.

"Run!" someone screamed.

Gripping Olga, and clenching her fist to marshal her defences, Jindabyne urged her horse into motion. The horse, shying and dancing at the clash of weapons, broke into a gallop heading towards the Mori forest.

"Hold tight," shouted Jindabyne to Olga. A glowing attack of magic shuddered against her defences, then a second, then a third, each blow a near miss. The horse, ears back with fright, surged headlong through a field of sun dried grass so tall that it whipped against Jindabyne's legs. She dug her heels into his flanks, driving him onwards toward the cover of the dark forest.

She gritted her teeth as two more magical blows smashed into them. Then they were in the forest crashing through undergrowth, trees looming up all around, and she knew she was safe, since her attackers could no longer see her to focus their magical attacks.

At last she unclenched her fist and relaxed her defences

and as if sensing safety, the horse relaxed with her and slowed to a trot before he stopped and stood blowing hard. Jindabyne coaxed him up against the trunk of a tree and, with a wide sweeping gesture of her hands, camouflaged them with magic so that they blended into the tree trunks and the undergrowth.

Olga was whimpering, tears running down her cheeks but she sobbed quietly, clearly understanding that they were in danger. Jindabyne gritted her teeth in anger. *That damned Lev putting Olga through all this!*

"Hush, it's all right," she whispered. "I've covered us with my magic. No one can see us now."

Nearby, steel rang against steel. Someone shouted and another yelped in pain. A horse crashed through the undergrowth past them. Serge was riding it and after him, so close their horses seemed to merge, came another rider, sword raised. Serge turned in the saddle to defend himself as the following horseman swung a mighty blow. Steel clashed, the blades sliding over each other as Serge tried to hold off the blow and the man pushed down into it.

"Serge!" squeaked Olga in Jindabyne's ear, forcing Jindabyne out of her magical detachment. Sweet life, she was watching them as if they were a kind of performance! Giving herself a mental shake, she reached out with her magic and threw the man's sword out of his hand, unbalancing him so that he fell off his horse. Serge swung his horse round to hit him, but the man was up before he could reach him, running away back towards the edge of the forest, keeping close to the tree trunks. For a moment Serge seemed about to follow, but the clash of swords and thud of nearby hooves made him stop. He stood up in his saddle, waved his sword and shouted, "Madragas! To me! To me!"

A moment later six more horses came crashing through the undergrowth, closely followed by several more. Confusion reigned as men and horses clashed together, grunting and yelling. Jindabyne saw Serge urging his horse forward to help his heavily outnumbered followers.

They're getting the worst of this, thought Jindabyne.

Still hidden, she threw a spell at a couple of the Petrus men, knocking them off their horses. With a huff of satisfaction, she threw another one and toppled three more men into the undergrowth. Their horses bolted into the trees away from the fighting. The remaining Mirayans must have realised they were the victims of magic - faces pale with panic, two of them wheeled their horses around and fled, shouting for the others to follow.

Several more of Serge's followers now came crashing through the undergrowth toward Jindabyne, just as a flight of arrows came hissing out of the trees and one man fell. Olga screamed as several more arrows whizzed past Jindabyne's hiding place and Jindabyne readied herself to disrupt the next flight. Then a horn sounded out at the edge of the forest sounding the call to regroup.

"Come on," Serge waved his arm. "We must get away. To me! To me! Jindabyne come on!"

He wheeled his horse around and rode deeper into the forest. With a shrug of her shoulders, Jindabyne dropped her camouflage and marshalling her magical defences again, followed.

***

Alyx Verdey, heir to the Mori throne was hunting with three of her Mori brethren. They were creeping silently toward a herd of hopping mice grazing in a glade near the outside border of their forest, when a shout rang through the trees and they heard the sound of horses and the ring of metal on metal.

The hopping mice fled from the sound. Alyx flattened herself against a tree trunk while her guardian, Didier dropped behind a bush. A horse whinnied and a man shouted. Horses - that meant Mirayans. Sweet life! What were they doing in the forest? Attacking? Was this the next step of their plan to destroy the Mori?

Didier, popped his head up above the bush and beckoned the others to follow as he crept through the underbrush toward the sound. Suddenly a couple of horses came crashing toward them, flank to flank, riders smashing at each other with swords. Silently the Mori group broke apart, all four putting trees between them and the riders. From where she was hiding, Alyx could see an old overgrown camp ground making a clearing in the surrounding forest. Several riders were fighting there and a couple more were hacking at each other on foot.

One young man stood up in his stirrups waving his sword.

"Madragas!" he shouted. "To me!"

Madraga! The surname of the Duke of Lamartaine, her father's killer. So was he invading the Mori after all his promises? It didn't look like it. It looked like his party was under attack by a superior force. The liveries showed them to be Lord Petrus' men, but Petrus was a loyal follower of Madraga. Cursed Mirayans. Why were they fighting each other? And why come into the Mori forest to do it?

Suddenly, several men in Petrus' livery fell from their saddles. Magic! Alyx looked around for the mage but he or she was keeping hidden. A couple more of Petrus' men fell and the rest turned their horses and charged away towards the edge of the forest, leaving only those wearing Madraga colours behind. The young man who had called out turned his horse around.

"Jindabyne, come on," he called. He was looking for a mage too and suddenly a woman carrying a child and crouched on the back of a horse, appeared. A Tari woman. She was so close Alyx would have walked into her had she crept a few steps further. Alyx had never seen this Tari before, even though she had thought she knew all the Tari outside Ermora! Jindabyne? That name seemed familiar.

A horn sounded nearby. Petrus' men were probably marshalling for another attack. Certainly Madraga's folk thought so for they turned their horses and fled away deeper into the forest. The moment the Madraga party had passed, Alyx slid round the tree back towards the place where her own group had originally separated. She spotted Didier among the ferns, caught his eye. After a quick exchange of signals, the silent language of hunters, Alyx and the others nocked arrows into their bows ready for when Lord Petrus men came into view.

"Are there Gibadgee in our forest?" asked one of her mother's guards, using the derogatory name the Mori used for outsiders.

"We drove most of them off," called Alyx over her shoulder as she entered the opening of the enclosure where her mother held court. "Only a few got through."

How did news spread so fast? she wondered. After they'd scared off Lord Petrus' men with a couple of flights of arrows, Didier had sent her and Seb back to the camp while he and Arlette had followed the Madraga group. For once she hadn't argued about being sent to safety. *Better this news comes from me than from someone who doesn't understand the Madragas' significance. Especially now that I remember who Jindabyne is.*

Alyx handed the guard her weapons and strode down the corridor into the centre of the enclosure. Her mother, Elena Verdey, was there with some of her attendants. Since the attendants were all female her mother was unhooded. Good, Alyx would be able to read her expression.

Her mother had a thin message paper in her hand and a couple of messenger birds sat on a bird feeder that hung over the side of the enclosure. So that was how the camp knew about the Mirayans in the forest. But a bird could only carry short messages. Her mother smiled at Alyx and Alyx's heart sank. Elena clearly didn't know. Alyx would have to tell her about the Madragas and break her mother's fragile peace. Talk of the Madragas meant reminding her mother of Alyx's father's murder and of the captivity and abuse Elena had suffered at the hands of his killers. Often as not these memories drew Elena into black moods, leading to days spent sitting silently in the corner of her tent, speaking only as much as was necessary to maintain her rule.

Alyx knelt formally, as was proper for a subject, and gave her report of the fight and of Didier's plan to follow the intruders.

"He has done well," said her mother, her eyes bright with exaltation. "Were there any indications of who they might be?"

"Their leader called out the name Madraga," Alyx told her mother carefully. "I don't know if it was his name or his chieftain's."

Elena clapped her hands, her face full of bitter triumph. "Ha! So they *have* ended up here."

Alyx blinked. Not the reaction she had expected. How did her mother know everything when she seldom left the enclosure?

"Our spies in Lamartaine say that Lev Madraga has taken over the Dukedom and driven out the youngest son Serge. So Lord Petrus has turned against Serge Madraga," Elena paused. "Unexpected."

"And Duke Wolf?" asked Alyx, feeling so confused by this news that she mentioned a name she normally never spoke aloud.

Her mother laughed mirthlessly.

"He's dead," she snapped. "He was killed five days ago with his two oldest sons. The Mirayans blamed us, of course."

Alyx's jaw dropped in amazement.

"Dead? Then he's gone!" Her sense of relief was quickly replaced by outrage. "And they blamed us!"

"Until Mage Lev accused Serge of killing his father. Though I expect that the Mori will still be held responsible for it in the end. Given what I know of Lev, he is probably attempting to conceal his own guilt."

Her mother's mood was so strange that Alyx hesitated to go on, but a ruler could not make proper decisions without having all the facts.

"There was someone else with them," she said. "A Tari. The leader called her Jindabyne."

"Jindabyne! Sweet life, Jindabyne here!" cried Elena. Her eyes narrowed. For a moment she almost wasn't beautiful. "So. I am to have vengeance after all."

***

The Madraga troops bashed their way along through the underbrush in single file behind Serge, the nervous horses occasionally shying at rustling shrubs or uneven ground under their feet. Here the mangiri trees grew as tall and straight as pillars, with few branches low enough to trouble the riders, but the undergrowth beneath them, tall tree ferns and prickly shrubs, was as high as the horses' heads and covered all manner of fallen logs or stones. Jindabyne was too busy trying to keep her mount under control to pay any attention to the birds nearby.

She was not the only one to heave a sigh of relief when the party suddenly came out onto a path. Serge stopped and the others gathered round him. Except for the breathing of the horses and the shushing of the wind in the trees, it was suddenly very quiet. They could not hear the sound of horns any more.

"Is Lord Petrus still following us?" Serge asked.

Jindabyne sent her magical consciousness back behind them. She could not sense anyone nearby. She sent out her thoughts to find a bird to send back for reconnaissance. To her surprise she found none. *But there are always birds and animals around.*

"I can't sense any life at all," she told Serge, confused.

"What possessed Petrus to attack us?" asked Alain. "I thought he was loyal to your father."

"He made the same accusation as my Uncle made. That bloody man has thought of everything, curse him!"

"What accusation?" asked Jindabyne.

"He accused me of murdering my own father," growled Serge through gritted teeth. "Petrus told me he understood it was all your plan, Lady. He said if I handed you over, Olga and I would be safe. May he rot!"

Jindabyne was too shocked to speak.

"He can't believe...?" whispered Alain Seagani. "Lady Jindabyne is Tari. She couldn't do such a thing. And he must know that your uncle would kill you."

"He honestly seemed to believe that I would be safe. And that part about Jindabyne? If you recall, Petrus doesn't have a high opinion of women." He shrugged. "There's nothing else for it, Alain. We will have to keep to the forest for now. Lord Petrus's fief borders it for a good ten more leagues."

There were nods of agreement, but Jindabyne couldn't help casting nervous glances around at the surrounding trees.

"The Mori do not like trespassers in their forest," said Alain. "That's probably why Petrus has let us go."

"My father never broke his peace treaty with the Mori," said Serge stoutly. "They have no reason to treat us ill."

He's doing a good job of hiding the uncertainty he must feel, thought Jindabyne.

"Perhaps if we travel fast they will not notice us," said Alain.

"Yes," said Serge. "We should leave the forest as quickly as possible. By the sun this path goes north. Let's follow it till we can find something that leads back to the forest edge. I think a river flows through here somewhere, doesn't it? If so, we may be able to find our way by it."

Only fifteen members the party were left: nine men, three women, Jindabyne, Olga and Serge. No one knew whether those they had left behind during the battle at the forest edge were still alive. The mood of the party was heavy.

They rode silently along the narrow path, keeping their eyes sharp for movement and their hands on their weapons. The Mori were swift, silent killers, savage in defence of their sacred forest and they liked neither Seagani nor Mirayan.

Jindabyne kept her magical sense open to the element of life, but could feel nothing sentient - there was only vegetable life, trees and ferns stirring gently in passing breezes. The springtime fronds of the ferns were unfurling like the fingers of babies and the trees were covered in flowers. Those trees should have been full of honey eating birds, but there was no sign of them. Even the life spirit of the plants seemed muted.

A deep darkness fell on Jindabyne's heart.

Wolf is dead. The thought so filled her mind that it was as if she was wearing a mourning veil made of lead. When the party stopped in a clearing to rest and get their bearings, she sat on her horse, too limp and heavy to move.

"Lady!" called one of the horsewomen, bringing her horse to Jindabyne's side. She held out a small cloth parcel. "Here, I have a little food. Give it to Lady Olga. She looks so pale."

Her words pulled Jindabyne out of her black daze. Olga did indeed look pale.

"I feel sick, Mumma," she whimpered.

Jindabyne felt nausea roiling around in her own stomach too - as if the black mood had become physical. What was this? She felt terrible - not just grief but a cringing feeling like fear or horror. She increased her magical defences over herself and the feeling subsided. She spread the defences to include Olga and soon the colour came back into her daughter's cheeks. A drink of water seemed to settle Olga's stomach and she nibbled on the food the horsewoman had given her.

They started moving again, following the path.

Jindabyne looked around. Still no birds... Sweet life! What was that smell?

"Eww, what stinks!" cried Olga.

"Some animal is dead nearby," said Serge. "A big one by the stink of it. We'll be past it soon, Ollie."

But instead of getting better the stench got worse and worse until it became strong enough to make their eyes burn.

"What the hell can it be? Has a whole herd of cows died?" muttered Alain.

"Smells like rotting fish," said someone else.

Despair was gnawing at Jindabyne's mind with small pointed teeth. Why did anyone bother fleeing? Everything was bleak and bitter. If Mirayans had attacked them now, she would have willingly thrown herself on their swords.

The sound of Olga crying jolted her back to awareness. She cuddled her, whispering soothing words, but Olga simply buried her head in Jindabyne's breast and wept.

Jindabyne was suddenly overwhelmed by the conviction that something was terribly wrong, and in that same moment she knew what it was. The life spirit was wounded - was being attacked!

She reigned in her horse so violently it reared slightly.

"Stop, Serge! You must stop. Something terrible is ahead."

Perhaps Serge felt the wrongness too. With no more than a quick questioning glance at Jindabyne, he gave the order to stop.

A sense of urgent determination gripped Jindabyne.

She kissed Olga and passed her to Serge.

"Stay with Serge, sweetheart. Here is my kerchief to cover the horrible smell. Serge, you must all turn round and go back. This is Tari business. I will meet you back beyond where the smell starts."

She slid to the ground and began to run down the path, certain of her course.

"What are you doing?" cried Serge. He spurred his horse to catch up with her.

"I have to go and help. The life spirit needs me."

"You can't ... Jindabyne!"

"Go back!" shouted Jindabyne. "This is no place for Olga or for you."

Serge's protests were drowned out by Olga's wailing and he turned back. In a moment Jindabyne had rounded a curve in the track and was out of sight. Even Olga's wailing was less distressing than the overwhelming sense of horror up ahead.

A short time later Jindabyne heard the sound of horses hooves behind her and Serge and Alain Seagani rode up.

"Where's Olga?"

"Don't worry, she's with the others. They've gone back, but I can't let you go on alone."

That was the only thing they said to each other, for now the stench was so strong that opening your mouth felt like you were eating something rotten. Tying handkerchiefs over their noses did nothing to help.

The horses refused to go on. Serge and Alain were forced to dismount, and the moment they set them loose, the horses fled away back down the path.

The sense of wrongness filled Jindabyne's body like a pain. Through eyes blurred with tears she saw that the leaves of the still and silent trees had turned a blighted black. The ground was littered with the rotting carcasses of small animals.

Then they came to an opening in the trees and before them was a red gash in the land, as bloody as a fresh wound. For a shocking moment Jindabyne thought she was looking at a huge piece of torn flesh, before she realised it was a river. A river of red slime.

The sight was as obscene as seeing someone pissing on the face of a baby. Her gorge rose and, falling to her knees, she began helplessly vomiting. Serge was at her side, wiping her face with a cloth which he had wet from a waterskin he carried. The water was a brief blessed touch of balance on her skin before the horror of what she was seeing swept over her again.

Death. The river, the element of water, which should be a force of life, was only full of death. The bodies of animals that had been poisoned by it were littered everywhere and the grass and flowers along the bank were blackened husks.

Jindabyne began sobbing. She tried to crawl forward and fill the wound in the life spirit with her own life spirit. Hands grabbed at her, but still she struggled forward. The closer she got, the more overwhelming the horror became. The stench of it filled her head, the physical anguish of it made her shudder all over as if afflicted by a fever. Then, mercifully, everything went black.

***

As Alyx's party prepared to go after the Gibadgee, her mother came out of her enclosure to wish them good hunting. She wore a black cloth mask over her whole head which left only narrow slits for her eyes and a hooded black robe that covered her body and her hair.

I wish she didn't have to wear that thing in public. She looks so sinister, thought Alyx.

"Another bird has come. They are taking the Wulpunya path towards the river," said her mother.

"Then they will see what has happened to it."

"Yes."

"We will have to kill them, then," said Alyx. The thought was frightening. She had always wondered what would happen to her if she broke this greatest Tari taboo.

"No!"

The party leader spoke up. "Do not fear Lady, I will not let the Forest Child pollute herself with human blood."

"You must bring them back alive," said Elena. "I have use for them."

The leader bowed her head, obviously troubled by the order, but the Mori rarely disagreed with Elena. They trusted in her wisdom, both because she was Tari and because she had proved to be a wise ruler over the years. The party leader turned and ordered her group to go.

Alyx could not help being afraid. She knew how her mother felt about these particular Gibadgee, and Yani wasn't here to keep things calm.

"Mother! Wouldn't it be better to kill them outright and be done with it? The life spirit doesn't allow vengeance. You have told me this often."

"Don't preach to me, child!" snapped Elena. "Go! Do as you are bid."

As she jogged away through the trees after the rest of the party, Alyx's heart was heavy. She had only been six years old when they had been captives of the Mirayans and her memories of that time were hazy. Sometimes in dreams she relived the terrifying night in a barn when she had seen an evil man kill a woman and threaten her mother. Otherwise she had been kept separate from her mother and her greatest suffering had been her fearful longing to see her.

The time after they were rescued had been much worse. Her aunts had taken them to hide with their foster parents on a swampy island many miles from other people and her mother had been like someone dying of an invisible wound - pale, staring at nothing, weeping when she thought Alyx couldn't hear.

She and her mother had shared a small room at the back of the farmstead. One morning Alyx had woken up in the grey time before sunrise to find her mother gone. Frightened, she had jumped up to look for her, and seen her in the distance walking into the sea with a heavy bag slung over her shoulder. Full of fear, Alyx had run after her. When she got to the shore, there was no sign of her mother and no answer to her desperate cries. Staring at the empty sea and sky, she was overwhelmed by the sense that she would never see her mother again.

Then suddenly the sun broke through the early morning clouds and turned the world as golden as the life spirit, and her mother's head broke the surface of the water. Much later, she realised that her mother had tried to kill herself that day.

How will her pain express itself when she is faced with the one who caused it?

By the time Alyx's party had reached the Wulpunya path and caught up with Didier and the others, the Gibadgee party had split up. The Tari woman, Jindabyne, had ordered them to stay and had gone on towards the river with only two companions. The rest of the party had set watch, settled down to wait and had been easily outnumbered and disarmed by the Mori. The only difficulty was the child's screaming, which their mage quickly stilled with a sleep spell.

"She wants the others alive, as well," said the Mori leader as she left to escort the prisoners back to the camp.

"I knew that when I saw the Forest Child," said Didier. He sighed. "We can ill afford so many extra mouths."

Alyx cursed silently. Who the hell would want to be half-Tari? Tari were forbidden to kill, forbidden even to collude in killing, though Alyx knew her mother had ordered attacks on Mirayan intruders before. How could one protect one's people against enemies under such circumstances? The Gibadgee were not so handicapped. If Alyx had had some of the Taris' great magic, the taboo might have been practical. But her only skill was the ability to pass her life spirit to others, a limited ability at best.

"Why do the Mori accept Tari rulers?" she muttered to Didier as they crouched together.

Didier smiled at her. Mentor, bodyguard, almost foster father, he could be very stern but he had a kind heart.

"Stop it," he whispered. "Tari are holy conduits of Labwa's love for his children. There is no shame in being unable to kill other men."

"What do you think my mother wants with these people?"

Didier's face clouded. He knew more of Elena's past than most Mori. "I don't know," he said, adding, "But she is still Tari. We must trust her to do right."

"What if...?" Alyx struggled to put her dread into words. She herself felt bitter hatred towards the people who had robbed her of her father and she had not been half as harmed by them as her mother.

"Ssh! Here they come." Didier's face became still and alert

Two young warriors came down the path. One had the facial tattoos and torc of a high-class Seagani and the other was a Mirayan, judging by his fair skin and hair. Their faces showed great distress, cheeks stained by tears. The Mirayan carried an unconscious woman in his arms.

Jindabyne! The woman who had delivered Alyx and her mother to their enemies. Alyx was aware of a feeling of satisfaction. Seeing the ruined river the first time had affected Alyx in much the same way.

May the life spirit give the bitch terrible dreams!

The moment the men stumbled past them, Didier rose from the undergrowth and gave the signal to move in.

As always in these situations, Alyx had been told to hang back, and this time she did as she was told. The rest of the Mori simply stepped out of the undergrowth with their swords drawn blocking all escape routes. Two young Gibadgee knew they were outnumbered and only protested when someone put an iron collar on Jindabyne and took her away.

Now was the time for Alyx to step forward. The others spoke only halting Mirayan, and of course the Gibadgee spoke no Mori. And trade talk was no language for speaking to enemies.

She looked at Serge Madraga, the son of her father's murderer, expecting to see what? Cunning? The signs of an evil spirit? Cowardice?

He was surprisingly good-looking and the frank admiration in his stare caught her off-guard, making her stumble over the vehement words she had been rehearsing in her head. Annoyed, she recovered quickly.

"You are Serge Madraga, youngest son of the late Duke Wolf and this is the Lady Jindabyne," she said in her fluent Mirayan, learned during her captivity.

The young Mirayan closed his mouth and the admiration went out of his eyes. She could see him thinking about lying.

"Do not trouble to lie. We have already mindsearched your companions."

"Then you will know we are a peaceful party seeking only to pass through your lands," said the Mirayan.

"So your people *always* say," sneered Alyx.

With visible effort the young man controlled himself.

"Where is the rest of our party? The little girl? Surely even Mori would not kill a little girl."

"You are a fine one to talk," snapped Alyx, suddenly furious at this fresh-faced young man with his blue eyes. "Murderer's son!"

Didier shot a warning glance at her. With difficulty Alyx controlled her feelings. A ruler did not bandy words with prisoners. To show anger was to show weakness. She turned on her heel.

"Bring them!" she ordered.

Chapter 5

In the dead land, shadows flew above Jindabyne and the stench of rot filled her nostrils. The shadows grew into birdlike things the grey-blue colour of veins with three wings and long misshapen necks. Their cruel black eyes glittered. Twisting their necks down at a painful angle, the bird things gouged their beaks into Jindabyne's shrinking flesh, leaving deep red gashes. Stringy red flesh dangled from their beaks as they pulled them up out of her. Their ice-cold claws dug in as they gulped the flesh down.

Suddenly someone threw open a door and light blasted the shadows away. Birdsong rang out bright and loud and the clean smell of sweet-oil overpowered the stench of rot. Jindabyne's eyes opened to see a man was leaning over her with his hands on her face. His healing power smoothed into her like warm, golden honey and for a moment she relaxed into it.

Only for a moment.

Braids interwoven with feathers. Sweet life! A Mori!

"What...? Where am I?"

"You are in the Mori camp," said the man kindly. "Rest now. You were exhausted and shocked."

He held a slightly salty drink to her lips. She was lying on a bed of skins and, above her, a huge canopy was stretched between trees. Its sides were open to the sky, and she could see four little green parrots chewing on the sweet-oil nuts in one tree. The sight of them busily climbing round the branches was very comforting. She didn't want to think about the reason she needed comfort.

Then she felt the cold weight around her neck. An iron collar to prevent her from using her magic. She was a helpless prisoner. Olga! Where was she?! The man did not try to stop her as she scrambled up from the pile of skins. A group of Mori were standing outside the tent and they turned to stare at her.

"Where's my daughter?" she stammered.

"Your daughter?" said a contemptuous voice speaking Mirayan. A tall dark-haired young woman stepped out from among the watching Mori. From her almond shaped eyes, she must be half-Tari; a very beautiful young girl but her expression was ugly. "How ironic that we now keep you from you daughter, Jindabyne Tari."

"I'm sorry? What do you mean?"

"You don't know me, Jindabyne? Alyx Verdey?"

Jindabyne could only look at her uncomprehendingly. She knew that Verdey was the name of the Mori ruling house but this girl was far too young to be the queen.

The girl made a contemptuous noise. "How well you feign innocence! Bring her!" she said to the others and two strong women seized Jindabyne's arms.

"Where's my daughter?" she cried as they dragged her across a clearing towards a huge enclosure made of skins. "Olga! Olga!"

She thought she heard a child calling out but before she could be certain, the women were hustling her along a corridor with cloth walls and no roof.

"Where are you taking me?" she cried to them in trade talk.

"Shut up!" snarled Alyx, who was striding before them. The corridor opened up into a wide enclosed space. At the end of this space was a tent open at one side and floored with beautiful skins.

The young girl went over to three who sat on stumps of

wood at the centre of the enclosure and took her place behind them. Two were Mori, a woman and a blindfolded man dressed in fine skins, hair decorated with bright feathers, and carrying staffs banded with copper. The central figure was a woman, though she wore breeches like a man. It was impossible to tell anything else about her for a black hood like a bag with slits for eyes covered the woman's head.

The hooded Queen! Even in the seclusion of the women's quarters Jindabyne had heard of the sinister queen of the Mori. A woman who never showed her face, a ruthless sorceress who had reunited the Mori tribes after their defeat at Wolf's hands, and who had forced the Mirayan settlers from their homes in the forest. She was rumoured to be a Tari, which accounted for why the Guardians favoured her so unfairly. Wolf had once told her that the Queen was so hideous that she hid her face. Wolf had hated the Mori Queen.

"Jindabyne! It *is* you!" cried the hooded woman.

This woman must know her from the forgotten time, but she did not sound as if it had been happy knowledge.

"Lady," said Jindabyne politely, curtseying and trying to hide the fear swirling in her gut as best she could.

"So now *you* are in my power."

"Have we met before Lady?" She couldn't stop her voice from trembling.

"How can you have forgotten?" snarled the Queen. She leapt up from her seat and suddenly she was on Jindabyne, her hands grabbing her shoulders, shaking her roughly. "I have not forgotten. I will never forget you and how you handed us over to him."

"Who lady? Please forgive me! I remember nothing of the past," Jindabyne cried. The woman had stopped shaking her. Her eyes glared through the slits of her hood. Over the woman's shoulder, young Alyx Verdey hovered, her face tense and fearful.

The Queen threw Jindabyne to the ground.

"My sisters told me of the mindblast," she said, spitting out the sour words. "You lucky bitch. I remember everything. Every *damned* thing."

"Lady, if I wronged you, I humbly beg pardon," cried Jindabyne. "Please forgive me. I was another person then."

The Mori woman was at the Queen's side, dragging on her arm talking to her urgently in a language that Jindabyne did not understand. The queen let herself be pulled away before suddenly turning back.

"Have you really forgotten me Jindabyne? I find that very hard to believe."

She ripped the covering off her face.

Jindabyne gasped. Before her stood the most beautiful woman she had ever seen. Utterly, utterly, breathtakingly lovely. How could she have forgotten her?

As she stared in open mouthed amazement, the woman's eyes widened and the glaring hatred on her face changed to bitter amusement.

"So! Marigoth was right," she said, her mouth twisting wryly. "Or I am less memorable than I thought."

"Lady, I am sorry," cried Jindabyne wringing her hands. "I always suspected that I did wrong in the past, but I am different now and willing to make amends."

The savagery of the woman's glare did not make her any less beautiful. For a moment Jindabyne thought she was going to leap on her again, but then she slumped back onto her seat.

"Take her away!" she said her voice heavy with disgust. "I cannot bear the sight of her."

"Lady please!" cried Jindabyne, as the guards dragged her away. "If you wish revenge... Do not harm the others. They are innocent of any harm to you."

Alyx found herself laughing mirthlessly at the irony of it all.

That was the great ruthless mage, Jindabyne? That weak cringing woman who was still apologising as she was dragged beyond the enclosure walls. Aunt Marigoth had said she was changed but that ... She was more Mirayan than Tari.

Alyx's mother let out a roar of rage and leap from her

seat shaking her fist at the sky.

"Sweet life! Why have you blessed her with forgetfulness when I remember everything?" Alyx, Warleader Inez and Shaman Jark sat open mouthed as Queen Elena, normally so controlled, kicked savagely at her tree stump throne, screaming curses until she was exhausted and panting, her fists still clenching with rage. Then suddenly she threw back her head and laughed.

"Oh no!" breathed Inez, a sentiment Alyx silently echoed. Laughter on the edge of hysteria - this couldn't be good.

"Oh I was a fool," cried Elena. "I was a fool to hope for vengeance. The past is dead and done for." Her face was bitter as she turned to the others, but she looked sane enough.

"Bring the boy to me, Alyx."

The two young men, Alain Seagani and Serge Madraga, had been kept separately from the other Gibadgee prisoners so that they could not tell them of the terrible pollution of the rivers. Both Seagani and Mirayan had long coveted the Mori's sacred forest and should they hear that the Mori were so short of water and game that they would very soon be forced to migrate to the foothills of the Gen Mountains where there were still unpolluted springs, their tribesmen were certain to take advantage of it. Most of the Gibadgee party would probably be blindfolded and set free on the edge of the forest but some other fate awaited the two young men.

Alyx felt queasy as she watched the guards untie Serge Madraga from the tree where he'd been bound. Her mother had the ability to command complete devotion, indeed love, from anyone who saw her face. Her Tari aunts had called this "the gift of fatal beauty." Those who looked upon Elena, especially men, lost all sense of self-preservation which was why her mother kept her face hidden as much as possible. Only Tari showed any resistance to her power.

Alyx had hated the few times when her mother had used her face to enslave people. So unfair. So ... un-Tari.

Was she about to enslave Wolf Madraga's son, by showing him her face? Alyx wanted vengeance as much as her mother did, but this didn't seem right.

But her mother always knew what she was doing.

Alyx ordered Serge Madraga to be brought to the Queen.

"Where's my stepmother? Why have you separated her from her child? It's inhuman," demanded Madraga. Always the Mirayans *demanded*. Alyx hardened her heart. He was her enemy and deserved no mercy just as his father had shown none when he had murdered her father!

"When I was her age, you Mirayans separated me from my mother and beat me if she did not comply with your demands," retorted Alyx. "Don't tell me what's inhuman. Bring him!"

When she entered the royal enclosure, Alyx was relieved to see that her mother was again wearing her hood. The Queen addressed the Mirayan coldly in his own language.

"So! A peaceful party travelling through the forest?"

"Yes, Highness," replied the Mirayan. "We mean no harm to the Mori and are very anxious to be on our way."

"Of course you are," said the Queen tartly. "We have heard of the political upset in Lamartaine and mindsearching your followers has confirmed it. I imagine the Mori would not be high on your list of enemies at the moment."

Dismay flickered briefly over the young man's face.

"Those who seek us may be inclined to come into the forest after us," he said. "It would be far less trouble for you if you let us go on our way."

"And the least trouble of all if we just handed you over to your uncle. We might even win his friendship."

"My uncle would never make an alliance with natives," snapped Serge. "He hates you all."

"Yes, indeed," said the Queen. "The return of Lev Madraga seems to have coincided with some interesting changes. Were you aware that your uncle Lev has a leaning towards death magic?"

The Mirayan had clearly not known of it, and it was news to Alyx, too. Did her mother suspect this boy's uncle of being behind the desecration of the rivers?

"What are you talking about? He would never...! A Madraga would never soil himself with such things!"

"It seems I know your uncle better than you do for he has most assuredly dabbled in the past," said the Queen. "According to your followers, your Uncle has accused you of killing your father. Of course, the penalty for this would be your death, which would leave your little sister the only Madraga left. And your Uncle in the position to take over as Regent on her behalf."

The Mirayan's face showed humiliation. He bowed his head and took a deep breath before speaking very carefully.

"I do not know my uncle's plans. But I know he is keen to war on the Mori, Lady. The nobles were full of talk of it. They blamed the Mori for my father's murder. So it would serve you better if my companions and I were let free to organise resistance and keep my uncle busy."

"Perhaps. Or perhaps you would just take advantage of our weakness. We have no reason to trust Mirayans."

Serge blinked, obviously not understanding what she meant.

Her mother laughed softly and shook her head. "You are not your father's equal, are you boy?"

The Gibadgee flushed, opened his mouth to protest against the taunt, closed it again, and then, with a visible effort, relaxed his face until he looked almost dignified.

"Since I am your prisoner, I can't stop you insulting me."

"Very good!" laughed the Queen. "Perhaps you do have some sense after all. Now it's like this. Something terrible has happened to our river." She paused. "It is death magic, but despite the rumours I am no mage and our Mori mages have not the skill or the power to make our river whole again. Your stepmother is a Tari mage. She can help us heal our river and unless she wishes to see your little sister blinded and crippled, she will."

"You cowards! You don't have to threaten Olga," cried

Serge angrily. "My stepmother would be willing to help in any way she could. The state of the river distressed her beyond measure."

The Queen shook her head. "Foolish boy. Your Uncle will eat you alive. Don't waste your time with talk and anger. You are in my domain and I can do with you as I wish. You will tell your stepmother what I want." She waved her hand dismissively.

"Why not ask her yourself?" snapped Serge, obviously furious at her dismissal.

Alyx's hair stood on end at the sound of the fury in her mother's voiced as the Queen said, "I never wish to set eyes on *that woman* again. Take him away! Now!"

The Mori had heeded Olga's cries and brought her to the tent where they were keeping Jindabyne. Exhausted by her upset, she lay fast asleep in her mother's lap with her hand tightly clasping Jindabyne's, and did not even awaken when Serge came in.

"Yes! I will help them," said Jindabyne, speaking softly in Mirayan so that no one could hear her. "It is the only thing I can do. I have already discussed it with some of the shamans here."

"That woman is your enemy," hissed Serge. He leaned close. "Surely we can escape somehow."

"No," said Jindabyne. Her sense of self-preservation told her that she should be worrying about the Queen and what had happened between them in the past, but it was so unimportant compared to the horror of that polluted river.

The life force was mighty -- a great circle that bound the whole world together. Surely it was more powerful than the magic that had befouled the river. Yet witnessing that red gash in the land was like watching a leech crawling up an arm, watching its narrow pointed head questing in the air. Like a leech this red gash would sap the life force if it were allowed to continue unchecked.

"You must leave me here, Serge. You must get out of the forest and start organising against Lev while there's still time. I'll be safe enough. The shamans favour me and Queen is also Tari. She, too, loves the life spirit. She won't kill me."

Jindabyne had no idea what the queen would or wouldn't do. She could only hope their shared race meant something.

"She really is Tari? She was more aggressive than I would have expected."

Jindabyne was relieved to realise that Serge had not seen the Queen's face. There was something dangerous about the Queen's beauty - she had felt her will being sapped by it. That was another reason why Serge must get away. Had Wolf seen the Queen? He had spoken as if he had. When? How? Why had he lied to her about the Queen's face?

"What's to stop her killing you once you've served your purpose? What makes you think she holds to your shared religion over her own wishes?" hissed Serge.

"It's more than just a religion. It's part of us. This is a secret and you must never speak of it to anyone. The Queen cannot kill me without feeling my death herself. And that journey into death harms us Tari - can even drive us mad."

"Sweet Mir, you Tari are very strange!" said Serge wonderingly. He was thoughtful for a moment. Then he said, "You can be harmed in many ways without being killed. And there is nothing to stop others killing you."

"Healing the river is more important than my life. The life spirit in me knows that." She touched Serge's arm gently. "Without your father my life does not seem to matter so much. But yours does. You must leave me."

"What about Olga?"

Jindabyne sighed and touched Wolf's sleeping daughter's cheek lightly.

"I think she will have to stay with me. She will slow you down if you take her."

"The Queen uttered threats against her."

"I know, but I think they're empty. She just wishes to frighten us. I injured her once."

"How?"

"I don't know. It was in the time before I can remember. Serge, I truly think Olga's safer with me."

Serge nodded unhappily. He could see all the complications of trying to escape with Olga but was ashamed at how much he wanted to leave her behind.

"That half-Tari girl, the princess. She said something about ... She said that when she was Olga's age we Mirayans separated her from her mother and beat her to make her mother comply."

"Which Mirayans?"

"She didn't say. People have often asked me why my father honoured the treaty so loyally when it was so unpopular. Was there something between him and this Queen?"

A horrible thought came to Jindabyne's mind. "That was because of the Guardians surely," she said softly.

If Wolf had seen the Queen's face... But Wolf would never harm a child to control its mother.

She could not share these suspicions with Serge.

"Serge if you ever have the opportunity to see the face of this Queen, don't take it. She was once very beautiful but someone wounded her grievously. She covers her face because she cannot bear to have people see such terrible wounds and she would never forgive you if you saw them."

Serge was silent.

"Did you wound her?" he asked at last.

He had taken up her lie up so quickly that his question confounded her.

She turned away, trying not to let her relief show. "I truly cannot remember. I hope not. Just get away from here, Serge. It's me they really want. You get that bastard Lev for both of us. And for your father."

It was only after he left her that Jindabyne remembered the Guardians. They were all powerful Tari mages. Surely the river pained them as it pained Jindabyne. So where were they?

Just after dawn the following day, Alyx was shaken awake by Didier.

"The young Mirayan's gone," he said. "We're going after him."

"What about the Tari woman?"

"She and the child are still in their tent. Several of the Gibadgee tried to escape last night. The young Mirayan must have got out while we were busy with them. He's got the other man with him."

"Curse him! Just let him get lost in the forest and die."

"I wish we could," Didier looked grim. "But we can't risk him getting out and telling the Mirayans of our problem."

The escapee's tracks were not hard to find. The two men had left the camp in the predictable direction - heading west towards the forest border, but they hadn't been stupid enough to travel in the dark. The Mori quickly found the place under a stand of ferns where they had spent the night. The freshness of their tracks showed they hadn't been gone long. They must be relying on speed.

Soon Alyx, always fleet of foot, was joggling along the path with six Mori hunters behind her.

Around mid-morning, Didier shouted, "Stop! They've left the path."

Alyx, a little ahead of the others, stood where she was uneasily scanning the forest.

"*There he is,*" yelled someone.

As Alyx swung round to give chase, she caught a glimpse of movement in the trees ahead.

"No," she shouted. "This way! He's here!" She took off after the man, who was sprinting away down the track like a startled animal.

The Mirayan ducked through some tree ferns, sending the branches whipping back at her as he ran. She leapt after him, sure footed over the rough ground, dodging the slashing branches. He was so close now she could almost ... He ducked away from her grasp. With a final burst of energy she threw herself forward and grabbed his legs. They fell together in a bone-jarring, struggling heap.

He was hitting at her, trying to push her away, but she held on with gritted teeth while he thrashed and kicked around. He was so strong, he flipped her over easily and suddenly she was under him and he was bent over her with his fist raised.

He stopped, his face shocked. For a moment they stared at each other. What blue eyes he had! He was really very good looking.

As she opened her mouth to scream, he clapped his hand over it. She kicked and struggled trying to bite and break his hold. Then suddenly he was off her. Two of the hunters had him round the neck, twisting his arms behind his back.

"You have to let me go. The resistance! I have to ..." shouted the Mirayan struggling between his two captors.

"Do you think we're fools?" shouted Alyx, scrambling to her feet. "You just want to tell your friends that we're weak so that you can prey on us."

She longed to hit him so much that she had to turn away quickly.

"Damn you! You're digging your own graves!" shouted the Mirayan. "You have a peace treaty with my father which I would honour."

Alyx turned and looked at him. "Mirayans have no honour," she spat at him. "Your father was a rapist and a murderer."

As she walked away, she heard a sickening thwack one of the others hit the Mirayan.

"You lay your dirty Mirayan paws on the Forest Child again, you'll die," she heard one of them snarl.

Alyx started to run blindly. Away from the Mirayan, away from her tribesmen, away from everything. But the past kept pace with her.

She had vague happy memories of her father - the smell of leather, the feel of his cheek pressed against hers and of wriggling and giggling at the prickliness of his beard. When she was six, Serge Madraga's father, Wolf, had raided their summer gathering at Fleurforet and killed Alyx's father. Alyx clearly remembered huddling among the other children at the top of the stone tower while her mother and the other women fired arrows out of the windows. She remembered watching her mother cry and a grey dawn full of smoke and black clad men who loomed over her like birds of prey. They were forced onto a ship where a fat man hit her mother and even Alyx's desperate bites and screams couldn't stop him.

The rest was hazy. Tall women dressed in black with white veils over their faces, her mother crying, a beating that she knew was unjust. She didn't want to remember that time. She knew from what Didier had told her that Wolf Madraga's liege lord, Alexi Scarvan, had taken them prisoner, that he had raped and beaten her mother and that he had had Alyx beaten to make her mother more co-operative.

She also remembered a tall cold-eyed Tari woman, who must have been Jindabyne, taking her away from the black and white ladies to a small cosy wooden room which proved to be on a boat. A nice man had played ball with her and spoken to her in halting Mori. She had asked him where her mother was and he had told her that she would see her soon. He'd kept his promise too. He had such kind blue eyes, just like that Mirayan boy, Serge, and she had really liked him. Later she learned that he was Wolf Madraga, her father's murderer.

She was still shaking with emotion, when she charged blindly into camp and almost knocked over a messenger crouching on the path gasping for breath while a woman splashed water on his face.

The woman turned to Alyx. "The Mirayans have come into the forest with their mages and are heading this way. You mother wishes your attendance."

Everywhere people were seizing weapons, gathering up belongings and loading supplies into packs. Being semi-nomadic the Mori were used to moving camp. They were just doing it faster than usual.

Alyx raced into the enclosure where she found her mother hooded and ready to travel.

Her mother seized and hugged her. "You found the boy?"

"He was no trouble. But the Mirayans - where do you

want me? I don't want to hide this time."

"I have an important mission for you, Alyx.

Alyx knew what was coming.

"No!" she hissed. Having lived most of her life in tents, Alyx had learnt long ago to argue with her mother in a soft voice to prevent the whole camp from knowing their business, but this didn't mean she wasn't furious. "You're sending me away again, aren't you? How am I to learn...?"

"Alyx! Please listen! The Mirayans are not much danger. We will just melt into the undergrowth and pick them off as we usually do. The river is the true danger." Elena put her hand on her daughter's cheek. "I have discussed the situation with the shamans. They all agree that the best plan is to take that Tari Woman to the source of the river where the sickness begins."

"Mother!" wailed Alyx, forgetting about possible eavesdroppers. "Please!"

Her mother pulled off her hood. "Do as you are bid Alyx! I order it! Select your warriors and go." Her face softened. "Please! My dear, this is the most important task. The only vital task. If we can cleanse the river we have little else to fear. The forest can protect us as it always does. But one of us should go with That Woman to see that she does not weave a spell over the Mori. You know how much they revere we Tari."

Alyx scowled, knowing her mother was right. Elena kissed her brow.

"Alyx, it would be irresponsible for my heir to risk herself against the Mirayans. We should separate so that we are not captured or killed together. We are the last of the royal Verdeys."

Alyx nodded and bent her head. She was the heir, and must be responsible. Always responsible.

Chapter 6

Yani had cut off the skirt of the gown she'd been wearing when she been captured and now, axe in hand, ready to fight, she travelled through the forest at scout's pace - ten paces walking, ten jogging. Shut up in Daria's carriage, she had no idea the direction they had taken from the coast so she headed for the nearby mountains hoping to find a hiding place and perhaps even some kind of border over which she might be safe. With any luck she would be able to find someone who knew whether the coast was north-east or south-east from here, so that she could reach a harbour and try and find some way to meet up with Marigoth.

For now the most important thing was to get as far away from Daria as possible. After the savage way Daria had treated her, she must have left lots of bits of hair and skin behind which were exactly the things Mirayan mages used to find a person nearby. Hunting dogs might be a danger, too. Yani had no idea how experienced Daria was in tracking escaped prisoners or if she even had hunting dogs, but it was best to err on the side of caution. When she came upon a large stream flowing from the mountains, she followed up its course walking in the stream bed wherever it was shallow enough so as to foil anyone who might follow her.

The landscape here was utterly different from the scented forests and Mangiri trees of Yarmar. This forest was made up of low green bushes and large leafed spreading trees, which were almost as wide as they were tall. The smells were mostly of good earth and rotting leaves. Everywhere she saw signs that people used the forest for wood and food collecting, but there was not a soul to be found.

Around midday she rounded a bend in the stream and saw a village ahead. She stopped to take stock of her situation. She couldn't just walk into that village and ask them to take her manacle off. If they were Daria's peasants, they might well be too loyal or too afraid to help and even if they were not, in a country where death mages roamed free, it made sense to be cautious of a strange person wearing witch manacles.

What she needed was a smithy with useful tools and a fire. Yani climbed into a tree and took a good look at the village. Scanning over the buildings, she was surprised to see no smoke coming from any of the houses. Even on a sunny day like this there should be cooking fires. What was going on here? The village looked poor but too well-kept to be abandoned. Climbing down from the tree, she circled the entire settlement, creeping along under the cover of the forest.

The place seemed deserted, but she could make out a building that looked like a smithy. The only way to find a trap is to spring it, and if she could only get these damned manacles off everything would be so much simpler. She slipped in among the little houses made of mud and thatched with grey mouldy-looking straw. A hunk of bread lay on a table in one of the huts. Hungrily Yani slid inside, ripped a piece off the loaf and stuffed it into her mouth. It was hard and stale, but it was food. Signs of hurried flight were everywhere. A pot full of stewed vegetables hung in the fire showing that people had been here in the last day. They had taken their animals too. Fleeing from what? Daria Symina perhaps?

She slid out of the cottage and crept carefully between the houses into the dark smithy. The fire was out. *A smith never lets his fire go out!* In the dim light she felt around on the benches. A file. She could file through the manacle clasp. It would take forever, but it was her best choice so far.

Standing fumbling round among the tools, she chanced to glance out of the window at the little sandy clearing between the houses and saw blood and flesh on the ground. Sweet life! Some kind of large animal had been killed here. A goat or sheep had been torn apart here - it bloody carcass lay there, its white ribs like a cage, and guts and limbs were strewn everywhere. Pray she didn't meet whatever had done that!

A couple of sacks hung by the door. Yani shoved several files into one and, in the spirit of groundless optimism, added a hammer and chisel in case she met someone she could trust enough to use it. Then she crept back down the street and into the forest again. Safely back under cover she straightened, leaned back against a tree-trunk and relaxed.

Crack! A terrible pain on the side of her head and briefly things went blank. She staggered, saw stars, hit out blindly. Then they were on her, too many of them to fight off and in a moment she was on the ground, a man kneeling on her arm and another holding a knife to her throat.

A wrinkled face glared down in hers and a constellation of dirty faces hung behind him. A mouth full of blackened and broken teeth said something in a language she couldn't understand. A stubby hand tugged at her neck manacle. The question was repeated louder. Yani still couldn't understand a word.

"Mirayan? Trade Talk?" she asked.

Another face spoke, this one younger, lean, with sunken cheeks.

"Who you?" said this face in something like Mirayan.

"Where you come from?"

Strange accent, but at least she understood.

"The Archipelago," said Yani. "I am not Mirayan."

Wrinkled face said something urgent. Yani couldn't understand a word. What was this? Wasn't she in Miraya anymore?

"You healer?" said Thin face.

"Yes," lied Yani, thinking they might take her out of the manacles. It wasn't exactly a lie. All Tari could strengthen people by channelling their life force into them.

The men had a heated discussion in the strange language. Yani thought she heard the name Symina several times. Were they Daria's friends or her enemies? She counted seven of them. Those she could see looked like farmers, an unkempt-looking lot with bad teeth and pinched faces. Archipelagan farmers never looked as miserable as this. Was this what the Mirayans wanted for the Archipelago? Pray she survived to stop them!

The thin faced man shook the manacle again.

"Daria Symina make this?" he asked. Sweet life. Should she lie? Or had she found friends?

"Yes," she said.

Suddenly there was a shout from behind them in the village. Fear lit in the faces of the men.

"Get up! You come with us."

Though the knife was suddenly gone from her throat, they kept firm hold of her hands, twisting them behind her back and tying them with a strong cord. Two heavily laden oxen waited in a nearby clearing. Moving quickly, her captors blindfolded Yani with a filthy scarf and bundled her onto the broad back of one of the oxen along with what felt like several bags of flour. *Wonderful! Captive once again!* She forced herself to relax and listen to the life spirit. The whispering of the life spirit of this strange forest sounded different from that of the forests in Yarmar yet its essential nature was familiar.

Several times she heard something howling in the distance. Each time the men around the oxen swore softly and muttered Daria Symina's name. The howling sounded like something much worse than hunting dogs. Fortunately the sound was a long way off and her captors were taking precautions. At every little stream they came to, and they crossed several, they turned and splashed along in the water for a while.

Up and up they climbed until at last they stopped and pulled Yani off the ox. One pair of hands took her round the shoulders and another round the ankles and she was carried into what, from the echoing of their footsteps and the cool damp air, must be a cave. She could hear the sibilant hiss of whispering voices in front of her and the oxen plodding behind.

Finally she was set down on the ground and someone unbound her hands and pulled the bandage off her eyes.

Even the dim torch light made her blink. A cluster of men were looking at her and talking intently amongst themselves. Their pinched greyish faces were shadowy in the flickering torch light.

As her eyes adjusted she saw that they were in a huge dark space. People were gathered around the talking men, but others, many others, sat around the walls on mats, their indistinct faces turned to Yani as if staring intently. Cages filled with small animals and chickens were arrayed among them and to one side Yani could see pens for larger animals.

The men seemed to have come to an agreement.

"Come!" said a man, whose face was fleshier than the others and who seemed to be their leader. He pulled her up from the ground and tugged her deeper into the cave towards some mats where two small bundles lay side by side.

Two children lay with the unnatural tidiness of the very ill, their faces and arms covered in bloody bandages. Where their skin was not bandaged, it was badly scratched.

Yani knelt down, carefully lifted the bandages on the first child, a boy, and sucked in her breath. Some large, vicious animal had savaged him, leaving such terrible wounds that he might not survive. The little girl beside him was less badly wounded, but she would probably never walk again. Even Yani, who had no significant magical powers, could feel the death magic about these wounds. It was obvious what these people wanted.

"I can strengthen the life forces of these children," she said in Mirayan. "But I cannot promise the boy will survive. The dead hand of the Abyss is on him."

"Try!" said the fleshy man.

"You must release me then," she said, holding out her manacled wrists.

More heated discussion. Even the three women who were crouched beside the children, their heads covered in scarves, took part in it. Who could blame them? How could they know that she was not some evil creature like Daria Symina? She looked down at the children again. She had only a rough knowledge of the art of healing so she was glad to see that the children had already been washed and skilfully bandaged. She had only ever used her healing power in the heat of an emergency to strengthen the life spirit of the injured until they could be treated by trained healers.

Even though she was wearing iron manacles, when she touched the boy, death filled her mind with its cold, unyielding power. She pulled away quickly, feeling unaccustomed panic and forced herself to relax and try again.

She touched the boy's bandages one by one and felt a cold, hard something that was part of the Abyss was lodged in the child's shoulder. That would have to come out before anything could be done for the boy, otherwise it would just absorb all the life spirit she gave him, like a sponge absorbs water. She looked up. The villagers were still arguing about taking her manacle off, but an older woman with a lean, brown face and bright eyes was watching her closely.

"This child has a piece of darkness in him," said Yani

The woman understood her immediately.

"Where?" she said, in the clearest Mirayan Yani had yet heard.

Yani pointed to the place. The woman pulled off the bandage and with expert fingers gently prodded the wound.

The unconscious child did not even stir under her hands.

"Perhaps you are right," she said. She must be the village healer. She unrolled a bundle of cloth beside her and brought out a long thin probe which she offered to Yani.

"Since you can feel it, it would be best if you dug for it."

Yani looked down at the boy. Through the taint of the iron, she could feel that his life force was a thread, stretched thin, ready to break. And if it did? These people would surely turn against her. They had already fallen silent, watching her and the healer.

"No," she said. "I cannot do it with these iron things on. The probing will surely kill him."

The healer sighed. Then she spoke loudly in the unknown tongue. Instantly people were galvanised into action. A man grabbed Yani and, leading her over to a rock on the other side of the cave, took the hammer and chisel out of her sack.

The fleshy man scowled at Yani. "If you treat us ill, we find revenge."

"I will not harm you."

The man with the hammer spoke. The fleshy man took her shoulder and pushed her down against the rock so hard that the manacle clanged.

"He say hold still less you want lost ear."

Pray the hammer man had a steady hand!

The chisel hit the manacle with teeth jarring blows, but it came off easily. So did the wristlets. Then the wonderful feeling of the life spirit free now of the taint of iron came flooding freely back into her.

Her first instinct was to flee, but she could not leave those children. Before she sat down to work on the boy, she drew the Tari sign of the life spirit on the ground of the cave, four concentric circles representing the four elements Earth, Air, Water, Fire with the cross of Life itself bisecting it. She whispered the morning chant to herself. The words brought the life spirit even closer, its gentle cleansing power washing away her fear. She could feel the earth all around her and somewhere behind her the air at the opening of the cave.

She called for a candle and a cup of water and placed the cup of water on one side of the boy and the candle on the other. Now with all five elements, Earth, Air, Fire, Water and Life present, her contact with the life spirit was strong and she picked up the probe and after giving it to the healer, took her hand and showed her where the piece of the Abyss was embedded in the boy's shoulder.

"You must dig for it. I shall keep the boy alive while you do."

The healer sighed again. "This boy's father is the village headman," she said. "Do *not* let him die."

Yani put one hand on the child's heart and another on the pulse in his neck. She let the life spirit flow over her like gentle waves in a summer sea.

"Begin," she said.

The healer was blessedly skilful. Only the boy's weakened condition had made her reluctant to clean the wound more deeply. Soon she let out an exclamation of triumph and held something up. The villagers shouted with pleasure. Yani was too busy to pay much attention to it. With the draining power of the Abyss out of his body, the boy could absorb the life spirit she was passing to him and Yani felt the thread of his life suddenly thicken and grow. Already his breathing was deeper. She sighed and relaxed for a moment. Now for the little girl.

But as she got up to go to the girl, the village headman caught her arm.

"No waste time with her. She not important. Spend healing power on son."

Yani couldn't believe her ears.

"Who are you to make such a choice?"

"I Father. Girls not matter."

Yani's mind filled with hot red light.

"What kind of father...? What kind of animal makes such a choice between his children?" She shouted. The man shrank back.

There was silence and in that silence, the woman

sitting by the head of the boy began to sob.

"Lady, don't harm us," cried the healer, catching Yani arm.

"Don't worry," said Yani. She turned back to the man. "And who is it who bears the sons that you find so valuable? The boy has had all the healing he can manage for the moment. I will heal the girl now."

"If son die, I kill you," muttered the headman.

"Go away you nasty man," snapped Yani, kneeling at the girl's side.

Afterward passing her life force to the girl she was tired to the bone. "I need food," she said to the healer who was hovering nearby. It was really sleep she craved, but she must leave here as soon as possible. If Daria Symina was looking for her, Yani's presence here would bring danger to these people.

A couple of women bought her food. One of them, who seemed to be the children's mother, kissed Yani hand's and wept. Yani blessed her more from force of habit than any real intention. The woman could not understand a word Yani said in any language.

"What language do you speak here?" Yani asked the healer, whose name was Mab.

"It is serf Mirayan, Lady," said the healer. "She is thanking you, and I thank you, also, for these are my grandchildren."

"Why are there two languages here? How is it you can speak the same as me and they cannot?"

"Only those who have dealings with the Princes of Earth learn to speak noble Mirayan," said Mab. "Once upon a time I worked in the Symina household as Lady Daria's nursemaid."

"Daria's nursemaid!"

"Yes," Mab smiled ruefully. "Such a sweet little baby. Now when she is here at the manor house she lets her blood beasts roam freely and her men raid our villages. They do not care that I once suckled her."

"They never find you here?"

"There are many caves in these hills," said Mab. "And

they do not really look so hard. We have an agreement..."
Her face changed as if she had said something wrong and
she looked quickly over her shoulder.

"The Symina are not fools," she went on quickly.
"Their wealth comes from lands such as these. Without us
there would be no wealth. They do not come here often.
The Pimenovs who own the lands over the mountains are
their deadly enemies. Lord Malov has taken land further
south which is much safer for them."

"Daria told me her brother killed their parents."

"I think that would be true. Malov Symina is a beast.
Far worse than Daria because he is colder."

"A death mage?" Yani asked.

"Yes. But he never had much power himself without
his demons. Daria has the magic in this generation. A cruel
family, the Syminas. Cruel even for the Princes of Earth.
They have always leaned towards the Abyss." She peered
into Yani's face. "You should sleep lady. You are tired to
death."

"I cannot stay here," said Yani. "I shall lead the lady
Daria to you."

Mab nodded. "When you leave, go over the mountains
to the east. Those are Lord Pimenov's lands. You will find
shelter there. I will get you food for your journey."

Yani's back ached. She lay flat for a moment to rest
her tired muscles.

It only seemed like a moment later that she opened
eyes again, but from the blanket that lay over her she knew
that she'd been asleep for some time. She sat up quickly.
Impossible to tell how long had passed in this dark place.
There was no sign of Mab, but a number of women were
seated nearby staring at her with a strange intensity.

"How are the children?" she asked.

None of them seemed to understand her, so she got up
and looked for herself. The little girl was now sleeping
quite naturally and the boy had some colour in his cheeks.
The children's mother was still sitting by their heads. She
took Yani's hand and kissed it again.

"Where is Mab? Mab?" she asked the woman, thinking she must surely recognise the name.

Was it the torch light or did anxiety flicker across the woman's face?

She pulled Yani down and said something urgent to her.

"I'm sorry. I don't understand," said Yani, unease growing. The woman repeated herself again even more urgently. Then suddenly she stopped, let go of Yani's hand and turned her face away.

Someone touched Yani's shoulder. A woman leaned down and passed her a bowl of stew. The hot savoury smell of it made Yani's mouth water. She took the stew and thanked the woman.

"Where is Mab?" she asked this new woman.

The woman merely shook her head and walked away, and Yani took a spoonful of the stew. The children's mother looked around quickly to see if anyone was watching, put her hand on the hand Yani was lifting to her mouth and said something urgent. This time she pointed towards the opening of the cave.

Did she want her to leave? Yani jerked her head towards the opening of the cave and the woman nodded vigorously and actually pushed Yani.

"Right," said Yani. "But first some food." She put the spoonful of stew to her lips.

The woman let out squeak of protest and dashed the stew from Yani hands. The earthenware bowl fell to the ground with a clatter.

"What?" cried Yani, but the desperate look on the woman's face told her that the stew had not been safe to eat and that she should go. Now!

She jumped up and made for the opening, wishing she had her weapons.

The cave was suddenly hushed. Yani's scalp tingled with the feeling of all those eyes watching. There was a flurry along the walls and a black mass rose to intercept her. In the torch light it resolved into a group of men, led by the fleshy-faced headman and the blacksmith.

"Where you going?" demanded the headman.

"It's dangerous for me to stay here," said Yani.

"Oh no Lady, do not go. Safe here. Lady Daria never find us,"

"Lady Daria can find anyone she likes," said Yani, edging forward round the group. She could feel the movement of air and, yes there, she could see the curve of an opening in the torch light. She edged towards it. The men moved and suddenly they had surrounded her. They were all a head shorter than her, but there were a lot of them.

"No lady!" said the headman washing his hands ingratiatingly. "Not here. Powerful spells have we."

"That so?" said Yani. All her senses spoke of danger, but she forced her body to relax. The men relaxed too. "Then perhaps I should stay here."

She stepped back so that she was out from among the men.

"Dangerous for you out there," said the headman. "I so grateful to you. Let I take care." He sidled forward and reached out for Yani's hand. She saw the smith at the back of the group grin. At the last moment she side-stepped so that the headman missed her. She jumped back, turned and ran back into the cave.

"Raven, Raven, Come!" she shouted, reaching inside herself to set free the Raven. She heard yells and heard the men come after her.

Suddenly the Raven was there and her humanity was sinking into it. Yani pushed her body forward into the Raven shape. With jagged pain her bones drew in and her muscles and skin changed to feathers. Suddenly she was flying instead of running.

She swerved and banked high into the air. She could not see well, but a draught of fresh air told her were the opening was. She swooped toward it, dodging past grasping hands, flapping her wings as hard as she could. From behind came shouting and the sound of running feet, and some thrown object whizzed past her. Light came to meet her and suddenly she was in the cool open air. She flapped her wings hard, climbing upwards in the sudden space, flying into a clear sky. Oh joyful, joyful freedom! She dipped and swerved for a few moments, familiarising herself with the different body shape, careful to stay as high as she could. Beneath her, she saw people streaming out of the cave mouth. One of them threw a rock, but it came nowhere near her. She let out a derisory cawing and flew upwards, enjoying the feeling of the late afternoon air beneath her wings. Far below two of the villagers had left the group and were running away along a pathway down the hill. The rest were rushing back into the cave. Yani turned and followed the pathway for a short way overtaking the runners. As she come out past an outcrop in the mountain side, she could see down into the valley to where the village was, just as a small group of horsemen headed by a veiled woman in gold brocade entered it.

They had sold her to Daria in return for safety. Ungrateful, cunning pigs! Even after she had healed their children, they had sold her. But after all she was a stranger and better to sell a stranger than someone you knew.

Yani turned in the air and flew back toward the mountains.

The problem with becoming a raven was clothing. Once your body changed, you shed clothes, armour and everything you carried. Mages had ways of dealing with this, but Yani was not a mage. When she had become the Raven - the Tari War Leader - the life spirit had simply gifted her with the magical ability to change shape.

Dusk was falling. She could find a safe roost and spend the night as a raven but spending a long time in raven form was...disturbing. While you did not forget your humanity, your mind was dominated by raven thoughts, simple thoughts of food and safety. On top of that, ravens were not great strategic thinkers, so if Yani wanted to plan what to do next she needed to resume her own shape. The moment she passed over the brow of the eastern mountains into the presumed safety of the Pimenov lands, she began looking for somewhere to spend the night. As dusk became darkness, she came upon little shelter full of hay, hopped inside and changed back into human form. The painful stretching feeling of changing into a bigger body left her shaken as always.

Fortunately it was a mild night and the little cocoon she made in the scratchy hay kept her warm. She lay trying to think about what to do next, but was so tired that she fell asleep.

Awaking in the grey light of dawn, she was quickly certain of her course. She could not leave Daria unchecked. She would go to this Pimenov fellow that Mab had told her about and try to join forces with him. Surely he must thank her for the information about Daria's proximity, and he should at least be able to tell her how to get back to the nearest port. She hoped she would not miss meeting Marigoth on her return journey.

After so much uncertainty it was good to have a clear path. She lay for some time in the warm hay enjoying her freedom and well being, until voices calling to each other somewhere in the distance reminded her that she could still be caught. Wriggling to the front of the shelter, she pushed herself into the painful change of the Raven.

Chapter 7

Yani flew east in big circles, keeping an eye out for any bird of prey that might be big enough to take on a raven and scanning the surrounding countryside. A river lined with villages sparkled through the trees below. The sky was overcast and as the morning went on the wind became chilly. Yani hoped she would not be spending another night in the open.

At last around noon she caught sight of a fortress set in the bend of the river. She had thought that fortresses the Mirayans built in the Archipelago were large, but this was enormous - a dark towering building with a strongly walled town nestled at its feet. Surely this must be the place were the lord of these lands lived.

As she alighted on the ramparts she felt the magical wardings around the place, but they were not the right kind of magic to bother her. When she changed her shape like this it was not a magical change, but a change of her nature from human to raven. All Tari magic was able to actually change things like this and because it was so different, Mirayan magic seldom affected it.

Patrolling guards walked past on the walls below, but despite the heavy guard, the fortress did not seem to be expecting an attack. The fortresses main gate was open and in the walled town below people were bustling about buying, selling, gossiping and working. Within the keep three women surrounded by playing children sat sewing in a walled garden full of roses. She was delighted to see that that shutters in the upper storey of the keep were open. Surely Mirayan lords lived in the upper stories of their fortresses, where open windows could catch the breeze and they could survey their domains.

Yani flew from narrow window to narrow window, resting briefly on sills and peering into rooms; staircases, a room where women lived, guard rooms and what smelt like a jacks. At last, hearing the sound of men talking and laughing, she landed on that windowsill.

Half a dozen well-dressed men were relaxing around a table eating meat from a cold roast joint and talking about hunting. Yani was relieved to discover that she could understand the Mirayan that they were speaking. That meant they were members of the aristocracy, or the Princes of Earth as Mab had called them. One of these must surely be Prince Pimenov.

"Look!" said a thickset man with curly iron grey hair, noticing the raven sitting on the windowsill. He tossed the piece of meat he was holding in his hand at her. Before Yani realised what she had done, she had caught it in her beak and swallowed. Delicious. She'd been hungry

"Highness, that's an unlucky bird," protested one of his companions.

"It's a clever bird that knows where the food is," retorted the grey-haired man. "Amazingly tame."

He picked up another piece of meat and came carefully toward the window. He had kind eyes. For a moment Yani thought to jump through the window and change there and then. Then she remembered that even the most serious message lost its impact when delivered by a naked woman. For the first time she regretted the torn and filthy gown she had left behind in the cave. Before the man could reach her, she flew off the window sill and went in search of clothes. The next window opened onto an empty bedroom. Someone, the lord probably, slept here, but at the moment the room was empty. She hopped onto the floor beside the bed and after changing back to her human form crept softly over to the big clothes chest in the corner and rummaged around in it. Yes, this would do - a long sleeveless blue tunic that should cover enough of her to save Mirayan sensibilities. Being a man's tunic, it was tight in all the wrong places, but she squeezed into it without too much difficulty.

Then she strode to the door and flung it open.

"My Lords! I have a message for Prince Pimenov," she cried.

The men stared at her in shock, before overturning chairs in their haste to leap up and draw swords. A tense half-circle of faces glared at her.

"Who the hell are you?" shouted the man with iron grey hair. "What are you doing in my best robe?"

The men looked ready to rush her. Were they going to listen to her? The only way through was forward!

"I am Yani Tari from the Archipelago and I have come to tell you that Daria Symina is at her manor house in the next valley with only 20 men for a guard," she said. "I heard Prince Pimenov is no friend of hers and that this information might represent an opportunity for him."

"Daria Symina!" cried one of the men.

The grey haired man put a restraining hand on his arm.

"Who sent you?" he asked.

"I came of my own will," said Yani. "Daria is a death mage. She held me prisoner but I have escaped. I came to you because they told me you were her enemy and would attack her if you had the chance."

"What is this? Who are you?" cried the grey-haired man.

"It's a trick!" shouted one of the younger men.

"Death magic," shouted another and they rushed her.

Judging it time to go, Yani swung round, darted back through the bedroom door, slammed it shut and finding the bolt, rammed it home. There came a sickening thud as the men slammed against the wood.

"Raven, raven," she cried. There came a moment of searing pain as she shrunk and suddenly the door looked terrifyingly huge, bulging under the blows of the men. She hopped up onto the window and launched herself out into the open air.

She flew around the steeply wooded hills until she found a lonely hay barn where she could hide and resume her own shape. With her own shape came an intense feeling of frustration. *Those damned men!* She still had no idea where she was. She supposed her appearance had been too precipitous, though she wasn't quite sure what else she could have done. At least she had done her duty to the life force. Surely they would at least check on her information.

Now she had to turn her mind to stopping Marigoth from falling into the hands of Daria's allies. Even though she knew the sea was to the west she had no idea what port she had entered the country from. What if she missed Marigoth while finding her way? Damn! Daria, curse her, was her only connection to Marigoth.

The straw itched and tickled her bare skin and it was chilly in this barn. She cursed the raven's lack of clothes. She cursed the Mirayan's fearfulness and she cursed Miraya for being so full of death mages that that fearfulness made sense.

Her instinct was to go back to the fortress and try to speak with its Lord again. He had seemed like a sensible man. Perhaps a more discreet visit to his chamber? Then at least if he attacked her they were evenly matched. Surely since she told him about Daria he would not treat her as a complete enemy. All she really wanted was information. She could think of lots of ways this plan could go wrong, but she couldn't think of a better one.

Ravens did not have good night vision so she returned to the fortress around twilight. There was no sign that an attack on Daria was being planned, but she was too much the Raven to really worry about the implications of that. She flew up to the top of the fortress and waited there. The ripe carcass of a pigeon lay in the guttering and she had difficulty in restraining her Raven self from feasting upon it. She'd eaten carrion as a Raven before and paid the price in human form later.

Night fell. Fortunately there was a moon. Unfortunately when she flew down from the tower hoping to get into the fortress all the window shutters were closed. She almost knocked herself unconscious against the wall squeezing in through one of the arrow slits and fell in a heap of feathers onto the stone staircase beyond. At least she didn't injure herself and the stairs were just outside the chamber where the men had been eating earlier that day, so she didn't have to wander all around the castle naked.

After changing back into human shape, she padded up the stairs and pushed open the door of the room. To her relief it was not barred, but the place stank of magic indicating that they must have been strengthening the wardings. Much good it would do them against a Tari shape changer.

Banked up coals in the fireplace lit the empty room.

Looking for something to wear, she crept across the floor, treading carefully to avoid squeaking boards, and found a pile of half-finished embroidery lying on a bench by the fire. She sorted out a good sized piece and after carefully feeling it over for pins or needles, wrapped the linen round her chest twice and knotted the ends together. The cloth was wide enough to hang to her knees. Surely now she was covered enough for Mirayan sensibilities. She crept to the door of the lord's chamber and carefully opened it a crack.

A light burned on a stand by the bed and the bed curtains were open so she could see the iron grey curls of its sleeping occupant quite clearly. But as she crept forward, someone seized her from behind. A hard hand clamped round one wrist and the cold sharpness of a knife pricked her throat.

"Stop right there, Lady," said a clipped voice.

Acting instinctively, Yani grabbed the man's forearm, ducked forward and threw him across her back.

Pin him down. Grab knife. Hold to throat.

As the dark-haired man on the floor stared up at her, she felt cold steel on her skin.

"Harm him Lady and you die!"

The man with iron grey curls was standing at her side holding a sword.

"I'm not here to harm anyone," she said.

"Let him go!"

Yani did as she was told. The man on the floor got up, and with calm deliberate movements, took a sword from a rack on the wall and turned back to Yani. He showed no sign of being hurt or even the least bit disconcerted by being thrown. Yani had to admire such professionalism.

Iron-grey curls backed away and sat down in a chair, putting his sword across his lap. He was fully dressed. Evidently they had been waiting for her.

"What are those marks on her shoulders, Ashana?"

"Tattoos, Highness," said the dark-haired man. "They're all over her back too."

"I never heard of anyone who tattooed their womenfolk. What are you doing here, Lady?"

"I thought you might talk more calmly with fewer companions."

"Did you? So tell me how you got into my fortress. Twice. And what are you doing wearing my sister's altar cloth?"

"Is that what this is? I don't have any clothes of my own. And you Mirayans are so prudish."

"What kind of people do you come from? And how did you get through my wardings?"

"I'm an Archipelagan from the island of Yarmar," said Yani. "I told you before. I escaped from Daria Symina yesterday and one of the peasants told me Prince Pimenov was her deadly enemy. Is that you and are you going to attack her?"

Amusement came into the man's eyes.

"Excuse me, but I'm the one asking the questions here. Notice my friend has a sword pointed at your throat. For what it's worth I *am* Prince Pimenov. So why don't you tell me in return how you got in here?"

"Look this is pointless. I just want to..."

"Tell me!" ordered Pimenov. "I have wardings against magic and you cannot have climbed the wall."

"Don't worry about that. As far as I can tell, your wardings are fine. You'll never meet another person with my powers and if you help me get back to the nearest port, you'll never see me again either."

The amusement had gone out of his eyes.

"Tie her up Ashana."

Yani darted quickly along the wall away from the sword and jumped over the bed.

"No you don't. I'm not letting myself be captured again."

Prince Pimenov had risen now. Both he and Ashana faced Yani with drawn swords. But she had managed to put the bed between them. They were all of them equal distance from the bared window.

"Lady we have you trapped here. We will inevitably capture you."

"What is it with you Mirayans and tying people up?" cried Yani. "Why can't we just talk politely like civilised beings? What's the nearest port from here?"

"Why? Did you come from there?"

"Yes, Daria captured me there and brought me here in a closed carriage. And I must get back there quickly. I haven't got time to play your little captivity games."

"Why?" asked the man.

"Are you going to attack Daria Symina? She needs to be taken care of."

"Would you attack someone on the say-so of a strange woman who won't say how she got through your defences?"

"You don't have to believe me. Surely you've got scouts."

"I've lost scouts to that bitch before," said Pimenov.

"This could well be some trap."

"Sweet life! You bloody Mirayans!" shouted Yani. "She's not that strong. And she only has twenty guards."

"All you have to do to make me trust you is tell me how you got in here."

It would be sheer folly to give away the Raven's secret.

"Where's the nearest port?" she asked.

"Tell me how you got in here."

"This is a waste of time."

"Agreed. Tell me how you got in here."

The moment she went for the window they would too. But there was a chance.

"I'm a mage," she lied, looking around.

"And you got through my wardings? Do I look like a fool?"

"Well you're certainly acting like one," she retorted. Seizing the coverlet from the bed, she cast it like a net at the two men. Of course they rushed her. As they did, she jumped the bed and darted towards the window.

Ashana had guessed her plan and was quick enough to duck the coverlet and seize her arm as she reached the window. She seized the wooden shutter bar and hit him with it. Then she pushed the shutters open with her body.

"No! Stop!" shouted Pimenov.

"Raven! Raven," she cried as she fell.

Thank life the change was quick!

The moonlight was bright enough for her to be able to make out the river below her as she flew, but as soon as she felt safe to do so she found a tree. She was tired so she nestled down into a fork in the branches and, listening to the soughing wind and the soft whispering of the life spirit all around her, went to sleep.

She'd been lucky that they'd wanted to capture rather than kill her, she reflected the following morning. She'd woken at dawn and after stealing a loaf of bread out of a peasant's cottage, and narrowly missing being hit by a flying stone, she'd flown to the lonely hay shelter where she had hidden the day before and changed back into human form.

There nestled in the hay she ate her bread and considered what to do next.

Any length of time spent in the shape of the Raven affected her thoughts. Animals, who mostly functioned on instinct, had a better sense of the life spirit than even Tari did. So while human logic told her that she should now fly to the west and find the sea, the instinct of the Raven was to return to Daria's manor house. The thought made her shudder, but she could tell that this course served the life spirit best.

And this unpleasant idea did have other merits. Marigoth would come looking for Daria so if Yani stuck close to her, then her chances of coming into contact with Marigoth were better than if she just hoped to meet her on the road. And if Mari got trapped before she reached Daria? Whatever the conspiracy was, Daria was a part of it so she was still Yani's best lead.

Seen from the outside, Daria's manor house did not look well defended - neither the house nor the high stone wall around it was in good repair. But Yani could feel even stronger magical wardings around it than had been round Prince Pimenov's fortress.

From the Raven's perch on the manor house roof, the layout of the house was simple. A great hall, with a shutter in the roof which kept out the cold but could also be opened to let out smoke, was connected to a newer building which contained three floors of smaller rooms. It seemed eccentric even dangerous to build a house like this in the middle of a forest with little defence and at such a distance from the surrounding villages, but if the Syminas had always had a yen for death magic, then it was very private. The grotesque faces carved on the roof edgings and window sills looked like the guardians of hell and perhaps they were.

For three days Yani hung around the manor, mostly in raven form and in all that time she saw no sign that Prince Pimenov had paid any attention to her warning.

In a place as loosely organised as Daria's manor house

there was plenty of opportunity for Yani to pilfer food from the kitchens, but though there were many hiding places in the manor grounds, she did not spend the night there, but flew away each evening to sleep more safely in human form in the loft of a barn near another deserted village.

Behind the house were huge roofed pens with tall fences which contained nine terrible dog-like beasts with huge fangs and wide staring eyes. These must be the creatures that had attacked the peasant children. They were far worse than just huge beasts, for there was no sense of the life spirit in them and Yani suspected they must have been born out of the Abyss. Even being near such creatures made Yani nauseous.

They were so vicious that every time something living passed the fence, even something as small as a raven, they would throw themselves at the bars and gnaw at them as if their will to destroy life was overwhelming. They were fed on live rats, which they did not eat but simply killed. The taking of life seemed to be what sustained them. Their carrion stench hung over the whole manor.

Daria was proud of her blood beasts. Every evening she fed and admired them as if they were finely bred dogs. Then a gate was opened in the back of the pen and the blood beasts rushed down a fenced run to spend the night roaming the forest. Every morning they were back in the pen, for they did not like sunlight and at the height of the day retreated under shelter. Yani could only be glad she had escaped during the day and had not had to face these beasts in the open.

Every day Daria's henchmen would ride out and patrol the area round about, visiting the villages, bringing back livestock and other food and occasionally setting fire to the buildings. The rest of the time they spent according to their taste; gambling, drinking, fighting or raping and torturing the young slave girls who were the servants at the manor. Yani tried not to go within earshot of these men, but there seemed no escaping the sound of children in terror and pain.

None of this seemed to trouble Daria and yet when she

found her men pack-raping two little girls that they had captured on patrol, she screamed at them like some demon spirit and cast a spell on the men that gave them severe pains in their bellies and sent them all running to the jacks. For a moment she seemed about to kill the little girls, but instead, after staring at the sobbing children for a time, she dragged them to the front gate of the manor house and threw them out. After the gate slammed shut, Yani flew down beside the children, pecked and harassed them to their feet and flew behind them until they reached a village and crawled safely up into a hayloft to hide.

Such sights left Yani filled with dark bitter anger, feeling sickened and dirty. Though it was always painful for a Tari to take life, even one gifted as she was, she longed to kill Daria and her men. Yet she could do nothing to help the slave girls without betraying her presence and Daria was the only connection she had to this plot to capture Marigoth. Was there any point to ripping out the plant unless you got the root as well? The cold instinctive mind of the Raven was a blessing in this time for it regarded human misery with detachment. "Wait," it said and though it filled her with shame, Yani waited.

A series of narrow triangular windows which were never opened let light into the room where Daria lived and slept. Yani could perch on the sills of these windows in her Raven form and watch. Daria's room was hung in red silks and velvets making it look like the soft inside of a mouth. Like a mouth there were teeth beneath. The death mage spent most of her time here playing with her fluffy white cats in the sullen glow made by sunlight or candlelight on the red hangings. She stroked them and dangled string before then. She caught mice and watched and clapped her hands as the cats toyed with them but when one of her pets scratched her, she paralysed it with a spell and pulled out its claws one by one while it yowled piteously. When she let it go, it ran away leaving bloody paw prints behind it.

Sometimes she locked the cats out of the room and cast herself naked upon the red silk bed. While smoking some kind of drug that made her languid and dreamy, she would titillate herself with a black feather until she writhed with pleasure. Daria was a pretty young woman but her back and breasts were patterned with the scars of whips. She slept unquietly, tossing and muttering in her sleep. Often she would call out the name "Malov," a sound of protest, and make the motions of pushing someone away.

At other times Daria would come to the window of her room and sit watching the road beyond the gateway, waiting for something. This could not be her permanent home. This was some kind of way station which meant that sometime, probably soon, Daria planned to travel onward.

On the fourth day Yani flew over the wall to find the maltreated and strangled bodies of two of the slave girls lying on the dung heap. Even with the coldness of the Raven's mind, she decided that she could no longer bear to witness their suffering.

She had located the keys to the cellar room where the girls were locked every night after the men had finished with them. That night she did not return to her hayloft. Instead she hopped through a space she had found in the roof tiles into an attic containing several chests full of mouldering old clothes. She often sheltered here in her human form during the day for the old clothes might be mouldering but at least they were warm. This night she slid quickly into an ancient green velvet tunic and hose and trying not to cough from the dust that rose from them, sat down with her back against a chest and dozed until the house beneath her was quiet. Then she crept to the door of the storeroom which was not locked but barred from the inside mage style, so that only a mage, who could move the bar without opening the door, could enter the storeroom. This made it easy for her to get out.

Relying entirely on Daria's magic, the men did not bother setting any kind of guard inside the house, leaving Yani free to creep downstairs, light a candle from the kitchen fire and pad down the greasy cellar steps. Taking the keys carefully from their nail, she opened the cellar door. The room stank of sweat and worse. The girls slept huddled on the floor, their slave manacles chained to the wall. They did not stir, though she suspected many of them were awake. She went quickly to one of the tiny windows and opened it in case she needed to make a quick escape. When she turned back, several of the girls were sitting up regarding her with wide frightened eyes.

Most were not yet women. Some were as young as twelve while the oldest could not be more than 17. They were dressed in tattered finery and all were pretty, with soft hair and what had been smooth fine skin before Daria men's had covered them with bruises and wounds. They sat docilely as she unlocked their manacles, but except for a couple of the older ones who went straight out the open door, the children clustered nervously around her with dazed expressions. Slavery and mistreatment had broken their spirits.

"Go!" urged Yani. "I've set you free. Now get out of here."

"But Lady where do we go?"

"There are horses in the stables," she told them. "And no watch on the gate. Ride over the mountains to the east. There you will be safe. Or walk if you are too afraid to ride. It will only take a day."

"What of the blood beasts, Lady?"

"Horses can go faster than them and by dawn they will be locked away again. I know it seems dangerous but if you stay here you will certainly be killed like your friends. Or worse. Sacrificed to the Abyss."

The girls fluttered and a handful more slipped through the door. But the younger ones clung to her hands. They were so little. One even begged her to lock them up again.

Yani groaned inwardly. She had had a feeling this might happen but had strenuously refused to face it. Marigoth always grumbled that helping people just made difficulties, but oppression of the weak by the strong was an affront to the life spirit which Yani found difficult to bear.

"Very well! I'll come with you and take you to somewhere safe. Come on." She herded them towards the door.

Suddenly a flash of white mage light blinded her.

Daria! *How?*

The high, light screams of children filled the room and the scatter of small bodies almost knocked her over.

"Raven! Raven," cried Yani. She ran for the window leaping into the change. There was a flash of light as something hit her and then darkness.

Yani awoke later to see shadows were dancing on soft red walls all around her. For a terrifying moment she thought she was in the Abyss. Big black bars stretched up and over to meet in a dome above her. Cold black iron pressed against the feathers of her back. Feathers?

Then she remembered that she was a raven and realised she was lying in the bottom of an iron cage. There was no way that she could change back into her human form surrounded by iron like this.

Even though her human instincts told her to lie still and feign unconsciousness, her bird self could not bear the exposure of lying on its back and she struggled to get up. The space was too small to spread her wings properly and it was difficult to turn without wrenching or breaking them.

As she settled on her feet and folded her wings behind her, she saw Daria sitting on a big chair by the fire, smiling at her. One of her cats was on her lap and as Yani watched, Daria deliberately let the cat go. With a deep-throated yowling it rushed to the cage, pressed its face against the cage and fished through the bars with outstretched claws while Daria leant over it smiling viciously. Yani the raven squeezed away, squawking with fright unable to but think of anything but escaping those huge claws. Then Yani the human got the upper hand. Anger filled her and with it, the will to fight. With a great leap she lunged over the reaching paw at the cat's eyes and felt her beak hit something hot and soft. The cat screeched and was gone and Daria threw back her head and laughed and laughed.

Yani called her a filthy name, but it only came out as cawing.

"Such fight," cooed Daria. "What a fascinating woman

you are Yani Tari."

She smiled silkily down at her. "I've been watching you, just as you have been watching me." She held up a black feather. Too late, far too late Yani realised that it was a raven's feather. One of her own. Daria would have been able to follow her movements using magic and that feather.

"You should never be kind to peasants, Yani. They only repay you with duplicity. Those crawling little worms had always planned to sell you out to me. They often give me travellers. It's an agreement we have. They told me all about your fascinating skill and gave me this feather so that I might find you. I didn't *have* to kill any of them.

"I assumed you would have run away by now. It's only a couple of days ago that I thought to cast the bowl of seeing on this little thing. I wonder why you hung around. Did you hope to kill me? Foolish. Very foolish indeed."

She put her hand on the cage and suddenly Yani couldn't move any more. Daria opened the cage-door and put her hand in.

"But what I really want to know is what you did to me that morning you escaped," she said, lifting Yani out of the cage. Bitter loathing filled her voice. "You damaged me in some way, meat. And now I'm going to find out how."

She sat on her chair with Yani still paralysed on her lap and put her thumbs like a vice on either side of Yani's small raven head.

"I could squash your brains out," she said. "But if you're good I'll refrain. *For the moment.* Now tell me what you did to me."

Daria's mind came into Yani's like the thrust of a dagger, but even so Yani felt only triumph. She repeated the words of the morning chant inside her head in order to strike back at Daria. Sure enough Daria screamed. Her mind pulled out Yani's like a dagger out of a wound and she flung Yani away from her. Though dazed with the pain of the mindsearch, Yani instinctively spread her wings to soften her landing.

Grabbing a poker from the fire, Daria came at her with savage intent. Screaming with fury she chased Yani round the room smashing at her with the poker while Yani flew before her, just managing to keep out of her reach and desperately looking for some escape. She flew up to a high window sill, but she could not resist Daria's magic. Daria drew her down to her hand and then flung Yani against the floor and Yani felt a terrible cracking pain in her left arm.

Daria came at her, poker ready to smash.

Change! thought Yani. *I must change!* As she thrust herself into her human form, pain made the whole world turn momentarily dark, but she came to herself in time to twist round with her good arm held up to ward off the blow. It didn't come. Daria had whirled away from her and screaming, flung herself around the room in an ecstasy of fury, smashing the poker against the walls and throwing the furniture about with magic. Chairs, tables, even a huge chest flew through the air.

Someone pounded on the door.

"Lady, lady are you safe?" someone was shouting.

Daria screamed at them to leave her alone and they went quickly.

Yani dragged herself upright. Her left arm hung useless. Her one thought was to kill Daria before she was herself killed. A heavy pottery bowl lay on the floor nearby, miraculously in one piece. She hefted it up with her good arm and swung toward Daria. But Daria turned too quickly and saw her coming.

When Yani woke again, she was lying on the bed - an iron manacle at her wrist and neck. Damn! Not again! For a moment she thought she was alone in the silent room, but when she turned her head she saw Daria was sitting crouched on the big carved chair beside the bed. Something in her face made Yani aware of her own nakedness. She pulled the red silk bed coverlet over her and tried to sit up. A stab of pain reminded her of her broken arm.

The room had been set right again, but signs of Daria's fury remained in the smashed crockery and dented walls. Her eyes were deep wells of darkness and her being seemed to be right at the bottom of them. For a long time she and

Yani stared at each other.

"What are those marks on your back?" asked Daria.

"Tribal marks. They mark me apart as a warrior."

"And a shape changer. They are the feathers of a raven."

Yani did not answer.

"Such barbarians!" sneered Daria

Something in Yani snapped. All the fury she had felt at Daria, all the things she had witnessed in this house welled up inside her.

"I'm not the one who rapes and strangles children," she shouted.

"You are in no position to pass judgement on me, slave," screamed Daria.

"If you kill me you'll only send me back to the Great Circle of Life, which I love. Why should I fear you?"

Daria lifted her hand. Suddenly Yani could not breathe.

"There are worse things than death," said Daria softly. *"And you know it."*

She leaned over Yani, watching her fall on her back and struggle for breath. Then with a click of her fingers, she released the spell and Yani took in a deep heartfelt breath.

"Keep a civil tongue in your head," said Daria softly. "You are at my mercy. And I have very little of that."

Yani returned her gaze directly. Something had gone out of Daria. She no longer looked like a predator. Instead she looked very, very tired and Yani felt vague foolish stirrings of compassion for her.

Beware, muttered the Raven inside Yani's mind. *A wounded animal is the most dangerous. Do not push her.*

Daria came to the bed and knelt down over Yani. Her hand slid round Yani's throat. "I have looked into the minds of many, many people but I've never seen a mind like yours. There was something terrible in there. Are you even human?"

Her fingers stroked Yani's throat, her thumb moving up and down over her windpipe.

"Something came into me. And you knew it was going

to happen. What are you? And what was it?"

"I am Tari. A child of the life spirit." There was no point in lying now. She was just giving names to what Daria already knew. "The life spirit flows very strongly in us binding us to the world, binding us to all life. You felt that in my mind. The life spirit can overwhelm those who are not used to it. I can imagine it would be very terrible to a servant of the Abyss."

She could not keep the contempt out of her voice as she said those last words.

Daria slapped her several times across the face. Luckily she was not very strong.

"You will tell me how to rid myself of this pollution," she cried.

"There is no way," replied Yani. She could not keep the smugness out of her voice.

"There must be a way, you lying bitch."

"Why would anyone want to be released from the touch of life?" snarled Yani. "Enjoy it!"

Daria let out a screech of fury and her fingers closed round Yani's neck.

"If you kill me, you will never..." croaked Yani.

Someone pounded on the door.

"Lady, is all well in there?"

Fear crossed Daria's face.

"Maggot bag!" She screamed at the door. "If you don't leave me alone, I'll make you shit blood till your guts fall out."

As footsteps went quickly away down the hall, Daria relaxed.

She was still sitting astride Yani, but now her fury was gone and she put out her hand and stroked Yani's cheek.

"Yani! Yani! Yani!" she said softly. "Let us not fight, Yani dear. Tell me of the weakness of this life spirit of yours. You know I can just rip the knowledge out of your mind if I choose. Do you really want to give me an excuse to hurt you? You know how much I'll enjoy it."

"I cannot tell you for I know of no weakness. If you don't believe me, you look inside my mind."

Daria made a disgusted noise, but strangely enough she didn't hit Yani again. She simply got up and began to pace the room.

Yani lay still listening to her pacing. Suddenly she felt very tired. Her broken arm ached savagely, she was covered in bruises and even if she got out of this room, she would have to get past the guards. At last she sat up, bound the coverlet more tightly around her and examined her arm. A messy swollen break. It would need healing. She could not ask Daria for help. If she knew Yani was in pain...healing would not be her first impulse.

Daria had paid no attention to her sitting up. Somehow a fire had appeared in the fireplace and Daria was sitting in her chair and smoking the sweet smelling drug that always made her languid and dreamy.

Both times she had come into her mind, Yani had felt how powerful Daria was. Why did she even bother with death magic? But she looked worried now, as well she might, for touching the life spirit usually made a person aware of the ways in which he or she had offended against it. What must that touch be like for Daria, whose very life was an offence?

"Come here," said Daria. She motioned with her hand and a chair was drawn close to the fire. "Sit. You will tell me about this life spirit. It must be a religion. How does it work?"

Yani sat down, trying not to wince at the pain of her arm, and began to answer Daria's questions. She told her about the Tari's beliefs, about the morning chant, about the way that the life spirit was a circle, which your spirit left to live in the world and returned to after it died and about how the life spirit connected you with every living thing. These were not secrets and the Raven, which was usually very vocal when the life spirit was endangered, was quiet.

But Daria was not, and her questions became increasingly agitated and angry. Suddenly she jumped up crying, "What is this sickly nonsense? Pale weak-hearted crap! What is sacrificed to this life spirit and what is gained? Where is the power in this?"

"Nothing but the will to violence need be sacrificed," replied Yani calmly. "Peace and unity are the gain."

"Pah!" spat Daria. She threw her drug pipe in the fire, pulled out a familiar looking vial and drank it down. As Daria drained the vial, Yani jumped up, looking for an escape even though she knew it was useless.

The Raven stopped her.

Stay, it whispered. *Take her within. Let the life spirit touch her again and again.*

Yani forced herself to stay still and meet Daria's madly glittering eyes, as the Death Mage pressed her thumbs into Yani's temples. Daria's mind came smashing in to Yani's like the blow of a blunt instrument, crashing though reality, into dreams and throwing Yani back into unconsciousness.

Chapter 8

Miraya was thirty days journey over the Western Ocean, too far to go in a small open boat driven only by magic. Ezratah and Marigoth stopped at the bustling port of Ishtak where the Tari's agents had already booked them passage on a fast ship to the closest port in Miraya. By then it had been ten days since Yani had disappeared.

The ship they were following was called *The Open Eye* and its home port was Cherabinium, well known as an open port - a fact which worried Ezratah. Open or neutral ports were the only places that death mages dared frequent and usually they bought the slaves to sacrifice to demons there. In return for the victim's life spirit, demons bestowed power on death mages. Marigoth and Yani's people, the Tari were more full of life spirit than ordinary people which would make them a great prize for a death mage. But as far as Ezratah knew, very few people knew of this Tari trait, so he tried to convince himself that the fact the ship came from an open port did not necessarily mean that Yani had fallen into the hands of death mages. Perhaps *The Open Eye* was heading for Cherabinium simply because it was the closest Mirayan port.

As a woman on a Mirayan ship, Marigoth was expected to cover her head with a scarf and have a veil over her face. This made a useful disguise and Marigoth accepted it with only the mildest grumbling and hardly a single insult towards Mirayans, which to Ezratah took as a measure of her concern for Yani.

Once the ship was under way, Ezratah, in his role as her proper Mirayan brother, took Marigoth to the prow so that she could introduce herself to the other women passengers. About 20 other people were travelling to Miraya on their ship, an even mix of Archipelagans and Mirayans. Only three of them were women; two quiet, shy Mirayan women, and a Seagani from Olbia. The Seagani was a merchant, travelling to Miraya with her brother, also a merchant, and, like Marigoth, was only veiled to protect Mirayan sensibilities.

Very quickly Marigoth and the Seagani struck up an alliance and abandoned the other women. They began chatting to the Archipelagan men. When Ezratah pointed out the impropriety of this, Marigoth retorted, "But the women are such dull creatures. I cannot spend 30-odd days talking of children and sewing. My brain will leak out my ears."

"Do you have to laugh so much when you talk to the men?" muttered Ezratah.

"Oh 'Tah. You *are* an old fogey," laughed Marigoth.

Soon Marigoth and her new friend became the natural centre of the group. Ezratah did not know if Marigoth was using magic or not, but she seemed to know just what to say to everybody to draw them out with remarks that could only be described as flirtatious. Archipelagans tended to regard flirting as a sport to be played by any and everybody so they regarded Marigoth as delightful. The Mirayans were clearly shocked. Ezratah remembered how disturbing he had found the freedom with which men and women interacted when he had first come to the Archipelago and now he could tell that the other Mirayans despised him for allowing his sister to carry on like this. He sighed but there was nothing he could do and secretly, he was relieved that Marigoth was acting so much like herself. At night in their cabin she slept badly and in the mornings she was often pale and heavy-eyed.

Not all of the Mirayans found Marigoth scandalous. A few days into the voyage, Ezratah was standing watching Marigoth with his usual mixture of amusement and exasperation, when a young Mirayan called Elius struck up a conversation with him. Elius was from a wealthy aristocratic family in the north of Miraya, "a part of the country which is now thoroughly subdued and safe". He always wore the finest brocade tunics over velvet breeches and very high red boots which disguised the fact that he was short and insignificant looking. His tunics were so splendid that Ezratah had dismissed him as a man with nothing but air between his ears. Over the next three days Elius told Ezratah all about himself, dwelling on the extent of his landholdings and of his family, leaving Ezratah mystified by this barrage of unsought information which he put down to the gaucheness of youth. Fresh-faced young Elius could be no more than twenty.

"She's wonderfully lively, your sister," he said to Ezratah on the third day. "I believe she is unmarried. As am I."

At this, the realisation dawned on Ezratah that he, or rather Marigoth through him, was being courted and for a very long moment he could only stare open-mouthed at the lad. He was disturbed to discover that his first impulse was to tell the boy in no uncertain terms to keep the hell away from Marigoth, but he bit his tongue and managed to reply politely, "My parents are unwilling to allow her to marry at the moment."

Elius looked surprised. "I had assumed you were taking her back to Miraya to find her a husband."

"Ah! Um! Well! We have an agreement with a cousin. He's expressed a willingness to come out to Ishtak for her. They can't face the prospect of her living back in Miraya."

"So you are going back to Miraya to...?"

All those of years of diplomacy came to Ezratah's

rescue.

"Grandfather's blessing. And we want to have the wedding there even though my parents are too old to travel now."

"Oh!" said Elius, managing to put a world of disbelief into that word. "Well I'm very glad for her. I think your sister would brighten up any household she lived it. I wish I could introduce her to my sister."

"I'm sure we would be honoured," said Ezratah, heaving a sigh of relief as Elius moved away and went to sit closer to Marigoth. Luckily he was clearly too well-brought up to approach her himself. *Damn Marigoth! If she's throwing charm magic about...*

But Ezratah knew that she wasn't. She was simply delightful company.

He avoided being alone with Elius after that and, except for one conversation where the young mage told Ezratah that he had several plantations on Ishtak and might be willing to settle there given sufficient incentive, the subject of marriage did not come up again. Ezratah would have felt sorry for the lad had he not been such an annoying little toad. He did not tell Marigoth about the proposal, even though it might have given her a laugh. Luckily for Elius, Marigoth was clearly too worried about Yani to notice her admirer.

One night Ezratah got sick of silently listening to her toss and turn.

"Is everything all right?" he asked, already knowing the answer.

Her voice when she answered him was croaky and she surreptitiously wiped her eyes. Surely Marigoth wasn't crying.

"I have such a dark feeling about this journey."

"Do you think Yani is...gone," Ezratah asked at last.

"The darkness I feel is different."

"What do you think it is?"

"Probably just fear," she said quickly.

"Marigoth, how is it you've come alone to find Yani? Surely they could spare someone else as well." Ezratah had been wondering about this for some time.

"The Guardians are down in numbers at the moment. A few months ago Mathaman went to investigate reports of bandits up in the Gen Mountains and he didn't come back. So Syndal's gone off to find him. Then Diyar disappeared with Yani. With me gone that leaves just four to keep you Mirayans under control. And you Mirayans take a lot of controlling, let me tell you."

Ezratah ignored the predictable old jibe.

"That's worrying. Mathaman disappearing."

"Yes, but things can happen even to Tari mages. I'm sure Syndal will sort it out."

"Could he have gone back to Ermora?"

This was the homeland of the Tari, a place now completely cut off from the outside world. Ezratah still remembered his brief time there with wonder - and with terror.

"That's what I think happened," agreed Marigoth. "He always longed to see it again. They all do. And it is in the Gen Mountains. Once he went in, maybe the stupid ninnies who still live there wouldn't let him back out."

"They forbade any of you to return at all."

"They can forbid all they like, but could they actually stop us? Ermora still welcomes us. I just hope Syndal doesn't follow him in."

A few days later he came into the cabin to find Marigoth leaning out of the window vomiting.

"Did you eat something bad? It's a bit late in the journey to get seasick, isn't it?"

"It's self-inflicted," groaned Marigoth. "I have been a very foolish impatient mage." She leaned against the port hole, her face green.

"What do you mean?" asked Ezratah.

"I made an imbalance. I deserve everything I get! Argh my head feels like it's in a vice."

"Hold on! I'll rub some healing magic on you. What do you mean self-inflicted?"

She protested but didn't push his hand away from her brow.

"I deserve this lesson. Oh, but that does feel nice. See, I've been trying to make the ship go faster and I've overdone it. Ooh! Look out!" She lunged over the porthole rim and vomited again. "Now I've made an imbalance in the Life Spirit and I can definitely feel it."

"I knew you could not kill without feeling the person's death. I didn't realise you could make yourself sick other ways."

"Oh yes. We Tari are as human as anyone else. Unfettered power would corrupt us into monsters unless the life spirit had ways of protecting itself from misuse." She groaned and lay down on the bed. "Ah! I think it must be righting itself a bit. If it wasn't for the fact that Tari can feel the outrage of the life spirit like this, there'd be imbalance everywhere. Curse it! I suppose this means I've done as much with the weather as I can."

"The captain said we would arrive at least three days early. We were ten days behind Yani. Now we are only seven. You've done well," he said consolingly.

"It only takes a minute to kill someone," whispered Marigoth.

Despite, or probably because Cherabinium was an open port, it was a thriving place, with a forest of masts filling the harbour and a good-sized, well-maintained fortress with impressive walls towering over the whole.

"Sweet life. It's enormous," cried Marigoth, when she first saw the port from the deck of the ship.

"Just a medium sized city by Mirayan standards," smiled Ezratah.

"To think there are so many Mirayans in the world," said Marigoth. "How ghastly!"

"Try to be brave about it," replied Ezratah.

As the ship slid slowly along a narrow channel through the mass of other vessels, there was an outcry from the other side of the deck. Both Ezratah and Marigoth turned and saw the half sunken hulk of an ocean going vessel sticking like a dead log out of the silvery harbour water, its burned masts black against the pale blue sky, a huge hole yawning in its side. Marigoth ran to the rail. When Ezratah followed and put his hand on hers, he could feel it trembling.

"We don't know which ship it is," he told her.

Behind them they heard Elius ask, "What happened here?" and the Captain reply, "The usual. A fight between death mages."

A couple of the Mirayans let out gasps and one of them said, "In this very harbour?"

"Aye! About time Lord Rayus closed the town to that scum. Pilot says they've put it down to Daria Symina. Seems she wanted something on this ship and instead of sneaking in to take it like they usually do, she made a big show of it."

"Stupid bitch," muttered Elius under his breath. He was glaring fiercely at the burnt out hulk, an expression which sat oddly with the outrageously feathered hat he was carrying.

"Yes," agreed the Captain. "The fire spread to several other ships, though this is the only one that sank. Most of the crew escaped, but since they were the kind of scum who work for death mages, they're in jail now."

"What was the ship called?" asked Marigoth. Her voice sounded quite normal.

"I don't know, little lady. But look, you can just make out the name on the bow there as we come round. What does it say? There you are. *The Open Eye.* A death magic name if there ever was one. What a place this country is!"

Silently Marigoth turned from the rail and walked away. Thanking the Captain, Ezratah followed quickly after her.

He found her sitting in their cabin, staring into space and shivering as if she had a fever. Without thinking twice, Ezratah put his arms around her and she leant against him, turning her face into his chest and holding his other arm with such intensity that afterwards he had bruises there. He held her, saying nothing, his cheek on her soft orange-blossom scented hair. At length Marigoth straightened up and shook herself.

"We don't know anything for sure yet," said Ezratah, cringing at the uselessness of his words even as he said them.

"True!" said Marigoth softly. She didn't even call him to task for mouthing meaningless platitudes. "Until I see her body, there is still hope. Sweet life, is this slug of a boat *ever* going to dock?"

To their great relief, once they had landed they quickly found evidence that Yani was alive, or at least had been when Daria Symina had taken her. The guards at the northern gate of the city had seen a fair-haired woman lying asleep in Daria's distinctive carriage as the death mage left the city. Daria had taken the trouble to show her to them.

"She won't be getting back in here quickly," said one of them. "His Lordship's real mad at her for practising magic in the city."

"Should have forbidden those two access to the city years ago," huffed the other.

"There are two of them?" asked Ezratah

"Yep, a brother and a sister. But the brother's busy in his lair in the west. He's carving out a fiefdom for himself there. You'd think he'd keep that mad bitch under control, but they say she's got the bulk of the magical power."

"Mir be merciful, a woman with power," said the other guard sucking his teeth at the enormity of it.

"This must be a trap," hissed Ezratah to Marigoth. "She must want us to follow. Why else would she show Yani off like that?"

"There's nothing else we can do but follow," snapped Marigoth. "At least Yani may still be alive."

If it was a trap, it did not have much chance of succeeding. Mirayan death mages could not know what sort of power they were facing in Marigoth and he couldn't imagine how they would capture her.

He and Marigoth discussed shape-changing into birds for the journey for that kind of magic was easy for her and she was powerful enough to carry luggage and clothing as well being able to choose any shape she liked. But in the end they decided simply to travel by horse. As birds, there was too much danger that they would miss Daria Symina's trail. Ezratah was secretly glad. Taking bird shape left your arms shaking with exhaustion and bird thoughts were easily distracted and confused. Also the few times Ezratah had taken that shape, he had had a disturbing attraction to beetles and worms for days afterwards

He went immediately to a livery stable recommended by the keeper of their tavern and bought horses and other supplies for the trip. To his dismay he ran into the annoying Elius as he left the livery stables. Elius had changed his brocade tunic for one of dark velvet, but he still wore the same enormously-feathered hat he had had on the ship.

"So you're joining the caravan north-west with us after all?" he said.

"No," said Ezratah shortly. "We are going in a different direction."

"Really? Where?" asked Elius, wide-eyed as if his was the only direction to go.

"I'm afraid I must get back to the tavern," said Ezratah. "I cannot leave my sister alone longer."

"See you later," said Elius, as Ezratah brushed past him.

Ezratah allowed Marigoth to persuade him to set out that very afternoon even though it was almost dusk. There was no point in insisting she stay in Cherabinium and get a good night's sleep. With her so worried sleep was unlikely to happen.

There was plenty of traffic on the road outside Cherabinium, but it was all very humble, mostly ragged peasants bringing in their meagre crops for tomorrow's market or simply trudging back from their fields to the safety of city. The houses along the road were all ruins and as they went further the fields became overgrown with weeds except for the occasional blackened patches which marked the places where magic had been detonated.

"Ugh! There's so much imbalance out here, it's making me queasy," said Marigoth.

This road ran through one of the most desolate and lawless parts of Miraya. Since very little large scale or luxury trade took place in this direction, Daria's rich carriage with its troop of outriders had been unusual and was well remembered by the few peasants they passed.

Eventually dusk fell and the countryside became entirely empty of people. Upon reaching a major fork in the road, they were forced to make camp in a burned-out inn rather than risk losing the trail by continuing. The camp could have been worse. Since Marigoth's magic was undetectable to normal Mirayan magic, they were able to use it to warm some food and then to move some of the broken furniture around so that they were hidden from casual searchers.

During the night wolves howled and several bands of men passed both on horseback and on foot. Once someone came into the inn and stood in the doorway for some time sniffing the air loudly, but Ezratah sat still, resisting the temptation to react and eventually the sniffer went away. At least Marigoth slept that night, a happy side effect of exhaustion. In the morning they discovered a family of gypsies sheltering in a nearby cellar who remembered Daria's passing all too well and were able tell them her direction.

Even though Marigoth and Ezratah were humbly dressed, shortly afterwards they were attacked by bandits. A large group of men, it must have been fifteen in all, came charging out of a copse of trees making their intentions clear by drawing their swords.

Marigoth simply flicked her hand and every single man and horse fell asleep. Then, as was the Tari way, she and Ezratah dismounted and checked the bodies of the sleeping men in case any of them should come to harm. Normally they would have pulled the men away from their horses, woken the horses up and driven them away leaving the riders stranded, but they were in a hurry and contented themselves with simply making sure that no one was in danger of being crushed under a collapsed horse.

Around midday they passed a fortified village and stopped to buy food and get directions before pressing on. The landscape remained much the same, fields around the village and then burnt-out houses, neglected farmland, destroyed villages and the occasional distant fortress.

Around mid-afternoon, Marigoth pulled up her horse and climbed off it and for the first time Ezratah noticed that the sky behind them had filled with heavy black clouds

"I don't think that's natural!" he said.

"I know it's not," said Marigoth. Ezratah, who had thought she was just answering the call of nature, saw that she was leaning against the tree with her face pressed against its bark. He jumped down, and found that she seemed to be breathing in the tree's scent.

"Is the storm making you feel sick?" he asked.

"Yes," snapped Marigoth. "Everything here is making me sick and now someone's creating a magical imbalance back there. This damned country! So beautiful, and yet so cursed." She took a deep breath. "I think we have to go back," she said.

"What!"

"I don't want to but the life spirit is crying out and I think it wants me to... It won't leave me alone. Curse it! I'm sorry, Yani!"

She shook off Ezratah's hand and strode back towards the horses.

There was nothing for Ezratah to do except follow. He understood how the life spirit called to Marigoth even though he could not feel it himself, but as he spurred his horse into a canter to keep up with her, he was aware of an odd lightening of his heart. Perhaps the life spirit was calling him as well and he had just been too insensitive to feel it properly.

"What the hell is going on here?" cried Marigoth, as they crested the hill and saw a thick black column of smoke rising from the fortified village that they had passed earlier. A glowing red rope came up from the fields near the village and at the end of it, a man hovered in the air like a malevolent kite, his arms outstretched and glowing with a sullen red fire. As they watched, he lifted his hand and shot bright red magic out of his finger making the log palisade around the village exploded into flame. Inside the walls, the tiny figures were scrambling round trying to put out the fire. A bolt of blue magic shot out of the centre of the village, but the mage in the sky just laughed crazily and deflected it away with his hand. The red glow that surrounded him meant he was full of demon power, puissant and reckless. Ezratah had seen such mages on the battlefield as a young man and remembered them being like men in a drunken frenzy, caring for nothing but destruction and the exercise of power.

As they spurred their horses on towards them he could see the source of the man's power. Another obscenely laughing mage was holding the end of the rope and he too glowed with magic. At his feet lay crumpled shapes which Ezratah knew must be the prone bodies of sacrifices to the demons, probably the unfortunate peasants who had been tilling the fields when he and Marigoth had passed earlier. Just as he was about to spur his horse forward to stop Marigoth from going in blindly, she swung round.

"What the hell's that?" She was pointing to the mage on the ground.

"He's got a demon stone," he told her. "He's drawing on the power of the abyss using it. You feed the life energy of a person to it and the demon lets you use a little of his power in return."

"How foul!" shouted Marigoth.

Ezratah seized her bridle.

"You need to make sure you don't touch it. A mage not consecrated to the stone will be drained by it."

"There's no way I'd touch something so filthy," cried Marigoth, and drawing back her arm, she threw a bolt of power that severed the glowing red rope between the two men.

The flying mage shot up into the air and the one on the ground sprawled backwards on the ground losing contact with his demon stone. Now was the time to attack him.

With a yell to Marigoth, Ezratah urged his horse toward the fallen mage. Several figures sprang up from among the wheat fields. Archers! Ezratah had forgotten that death mages always travelled with protective groups of thugs. As they loosed their arrows he threw up a defensive shield and swung round to see if Marigoth was safe. The flying mage had recovered and was plunging toward Marigoth like a burning hawk, his hands clawed out like violent talons. Marigoth threw a sleep spell, but the mage, still engorged with red demon power, merely spun it away with a flick of his hand. Meanwhile two arrows were heading for her.

"Look out," screamed Ezratah, as he tried to knock the arrows out of the air. Marigoth must have heard him because the arrows went as limp as two bits of string and dropped out of the sky, just as the flying mage grabbed her throat and hauled her up into the air.

Ezratah was so afraid for Marigoth that he let his own defences relax. It was only when an arrow grazed his cheek that he came back to his senses. He swung round and cast a sleep spell at the archers and one of them collapsed onto the ground. He may not have Tari power, but at least now he had his defences up again, the arrows thudded uselessly away from him.

Marigoth and the mage were wrestling in mid-air, tumbling over and over, seeming to be about to crash to the ground before rising each time. Each mage's power enhanced their blows so that the atmosphere thudded with magic and made them tumble even more crazily. Ezratah was sick with fear even though he knew Marigoth was probably much more powerful than this death mage. He forced himself to turn away. A series of sleep spells that left him shuddering with exhaustion dealt with the archers who had drawn their swords to oame charging at him. It would been better to have killed them with a fire bolt, but since his connection with the life spirit Ezratah found it difficult to call up such destructive magic.

As he surveyed the sleeping archers, Ezratah saw a movement in the corner of his eye. The death mage on the ground was lifting a small child up. Realising what he was about to do, Ezratah urged his horse forwards, putting all his remaining strength into a blast of power that would hopefully knock the death mage back off his feet again. But the man was still soaked in demon power and he brushed Ezratah's spell casually aside as he hefted the screaming child over to where the demon stone glowed redly on the ground. Torturing and killing the child would reconnect the mage with the power of the stone. As Ezratah struggled to produce another bolt of magic, the death mage dropped the child onto the stone and, undoing its bonds, put his foot on its chest, seized its arm and with a wrench broke it making the poor little mite scream in pain.

Ezratah heard an answering shriek from behind him as Marigoth, hovering just above the ground with the unconscious body of her opponent dropping gently from her hands, saw what the other death mage was doing and, without a second thought, threw out a mighty blast of power at him. The mage was flung through the air like a stone and plunged backwards into a pile of farm tools so hard that one of the scythes sprang up and pierced him through the chest killing him instantly. Marigoth screamed in anguish and, clutching her chest, fell out of the air.

Ezratah forgot everything, even the injured child, in his need to get to Marigoth. Seizing her in his arms, he turned her over.

She was dying. Even though she was still breathing, Ezratah could feel the life spirit ebbing out of her. This was the Tari's great weakness. They could not even accidentally kill without experiencing the pain, terror and separation from the life spirit that came with death. Marigoth's body would survive unharmed and the life spirit would come back to her in time, but when she awoke she would be weak and distressed. She might even go mad. Only Yani, linked as she was to the Raven, did not share this weakness.

Marigoth's death pangs lasted longer than those of her attacker had. Though she was already unconscious, her body twitched, gasped and shuddered. Ezratah wished he could take this burden from her, but he could do nothing except hold her. Hold her, make her comfortable, guard her secret. She had lost control of her powers and no longer looked like a Mirayan, so he drew her veil over her face.

Distantly he heard the gates of the village open, heard

people running towards him, shouting and laughing. They collected round them, patting Ezratah on the back, thanking him, offering healing for his companion. Ezratah waved them away.

"Just exhausted," he told them. "Just needs rest."

If they had touched Marigoth with magic the villagers would have found out she was dying and there would be trouble tomorrow when she was alive again. Luckily they accepted Ezratah's explanation and left her alone.

A woman touched him on the shoulder.

"Bring her into the village. We will find somewhere comfortable for her."

As Ezratah followed her, he saw the injured child being cradled in a woman's arms, a man who looked like the village mage hovering over them and several other people weeping over the bodies of the dead farmers. Then by the gate, they passed the bodies of two death mages lying in pools of their own blood, huge gashes across their throats. The villagers had shown them less mercy than he and Marigoth had and who could blame them? The death mages would have killed everybody long and painfully had they captured the village. Most of their henchmen were still alive tied up on the ground, but Ezratah doubted they would survive for long.

Rain began falling as Ezratah entered the village gates. He was shown to a large barn in which a number of people were sheltering and to a secluded bed of straw where he laid Marigoth down.

She was still now, but Ezratah was certain that in her mind she was still experiencing the horror of death, the loss and the separation. Not knowing if she could feel him, he kissed her forehead and murmured soothing words to her. The woman brought them food and under her insistence he stood up, stretched his back and let her tend to the graze on his check.

"Sir!" said a voice. "Fancy seeing you here."

Elius was standing nearby, not a feather on his outrageous hat out of place.

"What are you doing here?" cried Ezratah, so flustered

that he couldn't hide his annoyance.

"We were hiding out from the death mages," said Elius. "They attacked our caravan and this was the nearest shelter."

In other words his caravan had probably lead the death mages here. Ezratah thought, shocked to find himself thinking such an ungenerous thought. He wished Elius would leave them alone, but once again he couldn't bring himself to be rude to the poor young idiot.

"My sister is sick," he said politely

"My goodness!" said Elius, coming close to them as if he was about to peer round the wooden partition. Quickly Ezratah barred his way and Elius looked embarrassed. "Have you had a doctor to her? Ah I see you have had the village healer. I believe she is quite good considering what a benighted place this is. Where are you heading for? I thought you weren't coming north."

Marigoth stirred and began weeping. It wrung Ezratah's heart to hear it, though he guessed weeping must be a good sign - an expression of pain that prevented madness.

"Oh no, she's crying!" cried Elius, hovering anxiously.

"Please, leave us alone! I have to look after her." snapped Ezratah, unable to bear the lad any longer.

An expression of hurt came into Elius' eyes

"Oh, of course. Pardon me if I've been a pest."

Ezratah hardly heard him as he knelt by Marigoth, pulled her veil off and pressed her into his shoulder.

"Oh 'Tah. What have I done?"

"It was an accident. You didn't mean to."

"I wanted to kill him when I threw that power. I was so angry. I offended against the life spirit and it went away and I thought it was never going to come back."

"But it's back now, isn't it?" said Ezratah.

"I felt so abandoned," sobbed Marigoth. She wept and wept.

"Let me lay a sleep spell on you," he said at last, fearing for her white-faced exhaustion.

"I don't want to go there again."

"It's just sleep, Mari. You won't be aware of anything. You can't start being afraid to sleep. Best to do it now."

At length she agreed. She was so distressed that she longed for oblivion, might even have welcomed actual death. He laid the spell on her, stroking it gently into her face. As her eyes drooped, she could not help struggling fearfully to keep them open.

"Hush! Hush! I will be here with you all night. I will watch you and wake you if anything goes wrong."

"Oh 'Tah!" she whispered, drawing his face down to hers. "When I was dying, I regretted so much...that I wouldn't see you again." She kissed him softly on the lips.

Then she was asleep.

He rested her head on his shoulder, feeling strangely happy. How selfish he was to feel this when she was in so much anguish. But she had kissed him and said...

"Want some soup?" asked a voice. Elius, again! Sweet life, that fellow was a pest! Soup was the last thing he wanted.

"Put it on the ground," he snapped. Elius looked so wounded as he did so that Ezratah felt guilty.

"Thanks," he said, trying to smile with a warmth he didn't feel.

Elius shrugged. "Fine," he said and went away, obviously offended.

The healer had gone and so had most of the villagers, so that only the travellers who had been travelling with Elius remained in the barn, eating soup and bread and talking among themselves about the narrow escape they had had. Darkness had fallen and the barn was cosy with firelight. Outside a heavy rain was falling, caused no doubt by the unbalancing effect of the death magic. Several of the travellers were asleep already and most of the others looked very heavy eyed. Ezratah was glad to see that Elius was lying down. He settled himself against the wall so that he was comfortably seated, with his hand on Marigoth's shoulder so that he could feel her breathing. He was tired, but determined to watch over her. He closed his eyes, relaxed and dozed a little, but the seated position meant that he didn't actually sleep.

The sound of a splash made his eyes start open. He saw the barn door closing behind someone. It must have been Elius because his place in the straw was empty. Ezratah let his eyes droop again. Then he heard voices and opened his eyes to see Elius was standing in the doorway and was talking to a rough looking man.

Ezratah rubbed his face and looked around. The barn was quiet and still, full of sleeping bodies.

Elius and the soldier came over. *Uh-oh,* thought Ezratah. *He's going to try and make me join his caravan again.* He quickly moved the veil so that Elius couldn't see Marigoth's face.

"How is the lady?"

"Fine."

"You put a sleep spell on her?"

"Yes, she was too exhausted."

The young man smiled. "That's good."

That was the last thing Ezratah knew before something hit him hard on the side of the head.

***

"Right!" said Elius with satisfaction, looking down at the two prone figures at his feet. The woman hadn't stirred as her guardian had fallen.

"Give me the witch manacles, Argent!" he said to the soldier.

Scarcely daring to breath, he bent down and put the witch manacles around the woman's neck and wrists. When he had finished he let out a huff of relief. He let Argent put the manacles around the man's neck.

"Get them on the horses!"

"What about the rest?"

"What do you take me for? I've already fixed 'em. Poison in the soup."

Argent grinned, baring a set of sharp teeth.

"That's what I like to see, Lord. A nice clean job."

He heaved the mage up over his shoulder, Elius picked

154

up Marigoth and the two of them strode to the door, treading on the dead bodies of the travellers as if they were merely straw.

Outside three prisoners were huddled under the eaves of the barn.

"Hey!" shouted one of them. "What about us?"

"Oh, didn't you get any soup?" said Elius.

He put Marigoth down, trod over to the man and stood staring at him, grinning.

"Come on! Let us out!" said the man.

"I'm afraid you're surplus to requirements," said Elius. With one graceful motion of his hand, he caused a gash to sever the man's windpipe.

"Help!" shouted the others.

"Oh please, as if anyone's going to help you. You're gallows food," said Elius, cutting another throat.

"You lying hound," shouted the last. "You said if we helped you..."

"You really shouldn't have believed me," said Elius, and killed him.

Chapter 9

Jindabyne watched Alain and Serge being lead through the chaos of the camp by a group of warriors. Alain was hardly scratched but Serge was dazed, limping, his nose bleeding. Jindabyne pushed him down on a nearby log and helped him staunch the blood.

His eyes were troubled.

"Jindabyne," he whispered, "My father, did he..."

"Get up!" snapped the steely voice of Alyx Verdey. "If he can't walk, he'll be left behind."

"Don't you be so mean to my brother!" shouted Olga, surprising everyone and making a couple of the warriors smile.

"Hush, Ollie!" hissed Serge looking up at Alyx. "If your men wanted me to walk, why did they beat me up?"

Alyx turned away without even acknowledging him.

One of the group of warriors surrounding them said in trade talk, "We did not hit hard enough to hurt a real man."

Serge snorted.

"Come on," hissed Jindabyne, helping him up before he could retort. "I insisted you come with us, but don't push your luck. At least they're not handing you over to Lev."

In addition to Alyx, or the Forest Child as the Mori called their heir to the throne, their party was made up of ten warriors. They travelled light, carrying only their weapons, water skins and small packs slung across their shoulders. As they travelled, they gathered edible plants and sometimes stopped to dig up, or make Serge dig up, tubers. That night and every night afterwards they would set snares to catch game. During the daylight hours three or four of the Mori would leave the party all day, returning at nightfall with the birds, lizards or animals which they had caught. Though rations were not large, there were shared evenly and there was always something to eat before they lay down to sleep. No matter how little they gathered or caught, every evening and every morning they left some sacrifice of food to the forest Gods.

Despite all this hunting and gathering, at least two people were always watching Serge and Jindabyne. One of these was a woman called Sidore, who was a shaman, and the only person in the group apart from Jindabyne with magical powers. Every time Serge wandered any distance from the party, she seemed to know and would calmly and efficiently herd him back, thus putting a stop to any escape attempts before they started.

The party picked their way along thin, sometimes almost invisible paths. The tall trees grew so thickly along the paths that their smooth trucks were like canyons of wood. Often the party's way was blocked by fallen trunks or branches and every now and then they came to a patch of sharp-edged sword grass which would cut them if they brushed through it carelessly.

Jindabyne wondered aloud why they travelled on such tiny paths for it made the going slow.

"In the days before the poison we used to travel by boat on the river," explained Sidore. "These paths have never been well used."

Alyx shot her a warning glance but Sidore smiled back at her. The ordinary Mori seemed to trust Jindabyne even though she had been their bitter enemy's wife. They spoke to her with respect and helped her carry her child.

The way Olga would stump along sturdily for a couple of hours at a time, keeping good pace with the adults made Jindabyne very proud.

"I am a Madraga," she would say if someone offered to carry her. "Madragas do their part." But after a while it would all get too much for her and she would slow and finally let herself be picked up without protest.

The shaman Sidore was also happy to answer Jindabyne's questions about the Madraga's relationship with the Mori Queen. As soon as she got the chance, Jindabyne told Serge about Wolf's raid on the Mori.

"Oh, Hell!" said Serge. "Oh... I beg pardon for my language, Lady."

That made Jindabyne smile. Considering their situation, Serge's bad language was the least of her worries.

"No wonder they hate us. What happened to Alyx and the Queen afterwards?"

"Your father handed them over to Alexus Scarvan. I gather he was brutal to them."

Serge nodded knowingly and Jindabyne thought he looked relieved. She supposed under the peculiar moral code of the Mirayans, killing an enemy after a battle was no great crime. To a Tari all taking of life was wrong. For herself, she knew that there had been much fighting and killing in the early days of Mirayan settlement on Yarmar and on some level she had known that Wolf had done his share, but she must have repressed this knowledge for hearing of the raid and execution of Eldene Mori was a stain on her memory of Wolf, making her grief even more painful and she couldn't stop wondering about Wolf's relationship to the Queen, Elena Verdey. The shaman, Sidore, was unable to enlighten Jindabyne about her own offence against the Verdeys so she could only worry about what it was.

The Mori's kindness to Jindabyne did not extend to Serge. They had had an uneasy peace with the Duchy of Lamartaine for many years, but the Mirayan settlers were constantly making inroads into the forest to hunt or cut down trees, all with the tacit support of Lord Petrus of

Palffy and the other border Lords. Jindabyne sensed that only their respect for her prevented the Mori from physically mistreating Serge. As it was, they made him carry the heaviest pack, while at the same time keeping his hands bound unless there was any digging to be done. Once Alyx Verdey pushed him so roughly as she passed, that he went sprawling into a puddle.

He said nothing, but Jindabyne, who had witnessed the whole thing, said loudly that she was surprised to see one with Tari blood dishonour themselves, and their mothers, with violence.

Alyx turned furiously on Jindabyne.

"Don't you dare say anything against my mother!"

Serge sprang protectively to Jindabyne's side, though with his hands still bound there was little he could have done. All around there was a drawing of knives.

"I say nothing against your mother," said Jindabyne with dignity. "She is an honourable and true Tari and would not approve of violence either. That is all."

Alyx had the grace to blush. With dignity, Jindabyne drew Serge away.

"You are not making the situation easier," she hissed in his ear.

"That girl's a bitch," he hissed back "Does she have to gloat *all* the time?"

"You need to be bigger than this," replied Jindabyne. "Your father would be too busy finding some way to escape to waste energy bandying words."

"You're right," said Serge, shamefaced. He made a bigger effort to resist being needled, but an eighteen year old boy full of fight and sensitive pride does not take easily to being insulted by a sixteen year old girl and it was only a few hours before he was swapping snide remarks with Alyx again. If only she would ignore him as she ignored Jindabyne.

Jindabyne hoped Serge would be able escape once they reached the head of the river, when they would be close to the Gen Mountains and it would be easy for him to find his way through the forest using them as a landmark. At the base of the Gen mountains lived tribes of Seagani who had a loose alliance with the Mirayans and would give him shelter. From there he should be able to find his way back into Mirayan friendly territory and gather troops to oppose Lev.

But her worries about Serge were nothing to her worries for the Life Spirit. Always she felt the sick river's distant presence as a jangling of the nerves down her right side and at night she dreamed of red vultures eating her flesh and awoke feeling unrefreshed. The forest was being harmed by the poison in the river, for though the Mori continued to find enough game to eat, birds and animals were noticeably scarce. Jindabyne noticed most of all the missing bird song. The Mori must have known of hidden springs or water stores for they always had enough water to drink, but there were few opportunities to wash more than faces and hands with a damp cloth.

The pollution of the river had been caused by a plague of red fish. Mindful of her task, she asked the Mori to collect several samples from the river and they would bring back individual fish in bark containers. Jindabyne would send Olga off to play at a distance, for she did not want her exposed to such things, but the rest of the group would watch her examination. Even Alyx, who like Olga was half-Tari and obvious physically sickened by the fish, would watch.

Controlling her desire to retch as best she could, Jindabyne would pull the fish apart with sticks. She did not need stronger tools for the fish were always dead by the time they reached her and their flesh fell from their bones as easily as if they had been cooked. Though they were always small, red and fish-like, they seemed to come in an endless variety of shapes with different numbers of fins, eyes and even tails. Some were covered in eyes, some had strange protuberances growing off their foreheads and some had huge mouths full of teeth. Others had no mouths at all.

"How can it have no mouth?" wondered Serge, looking at one particularly misshapen creature. "How does it eat?"

"They live on the life spirit," said Jindabyne. This fact was quite obvious to her more attuned Tari senses. "You don't need a mouth for that. These fish aren't really alive. Just death magic given form."

"They looked alive enough to me that day we went to the river!" said Serge.

"They're not dead either. That's what's so horrible about them. In the natural world things are either one or the other. The life spirit flows smoothly through living things and the elements that make up dead things are also part of its balance. These things," Jindabyne gestured at the fish, "are outside that. Like leeches on the skin of the life spirit. Not part of it, yet sucking on its goodness. Because of this they create imbalance. That's why they come in this chaos of forms."

"I don't really understand," sighed Serge.

Alyx who was listening very intently made a scoffing noise. Serge ignored it - very manfully in Jindabyne's opinion.

"You have to be Tari or part Tari to really understand," said Jindabyne. "When you are able to feel the flow of the life spirit, then you can clearly feel how wrong these creatures are." She sighed. "But I learn little else from these examinations."

She put the two bits of stick neatly down inside the bark container and gave it to one of the Mori warriors. The Mori were very careful to put the fish and everything that had come into contact with them back into the river after Jindabyne had finished. Rightly so! The fish exuded a poisonous slime which burnt any living thing it touched and who knew what might happen if their bodies came into contact with other sources of water.

"Can't the water itself be cleansed?" asked Serge.

"I doubt it. The slime is very thick."

Jindabyne turned to the shaman.

"What happened when your people tried to cleanse the water for drinking?"

"It cannot be done. We tried herbs and magic and also magical filters, but still it was poisonous to drink. The river is worse than dead now. It can't nourish anything."

Things became worse. About eight days out from the Mori camp in the hilly terrain of the foothills of the Gen Mountains, they found the bloody remains of a taldra that had been killed very brutally. The unfortunate creature's limbs, head and tail been torn off its carcass and spread around the ground and the flesh had been shredded off its body. Its ribs stuck up like yellowed talons and its offal spilled limply out between them. Jindabyne could feel something wrong about it, but it was Alyx who put that wrongness into words.

"This taldra's been killed for the pleasure of killing. Look! Nothing's gone from this carcass. What animal rips open the belly and doesn't eat the entrails?"

Sidore put her hand on the Taldra's head and said what seemed to be a prayer to Labwa, the Mori god of forests before pulling out her knife. "We'll make sure this being did not die in vain. The meat will be useful for our journey."

"No!" cried Alyx and Jindabyne together, startling Sidore so much she dropped her knife.

"There's something wrong about this carcass," explained Jindabyne. "It won't nourish us. It may even harm us."

"This being was killed by death magic, wasn't it?" said Alyx.

"Yes!" cried Jindabyne in sudden realisation. "Some creature of death magic must have sucked the life spirit out of it. There's nothing here to nourish living beings."

Alyx looked at Jindabyne with uneasy respect.

"That is how I understand it too."

"Another creature of death magic?" cried Didier. He pointed at some huge paw prints. "Some kind of large dog did this."

Sidore sighed. She clearly thought Jindabyne and Alyx were depressingly right.

"You're both Tari. We must concede to your stronger senses in these matters."

"Come on!" said Didier. "Let's leave this ill-omened

place."

The party was subdued all the rest of the day and Alyx even refrained from needling Serge. Toward nightfall they blindfolded Serge, Jindabyne and even Olga and lead them for some time over rough ground. When at last the blindfolds were removed, they found themselves standing before a huge mangiri tree with a rope ladder hanging down its broad trunk.

"Climb Lady," said Didier to Jindabyne. "No harm will come to you."

"What about Olga?" she protested. "How will I carry her and climb?"

"We have a more amusing way for her to travel," smiled Didier who, like the other Mori, doted on the little girl. He strapped Olga into a large basket that dangled down through the branches.

"Climb now," he said. "The child will be safe."

After checking the knots that secured the rope to Olga's basket carefully, Jindabyne started climbing up the ladder and the basket was pulled up alongside her so that she could talk to Olga. Not that Olga needed soothing. She enjoyed the journey tremendously, leaning out over the basket's edge crying "Come on Mumma! I'm winning."

The rope ladder was secured to the tree trunk at regular intervals. At a large branch that ladder ended and another began. By the time Jindabyne reached the top of the second ladder she so was breathless that she could only lie on her back panting while an excited Olga jumped all over her.

She was lying on one of two wide wooden platforms fenced with strong wooden slats and completely hidden by the tree's branches. Serge and four other members of the party climbed in behind her. Serge's hands and feet were tied and he was tethered to a post. As dusk fell the rest of the party appeared bringing meat and vegetables which they had already cooked elsewhere. The night was chilly and the lukewarm food did not help. They did not light a fire as they usually did. Instead everyone huddled together under the skins which they brought out of a cache in the trunk of the tree. Despite this Olga fell asleep easily and, with her warm little body clasped in her arms, so did Jindabyne.

Then suddenly she was awake and very frightened. Blackness everywhere. Where was she? Something terrible was out there in the blackness and she couldn't see it. Olga whimpered in her arms and huddled closer.

There were other people nearby. She remembered where she was. On the tree platform with the Mori. Surely she was safe so high up. But she didn't feel safe.

Something was moving in the undergrowth at the bottom of the tree. The sound of the heavy body crunching twigs and small plants underfoot filled her with such a jangling feeling of horror, that she had to clench her teeth together to stop them chattering. She wanted to hide and at the same time she had to look, so gripping Olga tight against her chest she rolled sideways and looked through the slats of the platform.

Two glowing red eyes looked up at her. Whatever it was must be huge. The ground was a long way down and still its eyes were big red lanterns in the dark.

Squeezing her own eyes shut, Jindabyne could see the creature in her mind - a big black dog shaped hole in the world. The hole yearned toward her, bulging out at her and as she looked into it, she could feel the life spirit surging up inside her. That hole was an obscenity! She wanted to hurl it back into the abyss it had come from.

Then, as Olga whimpered and burrowed against her, Jindabyne came back to herself and remembered that wearing a neck manacle there was nothing she could do.

The thing below let out a deep thrumming growl and with a huge thud, hit the bottom of the tree. Even though it was an enormous tree, a faint tremor came up the trunk.

Someone on the platform cried out and Jindabyne felt the beast's attention turn toward them, drawing at her like a plug hole draws water. Olga squeaked and seemed about to jump out of Jindabyne's arms. Jindabyne clutched her tightly.

The beast let out a yowl that sounded horribly like the howl of a man and instantly the platform shook as people leapt up, drawing weapons ready to fight.

The beast threw itself against the tree again.

"What is that thing?" hissed someone. Suddenly a brilliant flare of mage light shone out all around them.

"No!" shouted Jindabyne at Sidore, feeling the beast-shaped hole bulging up towards them, drawn by the magic.

"Abomination!" screamed Alyx. She was standing at the railing of the platform gripping the rope that hung from a branch above them, her face suffused with killing anger. "You must be destroyed!"

"No!"

Someone lunged at Alyx but it was too late. She jumped out over the rail, throwing herself down the rope with such speed that she seemed to be falling.

"Stop her!" screamed Jindabyne. But everyone was screaming something. The shaman Sidore sprang to the rail, her body surrounded with the bright white mage light, and spreading wide her arms, jumped after Alyx, staff in hand. As she glided downwards, she took the light from the platform, leaving a chaos of cursing and shouting as shadowy figures leapt at ropes and onto ladders in the darkness.

Below the beast let out a loud yowl. An answering yowl rang out from further away. Another hole in fabric of the life spirit was nearby.

Jindabyne huddled on the floor of the platform, clutching Olga, horrified yet unable to tear her eyes from the scene below.

The brilliant white light haloing the shaman illuminated everything on the forest floor. Jindabyne could see the beast's outer form now. Its dog-shaped body was disgustingly pale and naked like skin and covered in tufts of hair. Its face was flat like a persons, but its gaping hole of a mouth was full of pointed teeth.

Alyx had flung herself on the thing and was slashing at it with the long knife that the Mori carried in their belts, but she was in some kind of frenzy and the blows were not well judged. The disgusting beast hit her a tremendous blow with one of its paws, knocking her to the ground.

"Oh hell!" cried Serge, who was suddenly beside Jindabyne. He must have broken his tether.

Alyx rolled away from the beast and held the knife above her. The beast leapt, flinging itself onto Alyx.

"No!" shouted Serge. "Jindabyne! For Mir's sake! Untie me so I can get down there and help them. We have to kill that thing!" Jindabyne, her eyes still fixed on the scene below, tugged at the knots at Serge's wrists. Above the roaring of the beast, they could hear Alyx screaming. The shaman threw a bolt of power at the beast that flung it backwards, revealing Alyx on the ground covered in blood, screaming and fighting as if the beast were still on top of her. The shaman bent over her while warriors swarmed everywhere.

Something yowled out in the forest and right underneath them, the beast yowled back. *Sweet life! Was it still alive?* The shaman turned in terror as the huge pale shape leapt on her, seizing her shoulder in its teeth. Screaming in pain, she was dragged backwards out of Jindabyne's sight line. Alyx, good for her, was up, staggering after them, hitting out unsteadily at the beast with the long knife still clutched in her hand. Another huge pale form lunged after her. Oh no, the second one had arrived! The other warriors were surrounding it, stabbing and slashing. The mage light was dimming. So hard to see now. Where were Alyx and Sidore?

"Jindabyne. For Mir's sake! Pay attention!"

With a great effort, Jindabyne tore her gaze away from the scene below and struggled with Serge's bonds.

"Yes! Yes! Olga, my little clever one. Can you untie Serge's legs?"

Olga was sobbing with fear, but she had managed to loosen the rope round Serge's ankles.

"That right!" said Serge. "There's a brave girl, Olga. There's a brave clever girl."

Just as he freed his arms, the light below blinked out and everything went pitch black.

"If only we could get you free, Lady," cried Serge. "You'd be able to defeat these things."

"I'm no use. Those beasts feed on magic. Magic and life spirit make them stronger. Didn't you see how the beast recovered after the shaman hit it? She's dead now. And they need light! Quick, where are torches?"

Beneath them, the beast's awful half-human yowling was drowning out the shouting of the warriors. Jindabyne had made a point of always remembering where the torches were in case Serge got the chance to escape. Now after what seemed like an interminable time of groping across the platform, she found them and the tinder box.

Together she and Olga lit several torches and flung them over the side of the platform. Some were still alight when they reached the ground. Meanwhile Serge had seized a rope and swung off the platform.

"No!" cried Jindabyne. "It's too dangerous."

But she was too late. With a quick apologetic grin, Serge dropped down the rope. She saw him land on his feet, but after that it was difficult to see anything from up on the platform. People were running everywhere in a chaos of growling, yowling and shouting. Were there two or three large dog shapes down there?

Suddenly light sprang up.

One of the beasts was on fire! And there was Serge. He'd found a weapon, clever boy. The beast didn't seem to care that its back was on fire. It had a warrior in its mouth and was shaking him back and forth like a rag, while three other warriors clung to its flanks ramming their knives into it like prisoners pounding rocks. Serge threw himself at the beast's neck where it should have been vulnerable and drove his knife into it, stabbing again and again. The knife went in easily but it was making no difference. The beast ignored both the warriors and the fire on its back and continued worrying at its captive.

Serge jumped back, stood still for a moment and then quite deliberately ran at the creature and drove his knife into its glowing red eye. The beast yowled and a stream of hot liquid spurted forth. Serge turned his face just in time, but the liquid drenched his neck and arm making him yelp with pain and stagger back.

"No!" shrieked Jindabyne, as he tripped over something and fell on his back.

Yowling, the beast lunged at him, black fluid eating away the side of its head as it streamed from the knife wound in its eye. Desperately Serge crawled backwards, trying to regain his balance, and get back on his feet. Two other warriors were dragging on the beast but it kept on coming until, with a sudden yelp, it collapsed like a mound of wet porridge on his ankles.

Three beasts had attacked and been killed and now their remains were beginning to dissolve into pale glutinous masses that shone with a dead, white phosphorescence and gave off a rotten egg smell. But the cost to the party had been enormous, with five warriors dead, including Sidore the shaman, and Didier their leader. Alyx lay unconscious and bleeding badly from a slash on the head. The remaining warriors carried her back up to the tree platform.

"The beasts' bites kill almost instantly," said a woman, whose name was Fredel.

"I think they suck the life spirit out of you to feed," said Jindabyne as she washed the acidic blood off Serge's neck and arm. His skin was burnt but it seemed no worse than a bad sunburn.

She turned to Fredel.

"Take my manacle off," she said. "Then I can heal you all and your Forest Child. You may close it again afterwards."

"We can't," said the woman. "We don't have the tools. It was the shaman's job to open and close the manacle and she's dead."

"Idiots!" shouted Serge.

Fredel shot him an angry look but did nothing. Like the others, she was too demoralised to bother with Serge for the moment.

"Serge!" said Jindabyne warningly. "It matters little. The magic would simply draw more beasts."

"I saw how Sidore's magic made them stronger. And how eager they were to consume her," said Fredel. "We

169

shouldn't have attacked it. And yet I felt driven to do so." She nodded at Alyx. "I think we all did. Will our Forest Child survive?"

"I can see little wrong with her," replied Jindabyne. "I think she has simply fainted. It's not surprising in one with Tari blood. Those things are a horror to the life spirit."

"Praise Labwa!" said another warrior. "Didier threw himself between the beast and the Forest Child and his sacrifice wasn't wasted. Our Queen chose well when she chose him to guard her child."

"The Forest Child must have a new guard," said one of the other warriors. They all spoke in trade talk. Clearly they wanted Jindabyne, included in the conversation.

"I'll do that," said Fredel. "I'm the oldest. Are we all agreed?"

There were nods all round.

"If the Forest Child recovers her senses and is able, I think it best we continue our mission," said Fredel. "Are we agreed on that?"

"What do we have to go back for?" said another.

"The Lady Tari might help our Queen to defeat the Gibadgee," said another.

"The Forest Queen told us this was the most important task before us," Fredel told them. "And most likely she can defeat the Gibadgee with no help from Tari mages. Our queen is very cunning."

"May your words sprout and grow in Labwa's heart," said one of the others.

"What happened to the Tari mages who helped your Queen in days past?" said Jindabyne. "Tell me truly."

Fredel and the others exchanged looks and muttered to each other in Mori. At last Fredel said shortly, "They left us."

"What? Why?"

Fredel would say no more.

Alyx wasn't badly hurt, but the moment she regained consciousness she asked for Didier and would not be put off until she learned he was dead. Then she curled up in a corner with her back to them. They all knew she was crying though she tried to hide it. She refused a sleeping draught and when Fredel tried tentatively to comfort her, Alyx snapped at her.

"She blames herself for Didier's death," whispered Jindabyne. "She was the first to attack the creature."

Serge looked astonished. "Why? We all wanted to attack it. That's the way such creatures work. Everyone knows that."

"What do you mean?" asked Jindabyne. "Have you seen such creatures before?"

"No but Father told us about the minions of death magic so that we would know how to deal with them if such creatures ever reached Yarmar. Mirayans call them bloodbeasts. They are the bones of a man and a dog ground together and resurrected with spells. We'll be safe at daylight. They don't like the sun and they don't see ordinary things well. Only magic is truly clear to them." He lowered his voice. "This should give me a chance to escape. The Mori won't expect me to try with those things around."

"I must tell Fredel about these creatures," said Jindabyne.

"Jindabyne! No!" hissed Serge, seizing Jindabyne's arm and pulling her back. "These people are our enemies. Don't give away our advantages."

"This is not something paltry like war," hissed Jindabyne. "This is death magic. All living things need to be allied against it."

"Hey! What's going on?" asked one of the warriors.

"I have something to tell Fredel," said Jindabyne.

Serge groaned and put his head in his hands.

Though it was still night, nobody slept much and they began their onward journey as soon as dawn came creeping greyly through the trees. For once the Mori did not tie Serge's hands, but they would not give him a knife either.

"You said they were nocturnal. If you told the truth,

what need do you have of a weapon?" Fredel told him.

"They're not nocturnal. They just dislike the sun," retorted Serge.

"If we're attacked we'll arm you, Gibadgee," she replied. She turned to the others. "I think this attack means we're on the right trail. Whoever poisoned our river likely put those beasts here to protect the head of it. When the red fish first came, our scouts told us that water flows cleanly out of the earth here. It's only when it falls into the pool that the red fish begin. I always wondered why our Queen didn't bring us here to the clear water, but I see now that she must have suspected a trap."

That day the forest was even quieter than usual as if it too had been frightened by the night's attack. The party travelled in close formation, gathering roots and berries along the way. No one left the group to hunt. There was no sign of more blood beasts, but well before nightfall they stopped to blindfold Jindabyne, Olga and Serge again and lead them to another forest platform.

Here a barrel had been set in the crown of the tree to collect water and they were able to drink freely for the first time that day. The water was full of insect larvae, but the Mori said none of them were harmful.

"Take a big gulp," said Serge to Olga. "Then you won't feel them going down." But Olga would not drink until Jindabyne had strained the water through her veil. While she was doing this, a group of four went out to forage for food, leaving Alyx and Fredel guarding the prisoners. They tied Serge up and Jindabyne wondered if she could try and untie him during the night. They were very close to the Gen mountains now, but would Serge be able to evade the bloodbeasts if he escaped?

Alyx and Fredel were making bird calls and after a short time several pale pink doves answered their calls. Alyx took some corn from a pouch on her belt and fed it to a couple of them. After eating the corn they became extremely docile.

She had written something on two pieces of bark and now she put the bark in tiny round containers and tied the containers to the dove's legs, before whispering in their ears and sending them to fly away.

"These doves have a partnership with the Mori," explained Fredel in answer to Jindabyne's question. "In return for this corn they will take messages to the Forest Queen for us."

"Do not give all our secrets away to the Gibadgee," said Alyx, shooting a sharp look at Serge.

Fredel turned away, slightly shamefaced while Serge glared at Alyx and she scowled back defiantly.

"How are you going to get my stepmother's neck ring off?" he asked nastily.

"We have a plan," said Alyx.

"I'll believe that when I see it. You Mori couldn't plan a drinking game in a brewery. You don't have any plan."

"That's for me to know," said Alyx calmly.

"Leave it!" snapped Jindabyne to Serge.

"How can you heal this river when they can't even get your manacle off? This mission is a failure already."

"How dare you! My guardian gave his life for this mission," shouted Alyx.

"He gave his life for you," snapped Serge. "Because you jumped in without thinking."

"Serge!" cried Jindabyne.

Alyx went white and slapped him across the face making Olga shriek with terror.

"No!" shouted Jindabyne, throwing herself between them so violently that she knocked Alyx over and the girl fell on her back. For a moment she lay there, her eyes sparkling with unshed tears, her mouth working with pain. With a growl of fury she leapt up, grabbed one of the ropes and swung off the platform and down into the foliage below.

"You deserved that blow," said Fredel to Serge.

"Yes you did, you stupid boy," cried Jindabyne, speaking in trade talk so that Fredel could understand her. "How could you say such a thing? After what you told me last night about bloodbeasts? Next time I'll just let them beat you. I only stopped them this time because of Olga."

"I... I'm sorry," said Serge. Jindabyne thought he looked ashamed. She turned to comfort the weeping Olga and did not speak to him for the rest of the evening. Unfortunately since the Mori kept good watch all night, she did not get the opportunity to set him loose either.

When they reached the head of the stream around mid-morning of the following day they could see immediately that the water coming down the low rocky cliff from above was clear, while the pool beneath seethed with a stinking mass of red fish. The Mori had approached by a roundabout route and for some time they hid in the undergrowth watching the clearing around the pool while a couple of them scouted the bushes nearby. They didn't find any sign of guards. Perhaps the bloodbeasts were the only guard.

"Or perhaps the death mage is confident there's nothing we can do," whispered Serge.

"Be quiet!" snapped Jindabyne, still angry at him.

In winter this waterfall must be a raging torrent, but now in late spring it slid like a thin layer of glass over the lip of the cliff. Behind the waterfall hung a deep green curtain of moss.

"There's a hollow behind that moss," Fredel told Jindabyne ignoring a scowling look from Alyx. "Just below the lip of the cliff. You can get there by following that shelf of rock. If we are attacked by the beasts, it will be a good place to hide and defend ourselves. Well Forest Child, there is nothing for it but to brave the clearing. You stay..."

"Wait!" cried Alyx. "Let the Gibadgee go first! If he's attacked, he will be no loss."

"Good idea," said Fredel, nodding quickly at the two warriors nearest Serge. Before Jindabyne could protest, the warriors pushed Serge out of the undergrowth. After an initial yelp of surprise, Serge pulled himself up straight and strode with defiant bravery towards the edge of the pool. He stopped short before he got to it, gagging at the smell of the fish. Moving back, he walked up and down around the pool, bowing and waving his hands to imaginary people with the kind of bravado calculated to make the Mori feel like complete cowards. Then, he began to do a jig.

"Come on," said Alyx to Fredel. To her obvious annoyance, Fredel pulled her back and only let her stand up and move out of the bushes after everyone else.

Serge left his jigging and climbed up the rock face behind the waterfall. By the time Jindabyne and Olga had entered the clearing, he was standing on a ledge and peering interestedly through the curtain of moss and water that obscured the hollow behind.

"This is great!" he shouted enthusiastically. "But I think it might be easier to drop down from the top."

Fredel grinned wryly and shook her head, but Alyx looked furious.

"Get out of there!"

"Yes, your majesty!" muttered Serge, just loud enough to be heard.

Alyx was looking distinctly green and Jindabyne knew just how she felt. The clearing seemed to focus the bad atmosphere of the fish.

"You two go to the top of the waterfall and keep watch," said Fredel nodding at Jindabyne and Alyx.

"No! I can do this," said Alyx. "I can conquer my weakness. A ruler..."

"This is no place for one of Tari blood!" said Fredel firmly. "And someone must watch this lady. You're the most sensible choice."

Shamefaced, Alyx turned away and made for the path that led up the side of the rock face, ushering Jindabyne and Olga before her.

From the top they could see a long way over the forest beneath, while behind them on the cliff top were scrubby trees. Beyond the trees lay tumbled rocks. Beyond that rose the towering cliffs of the Gen Mountains. Water flowed from a spring hidden among these cliffs and over a wide flat rock face to the edge of the cliff, where it fell into the pool below.

In discussions of what to do when they reached the pool, Jindabyne had come up with the suggestion that since the red fish started there, they should block the pool off from the rest of the river and see if by destroying the fish in the pool, they could cut off the source of them. The Mori warriors began collecting stones to block the lower end of the pool. Had it not been for the smell and the importance of not touching the water, it might have been a child's game.

Looking down from the top of the waterfall, Jindabyne could see the surface of the pool frothing with poisonous looking red bubbles as the red fish seethed around below the surface, thrashing their tails. The pool was almost solid with their bodies and occasionally they spilled out onto the bank.

"Ollie, let's see if we can find a good way to divert the spring," she said, hoping to distract the increasingly tearful Olga. But Olga would not be distracted and clung to her mother's skirt's making it difficult for Jindabyne to move. So Alyx started searching alone. Jindabyne moved back across the rock face until they could no longer see the red fish, but she still felt their presence.

"Do the red fish make you dream?" she asked Alyx. "Do you dream of red vultures?"

"Red birds, yes," said Alyx, surprised into a polite answer. "They have three wings."

"Yes. Mine have three wings too. This must be some vision of the Abyss. When I am so close to the river, I begin to fear I might have waking visions as well."

Alyx smiled at Jindabyne in fellow feeling. Then her face changed as if she was reminding herself that Jindabyne was an enemy and she turned back to her task.

"How can they bear these fish so close to them and do nothing?" she said suddenly.

"Who?" asked Jindabyne.

"The Tari. Ermora is so close," said Alyx pointing up into the mountains. "Just at the top of Gen Mountains. Less than a day's ride in distance."

"Perhaps they have not noticed. A day's ride away I would not feel the red fish either. The Tari do not leave Ermora any more, do they?"

"But the Tari are attuned to the life spirit. My aunts

told me that they commune with it in a place called the spirit cave, that it speaks to them even. And the life spirit must feel this attack on it. So why don't the Tari act? I mean I know they made a vow never to leave Ermora again but there are limits even to vows. Surely..."

Alyx stopped short. An expression of horror came over her face as she looked up at the sky to their right. Jindabyne followed her gaze. Two things flew towards them. Birds - no they were too big. Horror surged through her. Those weren't birds.

"What are they?" whispered Alyx.

"They are other," breathed Jindabyne. They are... Death."

Olga screamed.

"Run!" cried Alyx at the men below. But they were drawing their swords. So was she.

"No," shouted Jindabyne, knowing it was hopeless. "Don't fight! Run!"

The enormous speed of these creatures! Now she could see their blue-grey human shaped bodies. Grey bat wings spread out behind them. Their hands and feet had long scything claws. Evil angels. Angels of death.

"Quick, Olga!" she shouted, dragging her daughter towards the bushes.

With a thump and a cloud of sulphurous stink, one of the creatures landed beside her. Its face was a blank flat space with no eyes or nose, just a huge slit of a mouth. The outrage of it overwhelmed her like an oily tidal wave. She screamed without meaning too. Then it had her by the arm and she knew she was lost.

"Ollie, run! Hide!"

But Olga wouldn't let go of her hand. She dragged at Jindabyne screaming, trying to tug her away from the creature who held her other arm.

Somewhere behind her, Jindabyne could hear the sound of men screaming. Sword waving, Alyx was running towards the creature.

"Ollie! Let go! Run, please *run!*" begged Jindabyne as the angel gripped her neck, its touch stinging her bare skin.

Then as suddenly and as quietly as an eye blink, a woman was standing beside them. A tall, fair Tari woman dressed in green.

The death creature was so surprised that its grip on Jindabyne loosened and Jindabyne almost jerked free.

"Olga!" shouted Jindabyne.

As if she heard her, the Tari woman grabbed Olga round the waist and pulled her away.

"No!" shrieked Olga.

"Yes! Go, Olga Go!" *But Olga wouldn't let go! She must let go!*

Suddenly Olga went limp. The Tari woman had used magic to make her sleep. Now she scooped the little girl up in her arms.

The death creature turned and scythed at the woman with its long claws, but its blow hit empty air. The strange woman simply wasn't there anymore and neither was Olga.

The creature let out a raucous scream and, seizing Jindabyne in its sulphurous embrace, leapt into the air. The stink of its close flesh... As her feet left the ground, darkness came down on her.

Chapter 10

Alyx came to. Darkness. Falling water. Cold, damp, hard against her shoulder. Her back throbbed. Danger! Groping for her sword, she moved to get up and gasped with pain as her whole back seemed to split open.

"Stay put!" hissed a voice. A hand pushed her shoulder back against the wall.

"Wha..!"

"Shut up! They're outside!"

In the gloom she could see the face of the Mirayan.

"What?"

"Death angels, just outside. Be quiet!"

The urgency in his voice made her believe. Turning her head slightly she peered at him. Hard to see much in this greenish gloom. He was pressed close to the wall beside her, looking away behind him. Where was this?

Water falling. Greenish light was coming from somewhere behind the Mirayan. They were in the cave behind the waterfall.

Through the loud echo of water hitting rock, she could hear the thudding footfalls of something moving around above and she shuddered involuntarily. Now she remembered. She remembered running at one of those things on the rock above - the one that had seized Jindabyne. It had taken off and flown over her blinding her with its sulphurous stench!

She'd stumbled back towards the waterfall and something had hit her in the back. The pain of it! Then what? Had she passed out? Fallen?

The Mirayan leaned closer, touching her shoulder comfortingly. What the hell did he think he was doing? She shoved him away. The pain of the movement made her cry out involuntarily and the Mirayan over-balanced and rolled backwards with small choking yelp.

Outside something cackled, a loud sound of mad amusement. With a sharp intake of breath, the Mirayan pressed himself against the ground and covered his head. Alyx looked at the waterfall. Something was moving beyond it, a grey blue shape that leaned forward and peered in through the curtain of water, just like a person would. She froze, struggling not to panic.

A grey-blue hand thrust through the water and the creature hissed and pulled back, obviously stung by the touch of it. A sulphurous stench filled the cave.

Then came a hissing intake of breath and suddenly a blast of orange fire bloomed outside. A cloud of stinking steam filled the little cave, but there was still a lot of water falling over the opening. The creature let out a predatory screech of annoyance and was gone. As the steam settled damply over them, she could hear it back again just beyond the thin barrier of the waterfall. She heard its hand thrust through the water again, smelt the sulphurous stink of it, heard it hiss. But this time the hand did not withdraw. Claws scrabbled on the rock surface at the front of the cave, reaching out towards them, slowly deliberately scratching along the wall, feeling for them. Surely it could not reach them back here.

Alyx squeezed her eyes shut and fought down an almost overwhelming urge to scream. The blackness behind her eyelids was full of the sound and shape of those things. Angel of the Abyss! As suffocating fumes of sulphur filled the cave, Alyx's muscles began shuddering from the effort of staying still. The scratching seemed to go on forever and then suddenly there was a swirl of movement, an ear-splitting cackle of laughter, a whomp of wings and the thing was gone. Even then it was a long time before the Mirayan sat up. He shot a warning look at Alyx before creeping carefully to the front of the cave and peering out through the curtain of water.

"They're gone," hissed Alyx, certain of the fact. The Mirayan looked back at her, his stance questioning.

"I can feel them like your stepmother could," she hissed. "Where are the other warriors?"

The Mirayan crept back to her before he answered.

"I think they are all dead. I heard them screaming."

A cold stone filled Alyx's chest.

"Dead?" she echoed softly, remembering the screaming.

"They tried to fight... You can't... Death angels are the most powerful minions of the Abyss. Unless you have a whole phalanx of mages, the only hope is to hide."

"Death angels?" Alyx's brain didn't seem to want to work.

"My father told me about them. Back in Miraya the most powerful death mages use them as servants. He saw some once when he was a child. They're not created like the dog things are. They're actual projections of demon power into our world. As much as can pass into this plane without the destroyers actually being here. My father said their senses of hearing and sight are not good nor can they focus on any task for long. That's why hiding is the best way to deal with them. They are too powerful to fight and they feed on magic like the blood beasts do. Indeed they are attracted to it - attracted to any expression of the life spirit. That must have been why they chased that Tari woman and left you."

"There was a Tari woman, wasn't there? She took your little sister."

"Yes I saw her briefly, up on the cliff. I heard Olga and Jindabyne screaming and I just... I guess I would have been dead with the others if I hadn't come up after them. I pulled you over the edge of the waterfall. The ledge outside here isn't far below the lip of it."

"Why didn't she help us? Tari loathe the Abyss."

"They also loath us outlanders, so I've heard," said Serge. "We should just be grateful she saved Olga."

"But they're good! They wouldn't let..." In her distress Alyx moved and her back was suddenly agony.

"Careful!" said Serge. "As it flew past, it clawed you in the back. It's nasty wound. Lucky you were wearing armour. We'd better wash it."

"No...!" Alyx was about to tell him not to touch her, that she would get one of the others to wash her wounds.

But there were no others. Fredel and the rest - all of them dead? All of them? She put her face against her knees, ignoring the pain of the wound, overcome with grief and hopelessness.

Serge tugged at her shoulder.

"Come on, it's got to be washed. I expect those things have filthy claws."

Alyx couldn't bear to speak.

"We'll need to take off your shirt and armour. Do you have another shirt? No, I guess not. Umm... Maybe I'll go and have a look and see if anything's left," said Serge. "Maybe there'll be something for your back too. I expect you Mori travel with some kind of wound balm, don't you?"

Alyx nodded, still unable to trust her voice.

"Right!" said Serge. "Now just stay here, can you?"

Alyx nodded. Didier, Sidore, Fredel! Why had she survived when everyone else had died?

It was not until after he had gone that she considered the possibility that the Mirayan might be killed and that she might be left alone and so she couldn't help feeling slightly glad when he came back, even though his quest for healing potions had not been a success.

"They've destroyed everything," he said. "I guess that's their nature. All I could find was this." He dropped a bow and a couple of arrows beside her.

"You could probably wear my shirt," he said. "Or maybe yours won't be too torn to wear."

"What about the bodies?" she said quickly, trying to be hard.

The Mirayan's face showed distress. *Soft creature.*

"There are no bodies," he said. "Just piles of ash."

Overcome by shock, she gasped and put her face in her knees again.

The Mirayan sighed.

"Come on!" he said, gently pulling at her armour. His gentleness was an insult. Women of the Mori Royal house were not weaklings to be talked to in such tones.

"Don't touch me!" she snapped.

His face froze.

"Damn you," he snarled. "What do you think I am? Do it yourself then!"

He got up and went out of the mouth of the cave. Alyx realised he thought she had accused him of trying to molest her. She wanted to protest, but, after all, it didn't matter what he thought. He was just a stupid Mirayan.

Teeth gritted, she struggled out of her leather armour. Since it was buckled at the front, this was painful but not too difficult especially as the whole back had been torn out of it. But getting the shirt up over her head was so painful, she could not help crying out. The back of it was torn but not as bloody as she feared. *Stupid armour must have counted for something after all. Now to stand under the water fall and get her wound wet.* She knew that it would be better to have someone wash her wound carefully, but she was damned if she was going to call that damned Mirayan back.

Slowly, wincingly she stood up, but she misjudged the height of the roof and hit her head and then her shoulder on it.

"Arrgh!" she screamed as the bare wound grazed on the ceiling.

"What?" cried Serge, jumping in at the opening. He let out a sound of pain. "Hoooly Mir. What a mess!"

"Go away!" snarled Alyx between clenched teeth, as

she crouched on the floor, arms crossed modestly across her chest.

"Oh stop being stupid! I've got a cloth here. And it's all nice and clean and wet. Just hold still and try to be brave."

After that remark, Alyx couldn't allow herself to cry out and for several wincing moments, she allowed him to wash her back. The pain was so great that it was only when he had finished and she sat limp and sweating, that she realised that she should have had her dagger to hand. She should be treating him like the enemy he was, but it was hard to think of a man who said Hoooly Mir in that tone of voice as harmful. Such a boyish thing to say, the kind of swear words she suspected only Mirayan children used.

"Not deep," he said when he finally finished. "Not bleeding much. But it's already very inflamed."

"Poisoned?" asked Alyx. The Tari in her could usually tell poison, but this time she didn't feel sure.

"Can't say. I wish we had something to put on it. We need to go somewhere where you can get some healing."

"Most of the Tribe are down with my mother fighting against the Mirayans," said Alyx. "The old folk and children went further west. To the head of the next river."

"How far?"

"A couple of days walk."

The Mirayan sucked his breath in though his teeth. "I guess I can carry you on my back."

"No!" snapped Alyx. "I am a woman of the Mori Royal House. Not some weakling." Her strong words was marred slightly by her wincing as she straightened up. "Let's get going. There's a tree camp a half a days walk from here. There should be some supplies there. If we move fast we should make it before dark."

"Fair enough," said Serge. "Let's just get this shirt back on you first, hmm?"

"Princess! Princess!" cried a voice. "For Mir's sake, don't die on me."

She was lying on her stomach and water was trickling

down the back of her neck. She turned her head. The movement was agony.

Strong but gentle hands pulled her upright. Hands held a cupped piece of bark full of water to her lips.

"Thank Mir!" breathed the Mirayan. "Yes, good. Have a little drink. How do you feel?"

The light told her it was late afternoon, almost twilight.

Last thing she remembered it had been mid-afternoon under a hot yellow sun.

"Where am I? What happened?" The words came out in a kind of dry croak.

"You fainted."

Alyx was horrified. "No, I didn't!" she cried.

Then she remembered how nauseous she'd felt at the sight of the blackened patches of ash that had been the bodies of her followers and the dizziness that had started as she turned away. She had pushed herself onwards up the track that lead to the top of the cliff, across the flat rock and into the forest beyond. She couldn't remember what came next.

Serge rolled his eyes.

"As you wish. While you *weren't* unconscious, I carried you along the path until it forked, but I was scared of getting lost so I thought I'd better wake you up before I went further."

"You should have woken me up sooner," she muttered.

"But you're so much nicer when you're unconscious, Princess," retorted Serge.

Alyx didn't have the energy to give this the reply it deserved.

"Anyway I found a little spring." continued Serge. "Here, drink some more."

Alyx sipped at the wonderfully cold water. What to do now? She had a feeling they were still a long way from the tree house. She mustn't show indecision in front of the Mirayan, but her thoughts seemed to be clogged with soft moss.

"Let me have a look at the spring," she said.

He'd dug in a patch of boggy ground and the cavity

had filled with clear water. Despite herself she was impressed at his forest-craft. Which spring was this? After a moments struggle, her memory unlocked itself.

"Did we pass a big heap of rocks a short time ago?" she asked.

"Very round rocks? Like a giant's marbles?"

"Then this is the spring of Secret Purple Lilies. We've still got a long way to go to the tree house. Maybe we should just make camp here. Get some wood."

"I don't think we should risk a fire."

Alyx's hazy brain remembered the blood beasts and death angels.

"Something to eat would be good," suggested Serge. "Maybe you could show me how to make one of your Mori snares."

"There's plenty here," said Alyx, glad to be able to remember something. She crawled closer to the spring and dug around in the mud till she found a clump of bulbs.

"These are very good to eat," she said, rinsing them in the water.

Serge pulled a face, but ate one.

"Hmm! Not bad. You eat some too," he said. "You have to keep up your strength."

Alyx didn't want food. Everything seemed to be about pain and she felt like she was carrying a huge pounding pack on her back. Nonetheless she ate some bulbs to keep him quiet.

Serge looked around. "I think we should try to get off the ground tonight."

"Try and find a tree with a good fork," said Alyx. "One of these big ones with the white trunks should have something. We can tie ourselves into it with our belts. Or a hollow tree might do. We could stop up the entrance to keep warm."

"Right," said Serge. "There was a big old hollow tree a ways back. I'll go see if it's big enough."

"Good," said Alyx. As he disappeared through the trees, she crawled over and leaned her shoulder against a nearby tree trunk. After a while, she thought to check if she was still armed. He had taken her knife and there was no sign of the bow or arrows. She cursed him and then herself for being so off guard. She found a couple of good sized stones and, thus armed, she felt free to let the edges of reality get blurry.

Insane laughter shocked her awake. Dark. Night time. She was on her face on the ground. She grabbed for her knife and her hand hit somebody.

"Hold still!" hissed a voice.

Serge! He was lying beside her, his shoulder and hip pressed against her. Something firm lay on her other side. A fallen log from the smell and spongy feel of it.

An explosion boomed out, followed by another one. Bright light bloomed through the trees.

"Death angels attacking the spring," he whispered, his breath tickling her ear. "I thought they didn't come out at night."

"Where's my knife?" she hissed angrily back at him. Fear made her sharply conscious. "Give it back to me."

"Shut up! What are you going to do with it in your condition? Stab them by falling on them? It's lucky I got back when I did, otherwise you'd have been fried where you slept."

"Give it to me!"

"Stop being stupid!"

"I need something to defend myself."

Something heavy rustled nearby, pushing through the undergrowth behind the log and both of them froze.

Even had she not been able to feel the horrible wrongness of it, Alyx would have recognised the stench of a blood beast. It grunted and Alyx felt herself shrink back as it snuffled closer.

The undergrowth crunched and with a growl and a thud something heavy landed on them. Sulphurous breath enveloped her. She hit out hard with fists and feet as claws raked at her, caught a leg and tried to twist it away. The skin felt like dry leaves.

Suddenly it gave a high pitched squeal. She heard

Serge grunting with effort and a series of thuds. Something warm and stinking spattered her, making her skin sting. Hands grabbed her and pulled her away. *Sweet life!* She bit her lip to stop crying out from the pain.

"Quickly!" cried Serge, dragging Alyx upright. She forced her leaden feet to move.

As she stumbled away in the darkness behind Serge, the sound of insane cackling rose through the trees behind and suddenly a nearby tree exploded into flame. Serge dragged her down onto the ground beside him as another tree burst into flame and another, almost on top of them.

The bracken was waist high here, the delicate leaf fronds lacy silhouettes against the burning trees. Alyx prayed that the death angels would not set the bracken alight. As a screech like an angry parrot rang out on their left, another tree burst into flame, but it was a good distance away and the next was even further.

"Come on," hissed Serge. "There's a place to hide just ahead." Alyx crawled after him. Each movement felt like her back was bursting. The burning trees lit up the forest, making Alyx thankful for once that it had been a wet year. Otherwise a forest fire would have started and they'd have been done for.

At least the light of the burning trees made it easy to see their way. They stopped every couple of moments to listen for the sound of wings, but at last just as Alyx began to feel she could go no further, they reached a cluster of big boulders. A large tree had recently fallen over them making a kind of hollow where the tree trunk met the rock. There was just enough of a gap between trunk and rock for Alyx and Serge to wriggle under it. The hollow was only approachable from one side so that it would be difficult for anything to get at them from behind. Piles of bark and dead leaves had collected in that hollow between the tree and rock.

"Snakes," hissed Alyx.

"No, I checked earlier. Poke about with this stick if you don't believe me. There's nothing here."

He's a surprisingly good woodsman, thought Alyx, as

she lowered herself into the pile of leaves.

"As long as they don't set this tree alight we'll be safe enough," said Serge, heaping leaves over the pair of them.

Alyx gingerly leaned her shoulder against the rock, trying to find a position that didn't hurt. One certain thought remained.

"Give me my knife back," she hissed through gritted teeth.

"Don't be stupid! It's our only weapon and you haven't the strength to use it. I'll do what's necessary."

"What if something happens to you?"

They had argued back and forth in forced whispers for some time until finally Serge gave her a couple of stones.

"Anything to shut you up," he hissed. "Just don't have a bad dream and hit me with them."

Alyx was too tired to be insulted.

The night seemed to go on forever. Some kind of giant spider with claws like hot knives was digging into Alyx's back. Every now and then something horrible would howl nearby or fly overhead and Alyx soon lost count of the trees that kept exploding in the distance. She kept seeing blue-grey wings flying overhead spreading rubbery red particles of wrongness with every beat. Or did she dream that? Strangest of all was the sound of baaing and shouting in the distance, but when she tried to wonder about that, her thoughts got lost in the sludge in her brain.

She saw Didier walking away into the forest. He was just a dark figure against the green trees, but she knew his walk.

"Don't leave me!" she cried, terrified of being alone, but he just kept on walking without even looking back. She wanted to run after him but somehow her legs just dug hopelessly into the mud. She knew something terrible was going to happen to him and that it was her fault.

"Didier! Didier! I'm sorry I jumped. I should never have jumped. Please don't leave me."

Her face was wet with tears. Someone was patting her arm.

"Sshh! It was only a dream," said a soothing voice.

"I am such a fool," she said, thinking Didier must still be nearby. "I am not fit to be Queen. I will never be fit!"

"Hush," said a voice, as a hand gently stroked her hair.

Then she recognised the voice and froze.

"Stop that!" she shouted. "Leave me alone!" She rolled away from him, but the moment she rolled on her back she was overcome with pain.

"Ssh!" hissed Serge, clapping a hand over her mouth.

"Stop touching me," she hissed at him, when he removed it a moment later.

"I was just trying to comfort you," he hissed back. "You were crying in your sleep."

"I was not. I don't cry. Women of the Mori Royal house are not so weak," she hissed as she crawled away from him as best she could.

Then the Mirayan was shaking her and it was light. She'd had a vivid red dream, but she couldn't quite remember what it was. The Mirayan was offering her water and some berries and he kept asking her if there were sheep nearby.

"Seagani have sheep but they don't usually come up this high. They're not friends of the Mori."

"Do you mean there might be other people up here and you didn't tell me?"

"They are not friends of the Mori," she said again. She couldn't make him understand why she could not consider going to the Seagani for help. If only her mind was not so sludgy. After a while Serge seemed to lose interest in whatever point he was trying to prove.

"We'd better go," he said, crouching down beside her. "Come on! Hop on my back!"

"No! I can walk for myself!" She felt better. She did feel better. Just a bit of pain. She crawled out of the hollow and stood up carefully.

"Here," she said. "This is the path!" Walking just meant putting one foot in front of the other.

"It would be much easier if you'd get on my back

before you passed out," said Serge plaintively.

"It would have been so much easier if you'd got on my back before you passed out," said Serge, wiping her face with a wet rag. Hadn't he just said that? It was suddenly much later and they were in the shade of trees but looking up at a hill full of grass and a clean little stream that ran down the hillside past them.

"What happened?" she said. "Where am I?

"You passed out and I carried you. I told you it would happen. Perhaps next time you'll get on my back first."

Alyx managed to answer him. "You shouldn't have to carry me," she cried. "I should be strong enough to walk. I am a woman of the Mori Royal House."

"Yeah, well women of the Mori Royal house are pains in the arse," muttered Serge under his breath. "You've got a very ugly wound on your back that's making you sick. Why can't you accept that nobody can walk when that happens?"

"I am a woman..."

"Yes, yes," said Serge. "You are a woman of the Mori royal house. But you're only human. Don't you think it would be better for everyone if you just saved your strength for healing?"

Fear overwhelmed Alyx. The spider's claws were digging ever deeper into the flesh of her back and she was weak and sick and he was right - she couldn't walk.

"Shut up," she croaked. She curled away and put her face in her hands.

"Don't worry," said Serge softly. "Everything will come right, you'll see."

"I'm not worried," snapped Alyx. "I am no weakling. I will walk. I can." She tried to push herself off the ground, but the moment she got up, she started to topple and she found herself on her hands and knees.

"I can't stand up!" she wailed.

"It's all right," said Serge gently. He eased her down to lie on her side in the grass. "Just rest a moment. It's a bad wound, that's all. I've put some cobwebs on it and some of those leaves you told me about, but you won't really get better without time or healing."

"You should leave me. I'm done for," whispered Alyx.

"Oh Mir! Don't be stupid. You're a long way from done for yet. What's the problem with letting me carry you? After all you're still royalty. I'm a landless warrior now - pretty low in the scheme of the world. So isn't it right that someone like me should carry a princess like you?"

Why wouldn't Alyx's brain work? He must be making fun of her, but the look on his face was gentle.

"This is not how it works for the Mori. The Mori Queen must be strong," she said lamely.

"Well I'm glad I'm not a Mori royal!" He was being sarcastic. She just knew it!

Defiantly Alyx pulled herself upright, but almost immediately the world went round again and she found herself hanging on to Serge. He felt pleasantly strong and stable.

"Why are you are so stubborn?" sighed Serge. "Now listen. You will be easier to carry if you just get on my back while you're still conscious, and hold on. Please."

Alyx stared at him. "I don't trust you.

Serge sighed. "We come to it now, don't we? Look I know we are enemies but for the moment we are in this together. I can't survive out here without your knowledge and you need me to carry you. So let's just help each other. Hmm?"

"Very well," said Alyx. "But.... Don't think I'm weak. Or that I trust you."

"Never in a million years," said Serge kneeling down before her. "Come on. Put your arms round my neck."

Even on Serge's back, Alyx drifted in and out of consciousness. At first the light was dappled with leaf shade, but then it began to get bright. He seemed to have left the tree line and be walking in the mountain pastures. Seagani country. She asked him why but the question only came out as a groan and he didn't answer.

Suddenly armed figures were dark against the blank white sunlight and she was on the ground.

"HELP! SEAGANI!"

She groped for a weapon. The Mirayan was struggling between two of them. She shouted and threw a stone, hitting one of Serge's captors in the leg. Serge broke free only to be seized again. Alyx grabbed another stone and hit out with it as they closed in before someone threw themselves on her arm. A woman with Seagani tattoos on her cheek leant down to her. She put her hand on Alyx's face and a wave of gentle sleep carried her away.

Lying face down in something dry and soft. Wool and the pleasant scent of green wood and herbs. Warm torch light. Alyx lifted her head to look around, wincing as her wound hurt. *Life be praised.* The spider squatting on her back was gone.

A chain clanked as someone came to her side, squatted down beside her and smiled.

"Still trying to get up and walk?"

"Water!" croaked Alyx.

Serge lifted up a bowl and helped Alyx to drink from it.

"How are you feeling?" he said.

"Better," said Alyx. She lay back down and would have drifted off to sleep again but for a niggling thought, drawing her back to wakefulness.

Herbs, green wood, torch light. Wool!

"Seagani?"

"Hello! Back with us again?" Serge was sitting on the ground beside her.

"Seagani! They attacked us."

"'fraid so."

"Where are we now?"

"In a cave in the Gen Mountains. I thought if there were sheep, there must be shepherds so I set out to look for them and found the Seagani. Very fine healers, like all native Yarmarians."

Alyx groaned. "So now I'm a prisoner."

"Ironically, I'm the prisoner," said Serge. He held up his arms to show that a chain had been manacled to both wrists. "Hence the chains. My father always had good relations with them, but it seems my uncle has declared war on the Seagani as well as the Mori, which is why they're up here hiding out in these caves."

His cheerfulness irritated her.

"So you've landed us both in trouble, fool."

Her words wiped the grin of his face.

"Why you ungracious... I carry you for miles, putting up with your 'I'm a woman of the Mori royal house' and all you can do is call me names. You would have died if we hadn't found these people. Now at least you're healed and we have food and water."

He shuffled clumsily away from her and she saw his ankles were chained together as well.

Alyx lay there uncomfortably aware that he *did* deserve her thanks. But he was a Mirayan and not just any Mirayan, but Wolf Madraga's son. She had to hate him for her mother's sake.

"I beg pardon," she said at last. "I thank you for saving me."

"Think nothing of it," said Serge bitterly. "I did it for my own honour. Despite what you think of Mirayans, it is not our way to abandon a wounded woman to die alone in the forest."

As Alyx drifted in and out of sleep, she heard people and animals moving in the caves around them. One time she awoke to find Serge was playing peek-a-boo with two little children who were peering round the doorway at him. He gave a terrific growl and they ran away screaming and laughing, but a moment later they were back with another three. What a soft light-hearted creature he was! He was in a very difficult place, on the run from his uncle, separated from his friends and imprisoned by enemies, yet here he was playing with children, smiling and making the best of things.

Maybe he's just stupid, she thought, knowing even as

she thought it that she would just have to face the fact that the Mirayan had courage.

An adult's voice spoke and the children scampered away with guilty looks as a tall old Seagani woman came into the room and looked sternly at Serge.

"Your friend endears himself to our children as once his people endeared himself to ours," she said, leaning over Alyx.

Behind her, Serge said tensely. "She'll say she's no friend of mine."

"Well it *is* odd to find a Mori being friends with anyone except the Tari. Let us see how your wound heals, young Mori." She was kind and gentle in redressing Alyx's wound.

"Why do you think of them as enemies?" Serge asked Alyx after the Seagani healer went away. "They don't think of you in that way."

"Mori and Seagani have always been enemies," said Alyx shortly. "Their animals are slaves and they assault the sacred forest with their axes and try to steal our land."

"I see," said Serge.

Something in his voice made Alyx want to explain.

"It's true that some Seagani are not as greedy as others. But only a fool would trust them."

"She's back," said Serge quickly.

The healer had returned with a man and a woman, who both had red cheek tattoos faded with age.

"These Elders wish to speak with you and I deem you well enough, Alyx Mori."

"Did you tell them who I was?" snapped Alyx at Serge in Mirayan.

"Of course not," Serge snapped back. "They worked it out. There aren't a lot of half-Tari Mori in the world."

The elderly woman and man sat down nearby and the woman began to speak to Alyx in Seagani. Serge had spoken the truth. They were at war with the Mirayans, but at the moment they were much more concerned about the death angels.

"They come almost daily and burn our lands and kill

195

our sheep and at night those devil dogs prowl about and harry anyone they can find. We believe the Mirayans have sent them."

"No!" cried Serge who, though not part of the conversation, was sitting against the wall nearby. He seemed to speak Seagani better than Alyx did, which was odd for a Mirayan.

"We have no proof," continued the woman. "But its Mirayan magic, isn't it, young man?"

Serge looked away.

"From searching this young man's mind, we know that your mother is also under attack and we have seen the sickness of the rivers with our own eyes. We seek an alliance with the Mori Queen and even more we ask for the help of the Tari Guardians."

"My mother might welcome an alliance, but I do not know what help she or the Tari can give," said Alyx, wondering how she was going to keep the Tari's absence a secret.

"Surely the Tari Guardians will aid us against these creatures of death magic. Unless Mirayan magic is too strong for them. Is that why they haven't healed the rivers?"

"I'm not party to the Tari's plans."

The elderly woman nodded at the still scowling Serge. "This one's mind said that the Tari had left you. Why? Where have they gone?"

"We don't know," said Alyx.

The man sighed.

"You Mori! So untrusting. We have dealt honourably with you so far, but we will mindsearch you if we have to."

"Send the Mirayan away," said Alyx, accepting that the time had come to tell the truth.

"Good idea. He should not be party to our plans," said the man, nodding at the healer who took Serge by the wrist and led him out.

After he had gone, Alyx told the Seagani elders of the disappearance of the Tari.

"One went into the Gen Mountains after hearing a

rumour of death magic there. When he didn't return, others followed him. They too disappeared. A couple of others disappeared near the island of Tyronia. My aunt Yani and her guardian mage were kidnapped in Ishtak and my aunt Marigoth went to rescue them. There are no Tari to help us now."

"An odd combination of events!" said the woman, ironically

"A well-laid plan," agreed the man.

"When the rivers became sick after the last of them had disappeared, my mother also came to this conclusion."

"Does your mother think the Mirayans are behind it? We thought they hated death magic."

"My mother says that Lev Madraga once dabbled in death magic."

The elders looked at each other.

"We need the Tari. Only Tari magic can defeat all this evil. Lady, you are half-Tari and know more of them than us. Surely they must feel creatures of death magic so close to Holy Ermora. Yet three times we have sent messengers to the gates of Ermora and the Tari have ignored their knocking. The last group were set upon by death angels at those very gates. How can the Tari suffer this? Are they dead?"

"I don't think so," said Alyx. "Though perhaps I wouldn't know if they were."

"But surely... They must know that death magic is loose in our land. Surely the life spirit requires them to fight against it."

Alyx thought of the Tari woman who had taken Olga by the waterfall and how she had ignored the death angels.

"Truly, though I am half-Tari, I don't know why they don't act," she said softly.

The woman leant close to her. "Is it not true that those of Tari blood can still enter Ermora, even though it is closed to outsiders? Could you not go in and see what has happened and plead our case?"

Alyx was startled.

"I... I... I'm only half-Tari," she said. "I'm not sure I

could."

"From what we know of the Tari, it's always been possible for the half-Tari to enter Ermora. There are those of our tribe who have some Tari blood and we sent them to the gates of Ermora, but it's been several generations since the Tari mated with our folk and it was not enough."

"I... My mother sent me on an important mission," Alyx said, feeling as if she was being pushed too fast down a slippery slope towards a rash decision. "I... I need to think about it."

"Of course," said the woman.

"If your mission was to find a cure for the red fish, then surely your best hope is in Ermora," said the man.

Alyx thought she would lie awake and worry about the Red Seagani request but she must have fallen asleep the moment the elders left the room, because when she awoke, Serge was back in the room sitting by the opposite wall and a small boy was waiting patiently by his knee while he plaited some straw into a string and threaded it through a hole in a toy cart.

"There," said Serge at last.

"Come with me," urged the boy.

"No lad, I've got to stay here. And you should go back to your mother. It's dinner time. Can't you hear her calling?"

"Quite the nursemaid!" said Alyx, as the child ran away.

"It helps pass the time," said Serge simply. "I like them. They remind me of Olga. Do you think the Tari would hurt Olga?"

"No," said Alyx firmly.

Serge fell silent before abruptly asking,

"So are you going to go to Ermora to ask the Tari for help?"

Alyx turned her face away to hide her surprise.

"Why do you ask?" she said carefully.

"Someone in the main cave asked me if you were going to Ermora and it does seem the logical thing to do if the Tari are as strong as everyone says. Do you think there are many of them still left in there?"

"There were thousands when the Guardians left them seven years ago," said Alyx carefully.

"So did the Seagani ask you to go to Ermora?"

"That's not your business, Mirayan."

Serge was quiet again and Alyx drifted into wondering whether or not she should do as the Seagani asked. It *did* seem like a good idea, but would it just be a time-wasting distraction?

Serge broke into her reverie.

"If the Ermora Tari hate death magic so much, why haven't they come out already?"

"Perhaps they don't know."

"Do you really believe that?"

"Don't know." Their Tari Guardians had said the Ermora Tari didn't care what happened to people outside Ermora, but she wasn't going to tell the Mirayan *that*.

"So it might be worth going to tell them."

"I suppose it would be worth a try." Alyx couldn't bring herself to truly believe that the Ermora Tari didn't care. "I can't help worrying about my mother. I should be there with her, fighting Lev Madraga."

"You're only one warrior," said Serge. "If you persuaded the Ermora Tari to help you, you'd make a much bigger difference."

Alyx looked at him eyes narrowed.

"And why would a Mirayan want me to win against a Mirayan?"

"All living beings are allies in the face of death magic. My stepmother said it and it's true. Look at how well you and the Seagani are getting along."

"Huh!" said Alyx, for want of something better to say.

"I want this death mage defeated as much as the rest of you," he said. "If it is Lev, then I want vengeance."

She was silent, hoping he would give up, but instead he came over and knelt down beside her.

"Listen, Alyx! Lady! Forest Child," he said, putting Alyx instantly on her guard. "When you leave here what's going to happen to me?"

"I haven't even thought about it."

"I am just as big an enemy of my... of this death mage as you are and if I were set free, I'd be able to meet up with my Seagani allies and we could attack Lev too."

"How do I know you won't just go running to join him?"

"He killed my father and he'd kill me too. I don't know if he's behind all this death magic or not, but I do know that I must avenge my father and Paulus and Gideon. And that can only help you Yarmarians. You have to see that. You can't just leave me here to rot. I didn't abandon you back at the waterfall."

He was right.

"I saved your life," he hissed urgently. "You owe me. You have to help me."

Being told what to do always put Alyx's back up.

"Stop pushing me!" she shouted suddenly.

"I saved your life Alyx! Doesn't that count for something?"

"Maybe!"

"Maybe?!!"

"You talk of vengeance Serge Madraga, but your father killed my father. What do you owe me for that?"

"That's not my fault," shouted Serge. "Can't you see...?"

"What's going on here?"

A man had appeared at the door of room.

"Why are you shouting? Is he bothering you, Forest Child?"

"Yes," shouted Alyx. "Take him away."

The man grabbed Serge's shoulder, but the Mirayan struggled, red-faced with fury.

"You idiot! Can't you see your own advantage, you stupid girl?"

"You're the stupid one. Why should I trust a Mirayan?"

Two other men came to the first man's aid.

"You have no honour!" shouted Serge as they dragged

him away.

Alyx slept badly that night - drifting in and out of sleep, troubled by guilty memories of Serge, which turned into memories of Didier and how she had failed him and then into dreams of red vultures with three wings. She was woken from one such dream by an insane parrot shriek and knew that a death angel was passing overhead. She lay there on her stomach feeling vulnerable, whispering the morning chant to herself until she was sure the angel had gone. The idea that she should go to Ermora began to look good to her.

That day she sat up for the first time and broke her fast with a little cheese and meat. The strong food cleared her head and made her even more certain. If her mother had suggested a journey to Ermora, she would have had no doubts. Moreover it *was* the most useful thing she could do in her weakened state.

They did not bring Serge back into the room, but after midday the elders came to see her again and she agreed to their plan, asking only that they help her send word to her mother that she was safe. Then she asked them what they planned to do with Serge.

The man shrugged. "We haven't considered. He's the least of our worries."

"You've mindsearched him. Do you consider him a threat?"

"He is the enemy of his uncle," said the woman. "That is good for us. But these Mirayans... More loyal to each other than us. What if they're reconciled?"

"But you don't plan to harm him."

"No," said the woman. "Probably we will simply keep him here until we can ransom him."

Alyx lay back down trying to feel that she had done her duty, but she was still uneasy. If Serge fought against his uncle, he could ease the situation for her mother.

Oh Life! She couldn't decide. He had been decent to her out in the forest, but he was still a Mirayan. A Madraga. Son of her father's murderer.

She did not see Serge again for some days, but she thought of him often. Was she passing up the opportunity to gain a good ally? She remembered how harsh she had been with him on the journey to the source of the river. Why *had* he saved her?

With the benefit of healing magic, she was soon able to get out of bed and walk a little. She had been lying in one of a number of small alcoves leading off a huge cave. The cave itself was quite light because of a big hole in its roof. Sunlight came in and rain had formed a small pool, which had been modified into a water storage tank. Seagani families were camped in the shadows around the this pool and all day people plodded in through a tunnel at one end of the cave hauling huge bundles of cut grass which they carried to a tunnel on the other side of the cave. From the baaing, Alyx deduced they must be keeping at least some of their sheep in there. But they must have other caves nearby, for the whole Mori nation could not have lived in this cave, and surely this Seagani tribe was even more numerous.

Several times she felt the nearness of death angels. Once the shadow of a winged creature fell across the pool in the centre and the usually clamorous noise in the cave dropped, except for a baby that began shrieking. But as everyone stared apprehensively at the hole, a shriek of crazed laughter rang out and the winged figure disappeared.

"Why do the death angels not come into the cave?" Alyx asked the healer.

"How can you ask that?" replied the healer, pointing to the edge of the hole. The Tari symbol of four concentric circles bisected by a cross was carved all along its lip. They symbolised the five elements of the life spirit, the four circles of earth, air, fire and water and the cross of life binding them together.

"A long time ago the Tari made these caves for just such a purpose," explained the healer.

Even though Alyx told herself she did not care what happened to Serge, she kept looking for him among the

Seaganis camped around the wall until she located him. He was always playing ball or some other game with some Seagani children who were too small to help gather grass. The Seagani seemed to be trusting him to watch their children while they worked.

"He is a charming fellow, is he not?" said the healer, seeing where Alyx was watching. "Are all Mirayans thus?"

Alyx shrugged.

At that moment a couple of warriors came over to Serge and unchained him from the wall. As they lead him away, he looked distinctly worried.

"What's happening?" asked Alyx. The healer shrugged.

"A messenger came from the Mirayans this morning."

Alyx suddenly remembered the elder's words about ransom.

"What do you mean?"

"That's all I know. You should rest now."

"No! I have to..." Shakily she stood up and set off after Serge, trying her best to hurry even though her legs felt like they were made of wool.

"You're very pale. You should sit down before you fall down," said the healer behind her.

"I have to see what they're doing to him."

The healer sighed.

"Take my arm then," she said.

That made the going was much quicker, and it did not take them long to come out of the tunnel into a huge cave which opened to the outside air.

A wall the height of two men had been built across the mouth of the cave, with a barred wooden gate as the only exit into the outside world. The mouth of the cave was so huge that death angels could easily have flown in over the wall. Only the Tari runes all over the cave roof must keep them out.

The warriors had tied a veil over Serge's head and were now leading him up to the top of the wall, where Alyx saw the elders she had spoken to among a group of other elderly Seagani.

To her surprise, the warriors guarding the wall simply nodded at them as she and the healer climbed the stairs after Serge. At the top of the wall Alyx saw a wonderful view of the green rolling hills sloping gently down to an endless forest. But the lush land was dotted all over with blackened patches that Alyx knew must be caused by the feet of death angels and in the valley directly below them was a half ruined Seagani village. Horsemen were moving among the broken huts and Alyx could see the dragon banner of the Mirayans fluttering above them.

The elders were questioning Serge.

"Who is Guilius Appius?"

"He's a mercenary. An ally of my uncles."

"That's him down there in the valley. He offers us protection from the death angels in return for our accepting him as our overlord. He says the Mirayans have made a deal with their master, that all lands under Mirayan suzerainty should be free of their attacks."

"How convenient!" sneered Alyx.

Several of the elders looked askance at Alyx and she felt herself blush, knowing that she was interrupting where she wasn't invited. But now she had started, she might as well keep going.

"It's probably he or his masters who set these things on you."

The Elders exchanged looks. A kind of shrug seemed to pass among them, and Alyx sensed that they had already thought of this and no longer considered it worthy of comment.

"Does this Appius have enough power with the Mirayans to protect us?"

Serge had gone very pale. "I don't know for sure. But my Uncle is a very powerful mage and if he and Appius are still allies..."

Alyx could almost feel his shame as he hung his head. As well he should, when his own family was implicated in death magic.

"What sort of a man is he? What sort of an overlord?" asked one of the elders.

"I don't really know," mumbled Serge. "His father was wise enough to know you don't get the most out of your vassals by grinding them into the ground. Guilius himself is no fool."

"You're not thinking of submitting to this trick, are you?" cried Alyx.

The elders ignored her.

"The Red Seagani have never had an overlord," said one.

"Submission could buy us time," said another.

"You can't give in to him!" shouted Alyx. "By Labwa! You outnumber him!"

The Red Seagani elders gave her a cold stare

"Take them away," said one to Serge's guards. "Both of them."

"Did Appius ask after me?" asked Serge. "Does he know I am here?"

"He asked after you," said one of the elders simply. "We didn't tell him you were here. We don't think he expects to find you."

"Will you tell him?"

"We haven't decided."

"The Mirayans never keep bargains with natives," cried Alyx as the healer lead her firmly away. "Giving him up won't give you any advantage."

"Thanks for standing up for me," said Serge. They had chained him to the wall in her alcove again and he was sitting dejectedly on the floor, rubbing his face with his hands.

"Surely they won't hand you over to Appius. So stupid and pointless!"

Serge wasn't listening.

"If only I were a mage. I'd go down there and mindsearch Appius and find out what's happening. Find out if he was party to killing my father. Find out if it's true that my uncle... my uncle, a proud member of the Madraga family, has given himself over to death magic."

"Then you're starting to believe it?" said Alyx.

Serge nodded and put his cheek on his knees. "Do you think they plan to hand me over to Appius?"

"Unless he knows you are here, what can they gain?"

"Of course it depends on how sincerely they take this whole overlord thing... If they genuinely decide to throw in their lot with Guilius, they might give me to him."

"I don't believe they were willing to truly submit."

Serge sighed.

"They covered my face to protect my identity. But there're all kinds of ways Appius might find out I'm here. And if he does, he'll insist on having me and the Seagani have no reason to protect me."

How well he read the situation. Alyx couldn't think of anything to say, except that she was glad she wasn't in his position.

"Is there anyway you can get hold of a weapon for me?" he asked. "Something small."

Why?" asked Alyx. She had already considered the possibility of stealing a weapon and liked her chances.

"Well if they give me to Guilius Appius... I could at least try to kill him."

"That won't work," cried Alyx.

Serge gave a rueful grin.

"No! They'd search me before I even got to him."

"And then they'd kill you."

"They'll do that anyway. At least the honour of the Madragas is served if I try to strike back. God knows I've done nothing else to avenge my father!" He put his face back in his hands and sighed. "I'll just have to escape."

Alyx understood perfectly how he felt and before she knew it, she had put her hand out and squeezed his shoulder. He grinned ruefully up at her. She remembered then that he was the son of her father's murderer, pulled away quickly and went straight back to her side of the alcove. For a long time, they were silent.

I'm fed up with this, thought Alyx as the light in the cave darkened with evening.

She got up and demanded to see the woman elder. The elder was sitting quietly in a corner of the main cave, deep in thought, a woollen garment and knitting needles on her lap. A baby was sleeping in a cradle beside her and a toddler played with a cloth ball at her feet.

"What are you plans for Serge Madraga?" Alyx demanded.

The Seagani woman grimaced, obviously finding Alyx too blunt. *Bad luck,* thought Alyx. *If they want a favour from me, they can damned well do one back.*

"We haven't decided yet."

"You won't gain anything by giving him to Appius."

"What does a Mori care for the fate of a Mirayan? Especially one whose father killed yours."

"Serge Madraga saved my life," said Alyx firmly. "I owe him a debt of honour. When I go into the Gen mountains, I wish for him to come with me."

The elder considered her for a long moment.

"Prophecy would be served in that way. It is good," she said.

"Prophecy?" asked Alyx. The elder gave her an enigmatic smile. "You are a melded child," was the only reply she gave.

The Melded Child

Chapter 11

The Gen Mountains, a series of razor sharp peaks and sheer ridges, towered out of the middle of Yarmar and the path to Ermora wound steeply up the sides of these ridges through such difficult terrain that there was usually only one route to follow and little chance of getting lost. Had Alyx been going to Ermora alone, the Seagani would have sent a companion with her, but since she was taking Serge, they did not offer. Alyx did not ask even though she accepted that Serge would escape as soon as he could and climbing alone in her weakened state was a daunting prospect. Her back wound meant that she had to carry her pack over her chest instead of on her back and that meant carrying fewer supplies

Don't be a weakling, she told herself. *If Serge Madraga runs off to join his western Seagani allies - good for him. A Mirayan has no place in our affairs.* She had been alone in the forest often, and if she felt weak she would just have to take a bit longer about the climb.

Though they did not say so, Alyx was certain the Seagani Elders were keen for them to go, so as soon as she could walk across the cavern without help, she told the healer she was well enough to leave. Only time would make her strong again and she didn't have time. The healer looked doubtful, but didn't protest.

Serge was not so forbearing.

"You're not strong enough for mountain climbing!"

"We're a danger to these people as long as we stay here. If Appius finds out about us, he'll exact revenge."

Serge scowled and spent the rest of the day fussing about the disposal of the packs and pestering the healer for healing tonics. Alyx paid little heed to him beyond making sure the food was divided between the two packs.

The following evening the two of them and a small group of Seagani, slipped carefully out of the cave. Once outside, most of the group peeled away to keep a watch on Appius' camp and to distract any patrols, while Alyx, Serge and two guides went up behind the caves and into the foothills of the Gen mountains, creeping along among the rocks until they were a long way from the caves. Blood beasts howled in the distance, but they didn't meet any.

After walking all though the night, they took cover among some rocks just as dawn broke. Alyx, who had been in a haze of exhaustion most of the night, fell into a black pit of sleep and awoke mid-afternoon feeling much refreshed - refreshed enough to be annoyed that Serge had not woken her to take her turn on watch.

"Oh shut up! Why can't you just make the most of it?" laughed Serge good-naturedly, and when she scowled at him, went on, "If it means that much to you, take a watch now. I could do with some extra sleep."

He lay down with his back to her and appeared to go to sleep, leaving her feeling childish. Even worse, she had a struggle not to drift back to sleep in the warm afternoon and the struggle seemed to use up all the energy she had gained. She cursed herself for a fool. She had nothing to prove to Serge Madraga.

As the sun began to set, she roused the two guides. The Seagani pointed out the beginning of the path, described the few places where it diverged and made Alyx repeat their instructions back until she was word perfect.

"You should hide during the day," the Seagani said. "The death angels are attracted by movement. If you don't move, they should leave you alone."

They handed her a sword and a knife and left. They gave no weapons to Serge, but in her weakened state he could easily overpower Alyx. She honestly didn't think he would harm her, but the worry about when he would desert her and if she could manage the climb alone niggled at her.

At first the journey was easy enough. The light of the full moon made the path clear and the night was warm. They saw no blood beasts, but twice death angels flew over them in the darkness. Luckily Alyx could feel them coming in time to take cover.

Soon Alyx fell into a haze of tiredness, just concentrating on putting one foot in front of the other. Serge could have disappeared at any time without her knowing, but at dawn he was still there. When they stopped, she crawled under a rocky outcrop and curled herself round her pack before she fell into a deep pit of sleep.

Three-winged vultures pushed their beaks into the land and tore at its flesh. She was grabbed, lifted. A hand clamped over her mouth. Terrified she struggled.

"Ssh! Danger!" hissed a voice in her ear.

Rock. Sunlight. The sound of leather flapping.

Serge was holding her against his shoulder, his hand over her mouth, his mouth against her ear.

"Death angel!" he hissed.

Beyond the outcrop, Alyx's pack lay exposed to the sunlight and to anything watching from above.

The sound of leather flapping again. The shadow of the rock above lengthened and then a huge dark shape with wings separated from the rest of the shadow. The shape swept down the rocky path they had walked along the night before. Alyx caught sight of a trailing blue grey limb, before the shadow shape was gone.

Behind her Serge relaxed, but Alyx was certain the thing was still close by.

"Stop," she hissed at Serge, as he moved to get up. "It's nearby. I can feel it!"

Sure enough, a few moments later the dark shadow shape swept up past them. Four more times it passed back and forth along the path.

Then nothing for a long time and Alyx relaxed.

"They're gone."

Serge pulled the pack back in beside them, opened it, took out some food and handed it to Alyx.

"No travelling during the day then. Not that you could anyway."

Alyx pulled a face at him. "You let me fall asleep again."

"Yes and I will next time too," he smiled.

"You can't trust Mirayans," she said lightly.

His face froze and inwardly she kicked herself. How could she have made such a stupid joke! Of course he took her seriously. There was silence between them until seeking to break it she held a piece of waybread to him.

"Aren't you going to eat?"

"I've eaten," said Serge. "I'll sleep now."

Staying under the cover of the rock, he lay down as far from her as he could be. Alyx ate and lay down too, but it was difficult to fall asleep in full daylight. She could hear Serge moving tossing and turning. Was he going to get up and go? After a while she couldn't bear the suspense any longer.

"Are you really going to come all the way to Ermora with me?"

He turned his head and looked at her. She went on.

"This would be a good opportunity for you to get back to your allies. I wouldn't blame you. It's what I'd do."

"I've thought about it. It's going to be difficult to get back past Appius's troops. And the Tari can help me too.

So I thought..."

Alyx was quiet for a time. And then she said, "Thank you. I'd be glad of the ... the company."

He shrugged.

"I'm sorry for what I said before. About Mirayans. I..."

She stopped, feeling very flustered. Serge looked surprised and then he said, "Honestly, Forest Child. Haven't I earned the right to a little trust?"

"Sorry," said Alyx. "It was a reflex. I didn't think."

Serge grinned. "I noticed." He rolled over and put his hands under his head, looking much more relaxed. "You'll just have to accept that a person can be honourable no matter what their race."

"Fair enough," said Alyx softly.

She closed her eyes, unable to think of anything else to say and a few minutes later, or so it seemed, Serge was shaking her awake and it was late afternoon.

They hiked onwards up the now almost vertical path. Once again Alyx fell into an exhausted haze, but she still lost her temper with Serge when he let her fall asleep during one of their rest stops, causing them to miss valuable walking time.

"It is not for you to decide how much rest I need," she told him.

"I didn't," retorted Serge. "You decided by falling asleep. Stop worrying. I brought extra food. We can take a week if we want."

His calm in the face of her anger made him difficult to argue with and later, as they were toiling up the moonlit path, he had the cheek to tell her that she pushed herself too hard.

"I am heir to the Mori throne. I have to be strong."

"Tell me how that works," he said. "I'd heard that the leader of the Mori is not the battle leader but simply a decision maker and a spiritual guide."

"It works better if she can be both," said Alyx. "But even if she's only a spiritual leader as my mother is, she needs to be seen to be strong."

"I was not brought up to be leader," he said. "To be

honest, I was always glad of that. I never wanted all that responsibility. Now I am Duke of Lamartaine whatever that means. I'll do my best to defeat Uncle Lev. That's just a matter of survival. But I don't much want to be Duke. My poor father used to spend all day listening to people whine. Someone claims their harvest is bad so they can't pay any taxes, but they still want you to keep an army to defend them and fix their roads and then you discover that they spent twice their tax money on a dress for their second wife. Someone's great grandfather stole someone else's sheep and now they try to kill each other at every possible moment and injure some innocent bystanders in the process. What's the matter?"

Alyx had let out a groan.

"It's just so true. I've spent hours standing by while my mother decides which family can pick what berries where. She goes out of her way to make a fair judgement and later you have to listen to the muttering and moaning about her decision ... Why do they ask her if they can't accept what she's going to say?"

"Exactly," said Serge. "Why do they even ask when you know they're just going to brawl next time they meet or try and take over each other's land even after you've spoken?"

"Or argue about who gets what part of a hopping mouse when both their arrows pierced it. I remember two hunters coming to blows over a taldra and it turned out that they were really fighting because one's husband was sleeping with the other hunter."

"What? Oh they were both girls."

"Women, Serge. Girls aren't old enough to have husbands."

"All right, all right, women. Um... I suppose you've got a betrothed," he asked. "Someone your mother picked out?"

"No, it's not like that."

"Isn't it?"

"Well, I am supposed to mate with someone who'd make a good war leader. My mentor kept introducing me to men he thought might be suitable..."

She sighed.

"Boring?" asked Serge.

"Very."

"So what would you do if you weren't the Forest Child?"

"I've no idea," said Alyx, surprised that she couldn't think of anything. "I've been the Heir to the Throne since I was seven."

"That's why you're so serious and never laugh," grinned Serge.

"I do so laugh!" cried Alyx.

"Really? And when does this happen? Come on name the last time you laughed. There! You can't, can you?"

"Oh shut up!" said Alyx, shoving him but unable to suppress a grin.

The moon had set by then, so they were travelling by the light of a small lantern, and they were so deep in conversation that they did not notice they had taken the wrong path until suddenly Serge, who was in front, gave a yelp and disappeared.

Hearing a splash, Alyx lunged forward with a cry and found herself teetering on the brink of a high bank. She knelt and held up the lantern and the light glistened on disturbed water about half a man's height below.

Then with a splash, Serge's head broke the surface and he stood up, spluttering and coughing, in waist deep water. The moment she could make out his features, Alyx, intensely relieved, plumped down on the ground and laughed and laughed.

"What are you laughing at?" snapped Serge crossly.

"There's a frog sitting on your head," she spluttered.

"What?!" squawked Serge, flapping his arms, making the frog jump into the water and swim away.

"Sweet Mir! It's enormous. I'm lucky he didn't eat me." Serge looked so wet that Alyx couldn't stop the giggles bubbling up inside her.

"Hey!" he protested, grinning. "It's not that funny."

"No. I know," giggled Alyx. "Sorry! I..."

"When you've finished being amused, perhaps you could deign to help me out," he said, with such a wry grimace that Alyx fell into fresh paroxysms of laughter.

By the time she had mastered herself enough to help him climb out of the pool, the edge of the sky was turning grey with dawn light and they could make out that the pool was about three man lengths across and tucked into a fold in the cliffs where the sun rarely penetrated. Ferns clung to the walls around it and the path came right up to the lip where Serge, stumbling over the uneven stones, had fallen in. Beyond the rock pool was a brief tangle of bushes and then the rock platform dropped away to a sheer cliff.

"I don't remember this in the description," said Serge.

"I think we must have taken a wrong turn," said Alyx, still giggling and wiping tears of laughter from her eyes. "Oh well, we'll just have to go back tonight."

"Good idea! I'll get blisters if I walk in these wet boots." Squelching as he went, Serge marched round to the other side of the pool where the thick shrubs provided cover from the air. Here he pulled off his clothing, wrung each item out painstakingly and hung them on a bush making noises of disgust that set Alyx into fresh paroxysms of laughter. She could tell he was enjoying playing the fool for her benefit.

When he was down to his breeches, she handed him a blanket and he went modestly behind a bush to change. Then she spread his clothes out on a rock to dry, anchoring them down with stones so that there would be no movement to attract death angels.

Fortunately Serge had only been a short time in the water and most of his pack was still dry. In the early morning sunlight, they sat modestly on either side of a bush and and shared the food that had been water damaged.

"It wonderful up here," said Serge.

"Yes if only..." Alyx shrugged. "If only this was all there was."

"What sort of life would you lead? If you weren't going to be Queen, I mean."

"I don't know," replied Alyx. "I never thought about it.

When we were on the island I liked fishing and just being in the forest. I've always liked being in the forest."

"Me too," said Serge. "And horses. I like horses. My Seagani friend, Alain and I were going to run a horse stud together. Breed the finest horses in the world using Tyronian stallions and Mirayan mares. Mir! I hope Alain is all right! Do you think your mother set him free?"

"Probably," said Alyx, wondering herself how her mother and the Mori were doing.

Serge fell silent and Alyx cast round for a topic to lighten the mood again.

"So do you have a betrothed?"

"No. I'm supposed to... I was supposed to marry a Mirayan to make up for Paulus marrying a Seagani. I can't say I fancied marrying a girl... woman I hardly knew."

"You mean it would be arranged."

"Well not exactly. You can choose if you want. But high-bred girls... You never see their faces and you're not really supposed to talk to them too much or their father and brothers get angry!"

"What do Mirayan princesses do all day shut up in their towers?"

"I don't know. Learn to sew and pray and ... I'm not sure what else. Be mothers I guess."

Alyx pulled a face and told him about the hunting and fishing, the warrior training that were part of a Mori girls training.

"Sounds much like being the son of a Duke," said Serge.

"I guess so," said Alyx.

They lay there in the sun waiting for his clothes to dry and chatting companionably about forest lore, horses and hunting until Alyx fell asleep.

Over the following days as they toiled up the steep mountain ridges, Alyx suppressed her urges to snipe at Serge for being Mirayan. For hours on end she would forget that he was her enemy. Serge's good-nature made such forgetfulness easy.

Finally just as dawn was breaking on the sixth day they climbed round an outcrop of boulders and came out onto a high plateau filled with forest. Alyx felt such a sudden burst of happiness that she had to stop and catch her breath.

A line of low hills lay beyond the forest and she knew instantly and with complete certainty, that beyond them lay everything good - hope, joy, complete satisfaction, peace. Ermora - her true home. Unable to keep her joy contained, she turned to Serge, who was standing stock still, mouth open. "Can you hear it? Ermora? Over behind that line of hills."

"There is something...," he said.

"I never saw or was alive till this moment," Alyx cried. "Oh Ermora. How strongly the life spirit is singing! Come on! Let's find the entrance."

She started running as fast as she could even though she was quickly breathless and had to slow down again. The forest was thick, but they soon come upon a road. The paving was uneven where weeds had pushed through, and overgrowing branches and several fallen logs made the going difficult. Since the cover was good, Alyx insisted they keep pushing on instead of stopping to rest as they usually did at dawn. At last the trees thinned, only to be replaced by a thorny confusion of briar rose bushes, which were covered in blooms as if it were early summer instead of early spring.

"I guess we'll have to go over the top of those hills," sighed Serge, looking at the impenetrable thorny mass covering the path and the rock cliff beyond.

"We have to go through these brambles," said Alyx. "It's the only way in."

"How do you know that?"

"My aunts told me of this place. There is a gate in that cliff."

"Very well," sighed Serge. He watched as Alyx pulled out the short sword the Seagani had given her. "My swordsmaster told me to never use a sword for any thing other than fighting."

Alyx couldn't help grinning. "It seems sword masters

are all the same, no matter what their race."

Serge grinned ruefully back at her. "That was a more civilised time in my life." He bowed gallantly and held out his hand for the sword.

"I think it would be better if I did it."

"Alyx! Why not me? I'm stronger."

She realised the source of his wounded expression.

"It's not that I don't trust you. It's just... Here, have a go."

The brambles were fearsome things, with long viciously curved thorns. As Serge slashed out with the sword, they clung at him as if possessed of a mind of their own, scratching him through the leather cloth of his jerkin and breeches, while every time he struck out, soft pink petals rained down over him, tickling his face and getting in his eyes. After several minutes of hacking, he seemed to have gone no distance at all. Unaccustomed anger seized him and he redoubled his hacking, flailing about with his sword, wildly struggling with stems that seemed to want to strangle him.

Alyx shouted at him to stop.

"I think they're magical thorns. Why else would they be blooming so early in the year?" Gently she took the sword from Serge's hand and said the Tari morning chant over it. The instant she poked the blade into the briars, they seemed to shrink away from the metal. She stepped forward into the space and the briars parted before her.

"Here!" she said, taking Serge's wrist and drawing him after her. Within a few moments they had reached the rocky cliff that they had seen behind the briars. The cliff face was astonishingly smooth, except for a straight line down the centre. Silver lines were chased all over it.

Away among the mass of briars on either side of them, Alyx could see other lines in the rock that made it clear that this rock face was a door. They both put their shoulders to it and pushed. No hint of movement. Alyx stopped and put her eye to the straight line down the centre.

"I can see light beyond." She slid the tip of her sword into the gap as if to pry it open.

"Careful. You'll break it."

"I thought there might be a latch on the other side we could pry open. But it's useless. I can barely get the sword in."

"Hello. Are you the real Melded Child?" called a voice above them. A small fair-haired Tari boy was looking down at them from among the rocks above.

The moment he saw their upturned faces, he smiled brilliantly.

"It *is* you!" he cried. "They said you would come. I knew Kintora had the wrong one."

Serge and Alyx exchanged confused glances.

"We want to come in," said Alyx.

"Put your hands on those two curly things in front of you." cried the boy.

On the rock before her, Alyx could see the silver etching winding into two identical circles on either side of the opening, so she put her hands in the centre of each of them and pressed. The stones swung inwards as easily as if they had been wooden shutters.

"Hooray!" cheered the little boy. "You *are* one of us. They were right."

"Who?" shouted Serge. "Who was right?"

"See you inside!" called the boy cheerfully.

Serge shot Alyx a quizzical look.

Alyx shrugged. "My aunts say Ermora Tari can be very odd," she said, sheathing her sword. "Too much time apart from the rest of the world."

She pushed the doors further open and stepped in.

"It's wonderful! Suddenly I feel certain everything will be well!" she gasped.

"Yes! Nice feeling," agreed Serge.

Alyx's first impression was that they had entered some kind of forest. A line of huge gnarled tree trunks covered in vines stretched away ahead of them, but on either side a wide, dim covered corridor ran along the wall behind them. Either end of the corridor disappeared into darkness. A pale greenish light filtered in through the branches of the trees that formed the outer wall of the corridor. Drifts of dead leaves were heaped all over the ground, looking like the bodies of sleepers. A gust of air from the open gate rustled the leaves, as if the sleepers were restless. Otherwise all was still.

"Can this be Penterong, the great healing house?" murmured Alyx. Yani and Marigoth had told her of it often, but they had portrayed it as a bustling place and this was so desolate. Yet its beauty still filled her with wonder. Even the dead leaves in their sinister drifts were somehow beautiful.

"It's like an enormous cloister made of trees," breathed Serge. "Look! If you bend down you can see some kind open space beyond. I never saw one made of trees before though." He stepped forward.

A shuffling came from the darkness at one end of the corridor, sending a chill down the back of Alyx's neck. Then a small figure became distinct among the shadows, running toward them, cheerfully kicking through the drifts of leaves.

The boy, who looked about 12, was thin and delicate, with a dreamy face.

"Welcome! Welcome!" he cried, running up to Alyx, taking her hand in his cool, thin fingers and peering intently up at her.

"Yes, it *is* you," he cried. "You are the child of the Miracle Sisters, aren't you? They said you would come. Are you melded? You have dark hair!"

"Yes I'm a half-Mori meld," said Alyx, dazed by these questions. "And I believe the Tari did call my mother and her sisters, the Miracle sisters."

"Yes!" cried the boy. He jumped about in the leaves waving his fists in triumph. "I have the gift. I can see the path of destiny. They told me you would come and here you are."

"Then... you're a dreamer?" said Alyx.

"Who told you we were coming?" asked Serge loudly. "Was it the Seagani? They told us they had no contact with you."

"The who...?" The boy looked at Serge in amusement,

clearly astonished that someone didn't understand the situation. "No! The life spirit told me of course. It comes and speaks to me in dreams of prophecy. And I don't even have to take nectar to do it." His small face was as triumphant as if he was speaking about winning a running race rather than talking of spiritual matters. "So much for those who say that because I don't see demon fire, I can't tell the future. So much for Kintora and her pretender. I saw a melded girl at the gate and I knew it was *the* melded child, the true melded child and that the time of Three Sisters prophecy had come." Then suddenly serious he asked "Is the demon fire upon us? Can it harm Ermora?"

Alyx did her best to regain control of the situation.

"There are demon creatures loose in the world outside," she said. "They've been attacking people at the bottom of the mountains and they've done something to the water. We're here to ask the Tari to come out and help us against this. Can you take us to someone who can help us?"

"Help you! Oh!" said the boy. "I'm not sure ... They didn't show me what would happen next. I thought you'd know."

"We need to talk to someone who's willing to come outside and help us," said Alyx

"Sweet life! Outside? How could it be possible?" An idea occurred to him. "I know! We'll go see Kulde. He's quite intelligent sometimes. Come on."

He took Alyx's wrist and pulled her forward. Even though she ducked low as they went through the line of trees, she still got a face full of green leaves. She felt Serge's strong hand grab her other wrist as he followed her.

Then she was out in a great clearing, where tall meadow grass poked though heaped drifts of brown leaves. As the boy pulled her across the space she looked around. This must be a building. Though the sides of the clearing seemed to be covered in leaves, the space was too square to be natural and there were pieces of grey masonry showing through patches in the leaves.

"What a huge building!" she murmured to Serge.

"It certainly is impressive!" Serge murmured back.

A male voice came echoing through the space.

"Yundi! Yundeman!" it called.

"It's Kulde," cried the boy. "What can have made him leave his cooking? Kulde come here! Quickly!"

"Yundi, you stupid little rabbit!" came the voice. "I told you not to run away. There's been a breach..."

A young man about Serge's age ducked out through one of the leafy openings on the other side of the square.

The moment he saw them, he let out a yelp of fright and waved his hands at them.

"Why is he wearing an apron?" thought Alyx, as everything went dark.

Alyx awoke out of a deep soft sleep to the touch of something on her face. Sleepily she brushed it off. A leaf. She felt the secret moisture of more fallen leaves against her back. She was lying in a pile of them.

Above her the blue sky was marbled with wisps of white cloud. She felt deeply peaceful. Then she heard raised voices. Turning her head, she saw a crowd of people. Tari! Arguing!

Remembrance made her sit up quickly.

"What do you mean by putting me to sleep? We weren't doing anything wrong!"

The Tari turned to stare silently at her, except for the boy Yundeman.

"I tell you it's the Melded Child," he wailed to the sudden silence. "The true one!"

"Shut up Yundi!" said the young man in the apron, who had put them to sleep. He looked embarrassed. "You can't believe everything you dream."

"But I'm a dreamer. Why can't you believe...?"

"If you were a dreamer, you'd be asleep in the spirit cave with the rest of them," snapped a thin man. He turned and spoke to Alyx.

"Ermora is closed to outsiders. You are not welcome here. Especially when you bring one of the evil Gibadgee with you."

He nodded at Serge, who was still fast asleep his hands

clasped protectively like a child's. The dead leaves had drifted over him, covering his torso as if they were swallowing him. How long had they been lying here that the leaves had drifted so far? Alyx rested her hand protectively on Serge as she turned back to the Tari.

"He's not evil," she cried. "He loves the life spirit just as much as we do. And I'm Tari. I have every right to be here. Ermora opened itself to me."

"Nonetheless you are not welcome. Stranger Tari are dangerous. They turned their back on the right ways and bought pollution into the Holy Land. You must leave."

"If that is what you wish, but first I beg you to hear me. At the bottom of this mountain the rivers have turned red with poison fish. Terrible winged death angels fly through the air and death beasts roam the land preying on the people and their flocks. The Tari have always been enemies of death magic. I have come to beg you to help us against these evils."

"The outlanders have shown themselves evil and ungrateful to us on many occasions," said the man. "It is no longer our duty to help them."

"Yes it is!" cried Yundeman. "Can't you see how wrong you are? Ermora is linked to the Outlands. What affects us..."

A sudden cry of wild, insane laughter cackled through the building and echoed against the walls.

"Death Angel!" cried Alyx, jumping up and running back towards the gate. "Sweet life. We left the doors open! It'll get in!"

Through the open stone doors, she could see the death angel padding through the tangle of briars towards them. A sulphurous stench of rotten egg came off it and where its claws scratched the ground, little oozing black patches appeared while, as it passed, the green shoots of the briars shrivelled and the roses turned as black as bruises. As Alyx reached the doors, the death angel let out another insane giggle. Answering cackles came from the two others circling in the air above it.

The Tari behind her let out a gasp.

"Quick!" shouted Alyx, seizing the nearest door and pushing it. "Help me close it!

None of the others made any move to help her as she struggled to close the suddenly stuck door.

"Help me! Damn you!" she screamed at them. "This thing's dangerous."

Then the briars began to heave with life. With a loud rustling, a dozen tendrils raked out and their thorns caught on the death angel's flesh, making it shriek with pain. The briar tendrils curled and flexed and grew longer and longer, until the struggling angel was trapped.

Alyx stared open mouthed. Death angels were indestructible, yet here it was whirling and lashing around, yowling like a hurt puppy, its face clenched in pain and its grey tongue lolling out in agony from between its needle teeth. It fell to its knees as the briars thickened round it. Thorns as long as spears lanced into its flesh.

As the creature let out an ear-splitting yowl of agony, a green leaf burst out of a black oozing place where its nose should have been, heralding the appearance of a fresh green tendril of briar. Choking the creature's hands batted weakly as the tendril pushed vigorously outwards.

Then with a kind of wet splat, the creature's head burst spreading bluish-grey scraps of matter all over the briars. The grey lump of its body slumped backwards and disappeared into the writhing mass of thorny stems.

The death angels circling in the sky above shrieked and circled above the briars, spitting out blasts of sizzling ash, but the heaving mass of brambles were untouched by the ash and none of it penetrated in through the open gate.

Alyx, finding she'd been holding her breath, let out a relieved gasp. The magic of the life spirit really was as powerful as her mother and aunts had always said.

"Oh no!" cried the young man in the apron. Alyx spun round to see that the little boy who had let them in, Yundi, had fallen to the ground.

"Yundi, come on! Stay with us," said the young man kneeling over him. "Ah curse it. He's off."

Yundi was muttering and his head was rolling from

side to side. A couple of the other Tari gathered around him.

"That's interesting. Is he still having those fits?" said one.

A Tari man stepped past Alyx and pushed the gate till it clicked shut.

"There's no need for us to look at such nastiness," he said. "And I fear that in all conscience we can't send the outlanders out into that. That would make us responsible for their deaths and you know that is wrong."

The way the other Tari nodded at the man's words made them look as tall and bland as a field of lilies nodding in the wind. Their calmness went like a spike through Alyx's brain.

"Don't you see what horrors we face outside?" she cried desperately. "Don't you understand now why we seek your help? You must aid us!"

A look passed between the Tari. Only the young man, who was intent on his fallen brother, took no part in it.

"Well well, you're safe now," soothed a woman. "Despite the talk of some doubters, no death magic will ever come into Ermora. Of that you can be certain. Come now, you must be tired and hungry. Come."

"But what about the outlander?" asked the thin man who had closed the gate, grimacing in distaste.

"All in good time," crooned the woman. "My name is Jerandine. Come and have something to eat and drink and we can talk it over." She took Alyx's arm and gently led her back into central courtyard, where even now Serge was sitting up and sleepily rubbing his eyes.

The Tari confirmed that they were indeed in the legendary healing house of Penterong, but it had clearly not been used for many years. The dusty leaf strewn passages where puddles of stagnant water collected beneath fallen roofs should have been ugly, yet Alyx still felt that she was in a place of surpassing wonder. The piles of dead leaves were a beautiful copper brown colour and the stagnant puddles reflected the blue sky with limpid clarity.

Beyond Penterong, was a forest where garlands of delicately coloured orchids grew down the trunks of tall straight trees, tangled bark hung from the tree branches and a lacy froth of ferns surrounded the path they walked along. Sunlight slanted in golden rays between the trunks and the air sparkled with the delicious scent of damp mangiri leaves and an exquisite smell of baking. Nearby birds sang sweetly.

As they wound through the trees on a path that was damp and earthen without being muddy, Serge was open-mouthed with amazement and Alyx herself felt like she had been given a wonderful tonic. The world of past memory seemed like a poor pastel imitation of this reality.

"Kulde, have you been cooking again?" asked one of the Tari.

"Yes," said the young man in the apron absent-mindedly. He was concentrating on carrying his now sleeping brother in his arms.

"Well? Can we have some?"

"How can you think of food after...? That thing made me feel sick."

"Don't be a sook, Kulde! That things got nothing to do with Ermora. We're safe in here."

The young man's confused face hardened as he looked round at the group.

"Yundi says that Ermora is part of the Outlands, just as the life spirit is part of everything living."

"Kulde, he's a twelve year old boy with a vivid imagination!" said the thin man who had closed the gate.

The other Tari nodded, understanding looks on their faces and Kulde's shoulder drooped.

"I know you want to believe your brother is gifted and I'm sure he is," continued the thin man. "But let's not get carried away. Come now. I'll help you with him. Jerandine, you make our guests welcome."

He put his arm around Kulde's shoulders and drew him away through the trees.

"Let's see what Kulde has been cooking," said Jerandine, putting her hand on Alyx's arm and drawing her towards a place where the trees thinned.

"Kulde and his cooking!" said one of their companions. A ripple of laughter passed through rest of the group. "Why is he so wild to do everything by hand? He's perfectly capable of using magic."

"Oh come now," said Jerandine. "He does it for the challenge. I think it's very sweet."

In the middle of the clearing, chairs were set around a beautiful table made of pale sweet-smelling wood. Food, cooking bowls and trays were scattered all over the tables surface. Nearby, smoke was coming out of the chimney of an earthenware camp oven. As everyone took a seat around the table, Jerandine waved her hand and the oven door flew open. Little cakes flew out of the oven like a swarm of bees out of a hive, sailed over to the table and set themselves lightly down on a platter that one of the other Tari had placed in the centre. Yet another Tari was placing a large flat leaf in front of every person.

"Honey cakes!" cried the Tari, all lunging at the warm plate.

"No no! Guests first!" admonished Jerandine, holding out the plate to Alyx and Serge. "Careful how you eat them. There's a dollop of honey in the middle of each one and it will be hot."

Alyx and Serge each took a cake as they were bidden.

"These cakes are best eaten with matcha tea," said one of the Tari to Jerandine.

"What a good idea," said Jerandine. She put her hands on a big earthenware teapot and there was the sound of water being poured. A moment later fragrant smelling steam come out of the pot's spout.

Impatience gripped Alyx. Every day death angels attacked the Seagani, and who knew what was happening to her mother, while they were sitting round watching these layabouts discussing the best tea to eat with honey cakes.

"If they're not going to help us, we should go," she hissed at Serge.

"Let me ask them about Olga before we rush off. And we might as well eat. We haven't had anything since midnight."

He took a cake and bit into it carefully.

"Mir! That's delicious."

Alyx bit into hers. He was right. As warm syrupy honey filled her mouth with sweetness, every other thought suddenly receded.

"Have some tea," said Jerandine. "I've cooled it for you. It should be just right."

Alyx accepted the cup and took a sip. Its delicious warmth filed her with a relaxed golden feeling. Thirstily she drank it down.

***

As she puts down her empty cup, Alyx has an odd sense that there is something she is supposed to do. She can't seem to remember what it is. Does it matter? Probably not!

She smiles at the young man sitting beside her. What is his name? Serge? That's it. He smiles back at her. A delicious shyness fills her. He *is* very handsome.

Chapter 12

By the time Ezratah had regained consciousness, it was daylight. His head ached blindingly, his guts were churning and his nose kept banging against a hairy brown flank. He was face down over a horse behind a rider, his hands tied painfully behind his back and his feet bound. He could feel the iron witch manacles on his neck and wrists that prevented him from using his magic. The dizzying sight of the ground passing beneath him was making his guts even sicker so he closed his eyes and tried to work out how he'd got here. He remembered the magical battle at the village and the barn.

Marigoth! Oh Mir where was she? He opened his eyes and strained his neck to look around. There was another horse in front but he couldn't see who was on it.

The last thing Ezratah remembered was Elius smiling as he bent over him. All physical misery faded beneath fear. He squinted up at the man on the saddle before him, but couldn't even see his head. The man wore the strong battered trousers of a soldier with good but worn riding boots.

"What's going on?" he croaked. His mouth was dry

and full of grit.

The rider merely grunted and, when he asked again, told him to "shuddup" and kicked back at him, fortunately missing his face. Not Elius' voice. A southern serf's accent. A local then. No clues there.

Looking round he could see only two horses, his and another. They were riding along a small mule path. Looked to be in hills. Forest and sometimes earthen cliffs beside them. He couldn't tell much else about their whereabouts except that it felt like morning and they were riding away from the sun.

The horses stopped around mid-morning on the brow of a hill. The rider of his horse gave a yell and then laughed, a dirty guffaw deep in his belly before, ignoring Ezratah, he slid off his horse. As the horse turned and put its head down to graze, Ezratah could suddenly see another horse and beyond that a stream. There was Elius, standing thigh deep in the water and holding something - no - someone under. He and Ezratah's rider were laughing as if it was some great joke, but the person under the water was struggling desperately. As an arm came splashing out, groping for air, Ezratah instantly knew who was under there.

"Marigoth!" He screamed. He struggled and somehow managed to get off the horse, but it was no use. Since his feet were still bound, he simply lost his balance and fell over. Casually his rider kicked him in the belly, knocking all the air out of him.

The moment he could breathe again, Ezratah lifted his head and shouted Marigoth's name. By then Elius had pulled her up out of the water by her hair and she was coughing and gulping. She had also had iron witches manacles round her neck and arms. When she heard Ezratah's cry, she called back to him.

"Oh how sweet," said Elius. "Calling to each other like lovesick cattle across the fields."

"What are you doing to her?" shouted Ezratah furiously.

"Just teaching her a lesson. Sick little bitch threw up all

over me. And she did it on purpose."

That sounded so like Marigoth, it was almost reassuring.

"Bet you're sorry now, aren't you?" sneered Elius, using the neck ring to haul Marigoth out of the stream.

"Damn you! You'll hurt her!" shouted Ezratah.

"So? Doesn't matter how many pieces she's in as long as she's alive. And let me tell you this one's a long way from dead." He threw Marigoth on the ground and clicked his fingers. Instantly his black velvet suit was dry. He strolled over to where Ezratah was lying.

"I know..." He leant down and spoke directly into Ezratah's face. "...because I'm a death mage."

He gave a snort of satisfaction at Ezratah's expression and continued, "You can call me Lord Malov. Lord Malov Symina."

Ezratah could only gape at him. Even though he'd just seen this fellow mistreating Marigoth, he still looked like the fresh faced fool they'd known on the boat. Malov Symina? He was reputed to be the most vicious death mage in Southern Miraya. And Ezratah had felt sorry for him!

"But you were in Ishtak!"

"Indeed I was." His face was alight with a huge grin, as if he was a small boy who had just played the best joke in the world. "Waiting for my prize to come as was promised. I wasn't about to let such a precious treasure travel unprotected."

He turned and grinned at Marigoth, who was lying on the ground, shivering, eyes closed.

"Marigoth, are you all right?" cried Ezratah.

"'Tah, is this hell?" cried Marigoth in Tari. "Am I dead? Is this my punishment for taking life?"

"It's all right. We're alive. Just in great danger. Can't you feel the life spirit all around you? Say the..."

"Stop that," snapped Malov. "No foreign talk. Argent! Fix him, will you?"

The dark-clad henchman kicked Ezratah comprehensively in the balls.

When Ezratah could think of something other than

pain, Marigoth was kneeling with her face in the grass, shuddering and whispering. Hoping that she was saying the morning chant which always brought the Tari comfort, he started wriggling towards her, keeping his eye out for their captors.

The two men were sitting on a nearby rock, eating bread and cheese, Malov swinging his slim legs for all the world as if he was some kind of schoolboy on a picnic. He had removed his black tunic, and the white frilly shirt underneath it made him look almost angelic. The sight made Ezratah grind his teeth.

I'm going to break that boy the first chance I get.

He'd only wriggled forward a few inches before Malov saw him.

"Oops the meat's up again," he said to Argent. "What a good little friend you've got, Lady Marigoth. Just like a little dog."

"And what are you?" snarled Marigoth suddenly. "A rat. A sewer rat that lives on turds."

Malov looked startled. Then he grinned.

"Oh dear! Tut tut! Our little friend does know some unladylike words, doesn't she?"

He bent over Marigoth and said, "I'll tell you sweet darling. I'm a maggot. This earth is rotten to the core and humanity is just a mass of maggots wriggling away in its carcass. And now I, Malov Symina, am going to be the biggest maggot of them all. And you, sweetheart, are going to be my Queen Maggot."

"How romantic," sneered Marigoth. "But I think I'll pass on the wedding. You smell so much like a maggot, I don't fancy it."

"Ooh nasty," laughed Malov. "And here was I believing people when they told me I was so attractive."

"Who told you that? The other death mages? They probably just wanted to screw you."

Malov's jaw dropped.

"I can't think of any other way a fool like you could have got this far," she continued.

"Marigoth!" hissed Ezratah. Only an idiot would bait

Malov like this. Did she want to be killed? Actually, maybe she did. The realisation fell like a rock on Ezratah's chest.

"Oh, isn't she *spirited!*" laughed Malov, though his eyes were cold. "And so crude. Do all outlanders have such dirty mouths?" He pinched Marigoth's cheek viciously. "I'm going to so enjoy having you live with me. You're much wittier than my dear sister."

He turned to climb onto his horse. "You know I used to curse the fact that I looked so young. Used to wear a beard so that people would take me seriously. These last few months, it's been a real boon. None of those drool fools on that boat would have believed I'm twenty-three and made my first kill when I was thirteen. Pass her up, Argent."

The other rider lifted Marigoth and Malov pulled her up onto the saddle before him.

"How cosy!" he said squeezing her round the waist. "Just like lovers. Uh uh uh! No biting."

As they rode, Marigoth said the Morning Chant very loudly until Malov shoved a cloth in her mouth.

"What the hell was she saying?" he asked Ezratah later, when the horses were side by side. Ezratah was craning his head to see Marigoth. She kept her pale face turned away.

"A hymn to the life spirit," replied Ezratah. "That's probably why you didn't like hearing it."

"That's right!" mocked Malov. "And now I feel an overwhelming urge to give up my evil ways and wash the feet of the poor. Oh Mir forgive me!"

Argent guffawed. Malov stroked Marigoth's cheek. "You pray to your life spirit all you like, sweetheart. Just do it quietly. And try not to be too disappointed when it doesn't reach out and smite me."

Shortly before nightfall they stopped at a burnt-out monastery where Argent collected wood and Malov lit a fire in it. Watching the magic dance around in Malov hands, Ezratah could see that he had only minor magical powers. Death mages were often thus, weak mages who made pacts with demons to increase their power. Death magery could also endow long life - probably one reason why Malov looked so young.

Malov brought Marigoth close to the fire and as she was still bound, tried to feed her with his own hands. She clamped her mouth shut, refusing to eat.

"You are not going to starve yourself," he said firmly, and he ordered Argent to kick Ezratah till Marigoth submitted.

"I thought you'd prove useful," he said to Ezratah later, as he stuffed a piece of bread into Ezratah's mouth. "I'm glad now that you didn't eat my nice poison soup, though it was annoying at the time."

"Did you poison all those people just to get to us?" cried Marigoth.

"They were only meat," smirked Malov, as Marigoth began to scream abuse at him.

When a large group of horsemen came riding up shortly after nightfall, Ezratah dared to hope for rescue, but the leader dismounted and knelt in obeisance to Malov.

"We'll eat here and then ride to Golgarov," said Malov. He raised his voice. "Everyone is to have Elixir with their food."

"Your sister is still at Winterriser," said the leader.

"So? I don't need HER any more," Malov waved his hand carelessly. "Oh! What the hell! Ride down and tell her to meet us at Golgarov someone!"

***

A gentle hand stroked Yani's back, smoothing up and down her spine, a warm sensual, loving touch. She was lying face down on something soft and warm.

"Yani!" breathed a voice in her ear. "Wake up now."

Daria! Startled wide awake, Yani tried to roll away, but the pain in her broken arm made her cry out. A hand clamped hard around her mouth.

"Quiet!" Daria's voice was urgent. "My brother is here. He's downstairs. You have to change back into a raven."

Yani's arm throbbed and she felt weak and exhausted but Daria kept on shaking her.

"Quickly you must change into your raven shape. If he finds you, he'll kill you. But he won't know you as a raven."

"I can't change shape with this iron thing on," muttered Yani. Blearily, she pushed herself up from the bed.

"Then I'll take it off," said Daria sweetly. "There's no reason why you should wear it anyway." She took Yani's shoulders and looked down into her face with strange earnestness. "But I want no foolishness. I'm trying to save your life. We'll see my brother soon and if he knows about you he *will* kill you. But he never interferes with any of my animal pets."

The neck and wrist manacles snapped opened and Daria pulled them off. Suddenly Yani felt a lot better, a lot more alive and clear-headed.

"Now quickly, change! He's here. He will kill you. Come on, do it."

Yani had no doubt that she should do as Daria told her. Events had proved that she had no chance escaping her and her brother could only make things worse. She pushed herself hard into the change, but the pain in her arm as it changed into a wing was unbearable and she lost consciousness.

Then it was daylight. Yani was in the iron cage, in raven form, being carried downstairs by one of the men. Outside the manor house the carriage was being loaded and Daria was there in a travelling cloak, her face veiled with thin black gauze, busily swishing around shouting orders to the men. There was no other carriage - no sign of anyone other than Daria's party. As Daria took the cage from the man and lifted it up, Yani realised she had been tricked.

"There you are my pet. Just a tiny, teeny lie. We're going to see my brother and he would kill you if I let him. You'll have to forgive Daria for her naughty fib. It was for your own good."

She made kissing noises at the cage.

This sweet girlishness was so loathsome that Yani took a good hard peck at Daria's hand. Daria let out a very satisfying squeak as Yani made contact.

"You nasty thing! Just watch yourself. I don't really need you any more you know. You can ride outside with the cats and the dust for the first stage and see how you like that. Oh you've drawn blood."

She put her hand under her veil and licked it with an enthusiasm which was almost as revolting as her girlishness had been.

Yani's cage was tied onto the back of the carriage among various bags and travelling chests, beside the wicker basket containing the two white cats. The basket had a gap in the side and Daria made sure that Yani was as close as possible to it, so that even before the carriage began to move, she was forced to huddle against the iron bars of her cage to avoid the cats' furiously fishing paws.

The men mounted up and fell into place around the carriage and a small girl ran to open the gates of the manor. The morning was beautifully sunny and warm, but Yani, crouching in the bottom of her cage, with her feathers fluffed up around her, was overwhelmed with hopelessness. Captivity, white cats and Daria. Her broken wing throbbed. How many days had she been here? And where was Marigoth? Was she safe? Her plan of staying close to Daria had been stupid. Stupid! Stupid! Stupid!

Then as the party rode out of the manor gates, an arrow knocked the man riding just behind them off his horse. The carriage skidded to a stop and suddenly voices were shouting everywhere, men were falling off horses, and riders were spurring horses away. Steel rang against steel as figures leapt out of the trees and ditches at the side of the road.

Boom! Men and horses screamed as the carriage rocked with an explosion of magic. Daria came charging round the side, threw a blast of magic at something away in the forest, then spun round and began pulling at the ropes round Yani's cage. Yani threw herself at Daria's hands, scratching and pecking. With a scream of fury, Daria hit the cage, momentarily stunning Yani and making the cats' basket crash to the ground. As Daria swore and kept scrabbling at ropes, Yani struggled up again, clawing and pecking, doing her best to stop her.

Suddenly there came the womp of a fireball and the carriage burst into an inferno of flame, forcing Daria to stagger back. As she did, she saw something there that made her say, "Oh shit! Burn then, you stupid bitch!" Hitching up her skirts, she threw herself up onto a nearby horse and waved her hand as she kicked it into motion. It streaked like lightening off around the side of the manor house. Only magic could have made a horse move that fast.

Beneath Yani, Daria's white cats, clawing free of their fallen basket, streaked away into the road side grass, while all around men fought desperately and a clutch of horsemen charged past the carriage in hot pursuit of Daria. Yani smelt and felt her feathers singeing in the intense heat of the fire and her raven's mind filled with panic. Again and again, she threw her body against the hot iron bars of the cage, cawing desperately. The Yani part of her could see the fire burning through the ropes that bound the cage to the carriage and she kept on flinging herself about until finally they broke and the cage crashed to the ground. Someone picked her up.

"Hello there," said a voice. Prince Pimenov's face appeared against the iron bars.

Yani's heart sank. *This can't be good!*

Pimenov carried her over to a fallen log on the side of the road and taking off his cloak, he opened the cage, reached in with his gauntleted hand and picked Yani firmly up.

Good! Out of the cage! She waited until she was clear of the bars before she dug her beak hard into the narrow strip of flesh between Pimenov's gauntlet and his chain mail.

Pimenov yelped and dropped her and before she hit the ground she was pushing through the change into humanity.

The pain in her arm made the world swim.

Pimenov knelt beside her, putting something over her. Taking her captive! Yani forced herself through the pain and into the attack! Fist. Punch to the face. She seemed to be moving impossibly slowly and it wasn't her best arm, but it connected. He want over and the cloak round her fell away. He had a dagger at his belt. She grabbed it. His hand caught at her wrist but he missed her and she jammed the blade of the dagger against his throat.

He held up his hands saying something. Her mind was so cloudy she couldn't work out what the Mirayan words meant.

Someone grabbed her shoulder, sword drawn, coming to attack. Ah the pain! She jumped off Pimenov. Still too slow. Someone grabbed her ankle and she was on the ground.

She managed to roll so her arm didn't get caught, but someone was on top of her. They were shouting something. No damn it she wasn't going to go into witch manacles again!

The dark soldier from the bedroom pinned her down. Put a hand on her broken arm. Everything went black.

Chapter 13

Malov's party travelled for another day and night. Even when Ezratah could see Marigoth she would not met his eye. They made few rest stops. All the men drank regularly from some potion that made them shudder and then ride on with feverish intensity, but they did not give any to their prisoners and by the first sunrise Ezratah began dozing off from sheer exhaustion despite the discomfort of being slung over the horse.

In the middle of that second day's journey, he was jerked awake by the sound of Marigoth weeping.

"What's wrong?" he cried until Argent, his captor, hit him and told him to shut up.

But once Ezratah had taken a look at the surrounding countryside he knew the reason Marigoth was crying. Such destruction! They were crossing a blasted plain covered with piles of ash, craters and eroded fissures with no patches of green or signs of life. Runnels of rock, as hard and shiny as the skin over a wound, covered the earth, making the ground look as if it had melted and been poured chaotically out of a furnace. Against the horizon, mountains stood like broken teeth in a bashed mouth. The summit of each was a jagged crater and many leaked smoke, making the air sulphurous and gritty with ash.

Sometimes, in the natural course of things, the fiery blood of the earth breaks through its skin and destroys the surface of the land in order that it can be made anew, but the destruction here had been wrought with magic and its making had unbalanced the elements of life. That imbalance fell like a dark shadow on Ezratah's spirit and, if he with his dull non-Tari senses could feel it, no wonder Marigoth was weeping.

"This land is full of pain," she cried. Malov Symina threw back his head and laughed.

"Yes! It is! I wounded this land because I can. Because I am its master. And soon I will be even more its master. A master of the earth is more powerful than any mere Emperor of Miraya."

"Abomination!"

Marigoth whacked Malov hard on the side of the head and for a moment they struggled. Ezratah tried to push himself off the horse to help her, but his captor jerked his gauntleted fist back hard into his face and stunned him.

By the time Ezratah could see again, Marigoth was hanging unconscious in Malov's arms.

"If you've hurt her, I'll..." shouted Ezratah.

The only answer was another blow to the face. Marigoth remained unconscious or asleep and Ezratah concluded that Malov must have bespelled her. At least she was spared the pain of a desolate landscape that seemed to go on forever.

The stones beneath the horses' hooves were light and clattered like charcoal. As the day drew to a close, they began to pass little bubbling pools of hot mud. The scent of sulphur became so strong it tingled metallically on the tongue, and the surrounding air became hotter and hotter until sweat was trickling down Ezratah's face. Several times they passed places where liquid stone oozed along the wounded ground like a huge blind worm or lay steaming in a congealed mass. The sky was heavy with clouds of smoke and over-sullied by red light. They passed places where fiery lava had broken through the earth's skin and was spurting like arterial blood into the air or where it exuded like red hot pus from fissures in the ground. Ezratah was glad when night fell and softened this destruction, but the light of the lava flows still made the moon shine red.

Long into the night they came to a place where the whole landscape became burning red - a mighty river of lava. Malov shouted something and forced his resisting horse down the slope straight at the lava flow.

"Don't do it!" screamed Ezratah, fearing that this was some horrible death mage madness. But Malov's horse did not sink into the boiling mass. Instead it found a firm surface in the air above the lava flow, its hooves clattering as if it walked on stone, and Malov grinned derisively back over his shoulder at Ezratah as one by one the riders followed him out over the river of lava. When his rider's turn came, Ezratah could not tear his eyes from the terrifying sight of instant death swirling below his face even though the searing heat made them run with tears. Only one eye actually ran - the other was closed from Argent's earlier blow.

Then at last they were over the lava river, out onto a slope of ash and stone and riding towards a small hill where a low, stone building stood beside a single, tall, black tower which pointed like a contemptuous finger at the sky. This must be Golgarov then. Now things could only get worse.

In fact over the next couple of days, Malov treated them very well. No one beat or tortured them. Apart from being locked in witch manacles to suppress their magical powers, they were unbound and given clean mattresses to sleep on and clean blankets. Such was the heat in this place they hardly needed the blankets. Malov put them in two separate cages, close enough so that Ezratah and Marigoth could speak to each other even though they could not touch.

"My honoured guests," he called them in his revoltingly playful way, as he fed them good food from his own table.

"Hateful bastard!" Marigoth said behind his back. Malov had given her several healing potions and she was regaining her spirit, but she did not insult Malov to his face because the only time she had, he had walked coolly to Ezratah's cage and hit him hard enough to blacken his other eye.

Their cages were on a dais at the head of a huge hall. Ezratah could just make out a big stone altar at the other end of the hall, but he did not think Marigoth could see it and he did not mention it to her. Malov used the dais as a study so they were surrounded by shelves of books and two benches covered with the impedimenta of magic - globes, crucibles and jars of ingredients. Further away against the wall was another bench covered in metal instruments of torture - shiny and in good repair.

Malov had arrayed himself in his "death mage costume" magnificent long black robes embroidered with red sickle moons and every day he sat studying books, writing and "keeping a good eye on my treasure," as he put it. He didn't bother gloating. He kept busy studying a very complicated spell. Ezratah knew very well that it was a tapping spell, but he didn't tell Marigoth about that either.

He had two male assistants, one very old and the other grey-haired but still vigorous. Neither appeared to be mages, but they seemed very learned in the ways of mathematics and science and spent long hours poring over plans and making calculations. From listening to them, Ezratah realised that they were devising the best way to apply magical force in order to blow up yet another mountain. Apparently, from their work on other mountains they had discovered that if you used a silver pole to apply force in the right place, the effect was enhanced. Having seen the devastation that surrounded Golgarov, Ezratah was not surprised that Malov was feared throughout Southern Miraya and he shuddered to think how much more he would be able to destroy when he tapped into Marigoth's power.

Every day one of his guards would come to Malov and tell Malov a number, which the death mage would record in one of his notebooks. A short time later a long line of chained slaves - grey-faced people without hope - would file through the hall. Ezratah wanted to shout at them to have hope, for hope would protect them and make them tasteless meat for the Abyss, but how could he when he had no hope himself? He tried to persuade himself that someone would rescue them in time, but Yani was probably dead and who else was there?

He knew all these slaves must be here to be used in the spell to tap Marigoth - a spell which would enable Malov to draw on her resources of power for his own magical purposes, a spell which would bind them together so strongly that it would be impossible to part them without causing Marigoth's death. With such power as Marigoth had at her command, Malov would be able to blow open all the mountains he wished without resort to human sacrifice and demon power. Having her power used for such ends would surely destroy Marigoth.

Every chance he got, Ezratah checked over his cage for weaknesses, working away at any bar that seemed loose, trying to find a way to get out. But he was useless.

"Who are all those people?" Marigoth would ask, as the long line of souls who would soon suffer an agonising death, and who knew it, filed past.

"Workers in the mines around here," answered Ezratah quickly. His desperate lies made Malov grin with smug amusement but he said nothing.

On the third day Marigoth said, "You really should give up lying, 'Tah. You're rotten at it. They're here for some spell, aren't they? What are you going to do with us, Malov?"

"Do you really want to know? It's very nasty."

"What a surprise!" sneered Marigoth sarcastically. "No doubt I'll be sacrificed to demons and my spirit sucked into the Abyss and destroyed."

"Oh no, sweet darling! I would never waste you in that way. Shall I tell you? I don't think I feel like it today," he drawled.

"Oh please! Spare me these little games," said

Marigoth. "For a supposedly great man, you can be very petty."

"Petty!" snapped Malov. He took a step towards Ezratah's cage before stopping and smiling sweetly.

"I'll tell you what I've got planned, but in return I want to cut his hand off."

"Go to hell!" shouted Marigoth. "Don't tell me then! See if I care!"

Malov looked at Ezratah. "What about you, dear friend? Would you sacrifice your hand for me *not* to tell her?"

"No!" screamed Marigoth. "Don't do it! It's ridiculous!"

Almost Ezratah was willing to offer. He knew he should be willing to offer. But...

"She'll know very soon I think," he said, feeling ashamed of himself even as he said it.

"Tsk! Not much of a hero are you?"

"He's not a petty minded fool like some people," snarled Marigoth. "If you hurt him, I swear I'll get you even if it kills me."

"Talk! Talk!" said Malov turning his back on them. "I'd tear him from my heart now if I were you, lady. My dear sister is coming home tomorrow and she has some unpleasant habits. Perhaps I indulge her too much but I like to see her enjoy herself. I thought I'd let her play with your little friend."

"If he dies, how will you control me?" snarled Marigoth. "Because I swear...."

"Oh to play with, not kill," said Malov. "Daria has a very fine understanding of the difference."

"You know what's going to happen, don't you?" accused Marigoth, later that night when they were alone. "Why won't you tell me? You're beginning to frighten me. Surely it can't be worse than losing your spirit to the Abyss. Please 'Tah. Tell me!"

Ezratah's heart was heavy. Curse Malov! He had set things up so that Ezratah had to be the one to tell Marigoth.

"Well we aren't going to die," he said. And he told her all about tapping.

***

In the castle of Prince Pimenov, the bodyguard Ashana realised Prince Pimenov was not listening to him and stopped talking. The Prince was looking out the window at the torch lit courtyard below. Ashana had the sinking feeling he was thinking about the Raven-witch. He was a good man, Pimenov, and Ashana would happily die for him, but women brought out a chivalrous streak in him, which was an unfortunate weakness in times as difficult as these.

"My Lord, did you hear me?" he asked.

The Prince started.

"I beg pardon, Ashana. You were telling me that you could find no one in my service who knows anything about the Archipelago."

Ashana sighed. He had been talking of other matters for some time.

"What do you stare at, my Lord?"

"I was remembering that woman and how she jumped out of the window and how she turned into a raven as she fell. I saw it but I didn't really believe it. Thought it was some trick of the light."

Ashana grinned. He was rumoured to be the deadliest man in Southern Miraya, but he did have a sense of humour.

"That was exactly what I thought, my Lord. Even now I have seen with my own eyes how you were almost killed by a raven who turned into a woman, I still do not believe it."

"Yet it is true," said Pimenov. "What wonders must the Archipelago hold! The world is always stranger than one knows." He shook the thoughts out of his head and was suddenly all business. "What was it you have discovered about this Yani Tari, Ashana?"

"I have found out nothing more about the Raven-witch.

But I believe one of our agents has discovered something interesting about the Syminas. Malov Symina crossed into Golgarov, a couple of days ago with two prisoners. A fair-haired foreign woman and a Mirayan man. Both in witch manacles. The woman...”

Then Ashana heard the sound, the faintest creaking of a board in the corridor, where no one should be at this time of night.

Quickly but silently, he walked to the door, threw it open and sprang out into the corridor. He had the Raven-witch in his grasp before he realised who the intruder was. She was weaker than she'd been that first night, but she certainly knew how to fight, and he only escaped being thrown again because he remembered the move.

“What are you doing out of bed? You're still weak,” cried Pimenov. The woman stopped struggling and, instead of holding a warrior, Ashana suddenly found that he was holding a soft and curving woman, wearing only the thinnest of linen night gowns. The Raven-witch was a beautiful creature with her fair hair and exotic almond eyes. This thought startled Ashana, but fortunately all his years of training stood by him, so that he automatically kept a tight hold on her.

“Am I a prisoner?” she demanded in her blunt barbarian way. “Why are you keeping me asleep?”

“If you were a prisoner, you would be wearing manacles,” said Ashana's lord. “As for the sleep, we wanted to avoid something like this. Creeping round in the cold is not going to help you heal up. Go back to bed.”

“No,” cried Yani, twisting in a way that almost, but not quite, broke Ashana's hold on her. What warrior this creature was! “I have to find Marigoth.”

Pimenov regarded her. “What is this Marigoth that so troubles you? I might be able to help you.”

The woman glowered at Ashana. She made one more attempt to shrug him off and when she couldn't, her face broke into a charming smile.

“You are very good,” she said to Ashana, as if she genuinely appreciated his skill.

She turned her face to Pimenov. "You could give me some food," she said.

Pimenov laughed and, stepping back, motioned Ashana to bring the Raven-witch into the room. Ashana kept hold of her wrist until the door was safely shut and then he stood watch as the Prince guided Yani into a chair at the table where his untouched supper lay, cut some slices of bread and cheese for her and offered her fruit.

She ate very politely, just like a civilised person, even though she must have been starving.

"Lovely bread," she said at last. "Cheese is good too."

"Marigoth?" the Prince reminded her gently.

Yani regarded at him thoughtfully, showing no sign of fear at the potential danger of her situation. Ashana had to admire such élan and clearly the Prince did too.

"What sort of being are you, Yani Tari?" asked Pimenov. "You can change shape, but as far as I can tell you're not a mage, though you do seem to be healing up quicker than most."

"I am Tari," said Yani simply.

"I'm sure that means something to Archipelagans, but you'll have to tell me more."

"I have been gifted by the life spirit with the ability to change into a raven. That's all."

"And you are in our fair country because of this Marigoth?"

"Yes," said Yani. She was silent for a moment as if considering the pros and cons of confession. "My sister. Who is a real mage and very powerful. For some reason Daria and her brother were using me as bait capture her. I guess they want to make some great pact with their demons."

Ashana remembered the foreign woman he had been telling the Prince about earlier. From the briefest flicker of emotion across the Prince's face, he must have too.

"You have some news of Marigoth. What is it?" demanded Yani

"A woman who looks like you has been reported near here," said Pimenov, making no mention of the woman's captivity. "Everyone knows this is where you are, so I don't doubt that she'll find you. I suppose that like you, she'll have no difficulty entering our fortress."

Ashana thought the Prince sounded convincing, but Yani frowned at him as if trying to read something on his face.

Then her shoulders relaxed and for the first time the hand holding the cup trembled.

"You shouldn't be alarmed by her or me," she said. "Tari are forbidden to do harm. Don't attack her if she appears."

"I think you should go back to bed and rest. There is really nothing to worry about. From the looks of it, you will be back among your own people soon. Ashana, would you please escort the lady back to her room."

"Thank you," said Yani.

She made no attempt to escape as they walked down the corridor to her room. Ashana sensed that she was exhausted. Daria had treat her very roughly and her badly broken arm was still healing.

"Did the Prince really hear a rumour of Marigoth?" she asked him.

Ashana shrugged. "I am only the bodyguard," he said.

"Bullshit!" She smiled at him from under her lashes. "I would hate to have to play cards with you, Sir Ashana."

And she opened the door of her room to face the clucking of the nurse, who had not yet realised she was gone. Ashana waited in the ante-room, listening to the nurse trying to get Yani to take more healing potion, and Yani refusing but allowing herself to be tucked back into bed.

When Ashana returned to the council room, Pimenov was back at the window again.

"Wouldn't it be wonderful to live in a world full of benign mages forbidden to do harm?"

"But we do not, my lord. You are not falling into one of your chivalrous fits, are you? You should not be thinking of her as a lady in distress. She is far too dangerous for that."

Pimenov smiled. "Is she so dangerous, Ashana?"

"Anyone who can walk through wardings so easily is dangerous. This is not some foreign paradise. This is Miraya."

"Perhaps. I have a good instinct about this woman. If we had heeded her words, we might have destroyed Daria Symina."

Ashana shrugged. "Perhaps Lord. We have tried and failed before."

"Always so cautious. Well, perhaps someone has to be. But think how useful someone who could walk through wardings and change into a bird might be to our cause. We must try to win her to us."

He was right. A man could go a long way to find a cleverer lord. Once again Ashana thanked the day that Pimenov had bought him out of the Assassin's Guild.

"Did she take her potion?"

"No," said Ashana. "She lacks trust for us, that one. If you don't want her to escape, you should put her in a manacle."

"We cannot tame her in a manacle. She should be able to leave anytime she wants. With any luck she will be sensible enough to stay until she is healed and by then..."

"Is that why you lied to her about her sister?"

"She can do nothing with that broken arm except get herself killed," said Pimenov. "And she's too valuable to waste."

"You *are* falling into one of your chivalrous fits lord. Have care!"

Pimenov smiled again before his face became serious.

"You think that foreign captive of Malov's is her sister? In that case we do have a problem."

"Shall I send messages to the rest of the league?"

"Yes. If Malov successfully taps the woman he will be as powerful as his sister. Send a troop of men to Golgarov to make sure he cannot collect enough slaves for the task. And make sure anyone who knows about Yani's sister goes with them. We don't want her accidentally finding out." He shook his head. "Malov Symina powerful in his own right.

Whew! That doesn't bear thinking about."

Ashana kept an eye on the woman, who had a terrific gift for creeping past her nurse. Twice he caught her outside her room. Another time when he was checking the Prince's horse, he had the distinct feeling that someone was creeping round the stables, but couldn't find anyone. He suspected she must be reconnoitring her escape. It was what he would have done in her position. Under Ashana's suggestion, Pimenov put an extra nurse on at night, but he still would not put the woman in a manacle. "We want to make her an ally," he said. Ashana could see his reasoning, but it annoyed him that the Raven-witch probably had the run of the fortress.

The Prince found his own attempts to win her trust frustrating. He went every day to sit with her and they played a strategy game which he usually won, but his subtle questions, designed to find out more about her people, lead to nothing.

"We have much to blame our countrymen in the colonies for," he told Ashana.

A few days after they sent out the messages, one of the other lords of the Southern League arrived. Ashana always stood guard inside the door when this one conversed with the Prince, for he was a ruthless opportunist who would turn on the Prince as soon as it suited him. Unfortunately in such an unsettled country you had to take allies where you could find them. As the two men discussed how to deal with the possibility of Malov tapping a powerful foreign mage, Ashana heard a gasp outside the door and flung open the door to find the Raven-witch standing there. She was stronger this time and harder to hold, but he had seen the look on her face and was determined to prevent her escape. She could curse too. When the Prince put his head round the door to see what was happening, she called him a thrice-damned liar and some even worse sounding things in her own language.

The Prince excused himself to his guest, closed the door on him and together he and Ashana dragged the

Raven-witch back to her room. She must have heard most of Pimenov's conversation with the other lord for she kept screaming at them to tell her what tapping was.

"You told me I could trust you," she shouted, as they wrestled her back into bed. "Now I discover you have lied to me."

"I lied to you for your own protection. You cannot do anything in your state. Except get killed by bandits before you even reach Golgarov," cried Pimenov.

"Then give me some men. Let us go together. We must rescue Marigoth."

"It's all in hand. Trust me. Everything we can do for your sister, we have done."

The Prince called the nurse to fetch a Mage.

"If we can't trust you to be sensible we will have to hold you asleep until you heal."

"You bloody Mirayans! You always think you know best. If you must force me to stay here, at least tell me what tapping is."

The Prince sighed and rubbed his hand over his eyes, but he took comfort from the sight of the mage in the doorway. No one could resist sleep magic.

"Come on," said Yani in even tones, lying back against the pillows. "You want me to trust you. You want me to help you, don't you? Tell me what tapping is and I'll even take one of your horrible potions."

"Good," said the Prince. He picked up the potion from beside the bed and gave it to her. After a moment's hesitation, Yani swallowed it.

"Believe me, Lady," he continued. "This forced sleeping is for your own good. There's nothing you can do alone. Golgarov is impregnable and in one of the most dangerous parts of Miraya."

"Stop stalling. What's tapping?"

"Death mages have a way of binding themselves to other mages. They keep these mages alive and simply use their power for their own spells. It's a much more logical way to use a powerful mage then sacrificing them to demons."

"Sweet life! He'll be able use the life spirit for the work of destruction. But this is not so bad. Marigoth will live. She can be freed."

Pimenov shook his head.

"It is impossible to separate bound mages. The only way for Marigoth to be freed is if Malov frees her. And killing him will kill her as well."

"You mean... Earth and air! We have to stop him before..."

"We do still have time. He must sacrifice many, many slaves to perform this spell and we already have fighters out there stopping him from bringing any more in. And he must wait till the dark of the moon when evil magic is strongest."

Ashana knew this was an arrant lie, but he was almost certain that Yani did not.

"But how can you know...?"

"It's time to sleep Yani. You can't ride, you can't fight, you can't even safely change shape till you are healed."

"I can ride. I can heal while riding." She was struggling to get out of bed now, but the potion was dragging her down.

"No," she cried as she fell into sleep.

"Poor woman," said the Prince. "I feel for her." He stood up, straightened himself for business and nodded at Ashana.

"You and I must return to our friend in my room now and tell him of the poor mad woman we have been nursing. Though I doubt he'll believe that story." He turned to the mage and the nurse. "Keep close watch on her. She's very cunning."

Ashana woke the Prince in the early morning.

"She's gone," he said.

"What! But we gave her a potion. And the mage..."

"Clearly wasn't strong enough. When the mage left the room to piss, she tied up the nurse and put her in her bed and jumped some groom in the stables. She was out of the gate around midnight. The guards didn't stop her, because she said she had an urgent message for Atticus Darshanna."

"How did she learn the name of my neighbour?"

"She's a clever woman. You want me to go after her?"

Prince Pimenov sat up and shook his head to dislodge the sleep from it. Ashana had opened the shutters and seen dawn in the sky outside the Prince's window as he did so. That meant the woman had most of the night to get ahead of them. Yet she was not at her full strength.

"I should not say yes," said the Prince. "We have our own worries."

"I can ride with ten men. It is not a great waste of resources."

"Then you're in favour of this?"

"She is a magnificent creature," Ashana was surprised to hear himself saying. "And she would be a great help to us against Symina in the time to come."

"Then go," said the Prince.

The Melded Child

Chapter 14

Marigoth was very silent after Ezratah told her about the tapping spell though she answered his anxious questions with, "Fine. I'm fine."

Finally she said, "I've always enjoyed being with you, Ezratah. Thank you for being such a good friend."

Then Ezratah was really afraid. He sat up all night watching her even after she lay down and seemed to be asleep, only letting himself rest when Malov came back into the room the next morning.

He was awoken by shouting around mid-morning to see Argent on top of Marigoth's cage, and Malov was inside it holding Marigoth up, her legs clasped in his arms. Ezratah saw instantly that Marigoth had managed to hang herself from the bars of her cage using a strip of cloth.

Malov and Argent must have caught her quickly for Marigoth was still conscious, hitting, kicking and screaming insults at Malov as he laid her on the ground and untied the strip of cloth from her neck. Bruises were darkening on her skin, but otherwise she seemed unhurt.

"Don't bother doing that again, you tiresome bitch. I'm

expecting it. I've put wardings all over the cage and on you. The moment you stop breathing, I'll know about it. Next time I'll string your little friend up in your place."

She kicked at him as he left the cage, before curling up on the floor to weep.

"Oh shut up!" said Malov. "Did you think I'd let you deprive me of my chance?" He sat down and went back to studying.

"Mari! What were you doing?" said Ezratah in Tari. For once Malov didn't object to the foreign language.

"What do you think I was doing?" snarled Marigoth. "I will become a running sore in the life spirit. I mustn't allow that to happen."

"The life spirit is strong. Bigger than all of us. It doesn't need your death. You can survive this. Please, Mari."

"He'll use me to destroy. Force me to witness his tortures. Wouldn't death be better than that?"

The something in her tone of voice made Ezratah hope that Marigoth had no real wish to die.

"There's still time," he urged. "What if Yani comes and you've already killed yourself? At least wait till closer to the day."

"When is that day going to be?" snapped Marigoth. "Do you know?"

"No," said Ezratah quietly. "But he must speak to his demons first. Make a bargain for enough power to do the spell in return for all those slaves."

"I'm just one person," said Marigoth. "Isn't it better that I should die than all those people?"

"You won't save them if you die," said Ezratah.

She was silent for a moment.

"I've had a dark feeling about this journey from the start. That's why I asked you to come. I'm sorry, 'Tah."

"I'm not sorry," said Ezratah. "I'd do anything to help you."

Marigoth leant her head against the bars. Ezratah could almost but not quite touch her.

"You know, Malov wasn't even in the room when I

tied the cloth round my neck, but he still knew I was trying to harm myself," she said. "I shall have to think of something cleverer next time."

"I won't try to stop you," said Ezratah, hoping he would find the strength when the time came. "Just wait a little."

With her long black hair, pale white skin and rich red mouth, Daria Symina looked like something you might find wandering ravenously though a midnight graveyard. As she came into the room, she stared avidly at Marigoth. But she did not stare for long, because Malov was displeased.

"You failed me, sister," he snapped. "How could you let her get away?"

"Mari!" hissed Ezratah at Marigoth. "Listen! They're talking about Yani."

Marigoth's face seemed to gain some colour.

"They attacked me and took her," pouted Daria. "I didn't have enough men. If you had sent for me when you were passing close by, this would never have happened."

"Always full of excuses," said Malov coldly. "It was too much dream smoke, wasn't it?"

"No!" shouted Daria. "You didn't tell me about her. I thought I was just dealing with an ordinary mage. Not... She was a freak of nature! Why didn't you tell me?" Her voice rose to an angry yowl.

"You didn't need to know."

"Didn't need...!" screamed Daria.

Malov's hand shot out, seizing Daria by the hair and he pulled her to him.

"Now, now, sister. It's not nice to be angry at your loving brother. Why would I want to trouble your little head with details?" He stroked her throat. She hissed at him and for a moment, Ezratah though she was going to bite him.

"Sister, sister, be calm!" Malov crooned. He kissed her passionately on the lips, and after a moment she relaxed.

"Now look! I have a little toy for you, just for your pleasure."

"Mages!" Daria muttered in a disgusted tone. "Only two and I bet you won't let me play with the woman."

"Daria, I'm wounded. How can you be so ungrateful? Go on! Play with the man. I love to see you play."

"If you like," said Daria sulkily. "But I'm still annoyed at you, Malov."

She went over to the bench by the wall and inspected the instruments. At length she picked up a large metal needle and, with a dreamy smile, ran it over her lips. Then suddenly she darted over to Ezratah and dug the needle into the flesh of his arm.

Ezratah yelped, more from surprise than pain, and Marigoth screamed in protest.

"Don't worry!" Ezratah gasped. "She just startled me." Daria smiled at him sweetly and dug the needle in again. This second time he managed to stay silent, but the next time she stabbed him, she hit a place that was so tender that all his nerves jolted and he screamed before he could stop himself.

The look of pleasure left Daria's face.

"Shut up, you coward!" she screamed. "It doesn't hurt that much!" and throwing away the needle, she ran from the room.

"Tsk, tsk, we're moody today," said Malov, with a shrug. He turned back to his books.

Marigoth had covered her face with her hands.

"I'm not hurt," Ezratah whispered to her. "She just got me in a tender spot. Took me by surprise. You know what a coward I am!"

"Shut up you damned liar!" croaked Marigoth hoarsely. He could tell she was crying though he could not see her face.

"Mari, Yani is free. It means we've got some chance of rescue!"

"That's what I like to see," said Malov, without turning round. "Hope in the face of overwhelming odds."

That night lantern light woke Ezratah and before he was even fully awake, he found himself caught up in magical power, jammed up against the bars with Daria's face was pressed against his. Her breath smelt of wine, and that bitter elixir that they all seemed to drink, and her eyes glittered in the lantern light. She held the metal needle again, stroking his cheeks with it, and threatening his eyes. Though Ezratah's flesh cringed from the needles sharp point, he was determined not to scream and awaken Marigoth.

"Who is the master here?" asked Daria.

"You are," murmured Ezratah

"Good!" crooned Daria. "Now ask me what I want to know."

"What do you want to know?" said Ezratah. "Master," he added quickly.

"Tell me about these Tari. What's so special about them?"

"Nothing really!" said Ezratah. "They're just powerful mages."

"Wrong answer!" She jabbed the needle hard into the place that had hurt him so much earlier, but he saw it coming and though it jolted him, he managed not to cry out. "Don't lie. I'm not a fool. That Yani had no magical powers and yet she could change shape. How is that possible?"

"Their magic works differently from ours."

"How?" asked Daria, sliding the needle along his cheek bones.

"They draw on different sources of power from us. That's all I know."

"Liar!" Daria scowled into his face. She was silent for a moment. "I looked into that Yani's mind and I saw... What was it that I saw?"

"I don't know. I never looked into one of their minds."

"Oh very clever!" Daria jabbed the needle into his cheek again.

"Don't hurt him! I'll tell you," cried Marigoth, from out of the darkness. "You saw the life spirit. That's what you saw."

"You soft little bitch," crooned Daria. "So *you* will give me some answers then." She stuck the needle into Ezratah cheek again.

"Leave him alone," cried Marigoth. "I'm telling the truth."

"Don't tell her anything, Marigoth," gasped Ezratah.

"Her brother knows already," said Marigoth. "What's the point of keeping it a secret?"

"Yes. Why keep it a secret?" said Daria.

"Because he does," said Ezratah.

"Shut up," said Daria. She smacked Ezratah hard on the face, knocking him to the ground.

"Leave him alone or I won't tell you anything," cried Marigoth.

"An idle threat," said Daria. "You're too soft to carry that one out. Why don't you tell me everything, meat?" She strolled easily over to the Marigoth's cage as if she were a lady strolling in her garden. "Tell me why your sister's mind is full of life spirit. Is yours the same?"

"Don't tell her!" cried Ezratah.

"Do tell her," crooned Daria. She stroked the bars of Marigoth's cage.

"All the Tari are the same," said Marigoth.

"So you 'Tari' have a special relationship with the life spirit."

"Yes," said Marigoth. "And that is why your brother is so interested in us. We have more of what demons love to feed on. And we can be tapped. Which means more power for him. Which I notice he isn't going to share with you."

Ezratah shouted a warning, but too late. Daria's hand clamped around Marigoth's throat.

"Don't think you can come between me and my brother," she hissed, pulling Marigoth up against the bars and stoking her cheek. "Feel how powerful I am, meat."

"Yes, you are powerful. But were I free, I'd be ten times as powerful as you and my power would flow as long as the world existed. The life spirit makes me so."

"Rubbish!" said Daria, shaking her. "No one can be

that powerful."

"Why don't you set me free and try me out?" smiled Marigoth.

Daria laughed. "Do I look such a fool?"

Marigoth shrugged. "How can I tell if I don't try you? Tell me, did you like looking into my sisters' mind? It gives most people great joy and peace to touch the life spirit like that. But I wonder how it would affect someone like you. I bet you saw your true self, didn't you? And knew yourself to be an abomination. A hideous, foul..."

"Shut up!" screamed Daria, throwing Marigoth so hard across the cage that the whole thing shook.

"Stop it!" shouted Ezratah. "Guards! Guards! Help!"

His cries echoed feebly in the huge space of the hall.

Daria had taken a flask from a pocket in her robe and was drinking deeply from it. For a few long moments she leant against the cage breathing heavily, before telling Ezratah in a sleepy voice to be quiet.

"They're not going to come. They're afraid of me."

Marigoth had picked herself up and was crouching by the bars.

"You have hunger, don't you?" she whispered now. "Just like the demons you serve. You long to feel the sweet life spirit again, don't you? And I am full of that life spirit. If you look into my mind..."

"I don't serve demons! They serve me!" shouted Daria, storming from the room.

"You shouldn't have told her anything," groaned Ezratah. "Mir knows what she will do with the knowledge."

"How could things be worse?" shrugged Marigoth.

"She is worse than he is."

"I don't think so. He's coldly evil. She is creature of passions and such people can be played upon."

"She loves giving pain for its own sake."

"Yes, but... you know yourself that you cannot feel the life spirit and go unchanged."

"I was in the spirit cave. At the very centre of it. That's very different from a mindsearch. And it almost sent me mad. If Daria gets any more insane, she might harm you."

"Since I haven't got the strength to kill myself, it might be a good thing if she does," said Marigoth simply.

"Don't say that!"

"What other hope do we have, Ezratah? Can you promise me rescue? We don't know whose hands Yani has fallen into. Or how wounded she was when she got away. It would be better not to hope."

Ezratah put his face in his hands.

"I'm sorry. I'm no help to you."

"Oh 'Tah," said Marigoth softly. "I wish you weren't here."

Wounded he looked up at her, but her smile told him what she really meant.

"But for my own sake, I'm very glad you are," she added.

After a time they both slept. But in the grey light of dawn Ezratah awoke to see a hooded figure crouching by the next cage, gripping Marigoth's skull in the mindsearch position.

"Don't be so rough," groaned Marigoth. "Do you see it? Can you feel its beauty?" she continued.

"Yes, yes," crooned Daria.

Marigoth slid her arm round Daria's neck and put her hand up to stroke her face, but the moment the Tari touched her cheek, Daria screamed and flung herself backward, throwing Marigoth down and flouncing away in a swirl of black cloth.

"What the hell were you doing?" hissed Ezratah.

"Sweet life! That hurts!" panted Marigoth, wiping tears of pain from her face. Ezratah watched anxiously, knowing that too rough a mind search could cause damage to the brain, destroying blood vessels and shattering memories.

"I tried to give her my life spirit," she continued. "I thought it might affect her more strongly. But the iron makes it very difficult."

"Are you trying to turn Daria to our side? Do you think you can?"

"I have no clear plan with Daria. But Malov's had things too easy so far. I'm simply trying to throw some poison into his well and see what crawls out."

The Melded Child

Chapter 15

When Malov Symina saw the wounds that Daria's needle had made on Ezratah's face, he laughed and made insincere tut-tutting noises. "Has my naughty sister has been at you?"

"Your sister is a fiend," snarled Ezratah.

"Indeed she is. Dear little creature makes a brother proud."

He told one of his servants to put salve on Ezratah's face and turned to his studies.

Later when Daria came in and wandered round the room pouting and kicking her feet, Malov was so intent on his calculations, that he paid no more attention to her than he would to a restless cat until, just like a cat, she accidentally on purpose knocked over the stand that held his lamp.

"Daria, go away!"

"You pay me no attention, brother."

"I'm busy with these calculations. When the mage is safely tapped I'll have time for you."

"No you won't," pouted Daria. "You'll be off making your little volcanoes everywhere. You won't care about me any more when you have tapped her."

So she did listen to what we said last night, thought Ezratah.

"What a thing to say, my dear little beastlet," said Malov calmly.

"Why is it not me who taps her?" asked Daria sulkily. "I'm the one who does magic; you're the one who makes clever plans. That's the way it has always been."

"But you already have so much power, sister sweet. I'd like a little of my own."

"*I want to tap her!*"

"That's not fair Daria and you know it," said Malov sternly.

Daria scowled and kicked at the table with her foot.

"I don't think it's safe," she said. "There was something wrong about the sister and there's something wrong about this one. You should try it out on me first."

"How sweet of you to care!" He drew her to him and stroked her hair. "But how can I ask my little beastlet to risk herself?"

"These women are servants of the life spirit itself," said Daria.

"How did you know that?" asked Malov sharply. "Did the other one tell you?"

"Yes. And it seems to me that for servants of death such as us tapping the life spirit must be dangerous."

Malov eyes widened in surprise.

"How very lucid you are today, beastlet. But don't worry. I'm not tapping into the life spirit itself. I'll be drawing it through her. Her mind does not come into mine. Madraga and I talked it through. I see no risk."

She turned on him.

"So you already knew, didn't you? About this life spirit. Madraga told you when you plotted together, didn't he? Why didn't you tell me?" Her voice rose to shout.

"Why should I?" said Malov sharply.

"Because I looked into her mind and I saw... It was hell Malov. I felt that I was nothing. Even less than some peasant. Do you understand?"

"Well it's over now," said Malov. He straightened his robes so that they fanned out round his ankles properly. "Stop whining about it. I won't look into her mind so it won't happen to me."

"You should have told me," muttered Daria.

Madraga! Who was this Madraga Daria spoke of? Duke Wolf's family name was an unusual one and as far as Ezratah knew the only Madragas were those in the Archipelago at Lamartaine. If a Madraga had been visiting Malov Symina it could only be Lev Madraga, Duke Wolf's younger brother. But would he be having converse with a death mage? The more Ezratah thought of it the more likely it seemed. Lev was arrogant, angry and ambitious and he knew a lot about the Tari. Knew it because Ezratah had told him. They'd been close friends, before the Duke had announced his engagement to the Lady Jindabyne and Lev had stormed off to Miraya in a fury. Then he'd been gone seven years. Seven years when no one really knew what he'd been doing. A black weight fell on Ezratah's chest. Had he told Lev what he needed to capture Yani and Marigoth? Although he expected to learn little, he couldn't resist asking Malov. To his surprise Malov admitted openly that he'd made an alliance with Lev Madraga.

"It was he who arranged to have that Yani captured and handed over to me. He has a lot of influential supporters in your Archipelago. I wanted to take Yani's guardian mage, that fellow Diyar to tap, but Lev wouldn't let me have him. I guess he didn't trust me to carry through my part of Marigoth's capture." Malov grinned. "So I had to be patient. Lev insisted I take Yani to Miraya as bait to lure Marigoth away. But I didn't want to risk losing my chance at her so I persuaded another death mage to take Yani while I accompanied you and Marigoth on the boat. And a charming time we all had. I completely fooled you, didn't I?"

Ezratah found it odd that Lev was willing to let Malov tap Marigoth, because it would make Malov the more powerful mage.

"What did you give him in return?" he asked the death mage.

"One or two useful tricks. The Tari's days are numbered. This naughty world cannot accommodate such fine creatures. They are too much of a temptation for people like me and too much of a danger to us. Though it does seem a waste. All that powerful meat."

"What do you mean the Tari's days are numbered?" cried Marigoth.

"If I told you that you'd know, wouldn't you?" sneered Malov. "Now be good little creatures and shut up. I've got work to do." With a smile, he turned his back on them.

"Answer me," shouted Marigoth, shaking her cage bars "Tell me what you mean, damn you! Tell me."

Malov came back over to the cage. "I thought I told you to shut up," he said. "You're being very disobedient."

"Tell me what you mean about the Tari's days being numbered and I will be quiet," cried Marigoth.

"Tsk tsk! You still think you can make deals with me? There are only two choices here. Shut up or else." He went over to Ezratah's cage and grabbed the mage's arm. Malov might be a weak mage but he was strong enough to cause pain to jolt through Ezratah's nerves until his teeth began to chatter. When Malov finally let go, Ezratah's whole body was buzzing from the pain, his legs collapsed under him, and blood trickled down his chin from where he'd bitten his lip.

Marigoth crouched in the bottom of her cage sobbing.

"Hush!" whispered Ezratah. "I'm not truly hurt."

"I'm sorry to have caused your pain," said Marigoth through her sobs. "I have to know what he plans for the Tari. I have to." There was a desperation in her voice he had not heard before.

Ezratah woke in the middle of the night to hear Daria growling angrily beside Marigoth's cage.

"Leave her alone!" he cried. Daria ignored him and shook Marigoth roughly.

"Show me!" snarled Daria.

"Tell me what your brother gave Lev Madraga and I will let you see the place," said Marigoth.

With a howl, Daria threw Marigoth to the ground and rushed from the room.

"Are you all right? She pulled out of you pretty fast," hissed Ezratah.

"She went in roughly too! Bitch!" She gave a weak smile. "It's like having a hangover without the fun."

"She's back!" warned Ezratah, as the hooded figure glided back into the room. He braced himself to be hurt but Daria ignored him.

"Tell me what I want to know, Daria," whispered Marigoth. "Then I will show you everything. Everything easy."

In a pouty little voice, Daria said, "He showed him how to blow mountains apart and how to bring molten rivers of rock up from beneath the earth. Malov even lent him one of his scholars. And I showed him how to make bloodbeasts and death angels. And some small magics to poison waters. The pathetic creature knew nothing of the death arts. Are you happy now?"

Marigoth bowed her head in submission and soon Daria was cooing with pleasure. After what seemed like a very long time, she pulled out of Marigoth's head and went away, humming happily.

When she was gone Marigoth fell to the floor of her cage and wept.

"Hush, my dear one," whispered Ezratah softly, hating himself because there was nothing he could do but murmur platitudes.

"She forces herself in so hard that I can feel her mind. It's horrible - sharp with jagged edges. I can hear children screaming. Such pain. Such loss."

"What has she done?" wondered Ezratah.

"It's her," whispered Marigoth. "The screaming children are her."

The next day Marigoth was taken from her cage. She bit Malov, got free and ran, but since the witch manacles made her helpless, he caught her easily and, using magic, threw her right into the arms of his henchman Argent, who tossed her over his shoulder with a rough guffaw. Then Malov made her watch as he forced his juddering pain magic into Ezratah.

"I'll get you Malov, I swear! Even if it kills me!" was the last thing Ezratah heard before he blacked out.

By the time Ezratah become conscious again, Marigoth was gone and Malov had pulled aside the huge black curtain that hung on the wall behind them. Behind it towered an enormous silver mirror - so big that Malov's reflection was a tiny dark spot in its expanse. Ezratah lay huddled in the bottom of his cage, his whole body ringing like a bell from the punishment magic, while Malov assembled various items and the guards bought in a slave. When the frightened slave was tied spread-eagled on the ground and all the other preparations seemed finished, Malov came over to the cage and nudged Ezratah roughly with his foot.

"If you know what's good for you, you'll get under those blankets and hide."

Still dazed, Ezratah crawled obediently under his blankets. At least he did not have to see the subsequent torture of the slave, though his cries of pain made Ezratah clench his teeth and block his ears. But even with his hands over his ears, he could not shut out the terrible sound that suddenly cut through the room.

A voice.

A voice like a thousand stones grinding together. A voice that sounded like a whisper and yet was loud enough to make the whole room shake. Through his closed eyes, Ezratah could still see a hot red light. Waves of nausea and sweaty terror washed over him and a terrible emptiness tugged at his mind, worrying at it as a dog worries a captured rabbit and telling him there was no point in living - that he should die as soon as he could. Only one thing could radiate this hungry despair. A demon! Ezratah had never been so close to one of the denizens of the Abyss before.

The conversation between Malov and the demon seemed to last forever. Ezratah did not understand the language, though there were elements of Mirayan in it, but he caught the tone of the conversation well enough. They were negotiating. And the demon was laughing.

Not till the red light was long gone did Ezratah dare to peer out from under the blanket, and even then he did not come out till he had made sure the black curtain was back over the mirror.

Malov was sitting collapsed in his chair, clothes covered in blood, face grey with exhaustion, gulping down a bottle of elixir.

"How could you do that?" cried Ezratah, fury replacing his terror.

Malov jumped up and flung wide his arms, his face suffused with the excitement of the drug. "You would not dare it, would you? But I have greatness and greatness will dare anything."

"What could possibly be worth that?"

"Power!" shouted Malov. "I have the greatness to rule and soon I will have the means." He seized a poker and started beating on Ezratah's cage as if it were a musical instrument. "Power! Power! The power to be king! The power to be Emperor! The power to be a god!"

"Leave him alone!" shouted Marigoth from the doorway, as she struggled unsuccessfully to get free of Argent.

"Ah my Queen!" cried Malov, bowing mockingly. "Most fragrant of women!"

As Argent brought her past him, he pinched her cheek and ruffled her hair. She submitted coldly, all the time peering anxiously over at Ezratah.

"What happened?" she asked him, after they had put her back in her cage.

Ezratah told the truth, even though he could not met

her eyes.

"He spoke to his demon. That means he will tap you tomorrow."

"I see!" said Marigoth. Her voice shook.

"What was outside?" he said, hoping to distract her.

"They took me to a room full of cages. Horrible. Lots of prisoners who know they are going to die. I blessed them, but there was nothing else..."

She put her head on her knees and would say no more. Once Marigoth was bound to Malov, Ezratah knew of nothing that could separate them except death. Praying that this was merely his ignorance, he went over his cage again. There were a couple of bars that seemed a little bit loose and with pulling they might come away in time. In a very long time. If only...

Surely Yani would come. Surely this could not happen. Marigoth had served the life spirit all her life. Surely it would jump out of the air at the last minute and save her.

Daria came during the night. She ignored Marigoth's pleas to set her free. When Marigoth tried to shut Daria out of her mind, Daria simply thrust herself in, even though it made Marigoth lose consciousness. Sometime later in the night Marigoth tried to hang herself again, but Malov knew the instant she tried and guards were in the room before she could manage it. Afterwards Malov had Argent strangle Ezratah with the same piece of cloth that Marigoth had used.

When Ezratah regained consciousness again it was morning. Ten guards were pushing the great altar stone to the centre of the hall and Marigoth was standing in her cage watching, her hands trembling as they held the bars.

"Oh 'Tah. If only I could will myself to die. I guess I'm too weak. I've tasted death now and I didn't like it." Her eyes were glassy. "This can't be happening."

"If you're alive, there must be some reason for it."

"I don't know," said Marigoth. "Why should there be a reason for anything?"

Ezratah found that he was praying the morning chant.

Was this really going to happen to his precious indomitable Marigoth? Bound to Malov like a victim bound to a parasite? A Tari to be used to bring chaos to the world? And yet what was going to stop it?

Servants and soldiers were bringing slaves in from the other room, making a great commotion as they did so by knocking both men and women about. They chained ten of them to the altar and once they were chained, another guard came round with a large hammer and broke an arm or leg on each of them. The hall echoed to the crack of the hammer on bone and the sound of the slaves screaming. These slaves would be kept alive and in pain the whole time, their pain keeping the Abyss open while the life spirit of the rest of the prisoners was sacrificed to the demon beyond the gate.

Sobbing, Marigoth hid her face in her hands.

"I love you Marigoth," Ezratah said to her. "You are the most wonderful woman in the world. The strongest and bravest. You will rise above this."

Malov and Daria came into the room dressed in long red robes, Daria carrying several big sharp knives on a tray. At his desk Malov poured a mixture of wine and elixir into two goblets and together he and Daria drank them off. As they stood there, shuddering from the effect of the drink, a kind of hush fell in the hall. The guards ceased moving and came silently to attention and the whimper of the prisoners was the only sound. In that moment Marigoth sprang from where she had been huddled at the bottom of her cage and shouted something in Tari.

Ezratah had never heard those words before. The moment they were spoken, he felt as refreshed as if he had had a long cool drink of water and it seemed as if the prisoners whimpered less. Malov turned away with a disdainful look but Daria looked utterly sick. As Malov barked an order at her, she picked up the tray of knives and followed him down the hall to the altar. Behind him the guards brought forward several very frightened slaves.

Marigoth was already curled in the bottom of her cage, her face hidden in her knees. Ezratah turned his face away.

"You are strong, Marigoth. You will survive," he kept on saying.

Malov held up his arms, knife in one hand and shouted words. *This must be the ritual of summoning*, thought Ezratah. Even though he was talking to Marigoth, even though he tried not to listen to those words, each one seemed to burn itself into his shrinking memory so that he felt he would always hear them even in his dreams. At the end of the ritual, Malov stepped forward and slowly killed the prisoner on the altar so that the man screamed for a long time.

He killed three more prisoners and then as the fourth prisoner began screaming, there came the grating whining sound of a huge stone door opening and the altar began to glow with a sullen red light. A wave of horror made Ezratah crouch down in his cage and many of the prisoners cried out.

"The Abyss is open," Marigoth gasped.

"Don't look!"

"I don't need to," she whispered.

Malov let out a shout of triumph.

"Let us begin, sister," he cried and Daria stepped forward as the guards brought more prisoners up. Ezratah did not see what happened next, but there was the clatter of a falling knife, and when he turned to look he saw Daria running from the room.

"Come back here, you stupid cow!" shouted Malov. A horrible hungry yowl came from the altar behind him.

"Get her!" he ordered one of the guards, and then turned and resumed his butchery.

Ezratah did not look round again but he was certain that Daria did not return to the room. He suspected that Malov could not ask one of the others to help him kill the prisoners. The sacrifices would need to be made by a mage and the knives would be consecrated to that person. Twice the death mage sent guards to bring wine filled with elixir, but otherwise he did not slow or hesitate.

And on the slaughter went. Malov must have slowly

killed over two hundred people. The prisoners screamed and pleaded for mercy as bones cracked and flesh was cut. Demons loved the life spirit to be flavoured with strong emotions, so it was necessary that each victim die in pain and terror. A terrible yowling and, as time went on, the sound of slurping, like a cat or dog messily eating, came from the glowing altar.

At first Marigoth cringed with every scream, but soon she simply lay on the floor of her cage whimpering. As the light in the hall changed with the passage of the sun across the sky outside, she seemed to pass into a kind of faint where she did not move at all. Ezratah half hoped that she had achieved her wish of dying. He huddled against the bars of his cage, still telling her that he loved her and that she was strong and beautiful. He only noticed the guards coming to get her when they had opened her cage door.

He screamed a protest and grabbed at them, but they simply ignored him.

Marigoth hung limply between them, her eyes empty. Ezratah crawled round the bottom of his cage and saw that Malov was lying on the glowing altar. As the guards dragged Marigoth over the piles of butchered flesh surrounding the altar, paying no more heed to them than if they had been a spongy carpet, Malov stood up. He seemed have doubled in size and he glowed with hot red power. With his sacrificial knife, he slit his sodden robe open and peeled it off him. He was naked underneath but so soaked with blood that his skin glistened red. As the guards tore Marigoth's clothes from her, he held out his arms and they passed Marigoth up to him. Malov took her limp body in his arms and turned her so that he held her from behind. Marigoth eyes were open but otherwise she looked unconscious. Malov's hands left red smears on her pale white skin. He pressed his belly against her shrinking white back, folded his arms around her arms as if he were her bloody red shadow and squeezed her against him.

Lifting his head to the ceiling and screaming out some words, he bent and bit Marigoth hard on the shoulder, sinking his teeth in and holding on like a dog holds onto its kill. At this, a blast of red light rushed out of the altar, streaming up to the roof and engulfing them both.

Marigoth let out a guttural scream, while Malov threw back his head and howled triumphantly.

Letting Marigoth fall discarded onto the piles of bodies round the altar, he jumped down laughing, and turned and twirled across the hall, a joyous dancing red figure. Suddenly he stopped and waved his hands and Marigoth's unconscious body lifted up from where she lay and came flying into his arms and he clasped her to him.

"Yes! I have power!" he shouted. He flung out his arm over the room before him and shouted, "Be gone!"

Flames roared out of the floor. Guards ran screaming from the room with their hair and clothes alight. The sheet of flame blocked everything from Ezratah's view so he reeled back from the heat, thinking Malov had overreached himself and killed both himself and Marigoth.

But then Malov walked out of the flames with the limp figure of Marigoth draped over his arm like an old cloak - completely untouched by the inferno raging behind him. He let Marigoth slide out of his arms and turned and waved his hand again, clenching his fist in a pulling back movement.

"Stop!" he shouted.

The great hall was suddenly empty of flame leaving pillars and walls and roof blackened by fire and the chains round the altar glowing red from the conflagration. All the bodies were gone, but ash lay in drifts upon the floor - the only testimony to all those people killed.

Malov held up the palm of his hand and blew on it and a gust of air swept through the room, whirling up the ash and sending it flying out the hall's smoke hole in a great column. In a moment, the hall was swept clean as if the terrible slaughter had never happened.

"Yeees!" shouted Malov. "I am free of the foul smell of the maggots! It's so easy." He threw back his head and shook his fists in the air.

A guard came nervously across the hall to him. "My Lord, some of the men were hurt in the fire. Could you perform healing...?"

"I don't do healing magic. You weaklings. A little singeing and you come whining for healing magic. Go to my sister. She's the one with womanly virtues."

Ezratah hardly noticed any of this. Malov had let Marigoth fall very close to his cage and for the first time since they'd been here, he could touch her.

Her eyes were slightly open as though she was conscious, but she seemed to be in some kind of trance. He stroked her chill cheek and said softly, "Marigoth, my little love."

She did not respond, but he could feel her breath on his hand. He took a rag of cloth and soaking it in his drinking water, began to wash the smears of blood from her face.

Something hit him in the side of the head.

"Keep your hands off her, filth," snarled Malov, gathering Marigoth up in his arms.

"Please. Can't you see she's sick?"

"She'll live," said Malov. He picked Marigoth up and carried her into her cage, putting her gently on her blankets and covering her.

"Please! You've got what you want from her. Please let me care for her."

"What! So that you can kill her and rob me of my power?"

"I'd never do that."

"That's what she'd beg you to do," said Malov. "It's her only escape now." He pushed his face into Ezratah's. "I wonder if you would be man enough to do it." He strode from the room.

Malov was right. Marigoth probably would beg Ezratah to kill her. *But I will fail her in this too*, he thought.

Chapter 16

Yani Tari must have been riding like a mad woman, for although Ashana's party changed horses regularly and Mikhalus, the mage who accompanied them, used magic to give them greater speed, they did not catch her that day or the next. They saw signs of her passing. A horse had been stolen from a farm and Prince Pimenov's exhausted horse left in its place, and half a day later they came upon a bandit lying by the road with a broken leg. In return for a healing spell, he told them of the fair-haired hellion whom he and his mate had tried to rob and who had out-fought them and taken their horses, weapons and supplies.

On the third day the party came to the wasteland that surrounded the fortress of Golgarov. A stately mountain range had once stood in this region, but now most of the mountains were shattered craters, steaming with noxious vapours and surrounded by a wasteland of grey ash that was dotted with bubbling pools of hot muck or steaming green water.

It was easy to see where a horse had entered the wasteland and easy to follow Yani's trail through the ashy ground. Ashana was certain the trail was fresh, so despite the muttering of the rest of the men, he ordered them to cross into Symina land. Everywhere he saw the tracks of the large dog-like creatures called bloodbeasts that death mages used as guards. The party rode with their bows strung. By then , it was already afternoon and, though no one said so, no one wanted to spend the night in this bitter place.

Shortly after they entered the wasteland, the sound of screaming ahead made Ashana and his men dig their spurs into their tired horses and Ashana, the most daring rider, soon drew ahead of the others. Beside a huge blackened boulder, he saw a horse standing, foam-flecked and half-dead from exhaustion and nearby Yani, crouched on the ground, screaming and throwing handfuls of earth at the sky. Her face and hair were covered in black dirt.

At first the woman didn't notice Ashana but when he touched her, she turned on him, threw him to the ground, fled straight at one of the murky pools of stagnant water that lay all around and jumped into it. Without thinking Ashana leapt in after her. He could see nothing through the roiling greenish water, but he could feel her against his feet, so retching at the water's stench, he reached down and pulled her to the surface. She kicked and struggled and for a moment he thought he was going to have to punch her out, which was something he'd never had to do to a woman before. Then suddenly there was magic and she went limp in his arms. The group's mage, Mikhalus, helped him drag her out.

Night was coming. The Pimenov men took Yani back to the edge of wasteland and made camp in a small rocky gully. They dared not make a fire for fear of attracting the bloodbeasts, so they wrapped Yani in blankets and Ashana wrapped his arms around her till she felt warm again. The places where her arm had been broken were swollen, but Mikhalus decided against using healing magic on her for magic would also draw the bloodbeasts.

During the night, Yani awoke and wept inconsolably

and Ashana did his clumsy best to comfort her by rocking her and making soothing noises.

"Is it your sister? Has she been tapped?" he asked, suspecting the cause of her grief.

"Damn you!" she screamed suddenly. "If you stupid Mirayans hadn't kept me sleeping, I would have been in time. Damn you! Damn you to hell!"

She struck at him and when he rolled out of her way, she threw rocks and earth at him.

"I was so close," she cried, falling on her knees and then onto her face. She lay there weeping. The blankets had fallen away from her heaving shoulders and Ashana could see her dark tattoos clearly in the moonlight. He waited till she was quiet and then covered her against the cold again.

All night bloodbeasts howled in the wasteland and while nothing came up the gully, several times dark red-eyed shapes could be seen stalking nearby. The horses were restive, but Mikhalus was too experienced to fall into the trap of using magic to still them. Like most death-spawned creatures, bloodbeasts had poor eyesight and hearing, but magic drew them like a beacon.

At day break Yani was as limp and silent as a rag doll. Ashana's party moved camp again, riding to a hill overlooking the main road through the region. They set up under the shelter of some trees, where they could keep watch on the road without being easily seen. Here they were far enough from the wasteland to have more to fear from bandits than bloodbeasts. Mikhalus felt safe enough to set wardings around the camp and they were able to light a fire so that they could have dry clothes and hot food. Yani sat silent, wrapped in a blanket and staring into the flames.

In the late afternoon Ashana and Mikhalus was sitting on the other side of the fire, watching the road when Yani said suddenly, "So now Malov has bound himself to my sister, how can I stop him using her power?"

"The only way is to kill Malov," said Ashana, looking at her squarely. Like most Southern Mirayans, he was a man had faced many cruel practicalities in his life.

"But if he dies so does she, is that so?"

Ashana nodded.

"So she must die now no matter what. This tapping must be stopped. Is there no other way? No spell to free her? No magic knife that would kill him and not her?"

"The only way she could get free is if he set her free," said Mikhalus the mage. "The spell can be broken quite easily by the one who made it."

"He will never set her free. Why would he?"

"I can think of no reason," said Ashana. "Lady, do not torment yourself by thinking about it. There are still things you can do to prevent Malov becoming too powerful. We could join forces."

Yani shot him a cynical look and, to his own surprise, Ashana felt vaguely ashamed for being so opportunistic. It was far too early to be urging someone so deep in grief to serve their cause.

"My sister is Tari like me. We are stronger than other people."

"Yes truly. You're healing amazingly fast," said Mikhalus, who had also shot Ashana a cynical look.

"So perhaps... Do you think if he was killed, she, a Tari, might survive?"

Mikhalus shook his head. "I have no knowledge of the Tari," he said softly. "But if you're determined to kill Malov, I think you should try to accept the likelihood that your sister will also die."

***

In Golgarov Ezratah did not bother checking his cage for weaknesses the night of Marigoth's tapping. He just lay on his mattress trying not to think, until at last he drifted off into dreams that were too real and too full of screams and the cracking of bone.

He woke to the sound of Marigoth weeping.

"His filthy magic is all over me. I'm covered in death and the life spirit has abandoned me."

"No!" cried Ezratah, though this was very much what he felt. "That cannot happen. Let us say the morning chant together. It will bring us comfort."

He began the chant and soon her voice joined his until at last she seemed to fade into sleep.

When he next awoke from horrible dreams, he sat up immediately to check on Marigoth and saw a soft light surrounding her. At first he thought it was the grey light of dawn, but then he saw that the glowing shape of a raven was sitting on her chest.

He jumped up.

"Yani! Yani! Is that you?"

The raven looked at him and suddenly it was gone, but Marigoth still glowed with a golden light. Then he knew it was not a dream but some kind of vision. Despite himself he felt the faintest flicker of hope.

The golden light round Marigoth was long gone by the time morning came. She lay curled up like a baby, blanket wrapped tightly around her and her face pressed against her knees. Malov, wearing elegant new robes, breezed cheerily into the room as if going on a picnic,

"There, there, my little Queen maggot. Why so unhappy? We can't have that."

He put his hand through the bars to touch her and lightning fast, she turned and bit him hard on the wrist. As he squawked and pulled away, she sprang up, clawing and kicking at him through the bars, her bedraggled hair streaming down over her blood-stained body.

"What a little beast you are!" Malov's voice was admiring.

"Better than being an abomination," snarled Marigoth. "I stink of blood. I want some water."

"Surely," grinned Malov maliciously. "I'll piss in this bowl then. That's the only water I'm going to make for you."

"Oh funny!" said Marigoth. "You'd better not make my life too hard or I'll find some way of ending it. Then you'll have gone to all this effort for nothing."

"Full of spunk today, aren't we?"

"I've got nothing to fear now. The worst has happened."

"Just remember, if you're not good, our little friend here will pay in blood and pain."

"Don't be too sure of yourself, Malov," said Ezratah. "When I'm dead it'll be too late to threaten her."

"Such fighting words!" sneered Malov. He flicked a finger and power hit Ezratah with a smash of yellow light, knocking him to the floor and making his head ring.

"My, my, I am enjoying using your power, my little Queen Maggot."

Marigoth looked coolly at Ezratah's slumped body, obviously refusing to give Malov the satisfaction of showing fear.

"You'd better not let him die," she said. "Because I care nothing for my own life. Just get me some water. I need to wash."

She turned her back on him.

He laughed. "Women! You're all shrews at heart."

He picked up a water jug and shoved it through the bars of her cage. "Here, Queen Maggot, here's your water. Hurry up. I want to go out and play."

He turned and went out of the alcove, whistling happily.

"You all right?" asked Marigoth, as she washed herself under the blanket.

"Yes. Are you?" said Ezratah.

"I'm fine," said Marigoth. "My path has become clear."

"What?" asked Ezratah but before she answered Malov came back into the room carrying a red silk dress which he tossed at Marigoth.

"Isn't this your sister's favourite dress?" protested Marigoth.

"Time the stupid bitch did something useful," said Malov. "Come now. We have work to do."

As Ezratah lay on his mattress and stared at the ceiling, Daria came in and wandered round the empty and blackened hall looking like a hungry ghost. Finally she came to the cage and glowering at Ezratah, pulled him to her and put her hand on his head.

"It's no good trying me," cried Ezratah, as her mind spiked roughly into his. Marigoth had been right, the minute he felt her inside his head he could hear small children screaming in the distance. Daria pushed him away with a disgusted sound, leaving him dizzy, his vision shot through with bright lights. Amazingly he must have fallen asleep then, because he awoke later to the sound of distant explosions and the shaking of the fortress as Malov tested his new power.

As night fell Malov came back flanked by his two scholars and dragging a pale-looking Marigoth on a chain behind him.

"What have you been doing to her?" shouted Ezratah.

Malov simply smiled. "She's filled with envy to see me use her power when she cannot. I am King of the Earth now."

"I care nothing for your pathetic dreams of glory," sneered Marigoth. "Nor does the earth. Earth is far mightier than you can ever be."

"Manners! Manners!" laughed Malov. "Take care lest I make your little pet suffer."

Marigoth scowled at him, but when he had gone, she put her face in her hands and wept.

"Did he hurt you?"

"No," wept Marigoth and, between sobs she told him of how Malov, cheered on by his admiring scholars, had blown open the crust of the earth and caused its blood to seep out.

"I could feel its agony. And the horrible pig was delighted with how much destruction he could cause."

She fell quickly into and exhausted sleep, but not for long. A few moments later Daria came hurrying into the room.

"Leave her alone!" shouted Ezratah as Daria dragged Marigoth to the bars and gripped her skull.

"Go away and let me sleep, you stupid woman," mumbled Marigoth, batting at Daria.

"Let me see it," cried Daria. "I need to see it."

Marigoth shuddered as Daria's mind thrust into hers, but her eyes kept drooping closed and Daria had to keep shaking her to keep her awake.

"Why do you have to be so rough?" cried Marigoth when Daria had finished.

Daria skipped away from the cage bars, laughing uneasily.

"Do you feel pain?" she asked.

"Yes, because you are so careless," snapped Marigoth.

"Good. I like your pain!" snapped Daria as she ran off. But she was back again in the middle of the night, whimpering like a hungry child.

"Show me the place! I need it." Marigoth was too exhausted to even protest as Daria put her hands on her skull.

The days passed much as had the first, except that Malov took to wearing purple robes, a colour usually reserved for the Emperor. Every day he took Marigoth away and all day the fortress echoed to the sound of distant explosions. After nightfall Daria would come and mindsearch Marigoth, once at the beginning of the night and once and sometimes twice again later.

Ezratah sat forgotten in his cage. His wounds had healed and he should have been grateful to be left alone, but inwardly he was succumbing to despair. Listlessly he kept checking his cage for weaknesses that he knew were not there, but mostly he burrowed into welcoming sleep. He tried to be awake for Marigoth during the night but most of the time she was in her cage, she lay in an exhausted slumber. He was lonely when she was like this, but it was worse when she was not. One day she came back staring with horror, and told him of how Malov, his men and the scholars had met a troop of soldiers patrolling the edge of the wasteland.

"The soldiers shot arrows and bolts of power at us, but Malov turned everything into fireballs and sent them back. Many burned. There was death and screaming everywhere.

Then Malov's men danced about and hailed him as Emperor. This will happen again and again until he is ruler of Miraya."

Then after a long time she said. "Speak the morning chant for me. I can't remember the words."

The fierce Marigoth who had reappeared briefly that first morning after she had been tapped was gone, eaten up by the needs of the Syminas. As the days passed she no longer answered Malov back, but came obediently when he called. Yet although Ezratah was certain she loathed Malov, she touched him often - put her hand on his arm or back or leaned against him in a way that would have seemed affectionate, had she not worn a look of mute suffering on her face. Was she attracted to him in some way?

When he asked Marigoth about it, she smiled for the first time in days.

"Jealous 'Tah? Don't be. I do what must be done, that is all."

"What must be done?" he asked. "Is there nothing I can do to help?"

Tiredly she shook her head.

When Malov noticed the touching, he would slap Marigoth away, but he did not always notice it. He was too busy talking joyfully with his henchmen as they made measurements, calculations and diagrams, discussing what move they should make next. Should they cause an earthquake and volcano under Vulgate, one of the Southern League towns or should they blow up the town of Masum, a major centre of death magic? Typically of a death mage, Malov regarded other death mages as his greatest enemies.

However Malov also noticed how pale and wan Marigoth was becoming.

"She's fading away," Ezratah heard him mutter, as he stood by her cage one evening, watching her sleep. "She no longer fights me. So dull."

"The pair of you are wearing her out," snapped Ezratah. "Let me look after her."

"Not a chance. I'm..." suddenly Malov turned on

Ezratah. "The pair of us?" he asked.

In his heart, Ezratah was glad he'd let the secret out for there was no advantage to be gained from Daria now. If Malov had questioned Ezratah further, he would have told him everything, but Malov just stared at him before leaving the room. But later as Daria was crouching like a vulture over Marigoth, a voice rang out of the darkness.

"What are you doing, sister?"

Daria jumped back, leaving Marigoth clutching her head.

"Heal her!" said Malov coldly. Daria rubbed Marigoth's head with healing magic, her face torn between fear and longing.

"Now come here and tell me why you are mindsearching my source!"

Daria knelt before him. "I'm just curious, brother."

"Lying bitch," said Malov without heat. "You get some pleasure out of doing this, don't you?"

"It was when I had the other one," whined Daria. "She taunted me into mindsearching her and what I saw there - horrified me and yet... it's wonderful, brother. The most beautiful place. Such peace. You should try it."

"What? So that I can become weak and useless like you," snapped Malov, as he grabbed Daria by the throat and shook her. "You stupid little cow. Look how you've changed. You let me down on my great day and you've been useless ever since. Do you think I haven't noticed? Weakling! This is just as it was with the elixir. And the dream smoke. You have no self-control and I'm always forced to have it for you. So I will. You will not look into her head any more, Daria."

"I'll do as I want! You can't stop me!" shouted Daria.

"Yes I can and you know it! Learn to be strong."

"No!" shrieked Daria. She threw herself at Malov beating him around the chest. "I have to... I must!"

With a flick of his hand, Malov threw her to the ground.

"For too long I've put up with your wilfulness because you were more powerful than me! But I won't do it any longer. I am your brother and your master and now I have the power to enforce my will, I going to do so. Do you understand?"

Daria's face was white. "Yes brother."

"Good!" said Malov more calmly "You will forget about this place you saw inside Marigoth's head. That is no place for you. Today and every day you will commune with the demons until all this madness is washed from your mind. Now go to your room and do not come out until I call for you."

"No!" screamed Daria suddenly. She threw her arms round his legs. Tears ran down her face. "No! I must. I have to see it."

"You'll do as you are told!" shouted Malov. He waved his hand and still grasping at the air, she was propelled by magic from hall.

"Why did you let her go so long?" He snarled at Marigoth's half-conscious form. "You were trying to turn Daria against me, weren't you?"

"Of course we were! Why shouldn't we?" shouted Ezratah.

"Shut up, scum!" snarled Malov, punching him in the face, before stalking from the room.

"Are you all right, 'Tah?" asked a voice close by.

Marigoth was sitting in her cage watching him. She looked much better than she had for some time.

"I'm glad you told on Daria," she said. "Malov has become almost caring. He never liked using healing magic before, but now he gives it to me every day. I think it is beginning."

"What's beginning?" cried Ezratah, frustrated at these mysterious words. "You're just saying these things to keep my hopes up, aren't you?"

Marigoth shook her head. "Be patient. In time you'll see."

Chapter 17

An endless line of blue-grey birds filled the red sky above Jindabyne forever bringing rot to the land. The thick air stank and left the taste of bile on her tongue and she was too heavy hearted to move.

Something jerked her arm.

"Wake up, you lazy bitch," said a voice, and a slap stung her face. "Come on!"

The voice seemed to come from a place where there were no three-winged grey birds, so Jindabyne made herself go there and a handsome face with a sneering expression swum into focus above her.

"Good," said Lev Madraga softly, in a voice like vinegar. "Now bitch, tell me where Olga is."

"Olga!" cried Jindabyne. Terror made her sit up so fast, she would have butted Lev in the face had he not pulled back.

"Olga, where are you? Olga!" She tried to reach out with her magic but something stopped her. Iron at her neck and wrists - witch manacles!

"Thus the cow wails for her calf," sneered Lev.

"Olga!" cried Jindabyne seizing him. "What have you done with her?"

Lev pushed her aside with a look of disgust and Jindabyne saw a man - it was Guilius Appius - standing behind him.

"I've done nothing with her," snarled Lev. "You arrived here without her. *You* tell *me* what *you* have done with her."

"I don't know," wailed Jindabyne. "I can't remember."

"Women!" snorted Lev. "Animals have more sense. What sort of mother cannot remember her own child?"

Jindabyne put her hands over her face, finding strength in defying him and with that strength came memory; the dark shapes speeding through sky towards her, the thump as they landed, that thing looking down at her, Alyx drawing her sword. That thing had grabbed her. The crawling suffocating horror of its touch still made her shudder. She hadn't been able to breathe...

She had pushed Olga away telling her to run, but Olga wouldn't run. Then a woman had caught Olga by the arm.

"The Tari have her," she said softly. "They came when we were in danger and took her... Why?"

"Why indeed?" snarled Lev Madraga. "Damned meddlesome Tari. Why can't they stay in their own damned land?"

"She's out of your reach, Lev Madraga," said Jindabyne triumphantly. Lev's fair face turned pale and his jaw set and she saw that she had crossed some kind of line. With icy control, the mage turned to Guilius Appius.

"The minions were telling the truth."

"Astonishing," said Appius. "I thought there was no truth in those things."

"Get back to the Mori," said Lev. "Slaughter all you can. I'll think on your plan. A speedy solution may prove necessary."

"Setting the forest alight will kill them faster than we can," said Appius. He shot a worried frown at Jindabyne.

"What are you waiting for?" snapped Lev. "Leave her

to me."

With a shrug, Appius strode to the door and went out. The door slammed shut behind him and as Lev waved his fingers the bolts drew themselves. The mage turned on Jindabyne, a terrible fire burning in his eyes.

"The Tari!" he muttered bitterly. "Always the Tari. Tell me why the Tari took Olga? What's their interest in this matter?"

"I don't know," whispered Jindabyne, drawing away from him. "I've never had anything to do with them. She just appeared. I..."

"You bloody Tari! Why must you always interfere?" he screamed, seizing her.

Slapping her across the face, again and again, he shouted, "You Tari bitch. You came between me and my brother. You made him weak and foolish and you turned him against me! Arrogant bloody Tari!"

His hands seized her round the neck, crushing her throat till she couldn't breathe. She clawed at his hands but he was too strong.

"I'll kill you Tari if it's the last thing I do," he snarled, through clenched teeth. Everything went red, then black.

When she awoke again, every part of her aching, she was surprised she had awoken at all. Had he not said he would kill her? Her face was so bruised, it was difficult to open her eyes so she gave up the struggle and just lay there. Throbbing blisters on her skin reminded her of where the death angel had touched her and tormenting thoughts kept her conscious. Lev Madraga. Olga. The death angel. Serge. Olga. The Tari woman. Wolf, oh, Wolf.

At least Olga was safe! She tried to feel certain the Tari wouldn't harm her. Ezratah had told her they were a gentle folk and Jindabyne knew they could not kill, yet once upon a time they had mindblasted Jindabyne for breaking their laws. But Olga was innocent of any wrong doing, and surely the Tari would not punish her for her mother's crimes. At least, in the Tari's land of Ermora, she was safe from the death angels and from Lev Madraga.

The air in the small room was chill and the walls were made of dark stone but the straw Jindabyne was lying on smelt sweet and fresh, much fresher than the sweaty smelling blankets that covered her. After a time she heard footsteps outside. Bolts were drawn and a strange man in blue mage's robes came in. Through blurry eyes, she saw him looking down at her. He sucked in his breath thoughtfully, squatted down beside her and put his hand over her face. A moment later she felt healing magic flowing into her. Mirayan magic was never pleasant to feel, but it sparked off the life spirit within her and the swelling in her face subsided so that she could open both eyes properly. She was able to croak some questions out through her broken lips, but the man ignored her and when he had finished healing her, got up and went out of the cell without speaking. In the corridor outside she heard a low questioning voice and the mage spoke at last.

"She'll live," he said breezily. "Just keep her fed and watered."

How strange. Lev was keeping her alive. For what?

For two days she lay on the straw too debilitated by her injuries to do more than crawl to the slops bucket and the door. No one came into the cell, but twice a day a small door was opened in the bottom of her door and bread and water were pushed in. A narrow grill above head height let in daylight and she could see the moonlight at night. She had no idea where she was and didn't consider it much.

On the third day the door was opened and Lev came in, accompanied by a guard who put a stool on the floor and then went out again locking the door behind him.

Warily Jindabyne pushed herself upright trying to make a less tempting target.

"So! Still alive then," said Lev conversationally. "You don't deserve to be after gloating at me like that. I should have killed you, you cheeky bitch. Now tell me where my dear nephew Serge is?"

"I don't know where Serge is. He was with us when your death angels attacked."

Lev looked pleased at this.

"Yes, they said they killed everyone with you," said Lev. "So what were you doing at the pool with a pack of Mori?"

"Nothing special."

Lev threw back his head and laughed. "You fool. I don't really care what you were doing. Or rather I've already guessed. Did they ask you to heal their river for them? I believe they are mighty short of Tari help these days."

Jindabyne was startled at the level of his knowledge.

"I have taken the Guardians captive," said Lev airily. "So you were helping the Mori Queen. I must say I laughed when I learned that one."

"What if I was?" said Jindabyne. "I hate death magic as much as she does. Have you been dabbling, Lev? How could you?"

"Now, now, I'm asking the questions here," grinned Lev. "I suppose you know nothing about the Forest Queen and Wolf."

Jindabyne felt her heart cringing, suddenly afraid of what Lev had to say. She tried to hide it.

"Have you seen her face?" continued Lev. "I see that you have. Then you'll know how much Wolf loved her when they were married."

Jindabyne gasped.

"I bet she had a good laugh up her sleeve when she realised that Wolf hadn't cared enough to tell you," continued Lev. "He adored her. It was because of her that Wolf made peace with the Mori. So totally at odds with his own interests. A peace he lost good vassals over. It was nothing to her. The bitch enslaves men for the sheer pleasure of it, because she enjoys the power. After she left he was shattered." Lev's face took on a pinched look. "After making love to that... Everything else would be tasteless. But I wasn't surprised when he married you. You were the closest thing to her. Probably in the dark, he could pretend..."

"Shut up!" cried Jindabyne, even though she knew she should stay silent.

"Oh sister in law!" purred Lev with mock sympathy. "How wrong of my brother not to tell you the truth! After the Mori Queen, it wasn't possible for him to care about any other woman. His marriage to you was only to cement his power in Lamartaine. You poor fool!"

"Be quiet!" shouted Jindabyne. She pressed her hands against her ears, but she could still see Lev laughing as he picked up the stool and left the cell.

When he was gone, Jindabyne wept. She was certain that Lev hadn't really been interested in questioning her, but had simply come to tell her about Wolf and Elena Mori, to hurt her. So he have been must be lying. But in her heart she knew there was truth in his words. She had seen the Forest Queen's face.

A couple of days later, Lev came back and this time he bought a marriage agreement with him. He made her look at it, pointing out the contracts main features and laughing as he did so. There was Wolf's seal and his signature and there was another signature, one that read, Elena Mori. The script was delicate and flowing, as beautiful as the woman herself.

"He loved her so much," gloated Lev. Jindabyne tried to hide her pain, but it was all she could do to hold back the tears until after he left.

Had Jindabyne's marriage to Wolf really been a fraud? Had she just been a substitute for Elena or a political expedience? Their love had seemed so real to her at the time, but people could deceive themselves. The first time she had kissed him, Wolf had flushed and left her room immediately and she'd been worried that she had offended him and, at the same time, certain he was just being honourable. Only much later did he respond to her affection.

She was fool! Wolf had never told her he loved her. In fact he'd told her that he couldn't give her a whole heart, that he'd been wounded by another woman. She'd loved him so much, she hadn't cared. She'd kissed him again, overwhelmed his reluctance and offered to be his mistress, causing him to run away again.

"I've talked to him," Hierarch Taddeus told her later. She'd always assumed it had been something kind about trying to love again, but maybe he'd simply pointed out to Wolf the political advantages of marrying a Tari.

And if Wolf had been enthusiastic in bed, what did that mean? Everyone knew lovemaking was just a sport to men. They didn't have to care particularly for their partner. Those nights in his arms which had meant so much to her, had they meant anything to him?

How could she hope to compete with Elena Mori and her gift of fatal beauty?

She tried to comfort herself by thinking of Olga but that just made her worry about what might be happening to her daughter and even thinking of Wolf was easier than that.

The moon waxed and waned and waxed again, before late one morning Lev Madraga came slamming into her cell, his face like thunder. She shrank back, dreading some violence, but he did no more than seize her wrist.

"Come with me. This is your chance for revenge."

Throwing a veil over her head, he dragged her out of the cell, along the hallway and up out into the stable yard beyond, where a troop of mounted soldiers waited. As he hustled Jindabyne up onto a horse, she found herself looking round at the walls of Lamartaine in astonishment. She had been here in her beloved home all this time and she hadn't even realised it.

Lev flung onto another horse and the group set off out through the fortress gate at a quick trot and hurried along the very road Jindabyne had travelled when she'd fled with Serge - how long? - It must be two months ago now. Back in the days when she still had Olga and still believed Wolf had loved her.

After travelling all day, they spent the night in a small fortress where Jindabyne was locked in a tiny stifling cell and by the early afternoon of the next day, they had reached a part of the Mori forest, where sparse tree trunks blackened by fire, stood like bony fingers against the sky.

Jindabyne could hear detonations of magical fire for

some distance before she saw the tents and palisade of the army camp, but the crowd of men standing outside the walls were Mirayans not Mori and they were not attacking but milling about looking confused. Only Lev, sitting beside Jindabyne swearing under his breath, seemed to know what was happening. Soon he was surrounded by junior officers, all talking breathlessly.

"She came two days ago."

"Lord Lev, what's happening?"

"They've been fighting ever since."

"The mages went in last night."

"Now they're fighting too."

"We don't dare go in."

"My lord, what's happened?"

"Did you see the Mori Queen's face?" was the only question Lev asked.

"My lord she was veiled."

"Surely she can't have done this. She was alone, but for a couple of warriors. And they left as soon as she reached the commanders tent."

"She came under the green flag of truce."

"Shut up," snapped Lev, silencing them all. "That clever bitch!" he muttered softly, so that only Jindabyne heard him.

"Where's Lord Guilius?" he asked more loudly, and was told that he was in the camp with the Mori Queen.

"Stay out here. To look upon the face of the Mori Queen is disaster." He looked down at the questioning faces. "To do so will send you mad. Or turn you to stone."

From the looks being exchanged among the men, he had not done a very good job of suppressing their curiosity. Jindabyne felt an astonishing bubble of secret laughter rising in her throat as she remembered the face of Elena, the Mori Queen and the effect it was certain to have on people.

"Off!" snapped Lev. Jumping down from his horse, he pulled Jindabyne roughly off hers and, twisting her arm behind her back, shoved her in front of him.

"Come on!" he hissed in her ear. "I want you to see

this. I want you to know just how much that bitch deceived you, you poor stupid woman."

Inside the camp, a wooden building was burning and several of the tents had collapsed. The main street of the camp was strewn with recumbent bodies, most of them clearly dead. From the gate of the palisade, they could see living men too, hiding behind tents or barrels, occasionally throwing blasts of magic at each other, but the battle had clearly reached an impasse.

Dragging Jindabyne along behind him, Lev strode over to where a mage was hiding behind a pile of toppled barrels. The mage, who peering into the centre of the camp, not out toward the gate, was taken by surprise when Lev dragged him to his feet and shook him.

"Where's the Mori Queen?" Lev demanded of the man.

"You shall not have her," snarled the mage, preparing to smite him.

Lev squeezed his fingers into a fist and the mage's neck jerked round at an impossible angle and his face went blank. Jindabyne gasped and put her hands over her mouth, not sure which moved her more, Lev's callousness or this demonstration of what a powerful mage he was.

"Ah crap!" he muttered, dropping the limp body and stepping over it without a second glance.

"The commander's tent I guess," he said and, seizing Jindabyne's wrist, he towed her along a roundabout route through the camp being careful to keep under cover. They came upon four more mages, hiding from each other between the tents. The first three saw Lev coming and attacked him, but Lev killed everyone they met as quickly and calmly as if he were squashing ants, even the fourth mage, a very young man who was hiding in a basket and weeping.

"Why must you do that?" cried Jindabyne distressfully. She was lying on the ground, having tried to stop him and been knocked roughly aside.

"They're ruined now," snarled Lev, dragging her to her feet. "They can never be trusted again. She has that effect on men."

At last they reached the command tent. Three mages were still exchanging blasts of magical fire on the further side of it.

"I think I'll have to dispose of you for the moment, lady. Why don't you go and say hello to your rival?" said Lev, as he shoved her face first into the canvas wall of the tent.

Jindabyne opened her mouth to protest, but felt a sudden frisson of magic as the cloth gave way before her and she tumbled forward losing her balance and sprawling on the floor.

She sat up. Behind her the tent wall was whole again and the summer sun shone though the white canvas, showing a dappling of brown stains and making the air inside hot. As her eyes got used to dimmer light, she recognised Elena Mori sitting back in a huge chair with her feet resting comfortably on a foot stool. Jindabyne could only gaze open-mouthed at her as Elena's beauty struck her anew.

"What are *you* doing here?" cried Elena, leaping up and coming angrily at Jindabyne. "Betrayer! You were with him all along, weren't you?"

She dragged Jindabyne from the ground and shook her.

"Where's Alyx? Is she safe?"

Churning jealousy flooded Jindabyne's heart.

"I don't know," she shouted pushing Elena away. "And I don't care after what you have done to me. You are the betrayer!" She hit out at Elena, who ducked her blow with humiliating ease. A quick struggle and Jindabyne found herself face down on the floor again, with Elena kneeling on her back.

"How did you get here?" shouted Elena, twisting Jindabyne's arm. "Tell me!"

"I was taken by a death angel. I don't know what happened to the others."

Elena let her go.

"Using violence and yet you call yourself a Tari," sneered Jindabyne. The walls shook as magical power detonated outside followed by a strangled scream echoed.

Elena regarded Jindabyne coolly.

"You're the one who tried to hit me first."

"Who tried to hit who?" snapped Lev from the doorway. He held a sword in his hand.

"Lev Madraga," said Elena, and she turned to face.

Lev's jaw dropped and for a moment he just stood there open mouthed, the sword dropping from his limp fingers. Elena smiled and moved towards him, her hands outstretched, her face alight.

"My master," she said. "You have come at last." She dropped to her knees before him, a picture of submissive womanliness except that her face was upturned.

Lev stared and stared his mouth moving as if he was searching for words. The he closed his eyes and drew himself up with an effort.

"We meet again," he said softly.

Elena smiled up at him. "I have offered myself and my throne, the rulership of the Mori people and their lands, to the strongest man in this camp. I always hoped it would be you, Lev Madraga." She leaned forward to press her lips against his hand.

"No!" cried Lev and jumped away from her. "Get down on the floor, you," he shouted, panic in his voice.

"Whatever you wish, my master," purred Elena. Smiling seductively, she draped herself across the canvas floor.

Despite the jealousy roiling about inside her, Jindabyne felt a certain satisfaction. The great Lev Madraga was trembling, unable to deal with Elena Mori's fatal beauty. Flinging open a large chest that lay beside the camp bed, he searched feverishly among the contents and came back towards Elena gripping a set of witch manacles and a piece of cloth in his hands.

As Lev knelt to put the manacles on her, Elena raised herself from the floor like a stretching cat and smiling meltingly, offered her neck to the manacle as if her greatest pleasure would be to wear it for him.

"I'm so glad it's you," she cooed softly.

Lev flushed and looked away which gave a shy worshipful quality to the way he closed the manacles on her neck and wrists and the way he secured the veil over her face. Who is the true captive here, thought Jindabyne.

When they had returned to Lamartaine and Jindabyne was back in her cell, she could not help re-living that scene again and again, except that it was Wolf, not Lev, who covered Elena Mori so tenderly.

At least Lev no longer came down to her cell to stir the fires of her jealousy, but considering how bitter Jindabyne's own thoughts were, it was a small mercy.

Ten days later Jindabyne became aware of extra activity in the yard outside her cell and heard people shouting in the distance, as if a fair was going on outside the fortress walls. A couple of nights later, a huge crash awoke her. The flickering light of fires lit up her cell and she crouched in the straw listening to more crashes and shouts and screams. Puzzling over it made a welcome change from thinking about Elena and Wolf. Were they under attack? She dared to hope that Serge was still alive and had got an army together and that hope kept her awake the rest of the night.

"Please! What's happening?" she begged the warder who brought her food just after the sunlight crept through her window.

"Shut up," said the man shortly, as he shoved the bread and water through the opening. He would not have replied so brusquely to Elena Mori, thought Jindabyne bitterly. Then she noticed that one of the man's hands was newly bandaged.

Later in the morning the door flew open and, without ceremony, guards seized Jindabyne's arms and frog-marched her up through corridors and stairways until she found herself in a part of the fortress she recognised and then at the door to the women's quarters. The guards shoved her inside and slammed the door behind her.

She was in the small ante-room of the women's quarters, where people waited before a maid showed them into the main room beyond. The door between the rooms was open and she could hear people moving about in the next room and taste magic in the air. As she hovered there uncertain of what to do, Bebeth, her old housekeeper, appeared and beckoned her through the door.

Before Jindabyne could cry out her delight at seeing her old housekeeper, Bebeth put a finger to her lips.

"Hush! We mustn't be too friendly."

"Are you well?" whispered Jindabyne.

"Well enough."

Bebeth looked thin and had a healing cut on her face, but at least she was alive and Jindabyne could not resist squeezing her arm as she lead her into the inner room.

A large metal structure dominated the room. Jindabyne tensed as she recognised it as the cage that Mirayans sometimes used to hang prisoners from the fortress walls. Lev Madraga was crawling round the cage floor doing something magical. Carefully Jindabyne crept closer and saw that he was affixing strips of metal to the floor of the cage, using a heat spell to melt the strips onto the bars.

A hand touched her arm. A heavily veiled woman in a witch manacle was standing at her elbow.

"We are leaving this place today," she said.

Such was the rush of hatred that Jindabyne felt at the sound of Elena's voice, that she tried to think of a cruel answer to this innocent remark, even though she knew it would make her look a fool and bring Lev's anger down on her. Fortunately the moment Elena spoke, Lev looked up, his face sweaty and smudged with soot and his eyes fierce.

"Get over there. And don't talk." he said, nodding curtly at the wall. Both women quickly obeyed. Jindabyne looked longingly around the room. She had sat here often of an evening with Wolf. She squeezed her eye-lids shut on tears and turned her head away. Someone touched her arm. Angrily she shrugged off the hand, but it came back again.

"Leave me!" she cried, thinking it was Elena trying to offer her sympathy, only to find that it was Bebeth's hand on her arm.

"Sister-in-law. Watch yourself. I will not have such

behaviour." said Lev sternly, without even looking up. "Elena cannot help it if men love her more than you."

Bebeth sucked in her breath and scowled in Lev's direction, but seeing the mage was busy with his work on the cage, she pressed something into Jindabyne's hand.

"Right," said Lev, standing up. "You two, get in here! Get out, old woman!"

Quickly Jindabyne shoved Bebeth's gift into her bodice. Elena picked up a large bundle of clothes and pushed it into Jindabyne's arms.

"Put it in there!" she ordered.

Before Jindabyne could tell her what to do with her clothes, Lev said, "Do as you are told! She is mistress here now."

So Jindabyne climbed obediently into the cage and put the clothes down in one corner and Elena scooped up a pile of cushions in her own arms and followed. Once inside the cage she sat down on the cushion and slapped Jindabyne's leg until Jindabyne sat down beside her.

"Make yourself comfortable," Elena told her.

A huge lattice covered by shutters ran along one side of this main room, so that in good weather the women on the family could enjoy the sun and the fresh air without having to expose themselves to the eyes of the common people. The shutters that covered the lattice had been closed, but now Lev flung them all open. Jindabyne could see the sea in the distance, but the cage was too far from the window for her to see what was down in the fields directly below the fortress walls. With a hammer and a chisel, Lev broke the lattice free of its fastenings to the wall. Obviously, since he was using manual tools to do this task, he was saving his magical energies for a major spell.

When the lattice came loose and crashed into the courtyard below, Lev did not even look down to see if he had hit anybody. Instead he came over and chained Jindabyne and Elena's wrists to the bars of the cage. That done he went out and locked the cage behind him. Jindabyne longed to know what was happening but she wasn't going to speak to That Woman.

Lev lifted an ivory coloured whistle to his lips and blew on it. Though she could not hear the note, the moment he blew, a shudder of nausea went through her and Elena gagged.

"What's coming?" she whispered.

Unable to speak even had she wanted to, Jindabyne simply shook her head. She recognised the feeling.

Elena cried out as the blue-grey shape of the death angel came flapping in at the window and as it came toward the cage, she began to scream uncontrollably. Even though she had no magical powers, she was clearly just as affected by this avatar of the Abyss as Jindabyne. Lev peered in between the cage bars with concern, an expression that sat oddly on his harsh face and waved his hand. Instantly Elena fell asleep, sprawled across Jindabyne's lap.

"Don't make me sleep," cried Jindabyne, remembering how the proximity of a death angel had filled her mind with visions the grey three-winged birds devouring her and an overwhelming the sense of despair and nothingness.

"I wouldn't waste my power on you," Lev sneered. "Take care of her! If any harm comes to her, I will kill you."

Then with his mouth set into a thin clenched line, he climbed upon the death angels back. He shouted something in an ugly language and the death angel put its claws around the bars of the cage and dragged it to the open window. Even though its hard grey face had no eyes, it seemed to stare hungrily at Jindabyne and Elena. But it made no attempt to touch them.

Once in the opening, the angel clambered on top of the cage and seizing the bars in its claws, spread its sulphurous blue-grey wings and threw itself and the cage out of the window. For a sickening moment, Jindabyne thought both death angel and cage were going to plummet into the courtyard below. Then with a whomp of wings, the creature soared up into the sky and circled the tower.

When she saw the field below the fortress Jindabyne forgot her nausea. An army with the banners of Guilius

Appius flying above it was encamped outside the walls of the castle and, as they swooped over it, men scrambled to shoot arrows and launch stones at them, even though they were flying far too high in the sky to be hit.

Whoosh! Something bright sped down toward the ground, and a ball of fire briefly blotted out the camp below. Above, she heard Lev laughing triumphantly, before shouting another command in the ugly language. The death angel wheeled round in the sky and turned north towards the Gen Mountains at the centre of the island.

The huge granite peaks of the Gen Mountains dominated the island of Yarmar, just as the Tari who lived in those heights had once dominated its people. They said it took three days hard climb to reach the summit plateau where the Tari lived. Jindabyne couldn't remember the time when she'd lived there, but she'd always felt reassured when she looked to the Gen mountains.

The death angel swerved around side of the mountains and soon Lamartaine was out of sight behind the towering grey cliffs and peaks and they were over the forest that covered the whole western side of the island. Here the slopes of the mountains were weathered and folded, forming ravines, some of which were very long and deep. The angel flew onward with long steady wing beats until the sun was low in the sky. Then it plunged downward towards a wall blocking the entrance to one of the ravines beneath. Behind it was a squat square keep, its stone so clean looking that it must have been newly built.

Lev tenderly unchained Elena and carried her away without another word to Jindabyne. The close proximity of the death angel had left Jindabyne shivering so hard she could not call out to him or even stand up. But it seemed he had not forgotten her for burly guards came up and simply dragged her out of the cage, across the stone roof of the keep and down the several long flights of stairs to another basement dungeon. The cells here had barred doors instead of solid wooden ones so that she could see into each cell as they passed. Tari mages, manacled and huddled against the wall like bedraggled birds deprived of flight, sat in every one of them. Jindabyne counted seven in all. Few of them even moved as she was hauled past. Before she had time to wonder about the implications of all these captive Tari, she was shoved into an empty cell, falling into a pile of straw.

Captivity again.

Exhaustion made her fall asleep almost immediately, but her sleep was troubled by blood red dreams and when she woke, her mind was so muddled between dreams of the abyss and the tickling of the straw under her body, that for a few moments she could not tell which was real and which dream. Her head cleared, only to fill with questions. What was going on? Why had Guilius Appius' army been besieging Lamartaine? Who were all these captured Tari? Why did Lev keep her alive?

She had a horrible suspicion she knew the answer to the last question. She knew death mages fed their captives to demons to pay for mighty powers and that those with magical powers were demon's favourite food.

As she rolled over in the straw, she felt something in her bodice. Wondering what it was she reached in, and drew out a red rosebud and a locket. The locket had disappeared from around her neck after she had returned to Lamartaine. She was so delighted to see it again, that for a moment she forgot that Wolf had never loved her, and pressed it to her lips, her eyes full of happy tears.

Then she remembered and threw the locket and the rosebud at the wall and lay on the straw, feeling bitter. But slowly her mind changed. Wolf had deceived her it was true but despite his betrayal, she longed to see the lock of his hair again and smell his scent. She reach out for the locket and as she did so her hand brushed the rosebud. With sudden recognition she picked the flower up. It came from a bush that Wolf had given her. Roses did not grow naturally in the Archipelago and Wolf had sent all the way to Miraya for it. He had given it to her on their first wedding anniversary.

"For all the happiness you have given to me," he told her. "I never thought to feel such happiness again." He'd given her lots of gifts in a way that had always made her feel treasured. And he had never needed to. She was perfectly happy just to be with him. Had it really all been a lie? Lev said so, but then Lev wanted her to be unhappy. How the vindictive toad had laughed when she'd wept! Why should she believe a word he said?

Several times on the first day she called out to the other Tari and at last a woman's voice answered. But before she could find out more than the name Syndal from her, guards came storming down the corridor. She heard the Tari scream and then guards were in her cell, tying a gag round her mouth and slapping her around the face till she was dizzy. Even though they removed the gag the next day, she did not try to communicate with the others again. There was little privacy. Guards were always pacing up and down the corridor and several times every day a man in scholar's robes with tufts of grey hair sticking out all around his head, would come and stare as if she were some kind of scientific specimen. She remembered him - Lev's friend Neevus, who had been out hunting with Lev the day Wolf had been killed.

"Did you kill Wolf?" she asked him once, but he ignored her questions.

On the third day she was taken from her cell. Is this it? she thought. Am I to be fed to demons now?

She spent the whole climb up through the tower repeating the prayers to the life spirit that Ambassador Ezratah had taught her.

When she was shown into the room, Lev Madraga's eyes were as contemptuous as ever, but there was no sign he was carrying out a magical ritual.

"You are to serve my lady," he said briefly, after the guards had left. "But if she makes any complaint of you, believe that I will have you whipped as I did in Lamartaine and sent back to the cells. Do you understand?"

"Then send me back now," cried Jindabyne. "I won't serve That Woman."

Lev threw back his head and laughed.

"Oh my proud sister-in-law. How humiliating it must

be to be forced to serve your victorious rival. But I've changed my mind. If she complains about you, I'll have you whipped all right, but I'm not going to send you back to the cells. You should learn to bear humiliation with dignity like a proper woman."

Even though she was quivering with hatred and anger, Jindabyne kept her eyes lowered. She would not give Lev the satisfaction of protesting again.

"What do you say?" said Lev.

"Very well," replied Jindabyne through clenched teeth.

"Good!"

He led her to another door. Even though she was cut off from her magery by her iron manacles, she could sense the strong wardings of Mirayan magic upon it. Lev opened the door, pulled her through it and locked the door behind them.

A huge bed stood in the middle of the large room and beyond the bed was a collection of chairs made comfortable by big tasselled silk cushions and a weaving loom. The walls were hung with swathes of fine white linen so that though the windows were small, the room seemed bright and airy. A remarkably luxurious room for this little keep.

"She's here," said Lev curtly.

A graceful figure rose from one of the window embrasures and came towards them.

"I thank you, my kind lord," said Elena Mori, sketching a brief curtsey to him. She still wore witch manacles at her neck and on her wrists but she was unveiled.

"I must go," Lev said brusquely and went quickly out through the door, slamming and bolting it behind him.

The two women stood waiting. When they heard the door of the outer chamber shut, Elena relaxed and smiled wryly. "He's half afraid he won't be able to leave me."

"There is no need to gloat about it," snapped Jindabyne.

Elena was startled.

"I know you're irresistible to men."

"Ah, so he has told you about me and Wolf," said Elena. She sat down and looked at her thoughtfully. "I should have guessed. I've been asking for a companion and of course he has provided me with the one companion who can never be my friend. "

"Then it's true what he said?" snarled Jindabyne.

"What did he say?"

"That Wolf loved you beyond all reason."

"I don't know about that," said Elena. "I have this gift of fatal beauty, you see. People who are affected by it have to love me."

"I won't listen to this," cried Jindabyne, covering her ears.

Elena shoulders heaved with a sigh. She went over to a pile of cloth that lay by the window, picked it up and pushed it at Jindabyne till she took it.

"Good!" said Elena. "The best way to get Lev to separate us is to pretend we're getting along." She sat down at the loom and began to weave.

Sewing and weaving was what the Mirayan women locked up in the women's quarters always did. Jindabyne picked up the pile of cloth and found they were linen sheets. She had never been much good at the feminine skills, but hemming sheets was well within her capabilities.

They sat and worked in silence for a time. Then it occurred to Jindabyne what sheets were used for.

"Are these your bed sheets?" she snapped, suddenly tossing them down. "Do you mean to humiliate me?"

"I don't want to humiliate you," said Elena. "I want us to be allies. Lev Madraga is a far greater enemy to you than I could ever be. An enemy to you and your family and even our whole race. I understand that you must hate me. But we need to help each other none the less. The life spirit needs it."

Jindabyne turned away. Angry tears filled her eyes.

"I am truly sorry for what happened in the past," continued Elena. "What I said before... People don't really love me. My gift makes them do it. It's magic. It's not real. Wolf's feelings for me weren't real."

"Don't speak of it," shouted Jindabyne.

"As you wish," said Elena. She went back to her weaving and after a time Jindabyne went back to sewing the sheets. The feeling grew in her that there was logic in what Elena said but she could not bear the humiliation of admitting it.

They sat together thus all day.

As the day ended Lev came back, hustled Jindabyne out of the room and handed her over to a guard and Neevus with the tufty hair. This time Neevus was accompanied by a little Mirayan girl of about nine or ten carrying a box. A studded leather collar, that looked like it would have been more appropriate on a dog, was buckled around the girl's throat and the little man led her along by a leash. She was luxuriously dressed in silks and velvets like a tiny lady. Her face was elaborately made up, with coloured paint on her eyelids and lips as red as cherries, but under the paint, the little girl's skin was a sickly grey. Jindabyne could barely take her eyes off this strange little creature, but the child kept her face downcast.

They did not go back to the cells, but to a large room on the floor below. A straw pallet and blanket, a wash bowl, a slops bucket and a towel sat in the centre of the big empty space and hunks of bread and cheese and a jug of water sat in the wash bowl. The little man, his child and the guard followed her into the room.

"Hold her," said Neevus, and before Jindabyne could even flinch, the guard had caught her round the shoulders. Neevus opened the box that the little girl carried and took out what looked like an instrument of torture - a large clamp with pointed ends.

"Stay still, fool," he chided Jindabyne, as he came at her with the jaws of the instrument opened.

Jindabyne squeezed her eyes tight shut, but to her surprise there was no pain. She felt the instrument touch her scalp and chin lightly and when she opened her eyes, the little man was writing in a notebook.

"Fascinating, fascinating!" he said, holding up the

clamp again and placing it on either side of her face. Jindabyne realised that it was some kind of measuring tool.

"Once again the head of a Tari is of exactly the same dimensions as the heads of death angels. Are they extrusions of Heaven as the angels are extrusions of hell, I wonder?"

He didn't seem to expect an answer. That final measurement taken and a final note written, he dumped the notebook and clamp back into the box and turned and went out of the door followed by the little girl and the guard. The door was firmly locked behind them leaving it suddenly very dark in the room.

She could see the outline of a window on the other side of the room and she quickly groped to it and opened the shutters. But though the window was just large enough for her to squeeze through, it was stoutly barred. Below she could see up the ravine behind the keep. Dusk was falling but she could still make out soldiers standing here and there on the dusty ground. Over near the ravine wall were what looked like animal pens, some of them filled with figures huddled on the ground. Further up the ravine huge flares shone out, casting a harsh white glow on the cliffs above. Because of the way the ravine curved, she could not see what the flares were illuminating.

She sat down on her pallet and ate her bread and cheese, drank some water and tried not to think about Elena Mori and Wolf. Later when it was fully dark, the sound of shouting and whips cracking roused her and she peered out of the window again. Torches blazed over by the pens and by their light she could see thirty or so men filing out of it. Chains glistened and clanked as they moved. With the slow walk of the hopeless, they moved up the ravine and out of sight round the curve.

A short time later she heard the sound of shouting and clanking chains again and a group of men came round the curve of the ravine and were let into the pen. In the dim light she could not tell if they were the same men, but because their progress was much slower, she suspected not. What was happening further up the ravine that needed the labour of so many men? She lay down upon the pallet and wondered about it. But soon her mind wandered from those thoughts and returned to Elena Mori. She tried to shake off those thoughts. Olga had been taken by the Tari for who knew what purpose, she did not know where Serge was or even if he was alive, and Lev Madraga meant her and all Tari ill. This was no time to be indulging in jealous thoughts. But the certainty that Wolf had loved Elena Mori more than he had loved Jindabyne lay on her chest like a heavy stone.

Eventually she slept. Death angels must have been nearby for she dreamed red blood dreams of blue-grey birds and woke with her hand clasping the locket at her neck. It was dawn. She remembered waking up so many mornings with Wolf and how he had smiled and told her how much he cared for her. She reached into her bodice and touched the bruised rosebud. It was already falling apart in her fingers. She remembered once again all the trouble Wolf had taken to get it for her. He might have loved Elena Mori once but he perhaps had also loved her too.

That day Elena did no more than greet her calmly before they settled down to sewing and weaving. There seemed to be an endless number of things to hem.

"Who are all these things for?" asked Jindabyne at last.

"I don't think they are for anyone," said Elena. "Lev thinks this is how women like to pass their time. He does not seem to be thinking very far into the future. Whatever plan he has has a definite ending. Do you know anything about it?"

Jindabyne shook her head.

"He has slaves working on something at the head of the ravine," she told her.

"Mining perhaps?"

"Perhaps."

It was a small conversation, but Jindabyne knew it was a truce.

A couple of days later, Lev's face was like thunder

when he let Jindabyne into the Elena's chamber and Jindabyne found the beautiful Tari sitting by the window with her hand over one eye. As soon as Lev was gone, Elena said, "Put a cloth in water and bring it here." Jindabyne did as she was told and discovered that Elena had a rapidly blackening eye.

"Did he do this?" she cried.

"Yes!" said Elena, calmly pressing the cool cloth to her eye. "I pressed him too hard. He's very tight-lipped about his plans and he has a remarkable ability to resist my gift."

"But he adores you!"

"Yes, but he also hates that he loves me. Sometimes this hatred comes to the surface. I have seen it before. Properly managed it will not be a problem. Ouch! Get me another cloth, will you please. If only I could find out what he is doing." Jindabyne was ashamed to realise that the thought that Lev sometimes hurt Elena somehow lessened her jealousy.

"Knowledge is not useful if we are the only people who know it. Perhaps you should stop bothering to try," she said.

"What is wrong with you? Are you so little Tari that you care nothing that this man is dabbling in demon magic," shouted Elena.

"That's not what I mean," snapped Jindabyne. "But perhaps we should concentrate on getting out of here or getting a message to the Tari or something. I mean we know he means them harm. Why get yourself beaten up trying to find out the details?"

Elena snorted, a curiously ordinary sound in such a beautiful woman, and dabbed at her eye. Jindabyne turned away and went to her sewing.

"You are right," said Elena after a while. "It's just that at the moment I can see no way of getting out of here. Can you?"

"No."

"What is your room like? Are there wardings?"

For a while they discussed ways of escape. The discussion yielded no results but it soothed the tension between them. So much so that finally Jindabyne took her courage in both hands and asked,

"What happened all those years ago?"

Elena tensed and then relaxed. She suddenly looked very tired.

"I suppose it would be best to have it out. How to begin? Apparently there's some prophecy amongst the Tari that I'll bear some kind of saviour. A melded child - a half-breed. Actually the prophecy doesn't name me in particular, but your uncle Jagamar decided I must be the one because my gift means I can have any man I want. So you were sent to make the prophecy happen. A crazy idea. I think your uncle wanted to be the saviour himself. Did he resent that he had no magical powers of his own, perhaps?"

Jindabyne could only shrug. She didn't even have an echo of a memory of this despicable-sounding uncle.

"To bring the prophecy about, you handed me and my Alyx over to Wolf Madraga. Apparently he fitted the other conditions of the prophecy and those few Tari who cared about what went on outside Ermora saw him as a reasonable man. Wolf forced me to marry him." She looked steadily at Jindabyne.

Jindabyne clenched her fists, narrowly missing driving a needle into her thumb.

"Then it was you. You were the woman who broke his heart," she cried.

Elena gasped. Then she threw back her head and laughed a bitter mirthless laugh.

"I suppose you could say that," she said. "Though I have always thought of myself as the victim."

"How can you be the victim, looking as you do? With your power. What did you call it? Fatal beauty."

"Shut up!" shouted Elena suddenly. "If you knew what I had suffered because of this...this curse." Her voice broke. Jindabyne looked up and saw to her astonishment that there were tears on Elena's face. Elena turned away quickly but Jindabyne knew from her breathing that she was weeping.

"Your husband killed my beloved. I remember that moment every day," whispered Elena.

"Because of you?" asked Jindabyne in a small voice.

Elena was silent for a long time and Jindabyne kept her eyes firmly on her sewing, too overwhelmed to say more.

Then Elena said, "No. His quarrel with Eldene was simply over land. He killed him as a man kills an enemy after a battle. The rest came after. But Eldene was betrayed by a friend, a cousin, for my sake. The Mirayans killed that traitor. It did not bring Eldene back."

"And Wolf took you."

"No! Alexus Scarvan took me. The animal."

The bitterness in her voice told of a world of suffering. Suddenly she laughed bitterly.

"This is so strange! To be explaining this to you. You who took me from Alexus and gave me to Wolf."

"Shut up!" cried Jindabyne. Every fibre of her being rebelled against this idea.

A long silence hung in the room between them. Jealousy ate away at Jindabyne with needle teeth.

"In truth I should be grateful to you," said Elena suddenly. "Wolf was much kinder to me than Alexus Scarvan. He treated me with a certain respect, never hurt me..."

"Shut up! Shut up! Must you tell me about it! Must you rub salt into my wounds."

Someone banged on the door and a moment later it swung open and Lev looked in.

"What's all this shouting about?" he said sternly.

Elena's face had lit up. A soft smile played upon her lips.

"My lord," she cooed, as if seeing him was the most wonderful thing that had ever happened to her. As if he had not just blackened her eye.

Jindabyne could see that Lev's eyes softening, but he managed to maintain his stern tone.

"What's going on?"

"I was telling her how she once forced me to marry your brother," said Elena. "She was horrified."

Jindabyne saw the echo of her own jealousy in Lev's eyes. It made him look almost human.

"Do not speak of it," he said sharply.

"Forgive me," said Elena softly. She went to the door and touched Lev's cheek. "But you know it was against my will. He was not a strong man like you. He never won my respect and honour as you have. And my love," she whispered.

Such was the look of desire on Lev's face and the violence with which he seized Elena's arms, that Jindabyne thought he was going to couple with her in the doorway, but at that moment someone pounded on the outer door.

"Damn!" Lev was breathing heavily. "What is it?" he shouted behind him.

Jindabyne didn't catch the reply, but it made Lev swear again.

"I will be waiting for you," said Elena, sweet as honey. She dropped her voice. "Anyway we cannot with her here. She's so sour."

Lev scowled at Jindabyne as he turned away. He slammed and locked the door behind him.

Elena came over, knelt down beside Jindabyne and touched her arm.

"That was disgusting," said Jindabyne. "You were like that with Wolf, weren't you? And now you're like that with his brother."

"No," said Elena firmly. "I was never like that with Wolf. He always knew I didn't love him. In those days I didn't know how to use my power and so I was always the victim. Now I master it and Lev Madraga is so sunk in self-deception already that he's easy to play upon." She laughed wryly. "He actually believes that he can use death magic and not be a death mage. That he will give up after this."

"You can't count Wolf's love for me as a real feeling. Think on this. Didn't he say that he loved you? Didn't he marry you and make you his duchess and mother of his children?"

"Lev told me that was political expedience."

"He would, the bastard," snorted Elena. "Any advantage Wolf gained with the Seagani by marrying you, he lost with his own people. You know how Mirayans are about blood purity. He would've been much wiser to have kept you as his mistress. But he didn't. So he must have wanted to share his life with you. And you didn't have any way to make him love you except for yourself. That's worth so much more than a love that forces itself on people, isn't it?"

Jindabyne could not bear look at her even though she understood that she was right.

Elena leaned closer and dropped her voice. "We need to be allies you and I. I am afraid of Lev. I thought all he wanted was power over Yarmar. But now I think... He hates Ermora. He has some plan against our people there."

Jindabyne looked at her dully. Jealousy was roiling around inside her again and at this moment she could not bring herself to really care about Ermora, a place she could not even remember.

"He can hate us all he wishes. It will do him no good, if he cannot get into Ermora."

"He has created these terrible flying monsters and the bloodbeasts. Probably the red fish that pollute the river too. What else is he capable of?" Elena touched Jindabyne's hand.

"Think on what I have said," she continued softly. "And even if you cannot forgive me for Wolf, help me against Lev. After all, he killed the man you love. If we can bring him down somehow..."

She got up and went to her place at the loom.

After a time Jindabyne found her voice again.

"The hardest thing has been to find that my Wolf...that he could force himself on someone."

"Don't worry about that. He didn't. He treated me as kindly as he knew how. Tried to woo me. He didn't know much about women in those days - didn't realise that we were people just like men, so he didn't understand that it was impossible for him to ever make me love him. I saw him order my beloved's death. After that..."

She shook her head and was silent and Jindabyne didn't ask more.

Chapter 18

A group of men wearing the colours of the Southern League come riding down from the north past the place where Yani was encamped with Prince Pimenov's men. Ashana's harsh face was grim when he returned from talking with them.

"They're part of a patrol who were attacked by Malov yesterday. He showered them with fireballs and killed twenty men. They said they'd never seen one man muster so much power. Symina gave them an ultimatum for our Prince. Either the Southern League accept him as ruler of their province or he will destroy the city of Vulgate."

"Was my sister with him?" asked Yani.

Ashana looked away before nodding.

Later that day Yani went off alone. She found a large stone and worked through her swordsman's exercises finding a brief relief in concentrating on the movement. The arm was weak and tired quickly. As she set down the stone to rub the stiffness out of the arm, a voice called out.

"There's no need to creep away like this if you want to train."

Ashana was leaning against a tree, arms crossed, watching her. His harsh swarthy face seemed mild.

"Isn't there?" said Yani coldly. She picked up the stone again and started doing arm exercises.

"If you push yourself too hard you'll take longer to recover."

"Tari are stronger than other people," she said.

"Everyone needs to take it slowly after such a wound. Why are you in such a hurry?"

Suddenly she could not bear the way that Mirayans thought women were so helpless. She turned on him.

"I'm in a hurry because Malov Symina is using the life spirit to bring destruction and death. Such a perversion can only cause imbalance. I am the Raven. It's my duty to bring death to protect the life spirit."

"That is what the tattoo is for? Are you some kind of holy assassin?" He looked as if he believed her.

"I'm the only Tari allowed to kill without suffering," said Yani. She was already regretting her rush of anger. "And then only when the Raven wills it. Because of this I'm unclean and unable to enter holy places."

"What happens if other Tari kill?" asked Ashana.

"They share the death of the one killed. The life spirit turns its back on them for a short time. A terrible experience for us."

She put down the stone and stretched the stiffness out of her arm again.

"So what is your duty now?" he asked. Yani knew she was probably wrong about this, but she felt strongly that he was talking to her as one warrior to another.

"I don't know. I feel the life spirit but the Raven does not come to me." Her eyes prickled with tears of loneliness. She longed for the Raven's certainty. "Sometimes I am afraid... Perhaps Malov is already harming the life spirit so much that it can no longer form the Raven to speak to me. Perhaps someday we will not even be able to feel it."

Her voice betrayed her by breaking. She put her hands over her eyes to hide the tears. Feet scuffed in the dirt as Ashana came to her side. His hand fell on the shoulder, the warm hard tough of a warrior. She turned to him, her face clenched with grief.

"Perhaps the Raven does not come because it has nothing to say. My duty is so obvious. Malov Symina must be killed. And if I kill him, Marigoth will also die. HOW CAN I DO IT?"

Ashana held her while she wept, but the moment she was quiet again he pushed her away. She sensed he was uneasy with such close contact and did not meet his eye. To her surprise, he put his finger under her chin and turned her face to his.

"Do not be afraid," he said. "If it comes to that, I will strike the blow. I swear. You should not have to kill your own kin."

"Thank you," she murmured, blinking away more damned tears. "But this is not for you to do. The duty is mine."

The party stayed at the crossroads waiting for instructions from Prince Pimenov. During the next few days, several groups of soldiers galloped up and down the road near their camp. The Southern lords were putting their resources into guarding Vulgate and other towns near Golgarov, and making plans to assassinate Malov. Ashana trained with Yani every day, though he always urged her to stop before she wanted to and she still had to sneak away to do extra training. She could feel that the bones in her arm were finally becoming strong enough to bear her weight.

She tried to want to be first of the assassins to go against Malov. Better for Marigoth to die in the arms of her sister than some stranger. But as she worked with Ashana to regain the strength in her arm, memories of her childhood kept coming back - how the three of them, she, Marigoth and Elena had sailed boats, bickered, chased the chickens round the farm yard as children, how she and Marigoth had journeyed together to free Elena all those years since, how only five months ago, Marigoth had stolen her best green silk dress and spent all evening masquerading as her and flirting outrageously with the

Tyronian ambassador at an evening party. The man had sent her flowers for weeks afterward.

"She is no longer the Marigoth you knew," said Ashana after she told him this last story. "She is already gone, just a husk, a source." He never spoke much, but Yani always knew herself heard. Though she suspected his master had wanted him to bring her back to help with their cause, Ashana said nothing of it and did everything he could to aid her.

Despite the memories she worked dutifully to regain her strength and within ten days she was able to fly again. After fifteen she could fly as well as ever.

On the sixteenth day she bade Ashana farewell.

He surprised her by catching her arm.

"Let me do this for you!" he said. "You are too valuable to spend yourself in this way."

She shook her head. "How could you get into Golgarov undetected? Thank you for everything," she said and she leaned over and kissed him on the lips. There was enough of the old Yani in her to enjoy the slightly dazed astonishment on the bodyguard's face, but she walked away without further ado and after changing shape, she flew out across the wasteland.

The sky here was an angry mass of sulphurous cloud, incarnadine with the glow of lava spewing forth like arterial blood from the wounded land. On every side, the smoking remnants of mountains filled the air with dust and sulphur and molten rock oozed from new cracks in the earth. Malov had been at work here recently, moving in the direction of the town of Vulgate as if making some kind of supply line.

By the time Yani came upon the fortress of Golgarov, a low building with an enormously high tower, her heart was filled with animal hatred for the man who'd deprived her of her sister. She lit upon a window sill where one of the shutters was broken, completely focused on killing Malov, with no other thoughts or regrets.

Her wing brushed against something sticky as she hopped in through the window, and she shrugged it off thinking it was just a spider web. It clung. Sshe tore at it with her beak and then her claws. Soon clinging sticky threads were all over her. Yani ruffled her feathers and launched herself in through the window, spreading her wings to fly free of it.

But the web pulled taut and suddenly she was caught in a sticky net, wings flapping helplessly, dangling high above the stone floor of the hall.

Whoever had set this magical trap would know it was sprung. Knowing she must move fast, Yani snapped and clawed at the net, but every movement made the threads tangle her tighter. There was nothing for it but to change shape. To her horror the web grew with her. She struggled to tear it apart, working more methodically now, but still unable to break out.

"Oh good," said a familiar voice beneath her, as a hand reached up to snap cold iron around her neck. "You've changed shape already. That'll save trouble."

Daria's room at Golgarov was very like her room in the manor house at Winterriser except that the red silk hangings were relieved by gold tassels. Still Yani felt as if she was inside a mouth and Daria certainly treated her like a piece of food. She was so hungry to touch Yani's mind that she did not even clean the web off her, let alone give her clothes. She shoved Yani across her red silken bed and leaping astride her, seized her head in her hands. When she has finished, she curled up on Yani's breast.

"Ermora! Beautiful Ermora! You came back to me," she crooned under her breath, stroking Yani's breasts and flanks in a way that was both horrible and deeply sexual.

Ermora was Yani's homeland. A paradisiacal place, which Yani had never seen. There were no memories of it in her mind. Where had Daria learned to call the life spirit Ermora? Yani suspected that the death mage had been looking in someone else's mind and the logical person would be Marigoth. Yani judged it best not to ask Daria, for Daria was capricious enough to harm Marigoth.

The death mage had changed since Yani had left her at

Winterriser. She had been a fastidious creature, but now her hair and clothes smelt unwashed and her face had become hollow-eyed and pale. All her savagery was gone, leaving a Daria that Yani had never seen before.

But even though she seemed to have lost touch with reality, Daria was still sharp enough to keep Yani prisoner. She chained her on a long chain to a staple in the wall of her room, kept all potential weapons out of her reach and even the food she brought came in light wooden bowls with light horn spoons.

Tenderly she bathed Yani every day, more than she bathed herself. Her hands were fascinated by the Raven tattoo on Yana's back and she would trace it for hours as they lay on her bed together. She would lie Yana's head on her lap and feed her sweetmeats. If Yani told Daria to eat or bath or change her clothes, she did so docilely and it was easy to fall into the illusion that Daria loved her.

Yet all tenderness disappeared when Daria wanted, needed to look inside Yana's mind. Several times a day without any warning she would seize Yani crying, "I have to have it, I need it," and hold her down while her mind came bursting into Yana's, leaving Yani with a constant pounding headache. Daria loved her like an addict loves a drug, no more nor less than that.

Once Yani tried to knock Daria unconscious as she lay relaxed after a mind search. In revenge Daria sent Yani down into a sleep full of the most terrible dreams, dreams in which children screamed and people were tortured to death, dreams that left her shaken and unwilling to try attacking Daria again. Yani suspected that the dreams were caused by Daria's own memories and Yani wanted no part of them.

Since Yani was far taller and broader than Daria, she spent her first couple of days in Daria's room wrapped in a silken cloth, but Daria went to considerable trouble to get clothes for her, bringing her men's clothing and even trying to make her a dress. Clothing could not be made with Mirayan magic, for the seams would come apart as soon the mage who had made them lost concentration. Daria tried to sew the dress by hand, but was quickly confounded. Yani who had a workmanlike knowledge of sewing, which had stood her in good stead in the barracks room, had to take over. Daria had chosen red silk. Perhaps it was all she had.

"It will make you look like a rose," she crooned in Yana's ear as she leaned against her watching her sew. "Like a precious rose."

Then something about the way the needle dug into the cloth troubled her. "Stop it," she cried. She snatched the sewing and threw it away.

"Horrible sharp thing," she cried. "Digging into flesh."

She turned and came at Yani, hands outstretched to grasp her head, eyes desperate and hungry. "Show me the place!" she cried. "Show it to me."

Yani let Daria push her back on the bed. She relaxed opening her mind to Daria's. Resisting just made the pain worse.

Whenever Daria's mind entered hers, reality suddenly become as hazy as a dream. This day Yani saw keys dangling over her, but her mind did not register what she had seen. Reality was inside her head where Daria was pawing through her memories as if they were clothes out of a chest and trying to fit herself into them. Soft spongy memory - it still hurt when Daria squeezed and tore at it.

Only after Daria lay drowsing, relaxed and satiated and curled against Yana's breast, and the jangling pain in Yana's mind had subsided, did Yani remembered seeing the keys round Daria's neck. Could one of them be the key to her chain? So close? Yani slid her hand against Daria's neck. Yes there was a chain here. Casually she let her fingers slide downwards. Daria stirred and turned in Yana's arms, before starting awake, shoving Yani away and flouncing off. Yani lay back on the cushions. All this time freedom had hung just under her nose. All she had to do was get the keys off Daria somehow. Then she could get to Malov and...

She should feel excited but she just felt disheartened.

She didn't want to kill Malov and she knew it. Was this why she had never noticed the keys before?

Chapter 19

Time passed. Marigoth watched Ezratah fall into despair. His beard grew and though he was only in his thirties, it was flecked with white. He lay all day and night on his mattress sleeping or staring into space. He seemed to be eating his food and his muscles did not seem to be wasting away. Somewhere at the back of her mind she wanted to speak to him, to help him, but her mouth was weighted shut by the burden of Malov.

He spoke to her often. Keeping the faith. Telling her he loved her. Once such words would have startled and delighted her, but now she was just a piece of jetsam moving down a drain toward a place where she would no longer carry the burden of being. She was tired and sick to the depths of her soul; sick of watching Malov yowl with joy every time he made the life force groan and sick of seeing people die in pain.

Malov didn't have to take her with him but he liked to keep an eye on his "treasure". He chivvied her about, slung her on horses, pulled her off horses and made her stand and watch as he drew magic out of her and used it to plough great deep gashes into the earth.

He would crouch down to press his ear against the ground. "I can hear the lava flows and feel where the crust is weak," he would cry with pleasure. How could he feel the land's life spirit and yet endure its pain?

He and his scholars tested out a silver pole to which extra lengths could be added. Silver conducted magic well and, day after day, Malov used that long silver pole to drill deeper and deeper, driving explosions of magic further underground until he tore open a vent in the earth's skin, and steam and smoke and hot red lava/blood spewed forth.

"Vulgate is mine!" shouted Malov as he and his scholars danced around. "Miraya is mine!"

"Hail Malov Symina, emperor of Miraya!" shouted the scholars and soldiers. Even in her deadened state, Marigoth could feel the anguish of the earth when Malov broke it open. She was too sad to weep. She did not even respond when Malov got angry, taunted her and, driven to frustration at her lack of response, slapped her face.

He only did that once though. After that he contented himself with insults.

"You're such a dull bitch, Meat," he'd say. "It's as bad as having a wife. A little meat wife."

Just words.

Malov became careless of her and several times she'd had the opportunity to throw herself into a crevasse or lava pool. But the Raven who had come to her after the tapping had told her that she must not take her own life, but must endure to the end. She hoped the end would come soon.

The day Malov chivvied Marigoth onto a horse and they rode for a long time until at last they came to a place where Marigoth could see refreshing green hills beyond the ash fields.

Malov was dressed in magnificent purple robes and he had brought his own throne along strapped to the back of a pack horse. His men set it up and he took his place upon it, pushing Marigoth on to a cushion at his feet. Meanwhile some strange soldiers waited nearby

When he was settled to his satisfaction, he beckoned the soldiers forward. He instructed them to kneel and offer him their loyalty, but before they could do so, the mounds of ash on either side peeled open. Mages came pouring out.

Three phalanxes, over thirty mages had been hiding in low trenches covered with cloth, sticks and earth.

Marigoth sat calmly on her cushion watching the fight, not even ducking the bolts of magic that rocketed back and forth over her head. Malov made short work of them, just as she had made short work of phalanxes of mages in the past. She could feel the life spirit streaming through her as Malov threw the mages around like dolls and burned them with fireballs. Her skin tingled as Malov's victims were burnt and she noticed that Malov also rubbed his arms and chest uneasily. Soon the ash field was covered in dead or groaning bodies. The mages fought to the last man.

The group of soldiers who had come to parley had also attacked, but Malov's guards fought them off, capturing the leaders and killing the rest. When the battle was over, Malov raged at the captives and grabbed the leader by the head intending, Marigoth was certain, to crush his skull. But suddenly a look of nausea came on to his face and he flung Prince Pimenov to the ground.

"Go back to your people and tell them of what happened here," he snarled. "Tell them I accept their submission and will regard them as my vassals, my taxpaying vassals, from now on. I shall consider further how I will punish your disloyalty."

Seizing Marigoth by the arm, he bundled her back onto her horse, and whipping both it and his own into a gallop, thundered away. When they were well ahead of his men, Malov pulled the horses to a stop, leaned out of his saddle and was comprehensively sick. Then he put his head on the horse's neck and lay there shivering. Marigoth sensed him using healing magic on himself and felt a faint flicker of satisfaction.

"My lord you should have finished them off," said Argent back at Golgarov.

"I didn't feel... It pleased me not to. Who are you to question me?" snarled Malov, throwing himself down at his desk. "Get out!"

Argent shrugged and sauntered away and Malov

opened one of his notebooks and sat staring at the diagrams he had made of the hills around Vulgate. The scholars had been advising exploiting a weakness in the earth's crust 10 miles away to cause a catastrophic earthquake. As his breathing calmed and he relaxed into his columns of figures, Marigoth leaned against the back of his chair and put her hand on his shoulder. At first he didn't notice. Then suddenly he leapt up and pushed her away so violently that she was knocked to the floor.

"What are you doing? Always touching me. What do you mean by it?"

"Nothing," said Marigoth, lying calmly where she had fallen.

"Well stop it, do you hear? I don't need comforting or anything else from you, Meat." He kicked her in the leg and stalked from the room.

"Are you all right?" cried Ezratah. "Did he hurt you?"

"I'm perfectly fine," said Marigoth, sitting up so that Ezratah would stop worrying. "He didn't kick hard. I don't think he can any more."

"Mari." Ezratah put out his hand and seeing what was expected Marigoth went over and took it. He seemed to derive much pleasure from her touch. He drew her down to him and took her in his arms. The cage bars were cold against her cheek but this was a lot pleasanter than most places she had been lately. She felt him stroke her hair and kiss her brow.

"What wrong with "Mighty Malov" today?" he asked.

"The same thing as is wrong with his sister."

"Which is?"

"You can't use the life spirit to serve death. Malov begins to appal himself."

Delight dawned in Ezratah's face.

"So there's a sting in the tail after all! What'll happen? Do you know?"

"No. But it's a beginning."

"Of what? Is he going to turn from death magic?"

"Who can say? More likely he will go mad. That is what happens to Tari when they wrong the life spirit. Here,

I have this for you." She took the key she had stolen out of her bodice and unlocked the cage.

"The manacle keys are out in the slaves' quarters. Get yourself out of here."

"I won't leave you," said Ezratah.

"I want you to. It's too late for me."

Ezratah put his hands round her face.

"Please don't say that," he said, eyes full of tears.

She touched his cheek. "'Tah, I'm ruined. I just want to come to the end. But I want you to live. Please! Take this and go. Live!" She pressed the key into his hand and left him.

Ezratah was still there the next day and the next.

"I'll go after it ends," he said, after Malov had left them for the night and she was locked in her cage.

"What if that's too late?"

He shrugged.

"Please go," she said.

*　*　*

For many days after the soldiers' attack, Malov did not go out. He sat in his study or wandered the corridors of Golgarov, his imperial purple robe hanging limply from his shoulders.

"That Southern League needs a real lesson," urged Argent.

"All our calculations are done. It only needs for you to ride out and set off whatever disaster you wish," urged the scholars.

"Shut up!" snapped Malov. "I'll go when it pleases me." He would make some demonstration to scare his scholars such as setting their clothing alight, though he usually dowsed them in water before they got hurt.

"On who's sufferance do you live, meat?" he would growl, as they crept away whimpering.

He should hurt them properly, thought Ezratah, for they had begun to mutter about him behind his back. He tried to keep out of the scholar's sight, but one evening the younger one noticed Ezratah watching them. He hit Ezratah to remind him to keep a civil tongue in his head, while the other scholar watched licking his lips.

"You're free now. Why don't you go?" hissed Marigoth, when she saw Ezratah's blackened eye. It was the most emotional he had seen her for a long time. She nagged Malov to heal Ezratah. Malov sneered and sent for Daria to do the healing, but he also had his men beat the scholars and lock them in the slave cells for the night.

"I'll get you for this," hissed the younger scholar at Ezratah.

"You must leave," urged Marigoth. "There's nothing but danger for you here."

"I don't want to," said Ezratah.

"You're just making this harder," said Marigoth shaking her head.

She was right that he would be safer gone, but a world without Marigoth was too bleak for Ezratah to face.

One evening as Malov sat at his desk looking at his figures, Ezratah saw Marigoth look up sharply. She stared hard into the darkness and then she got up from the chair she was sitting in, went into her open cage and lay down on her blankets. Ezratah scanned the darkness in the hall to see what had brought on this tiredness.

Suddenly someone came charging out of the shadows, arm upraised to strike.

"Look out!" shouted Ezratah without thinking.

Malov whirled round. Metal flashed and he cried out in pain, as suddenly a knife was sticking out of his upper arm. Next moment he was up from his chair, lunging at the figure who had attacked him.

Yani! Yani had been wielding the knife! She turned and fled back into the shadows again

Malov was wounded, but by no means dead. He flung out his arm.

"Light!" he shouted, flinging out his undamaged arm and a burst of unearthly greenish light filled the hall. A large black bird was flying away through the columns.

Malov lifted his hand to strike.

"Stop!" screamed a woman's voice. A bolt of magic struck Malov, knocking him backwards into Marigoth and Ezratah who had both left their cages. The black bird soared out through a window.

"Ermora! No!"

Daria ran up the hall after the bird, her arm outstretched.

"No!" she howled up at the now empty window. "Ermora! Don't leave me! I need you! Ermora!"

The knife clattered to the floor.

"What the hell is this?" shouted Malov, striding down the hall, clutching a blood stained cloth to his upper arm. "What have you done, sister?"

"You bastard, Malov! You've driven her away!" Daria turned and flung a bolt of magic at him.

"Useless, bloody bitch," roared Malov, deflecting Daria's blow and making it hurl her across the room towards the wall. Daria only managed to stop herself at the last moment. With a twist and a kick of her legs, she pushed herself up the wall towards the window were Yani had escaped.

"Stop!" commanded Malov.

With a shrill scream of pain and rage, Daria crashed to the floor.

Then, just as Ezratah had gathered his wits enough to consider running for it, guards came charging into the room.

"How the hell did you get out of your cage, mage?" snarled Malov. "I shall deal with you later. Lock them both in."

Marigoth calmly returned to her cage, and wearing witch manacles, Ezratah was no match for three big guards. Daria howled with rage and frustration as Malov shook her.

"You stupid little cow!" Malov shouted. "How dare you hide a Tari here! Couldn't you see this creature was a danger to me?"

"Why should I care about you? You took the other one.

It's your own fault!"

Malov began calling her terrible names and slapping her around the head and face with his free hand, and when she tried to defend herself with magic, he made her fall helplessly to the ground and kicked her in the ribs.

"You bastard! Let me go! I have to find her!" Daria screamed.

With a snarl of anger, Malov took some scissors from the bench, seized Daria, and with a few savage blows, cut off her long black hair. Daria wailed and wept, begging him the whole time to let her go after Yani.

"Put her in manacles and lock her up in the slave quarters," snarled Malov, when he was done. "I don't want to see her again."

"I'll get you for this, Malov!" screamed Daria. "I needed her."

"I don't have to pander to your whims any more, little sister. I'm stronger now and you'll do as I say."

As the door slammed after them, he turned to healing the wound in his arm. Too soon it seemed, for was a commotion out in the corridor and Argent rushed in crying, "She's escaped, my Lord. She's turned into a hawk and flown."

Malov turned on him.

"Do I look like I care? Let her go where she likes. I'll put wardings up so that she can't bother us any more. She's useless now. She's lost her taste for the work."

Argent dropped his voice.

"My lord! If you let her free, she'll be a danger to you! Mark my words!"

"Don't be ridiculous! I'm not just more powerful than her, I'm smarter too."

"She was cunning enough to keep that woman concealed from you. She's had that raven for weeks."

"Shut up Argent! I can't be bothered with her any more. Here, tie this bandage."

"Can't be bothered or is it something else?" snarled Argent.

Malov didn't answer.

"You haven't been the same since you tapped the bitch, Lord," said Argent harshly. "Have you too lost your taste for the work?"

"What are you talking about?" snapped Malov.

"For two weeks our plan for Vulgate has been perfected and yet you do nothing. The Southerners will be wondering why you have not punished them. And I wonder also. I have no wish to serve a weak master."

"How dare you!" screamed Malov. He threw out a bolt of power that knocked Argent to the ground and sent him skidding across the floor. The soldier's body smacked hard against the wall.

Malov's gasp of horror was loud in the suddenly silent room. He leant against the table breathing raggedly. But Argent was wearing armour and after a moment of lying still, he staggered to his feet.

"Before you tapped that woman, you would have killed me for what I just said."

Malov was silent for a moment then he said, "You are useful to me Argent, but beware... I may still kill you."

"Will you just?" sneered Argent, in a voice full of disbelief. He limped painfully out the door and was gone.

Malov stayed leaning against the table.

"He's right," said Marigoth. "You have lost your taste for killing. I see how it sickens you. Just as it sickens Daria."

Malov swung round to face Marigoth.

"What have you done to me?"

"Nothing!" said Marigoth. "You do it to yourself when you draw power from me. You touch the life spirit and to touch the life spirit is to touch all living things. Do you remember how sick I was after I fought those death mages? That was because I had killed someone. That was why you were sick when you burned Pimenov's men."

"Shut up! I never touched your puerile life spirit!" shouted Malov.

"My skin tingled when you burnt all those mages. Did your skin tingle too? Or perhaps it burned as theirs did, because you were closer. I saw you use a healing spell on yourself afterwards. It will only get worse, Malov. Soon you'll have to actually share the deaths of those you kill."

Red faced with fury, Malov seized Marigoth by the arm and slapped her. "I'm no weakling. Not like my sister. I'm master here. Master of you and master of your magic."

"Stop!" shouted Ezratah.

"Your killing days are over, Malov. Get used to it," sneered Marigoth.

"Shut up!"

"My mother killed over one hundred people and she had to feel every one of their deaths one by one. Afterwards she wanted to die herself."

Malov threw Marigoth to the floor.

"That's not going to happen to me, bitch. I love the power of death and I am master here."

Later guards came and took Ezratah and Marigoth from their cages and locked them in the now almost empty slave quarters. As night fell, screams of agony from the Great Hall indicated that Malov was performing some kind of death magic spell.

Marigoth was lying on her mattress with her eyes closed, when Malov came bursting into the slave quarters.

"Did you know about this, bitch?" he screamed, flinging open her cage door, seizing her by the arms and shaking her. Marigoth stared at him expressionlessly and it was left to Ezratah to ask Malov what was going on.

"The great ones told me I was doomed, that you can't use the magic of a Tari mage for acts of death and power. That it leaks into you, pollutes you, makes you weak. Did you know this?"

A vengeful look came over Marigoth's face. "No! But I suspected it."

Malov put his hands round her throat squeezing just enough so that she could feel his strength.

"The great ones told me to kill you to stop the rot."

"Why don't you?" she murmured.

Malov squeezed harder.

"No!" shouted Ezratah. "If you kill her you lose all

hope. Think man! Use your brain."

Malov seemed not to hear.

"Will the rot go if I kill you? Or will it stain me forever?" he asked Marigoth, squeezing ever tighter.

"To touch the life spirit is to be changed for ever. Look at your sister!" shouted Ezratah.

Marigoth's eyes were dimming. Despite her brave words, she plucked at Malov's hands.

"If you kill her, you will have no power at all. Your enemies will fall on you. Think! Think before you go too far!"

Malov threw Marigoth away, and with a snarl, flung himself back out of Marigoth's cage.

The rush of relief bought a realisation to Ezratah's brain.

"Lev! Lev Madraga must have known this would happen. He must have. Think about it. Why would he have let you tap into such power otherwise?"

"Did he tell you, damn it?" snarled Malov

"Of course not! But it makes sense. Tapping Marigoth, you are much more powerful than him. He'd be insane to let that happen. He trapped you."

"I had no interest in the Archipelago," snarled Malov. "He knew that."

"As Emperor of Miraya, your eyes would have turned to it eventually. Cunning Lev Madraga would have thought of that. If your demons knew that tapping a Tari would send a death mage mad, his must have too. You gullible fool, Malov Symina. He's destroyed you and he hasn't even had to lift a finger. And you thought you were so clever. I bet Madraga is laughing at you even now."

Malov gave a yell of fury and used his power to throw Ezratah to the floor. The door of the slave quarters slammed shut and he was gone.

A palpable hit thought Ezratah with satisfaction, as he picked himself up off the floor.

Two days later Malov ordered the guards to start preparing for a journey.

"We're going to your little Archipelago," sneered Argent, when Ezratah asked him about it. "We're going to enslave your people and feed them to demons."

Ezratah hoped that it wouldn't be that simple - though he hid his satisfaction from Argent.

Chapter 20

Beautiful Ermora where the sun slants golden through the lush trees.

In Ermora Alyx sleeps on soft moss beneath silken sheets, protected from the morning showers by a bower of green leaves and roses. When she awakens refreshed, she can see clear blue sky through the branches. Soft rose petals have fallen on her cheek and she rubs them on her lips to feel their silkiness. Bruised by her touch, they melt and their sweet scent covers her skin and fills the bower. Then someone young and beautiful - for everyone is young and beautiful in Ermora - calls from outside and she crawls out to dance and sing and feast in the golden afternoon light. It is always afternoon in Ermora, except sometimes when it is night.

Warm velvet night. People hung about with garlands, come dancing and singing through the trees.

"The festival!" they cry. "Come on!"

Soon they are all dancing hand in hand. All the young men are looking at Alyx, which makes her shy but is also delightful. The one who attracts Alyx's eye most is Serge, who is fair like the rest of them, but looks stronger, more vigorous, and has a different cast of face.

The revellers dance and run until the tree trunks part and they are on a mountain top. A great river of molten rock runs out of a low broken-sided crater at the centre of the mountain and away down the mountain side to disappear into darkness.

"Blessings on the earth!" cry the Tari as they cast wreaths of flowers into the lava. Using magic they lift glowing balls of lava up onto the solid ground and mould it into wonderful shapes; sometimes figures, sometimes just sinuous forms. All night they compete over who can make the best statue. Along with the rest of the crowd, Alyx and Serge clap and cheer at each new wonder until the dawn shows pale over the mountains. Then they help the others push the now cooled stone statues back into the lava flow.

Dancing, singing and running beneath green trees - this is the life of the Tari. And Serge is there. Handsome Serge with his warm smile and laughing blue eyes. Seeing him makes Alyx feel both happy and shy. They try to talk to each other, but can't think of anything to say.

"You're beautiful," whispers Serge, blushing.

"So are you," murmurs Alyx, unable to meet his eyes.

Their hands seem drawn together and they dance closer and closer until other Tari catch up and whirl them apart.

Warm velvet night. Alyx swims in a dark pool, sprinkled with the reflections of stars. The refreshing water is like crystal against her hot skin. She is naked, relaxed and unashamed. Everyone is naked here. Candles float in the dark water and so does she, her hair brushing gently on her shoulders like soft water-weed. The bottom of the pool is soft smooth mud, sprinkled with little bits of glitter.

Jerandine draws Alyx gently from the water, helps her dry herself with pleasantly rough towels and she and another woman drape Alyx in the most gossamer of robes. The silk drags deliciously over the skin of her shoulders, her belly and her nipples.

With tender hands they bind the gown under her breasts and dry and comb her hair which they decorate with flowers and golden threads.

"How beautiful you are!" they cry, holding up a mirror.

"The red fish are not beautiful," says a little boy, appearing beside her in the mirror. Pretty little boy with dark serious eyes.

... "The red fish?" asked Alyx. "What fish?"

She struggled to remember.

"Go away Yundeman," said Jerandine. "Stop being a pain." She rubbed fragrant oil on to her palms and smoothed it over Alyx's face, especially the delicate skin of her eyes.

Alyx lies on soft moss, licking nectar from the ends of big purple trumpet-shaped flowers. All around her, the laughing Tari hold flowers out for each other to lick and a handsome young man called Tarwon reaches down a flower for Alyx. The nectar drips on to the palm of her hand and Tarwon licks it off, his tongue and lips deliciously soft against her skin. She tosses a handful of used blooms at Tarwon's golden head and he laughs and shakes them aside.

"Isn't he handsome!" whispers Jerandine, her sweet breath tickling Alyx's ear.

"Mmm!" sighs Alyx. Tarwon is stroking the inside of her arm and it feels delicious. She leans her head against Jerandine's breast while Jerandine strokes her hair.

"Come," she whispers into Alyx's ear. "Walk with us."

Alyx feels lazy, but somehow Tarwon and Jerandine have pulled her up from the ground and they are walking hand in hand through the sweetly-scented trees. The moonlight is almost as bright as day, but softer.

"So beautiful," says Tarwon, stroking Alyx's hair.

"A dark-haired Tari," says Jerandine, rubbing her cheek against Alyx's shoulder. "Such an exotic look. Do you think I should blacken my hair, Tarwon?"

Suddenly they're in a clearing - a low hill covered in

grass and flowers, all rippling in a breeze which doesn't exist. Alyx's eyes are drawn to an opening in the top of the hill, a cave mouth flanked by four tall crystal spires which glisten in the bright moonlight. The cave mouth glistens too. An irresistible urge fills Alyx. She lets go of her companion's hands and gathering up her gossamer skirts, runs headlong up the hill.

"Not that way!" shouts Jerandine behind her.

"Damn you! Don't go up there!" yells Tarwon.

Alyx quickly reaches the top of the hill and the mouth of the cave. She is desperate to go in, but her way is blocked by a huge lump of crystal. With a moan of disappointment Alyx presses herself against the crystal. In the moonlight that streams through it, she can make out the sleeping shapes of people in the cave beyond.

Tarwon and Jerandine arrive beside her, panting and flustered.

"Come away from there!"

Tarwon seizes Alyx's arm and pulls her away from the cave mouth.

"I want to go in! Why's it blocked? It shouldn't be blocked. I want to go in and commune with the life spirit."

"Those who go in no longer come out. So we blocked the entrance to make sure no one else can go in."

"Please, won't you let me in!" cries Alyx, bereft, banging at the unyielding crystal as tears flow down her face.

"Oh come, come," said Tarwon. He enfolds Alyx in his strong arms and Jerandine too throws her arms round Alyx and nuzzles her face.

"They're salt," she says in surprise. "Tears are salty."

"Really?" says Tarwon, pressing his lips against Alyx's face. "So they are. I'd forgotten."

Both Tari lick Alyx's cheeks as if they were dogs and it tickles in much the same way. Laughing now, Alyx pushes them away and runs off around the hill. In the back of her mind, she knows she is seeking a way into the spirit cave, but as she rounds the top of the hill, something else catches her eye. At the bottom of the hill stands a grove of dark straight trees and among them, torches show a group of dark-robed people. Dark robes are unusual in Ermora. Must be some kind of ceremony.

As Alyx runs down the hill to join them, she sees that the people are dancing round a huge white stone altar. Serge is tied to the middle of the altar, with garlands of flowers and silken ropes. Round him the dancers spin, singing what sounds like a dirge. Troubled now, Alyx stops at the edge of the trees to watch. Serge seems quite happy lying tied to that stone, singing to himself, looking up at the stars, but the dancers are robed in black and they seem to dance with a sinister intensity.

Suddenly one of them lunges at the altar and rears up over Serge, holding a black silk pillow in both hands.

"To the crisp, clean pain of death!" he cries, and he brings the pillow down on Serge's face.

Serge starts to buck and struggle, obviously smothering under the pillow. Alyx rushes towards the altar and the black-robed figures cry out. Hands clutch at her but are easily pushed aside. She leaps at the figure leaning down on Serge and kicks him hard in the side, so that he falls away from Serge. A punch to the head and the figure is gone...

...and she pulled the pillow away from Serge's face.

He still breathed, gulping now at the fresh air.

"Alyx! What..." he gasped.

"Come on," she cried, pulling at the silken cords around his arms. "Let's get away from here."

"Look out," shouted Serge.

Several angry looking black-robed Tari came at Alyx. She turned to face them, fists raised.

"Sweet life! What violence is going on here?"

Jerandine and Tarwon stood at the edge of the circle, their bodies stiff with outrage.

"They tried to kill Serge," cried Alyx.

The two older Tari glared at the shamefaced Tari in the black robes.

"Mundru. What are you doing to the outlander?"

The man Alyx had kicked was sitting on the ground, his hood thrown back to reveal a disgruntled face.

"Nothing," he said defensively. "We weren't going to hurt anybody."

"You were playing that damned morbid game of yours, weren't you?" snapped Jerandine. "It's dangerous."

"We know what we're doing."

"But did the outlander? I think not. How dare you involve someone without their consent!"

"He's only an outlander!" cried Mundru.

"We wanted to see if he felt different," cried someone else.

By now Alyx had got Serge free of the flowery ropes that bound him and helped him to sit up.

"Let's go!" he muttered, staggering shakily to his feet. Alyx put an arm round him and helped him out of the grove. Together they went back into the forest, Serge's steps becoming stronger as they went.

"Stop my dears," called a voice behind them. Jerandine had followed them. Alyx turned on her.

"What the hell were they doing back there?"

"I'm sorry" said Jerandine, her head held winsomely to one side. "It's just a silly game they play."

"It didn't feel like a game," cried Serge.

"They tried to kill him!"

"Here," said Jerandine soothingly. "Sit down." She pulled them gently down onto a rock. "Rest. Have some water. You'll feel better."

She held out a crystal cup.

"What game?" insisted Alyx.

"Some of the young ones have a morbid fascination with death. You know how the Tari must share in the death of those they kill. Well, they smoother each other so that the killer can share in his victim's death and then the others revive the victim before he actually dies. Just a silly game."

"A damned dangerous one," said Tarwon behind them. "The mind can be permanently fuddled if you wait too long to revive the victim. There have been accidents. It was very wrong of them to involve you without your consent."

"What's wrong with you people?" shouted Serge. "How can you treat death as a game?"

"Shh shhh!" said Jerandine, running her hand down Serge's face and over his eyes. He fell silent.

What's going on here?" cried Alyx. "The spirit cave closed, Tari playing with death."

"Hush, Hush!" said Jerandine, now stroking Alyx's face. She had some kind of scented oil on her hand.

"This is Ermora! There's nothing to worry about here."

A clearing filled with a thousand flickering candles. Sweet music floats on the air, the melting sounds of stringed instruments, and the woody tones of flutes. The gossamer robes feel delicious brushing against Alyx's legs as she dances in Serge's strong arms. Serge is so much more energetic than the soft languid Tari. Slim-hipped, graceful. Masculine.

The admiration in his eyes fills Alyx with a delicious fluttering.

"You're beautiful," he whispers.

"Thank you." She is shy, but overwhelmingly happy to be with him.

She tries to keep her mind on the steps, but she longs to run her hands over his hard chest and arms.

"Serge!" cries a voice.

Serge turns. A little girl is rushing across the clearing towards them, disrupting the pattern of the dance.

"Hello Olga!" smiles Serge. "That's right, you're here too." He lifts the little girl into his arms and hugs her tenderly. "Are you having a lovely time?"

"Where's Mumma?" asks Olga urgently.

"Oh!" says Serge struck by this questions. "You know I..."

"She's safe," coos a voice beside them. Jerandine is there. She brushes her hand over Olga's face. "She's perfectly safe. No need to worry."

"Is she?" asks Olga. "Is she really?"

"Of course!" coos Jerandine, stroking her face again. The fragrant oil on her hands smells delicious and makes

Olga's skin shine.

The little girl relaxes and leans against Serge's neck.

"Come and dance with us, Ollie," says Serge, and he and Alyx waltz with their arms round Olga.

"Oh look she's asleep," says Jerandine. "I'll put her to bed. Here!"

Serge is reluctant to let his little sister go.

"She'll be fine with me," reassures Jerandine, who, somehow, is now holding Olga's sleeping form in her arms. "She knows me well. And look! It's midnight."

"It's midnight! Midnight!" cry the other dancers and suddenly a crowd of them swirl around Alyx and Serge carrying them along. They dance together among the trees, brushing aside flowering branches, laughing as the petals rain down over them.

Alyx and Serge fall behind the others.

"You look like a beautiful bride," says Serge, brushing her hair out of her face. Startled she looks up into his eyes. The way he is looking at her makes her want to run away, and at the same time to be closer to him. A scary exciting feeling.

"Alyx," whispers Serge, as his hand slides over her cheek and he kisses her very gently on the lips.

Alyx leans her head on Serge's shoulder. Somehow they are getting closer and closer, hands touching, cheeks touching, lips kissing. She wants to be even closer to him. She puts her arms round him, feels his go round her waist. They lie down in the soft grass together. Her hands run down the muscular curve of his back.

Alyx lies watching Serge sleep, the slow rise and fall of his chest under the gossamer covering. His bare skin is pale except for where his arms are brown from the sun. The vulnerable sweetness of his eyelashes, long and dark on his flushed cheeks, delights her.

A small boy pushes aside the branches at the opening to the bower.

"Hello!" she says. "Do I know you?"

"Yes," says the little boy. "We're good friends. Let's

wake your lover."

He shakes Serge, who stretches and opens his eyes. The curve of Serge's stretching body fills Alyx with desire. She wishes the little boy wasn't there. Smiling sleepily, Serge puts his arm round her and draws her down to him.

"Stop that!" cries the little boy. "This is no time for lovemaking. I brought you a morning cup. It's the Tari custom. Take it! Drink! Then I can go away with a clear conscience."

Absent-mindedly Alyx takes a drink from the cup the little boy holds out. Surprised, she exclaims at the bitter taste of the drink.

"Yes but you will find it very invigorating. Here."

The boy offers it to Serge who takes a cautious mouthful. "Now how do you feel?"

... Alyx felt a lurch of nausea and a pain in her head, but before she could cry out, reality peeled open. Suddenly everything was sharp and clear and the breeze, which had seemed so gentle, was chill through the silken bed clothes. She remembered everything - the red fish, the blood beasts, the death angels and how much depended on her. She looked down. She was naked and so was Serge! Pressed together under the same coverlet.

"Sweet life! What have I done!" she cried, clutching the bed clothes round her.

Serge looked hurt and Alyx was instantly sorry.

"I..."

But Serge's face had hardened. He turned away and suddenly it was too difficult to say anything. He looked as embarrassed as she was.

How had this happened? She didn't even like Serge! He was a Mirayan and he didn't like her either.

"Enough of this!" said the boy brusquely. His name, she remembered, was Yundeman. "You've got lots of important things to do! Get dressed and let's get going!"

"The Red Fish!" cried Alyx. "Earth and air how long have we been here?"

"A month or so."

"Oh Mir!" cried Serge, looking as shocked as Alyx felt.

"Exactly!" said Yundeman. "I'm afraid Jerandine bespelled you so that you'd forget. Come on. We must get going before she wakes up and does it again."

Too embarrassed to look at Serge, Alyx scrambled into her clothes while Serge did the same at the other end of the bower. They were the clothes Alyx had been wearing when they came into Ermora, but they had been washed and now smelled pleasantly of lavender - the only pleasant thing about the situation.

"Come on," said Yundeman.

"Wait, where are you taking us? We have to get out of Ermora," cried Alyx.

"Yes, yes, that's what we're doing," said Yundeman irritably, as if he were talking to a difficult three year old. "Come on."

"We can't go yet. I need to find Olga first," said Serge.

"Fair enough," shrugged Yundeman. "Actually that'll be good. That'll show her who the real dreamer is!"

The grass still sparkled with dew. Yundeman avoided those few Tari who were awake this early by leading Alyx and Serge along tiny forest paths. Everywhere among the trees and bushes were little flower covered huts or bowers much like the ones they had woken up in. Woken up together in.

Alyx was very aware of Serge walking behind her, even though she couldn't bring herself to look at him. Certain things kept coming back to her with embarrassing clarity. How could she have done *that* with Serge? He was a Mirayan. Son of her father's killer. Her enemy.

She was so caught up in these thoughts, that she didn't even notice where they were going until they came to a pair of huge metal doors that stood among a grove of pines. They were unattached to any wall and hung slightly open, just open enough for a person to slip between them. With a blithe "Come on," Yundeman slid between the doors into the darkness beyond and Alyx and Serge followed to find themselves standing open-mouthed inside a huge room. Why hadn't they seen such a huge building through the pine trees beside the door?

Shelves of books and scrolls filled the walls of the room. Alyx had never seen so many works of writing in one place and even Serge looked impressed. But the writings were not well cared for. Dust lay thickly on the surfaces and cobwebs festooned the ceilings and hung in limp grey curtains from the softly glowing lamps that sat on a series of pillars along the centre of the room.

"Hey! Don't dawdle!" called Yundeman from the other end of the room as he disappeared through an opening. They followed him through another couple of rooms, each filled with monumental furniture and beautiful but tattered hangings. Then they passed through another door and found themselves in a pine forest again. Row upon row of pines stretched away like corridors, their branches meeting overhead to make a dark canopy above the bright green carpet of moss covering the ground below. A short way ahead Yundeman was just turning left between two tree trunks. As he did, they heard him say, "Look. This is the real melded child!"

Hurrying to join him, Alyx found herself in a far more traditional form of Tari dwelling, a bower made from tree branches. Yundeman was speaking to a woman who sat hunched on a stool in the centre of the bower. She was gripping a tattered book bound with wooden covers as if it were vital to her life. Sitting on a stool beside her, eating porridge from an earthenware bowl, was Olga.

"Serge!" she screamed, dropping the bowl, rushing at Serge and seizing him round the legs so tightly he almost fell over. And Serge being Serge, of course, laughed at this. He lifted Olga up and hugged her. How he adored his little sister. So kind-hearted he was. Alyx remembered him playing with the Red Seagani children.

He was still a Mirayan.

Yundeman had seized Alyx's arm and was shaking her.

"Look!" he cried to the old woman. "This is the one I see in my dreams. I tell you, this is the real melded child."

The woman gave him a disgusted look.

"Dreams!" she said nastily. "What are your dreams worth? You're making it all up."

Yundeman pulled Alyx toward the woman.

"Yours is completely wrong. She's not even a child of the Miracle sisters."

"You stupid little boy," snapped the woman. "For six years I have watched this child. A meld and in the time and place that the Master predicted before that useless Jindabyne destroyed his great mind. Of course this is the melded child. And I know because I have studied the Master's words long and hard. Not because of some wishy-washy dream."

She was no more than middle-aged, but she was still the oldest person Alyx had seen in Ermora. She had white streaks in her golden hair and lines around her eyes.

"I *am* a dreamer, Kintora," insisted Yundeman. "The life spirit speaks to..."

The woman interrupted him with a harsh shout of laughter.

"You a dreamer? Don't make me laugh. Why aren't you asleep in the spirit cave with the rest of them if you are a dreamer? You're just a jumped-up little snot-nose."

"I'm right!" shouted Yundeman, his face flushing with anger.

"Rubbish!" sneered the woman, with a contemptuous smile.

"I am, I am," shouted Yundeman, stamping his foot. "You stupid old woman."

"Rude little beast," snapped the woman, clapping her hands. With a rush of air, the bower seemed to fold in on itself. Before Alyx could even cry out, the woman, Olga and the bower were all gone and they were standing in an empty corridor of pine trees.

"Stupid old woman!" shouted Yundeman, shaking his fists at the air. "Why doesn't anyone ever listen to me?"

"Olga!" Serge was running along the corridor, peering between the trees. Seeing his distress, Alyx ran the other way, calling Olga's name.

"What are you doing?" cried Yundeman, irritably.

"Where's she taken Olga?" cried Serge.

"She's safe enough," said Yundeman.

"Tell me!" Serge seized Yundeman's shoulder and shook him. "How do we get her back?"

Yundeman gave Serge a look of mystified exasperation.

"Well you're not going to do it by running 'round shouting," he said tartly. "Kintora's taken her elsewhere. You'll need a strong mage to reach her now."

"But we have to... I'm not going without Olga."

"What?" cried Yundeman, looking even more exasperated. "What are you talking about? Why would you...?"

"Where can we get a strong mage?" insisted Serge.

"I guess Kulde's a strong mage if that's what you want. But why..."

"Then let's go to him now," said Serge.

With a groan, Yundeman turned on his heel and started stomping away through the trees.

"Come on then," he said. "That's where we were going anyway."

"She looked well, did you think?" said Serge to Alyx, as they followed Yundeman through the forest.

"Yes," said Alyx honestly. Then she caught Serge's eye and saw him blush and blushed herself and looked away.

Soon after, the forest opened out into a clearing. A long table stood in its centre, groaning with food as if for a feast. Huge cakes and pies were crammed against plates piled with little cakes and scones, candied fruits, fruit salads, trifles, stews, fritters, savoury breads, fruit breads, egg cakes, tarts and sweetmeats. A few of the dishes showed signs of being sampled, but mostly they were untouched. Near the other end of the table, a figure was bent over a large oven that stood alone on the grass. Smoke came out of the oven's chimney stack.

"Oh good! He's started," said Yundeman. "We can

have something fresh to eat.

Alyx, suddenly ravenous, reached out to take something from one of the plates. Yundeman slapped her hand away.

"Not here," he said. "Up at the other end. It's fresher there."

At the head of the table, a young man, the same one that they had met with Yundeman on that first day, was bent over a stove making pancakes. He was still wearing an apron.

"Pancakes! Great!" cried Yundeman, seizing one from the teetering pile at the end of the table

Kulde turned.

"Yundi, you stupid rabbit. Where have you been? I've been worried sick."

"So I see," said Yundeman. "He always cooks when he's upset," he said to Alyx and Serge. "What's fresh? We're all starving."

"Put on the kettle then. The apple pie and the egg-cakes were made yesterday, if you don't want pancakes." He looked shyly at Alyx and Serge. "So the potion worked. I'm so glad. Jerandine's a much more experienced mage than me."

"Kulde, we need some space!" interrupted Yundeman.

"Yes of course," flustered Kulde. He waved his hand in a kind of pushing gesture. All the plates slid a few inches down the table leaving a space and several plates of food fell off the other end.

"Oh dear, it's rather full, isn't it?"

Kulde gestured with his hands and several things, including an enormous decorated cake, simply disappeared.

"It's been full for weeks," explained Yundeman, setting cutlery on the table. "He's been upset ever since he saw that horrible thing at the gate. That Death Angel thingy."

"But now I've decided," said Kulde. "And I do feel much better. It's always easier if you follow the prompting of the life spirit. I'm a capable mage and you won't find anyone else prepared to go outside. So it must be me. I'm even beginning to look forward to it."

Yundeman had put a huge flat leaf on the table in front of each chair and now he sat down and began stacking hot pancakes on the leaves and slathering them with butter, lemon and honey which he had unearthed from among the pots on the table.

"Eat up! It's getting cold," he said, as he shovelled one into his mouth.

"Have you no manners, you horrible little beast?" snapped Kulde. He ushered Alyx and Serge towards chairs. "Please sit down. We'll have a bite to eat and then we must get going before Jerandine wakes up."

Alyx took a pancake off the top of the heap.

"Going?" asked Serge. "Going where? Back to that bower for Olga?"

"Outside of course!" said Kulde. "Who's Olga?"

"That's the melded child Kintora's got. The false one," explained Yundeman.

"Oh her. What about her?" asked Kulde.

"I'm not leaving here without Olga," said Serge firmly.

"What? We don't want to take a little child out among those awful flying creatures. Do we? Yundi?"

Yundi shrugged and kept shovelling pancakes into his mouth. He seemed to think sorting this out was Kulde's problem.

Kulde's brows creased.

"I don't think Kintora would give her up without a fight, and we really don't have time. If Jerandine gets her hands on you, she'll drug you again. She's determined to have you stay here."

"I don't know why you want to take her anyway," grunted Yundeman through a mouth full of pancakes. "She'll just be in the way."

"But I can't leave her." Serge's voice trailed off. "Can I?" he asked no one in particular.

Alyx could see his dilemma. Having found Olga, he wanted to keep his eye on her. But the world outside Ermora, with the blood beasts and the death angels, was no place for a little girl.

"She might be better off here, Serge," she said. "At least we know she's safe."

Serge put his face in his hands

"Oh Mir," he said softly. "I don't know."

Without thinking Alyx reached out and touched his hand. Then realising she was touching him, she jumped back in embarrassment.

Serge shot her a quick startled glance and shook his head as if chasing out a thought.

"Is this Kintora looking after Olga?" he asked the Tari.

"Oh yes," said Kulde, putting a fresh pancake on his leaf plate. "She believes her to be the melded child. The one who'll save Ermora from the Demon fire. She's a bit mad, but she's not a bad sort at heart. She often helped me with Yundi when he was younger."

"Of course she's wrong," said Yundeman thickly, through a mouth of pancake. He pointed at Alyx. "You're the melded child."

"Don't talk with your mouth full," said Kulde.

"What do you mean, melded child? What's this all about?" cried Alyx.

"Yundeman will tell you all about it. If he can stop feeding his face long enough."

Yundeman swallowed a lump of food so huge that he should have choked.

"And don't swallow without chewing," said Kulde.

Yundeman ignored his older brother. "It's to do with a prophecy," he explained.

"Prophecy!" cried Serge. "This Kintora grabbed Olga because of a prophecy? She must be mad! We have to get Olga away from her."

"Actually all Tari believe in prophecy," said Alyx. "Including me. And some Tari are quite good at telling the future. That's what Yundeman means when he says that he's a dreamer."

"And the melded child is one of the great prophecies," said Kulde. "Made at the birth of the three Miracle Sisters." He nodded at Alyx. "Your mother and aunts, Elena, Yanimena and Marigoth, I believe."

"This is how it goes," said Yundeman.

"Three children born of life force
A bridge from death to life,
from imbalance to harmony.
The warbird flies at their command,
to reign in the people of the dragon.
A demon fire that burns toward Ermora,
yields to their quenching.
A melded child of their making
is born to rule the dragon,
to bring harmony in clasped hands."

"Triplets are unheard of among the Tari," said Kulde. "The older folk regarded the Miracle Sisters as a Holy message from the life spirit."

"This is the first prophecy that mentions the demon fire which has dominated the visions of dreamers ever since," added Yundeman.

"No one ever told me about this," said Alyx. "Why not?"

"Knowing about prophecy can affect the way you live," said Kulde. "From what Kintora has said to me, her mentor Jagamar tried to bring the prophecy true with disastrous results."

"Really?" said Yundeman. "She never told me that."

"Well, why would she? You're still a child."

Yundeman threw a roll of fruit bread at Kulde, who laughed as he ducked it.

"So that's why you and Olga are considered important. There aren't many half-Tari children now that we no longer go into the outside world."

Such wild talk. Such actions. They seemed crazy even for eccentric Ermora Tari. And as for drugging them and keeping them prisoner and the business with killing Serge....

"What's happened to Ermora?" cried Alyx.

"Yes. That Kintora is the oldest person we've seen here. Where are all your old people?" asked Serge.

"I think Jerandine said something about the spirit cave closing," added Alyx, frowning in the effort to recall her muddled impressions of the past month. "There was some kind of crystal blocking the door."

Kulde and Yundeman looked at each other for a long moment.

"I'm not sure we should...," started Kulde. Suddenly he jumped up.

"It's Jerandine. Curse it! I got distracted. She's coming this way. Quick! Hide!"

Yundeman, Serge and Alyx leapt into the bushes surrounding the clearing and crouched under the branches.

"Shouldn't we run?" hissed Alyx.

"The aura from Kulde's magic will cover us better here."

Out in the clearing, Kulde was making the remnants of their meal melt into air. The he started making the other dishes disappear as well.

"Sweet life Kulde! What've you been doing?" snapped Jerandine, as she came charging into the clearing followed by several other Tari.

"I like cooking," said Kulde soulfully. Jerandine wasn't listening.

"Where's that brother of yours?" she demanded.

"Yundi? He was here just a moment ago. Have a pancake. They're still warm." He held out the heaped plate to them.

Jerandine's companions gathered round with exclamations of pleasure and started taking pancakes from the pile, but Jerandine was clearly made of sterner stuff.

"Stop that!" she snapped at her companions, who looked annoyed and kept on eating. "Did Yundi have anyone with him?"

"Those outlanders. Charming people. Have a cheese pie. I made them yesterday."

"No!" shouted Jerandine so loudly, that her companions stopped eating pancakes to look at her in reproachful surprise. "Where did they go?"

"Who?"

"Yundi and the foreigners."

"They went to see Kintora, I think. Are you sure you won't have a pie?"

"Come on, you lot!" cried Jerandine, charging away. The others followed more slowly, each taking a couple of cheese pies with them.

"Just like magical ones," said one of them, as he shoved a couple into his robe for later.

As soon as he was sure they were gone, Kulde beckoned to Yundeman and the others.

"Brilliant, Kulde! Kintora hates Jerandine. She'll keep her there for ages."

"Let's get going," said Kulde, pulling some packs out from beneath the table. To Serge and Alyx's delight, these were their original packs which seemed to have been restocked with supplies. Yundeman and Kulde had similar but slightly bigger packs.

As they shouldered them, Kulde gave everyone a small bundle to carry.

"We might as well take some of this food," he said. "Come on! This way!"

Chapter 21

They followed more narrow empty little paths and soon came to a circle of standing stones.

"Is this a circle of power?" asked Alyx, who had heard of this Tari method of travel from her aunts. "I thought they would all be closed."

"They were, but Kintora opened them up for her own purposes a few years ago. No one even noticed that she was using them."

"What *has* happened to the Tari?"

"This circle takes us to another at the bottom of the mountains," said Kulde, ignoring her question. "Much quicker and safer than walking down hill."

"You mean you're going to take us out of here instantaneously? Using magic?" asked Serge. He shrugged his shoulders. "I guess this means I'm going to leave Olga behind. I didn't even get a chance to say good-bye."

"I think it's the right decision," said Alyx softly.

He looked at her and looked away quickly, flushing.

"This is going to be fun!" cried Yundi, running to join Kulde in the centre of the circle.

"Stop!" cried Alyx. "Before we go charging off, we

should talk strategy. Do you have some kind of a plan? Some way of dealing with the death angels."

"Of course. I read all about death minions in Kintora's library and I know just how to deal with them."

"Don't you have to have a special knife or something?"

"No," laughed Kulde. "It's simple. So very simple."

"Yes, and so appropriate to Kulde," grinned Yundi. "Apparently you just overfeed them."

The two of them started to giggle.

"What?" snapped Alyx.

"Come on!" laughed Yundi, grabbing Alyx and Serge by the hand and towing them into the circle. "We'll show you when we get there."

"But..."

Kulde took a deep breath, spread out his arms and suddenly everything went black. Then the ground lurched. Serge and Alyx yelped and both lost their balance and fell over. Even as they hit the ground, the sun came out again.

"Can't you get out?" cried Alyx.

Her voice trailed away as she realised that light was different and so were the trees outside the circle. They had been on level ground, but now they were on a hillside. Somewhere else entirely.

"Wow! That was quick," cried Yundi.

"It wasn't hard at all," said Kulde. He shivered and flapped his arms. "Oooh I'm juddering all over as if I was a big elbow and someone had hit me. Hey, don't go running off, Yundi!"

"I'm just looking." Yundi had charged to the edge of the circle, but stopped suddenly before stepping out. "So this is the outside world. Not a very nice colour, is it? Oooh! It's so hot!"

The white morning sunlight had washed the colour out of the world. Dizzily, Alyx realised that it must be the middle of summer now. She realised something else too.

"Come on! We should get out of here. The death minions will have sensed the magic."

"Yes, come on," said Serge, pushing Kulde and Yundi before him into the nearby scrub, ignoring their loud complaints at its prickliness. Not a moment too soon. Dark shapes had appeared in the sky overhead, winging swiftly toward them.

Alyx and Serge kept dragging the now unresisting Tari through the prickly little trees.

"Where on earth are we?" Serge hissed. "We have to find somewhere..."

"I think I know... Yes!"

Suddenly the scrubby trees opened onto a large flat rock. Beyond was sky, below a cliff. "We're back at the source of the river," cried Alyx. "We can hide in the cave."

Something shrieked with laughter behind them and a dark shape covered the sun. Screaming, Kulde cowered backwards. Yundi went pale and dropped like a stone and suddenly Alyx really was dragging him. Serge darted forwards and scooped the boy up while Alyx grabbed Kulde, who was now staring white-faced at the sky and hustled him to the edge of the rock.

A stinking shadow fell over them and Kulde screamed again. Alyx jumped down onto the ledge below and took the unconscious Yundi from Serge. She shoved him in through the curtain of moss and turned back to help Serge with Kulde. As Serge lowered Kulde down onto the rock ledge, a death angel swooped them.

"Serge!" shrieked Alyx as Serge threw himself face down on the rock. The death angel's blue grey claws narrowly missed him and Alyx smelt the hot sulphur of its skin as it swished over her. As she dragged Kulde toward the cave mouth, Serge half jumped, half fell onto the ledge behind them. The death angel was zooming up into the sky above them but any moment now it was going to turn. And then...

They managed to get into the cave under the waterfall before the angel turned. Except that there wasn't a waterfall any more. Now it was high summer, the stream had slowed to a trickle of water dribbling down through the curtain of dried out moss.

While Serge settled Yundi gently at the back of the cave, Kulde huddled against the wall, his face pressed against his knees, sobbing hysterically.

The sight turned Alyx cold with embarrassment.

"Shut up!" she hissed kneeling down beside Kulde and shaking him. "It'll hear us."

"Oh life," moaned Kulde, burying his face in Alyx's shoulder. "It was so horrible! So horrible! Like a gash in the world! Oh life! Oh life!"

"Stop being such a baby," shouted Alyx. She pushed Kulde away and slapped him on the face, as she'd seen her mentor once do with a hysterical young man whose wife had just died in childbirth. Kulde was so shocked that he did stop sobbing, though tears kept running down his face.

"Oh life," he moaned. "I'm sorry. I'm so sorry."

Alyx felt Serge pushing her aside. He put his hand on Kulde's shoulder.

"Kulde, we need you to stop this. That thing hasn't got very good senses, but it can hear well enough to hear you crying like this."

"Yes, yes," whispered Kulde. I'm sorry. I'm sorry. It was just so horrible."

"Yes I know," said Serge, squeezing Kulde's shoulder. "But you cannot give in to it. You are stronger than this." He jerked his head at Alyx, obviously meaning for her to leave them alone.

Alyx crept over to Yundi's side. His skin was pale and covered in sweat and he was moaning and moving his head from side to side. His eyelids were fluttering as if he was trying to wake up, but couldn't. At least his moans were soft.

The death angel might not be able to see or hear very well, but it wouldn't be hard for it to find the cave. Alyx burrowed round in her pack and was relieved to find the sword that the Red Seagani had given her.

Kulde had crept to Yundi's side.

"Earth and air!" he whispered. "He's having one of his dreams. Life only knows what he is dreaming about. Oh Yundi, Yundi. Why did I bring you out here?"

Something laughed raucously nearby and another laugh answered.

Kulde gasped.

"It's them."

"Yes!" whispered Serge. "They're looking for us now and, I can't lie Kulde, they'll probably find us. Last time Alyx and I hid here, there was a waterfall over the front of this cave and that discouraged them from coming in. But this time, if they find the opening..."

Serge shook his head.

"You said you knew how to deal with these creatures," hissed Alyx. "This is no time to be weeping and moaning and letting us down."

Serge shot her a warning look.

"I know," murmured Kulde. "I'm a coward. I do know what to do. It's just..." He gasped again as another shriek of laughter rang out just outside the cave. "They're so horrible. I didn't realise how awful they would feel." He fell silent for a moment. "I can feel them walking about up there. Each footstep is like being touched by something...loathsome."

"Then tell us how to deal with them and we'll do it," hissed Alyx.

"No. It has to be me." Kulde took a long shuddering breath. "Sweet life. It seemed so easy back in Ermora."

Alyx drew her breath to retort, but before she could say anything, Serge had clapped his hand over her mouth.

"I have faith in you, Kulde," he said calmly. "I know you will do your best to protect Yundi from them."

Kulde put his hand on his little brother's forehead and sat there silently, shivering, tears dripping down his face.

Fury and disgust filled Alyx. She wanted to shout at Kulde, but Serge's hand was still over her mouth. For what seemed like millennia, they listened as the insane laughter of the angels continued and the rock above shuddered under their footfalls.

Then came the noise they had all been dreading - harsh laughter just outside the mouth of the cave. Kulde hardly reacted to the sound, but Alyx drew her sword and Serge pulled out what looked like a food knife.

"Kulde! Do they have some weakness we can use

against them? Please Kulde!" whispered Serge.

Kulde drew a shuddering breath.

"No," he said. "It's up to me to stop them. I can't let Yundi down now. I must do this. For the sake of the life spirit," he added more to himself than the others.

He wiped the tears from his cheeks and stood up.

At that moment something hissed outside and a blue grey hand came sliding round the side of the cave. Kulde clung to the wall of the cave as he watched it.

"Oh life! Help me!" he whispered softly. "I'm so scared. I don't want to do this."

"I know," said Serge, standing up beside him and squeezing his shoulder. "But you have to. It's only fear. Once you face it, it'll go away."

Kulde took another deep breath, and at that moment the death angel slid past the fall of moss and into the cave. Its needle filled mouth yawned wide, almost splitting its head in half and its blue-grey tongue snaked out, tasting the air.

Serge and Alyx help up their weapons ready to strike. Kulde didn't move at all. Instead he began to mutter something under his breath. Then with astonishing calmness, he stepped forward and held out his hand. The angel lunged forward and seized him by the wrist. Kulde gasped but kept moving forwards, his other hand outstretched as if in greeting. The sulphurous scent of the creature and the black miasma of dread that seemed to surround it, filled the cave and Yundi cried out in his delirium. Kulde kept moving forward until his other trembling hand touched the angel and then he flung his arms around it.

Alyx was not sure what happened next. For a moment they embraced as fiercely as wrestlers. But even as Alyx and Serge jumped forward to separate them, the angel let out a howl of what sounded like pain and with a puff of smoke and the sound of dust falling on stone, it disappeared. With a gasp Kulde fell to his knees and began to vomit.

"Sweet life! What happened?" cried Alyx.

Even as she spoke another shout of laughter rang out

and the second angel crashed through the curtain of moss.

Still retching, Kulde staggered to his feet and threw himself at it, open armed. It hissed with satisfaction as it embraced him, but within a moment it, too, had howled and turned to dust. Covered in the dust, Kulde sank to the ground again and lay there shuddering and gagging.

"That was great!" cried Serge, clapping Kulde on the back.

"Well done!" said Alyx, who appreciated how hard it must have been for him to embrace those horrible creatures.

"Oh life, I shall never be clean again," choked Kulde.

They had only seen two death angels and there must only have been two, because no more laughter came echoing into the cave.

Serge helped Kulde up and laid him down beside his brother, while Alyx took cloths from their packs. Together she and Serge washed as much of the vomit and the dust of the death angels off him as they could.

"We should move," said Alyx. "There is a tree house half a day's walk from here."

But though Kulde tried to get up, his legs gave way under him.

"We can stay here tonight," said Serge. "We're up off the ground. Safe from blood beasts."

"And I guess we are safer from death angels in here than we are out there," agreed Alyx. "Do they communicate with each other?

"Death creatures never co-operate well. I don't think the others will know what happened to their fellows. What did you do to them, Kulde?"

"I channelled the life spirit into them," he croaked. "They are creatures of death and too much life spirit at any one time destroys their nature."

"Overfeeding them," said Serge softly. "Of course! That's so clever."

Kulde smiled weakly. "It would be if overcoming them hadn't exhausted me so much. Tari and Death Angels are almost equally conduits of life and death. We must hope no more come before I recover."

"Is this something I can do?" asked Alyx. "I'm half-Tari."

"You have to be a mage," whispered Kulde.

His teeth started to chatter and Serge got a blanket out of their pack and covered him up. He was frighteningly white, but he kept muttering that all he needed was rest. He curled up against Yundeman and went to sleep.

"This cave stinks," said Serge. Together, using water and a broken branch, he and Alyx cleaned the vomit and sulphurous dust of the angels out of the cave. Alyx was astonished to realise that it was not yet noon. She peered into the pool beneath. It had shrunk with the summer but it still seethed with red fish. Yet the miasma of dread that surrounded the death angels, which had made her feel that all life was doomed, lifted.

But there was still a black feeling in her chest.

This morning she had woken up naked in the arms of her enemy. Of a Mirayan. What would Didier have said? And her mother? She kept remembering the pleasure of Serge's touch. She still wanted him to touch her. The thought made her furious. By the Abyss! He was the son of her father's murderer. A Mirayan. She should be ashamed.

"Alyx," said Serge tentatively.

This damned Mirayan! Couldn't he just leave her alone?

"I'll better take a look at what the Tari have put in the packs. Kulde and Yundi's seem very heavy." She hurried over to the packs and started pulling them apart.

Serge came over and crouched down beside her.

"Alyx. About this morning...?"

"I don't want to talk about it. We... It's just too embarrassing. Sweet life! They put a butter crock in here. A butter crock of all things."

"But..."

Alyx stopped pulling at the packs.

"We were drugged," she said firmly. "I didn't know what I was doing. Best to forget the whole thing."

"Yes. Of course," said Serge hollowly, after a moment of silence.

"Yes," said Alyx firmly.

"Right," said Serge. He moved away and sat down on the opposite side of the cave, looking out through the opening. Alyx busied herself with the packs. Her face felt tight and her eyes prickled as if she wanted to cry.

Chapter 22

Jindabyne forced herself to accept that getting free of this trap was more important than any feelings she might have about Elena.

Every day the two women discussed escape, but to no avail. Nor could they find out what Lev was up to. From the dusty state of the men in the enclosures, Jindabyne was certain that they must be mining for something. But what? And how had so many men got here in the face of the Mori patrols in the forest?

"If you are hardy you can get into these ravines from the Seagani lands on the other side of the Gen Mountains," explained Elena. "Seagani prospectors have always used those routes looking for valuable metals. In the old days we kept an eye on them, but since the Red Fish came in early spring...."

She touched the stone wall. "With the magic he has at his command, Lev could easily have thrown this place together in the months since our attentions were turned away. Now he acts with impunity and no one realises that he must be stopped. Clever, clever man. I am working to find out his secrets."

Lev continued to maintain a level of control in the face of Elena's gift. He could not be brought to the stage of confiding in her.

"He doesn't believe it appropriate to discuss business with women," Elena said. "He reads me love poetry. As if locking me in this tower has anything to do with love." She pulled a face. "At least he doesn't write it."

"Wolf asked my advice often," said Jindabyne. Immediately she was embarrassed by how self-righteous she sounded. But Elena simply said, "I'm sure he did. He loved you Jindabyne and relied on you."

The way she said it and sighed afterwards assuaged Jindabyne's jealousy. But was Elena simply manipulating her as she was trying to manipulate Lev? She was like a closed window with black shutters.

Lev was seldom there during the day, but that gave them little advantage. Jindabyne's witch manacle was warded against lock picking and so were the locks and bolts on their rooms. The sewing needles were made of bone and they were not given scissors so they could not work away at the bars on the windows. Anyway the windows were too small to climb through and the tower walls were sheer below it.

Jindabyne searched the room she slept in for a tool that might have been forgotten by the workmen, but could find nothing. Guards always escorted her to and from her room. Lev always let her into Elena's room himself. He was extremely careful that no one else should set eyes on Elena and neither she nor Jindabyne could work out a way to undermine this caution.

There was only one sign of hope and that was a small one. Neevus with the tufty hair started to come into Jindabyne's room at night. At first she was afraid he wanted sexual favours, but he always brought the little girl with him. He would sit upon a stool which the little girl carried in for him and ask Jindabyne about herself and about the Tari, but it soon became clear that he was really interested in Elena. Hoping to sew trouble for Lev,

Jindabyne told him all about her and how beautiful she was. She warned Elena that she had an admirer elsewhere in the tower.

"Such powers you have. He hasn't even seen you."

"Are you sure he's not interested in you?" asked Elena.

"No, he always brings his little daughter with him."

"Daughter? The fellow has a daughter? Here?"

But when Jindabyne described the little girl to her, Elena looked wise and said, "That sounds more like a plaything than a daughter." She caught Jindabyne's questioning look. "Bed-mate, you innocent!"

Jindabyne was sickened.

"But she's only nine at the most! Surely that's too young."

"Not for some," said Elena grimly. "Lev says that when you dabble in death magic, you must sup with scum. But if this Neevus likes little girls, I wonder why he's interested in me."

She was deep in thought for the rest of the day. Just before Jindabyne left she said "You must tell this Neevus about my gift. About how dangerous I am to Lev and how much power I'm gaining over him. That is the way to go. Perhaps we can persuade him to help us escape."

Jindabyne did as she was told, though it occurred to her that this was a dangerous game that Elena was playing. The Mirayan women's quarters, where she had spent the last six years, had been full of stories of those who assassinated other women to gain power over their lords. What if Neevus decided to have Elena assassinated?

Elena did not think this was a problem. "This room is covered with magical protections," she said the following day. "No man can get in here without an alarm warning Lev. And you and I are the only women in this compound. Except for Nevus's little slave." Her face hardened. "I asked Lev if we could have that little girl up here to keep us company. I told him I missed my daughter. And he said that she was a whore and not fit company for me. As if it was her fault that Neevus uses her ill. I was so angry I almost smothered him with the pillow."

Life in the keep was like life in the women's quarters at Lamartaine, only even more boring. They wove and sewed and when Jindabyne's jealousy of Elena was weak enough for them to be on easy terms, they taught each other songs. Several times a day they walked up and down the room so that they would not lose their strength. The windows of the tower looked out over the keep wall and the sight and smell of the distant forest was both a joy and a torment to both of them. Jindabyne tried calling birds to the window, but the death angels that flew in and out of the tower above scared them away.

One afternoon as they were each standing at one of the small barred windows, enjoying the scent of the forest after a recent shower of rain, Elena cried, "Someone's coming."

Jindabyne opened her eyes to see a lone rider heading towards the keep wall.

"Is that a woman?" asked Jindabyne as the figure got closer.

"Maybe..."

Before they could be certain, the figure was obscured from view.

The forest, full of death angels and blood beasts, was no place for a lone rider and a woman travelling alone in these unsettled times would draw all kinds of unwelcome attention. She must be some kind of mage. As if to confirm this, after they heard the small door within the fortress gate open, there came several blasts of magic and some kind of clamour. The clamour died down quickly and all was quiet again. Though they took it in turns to watch at the window for the rest of the day, there was nothing more to learn.

That night Elena was able to discover that another mage, an ally, a woman, had come from Miraya. She was a specialist in the creation of beasts and Lev had set her to nurturing his death angels. He seemed pleased.

"Another death mage to contend with!" sighed Elena the next day, as the two of them returned to their cloth work.

The day was humid. Elena set her spinning wheel near

the window to catch what breeze there was. Outside the sentries paced the walls, but after midday they simply stayed out of the sun in their guard towers. The distant hum of cicadas rose from the trees beyond the wall, but it was quiet inside the fortress.

Suddenly Elena gave a little gasp and the spinning wheel stopped with a clatter.

"Outside the window!" she whispered. "I saw something!"

The scrabbling sound of claws came from the stone outside the window.

"Don't scare it," cried Jindabyne, running to the window, making the soft cooing sounds you used to call a pigeon.

The face appeared in the window so suddenly that both of the women jumped back in shock. A woman's face with Mirayan features and a spiky halo of coal black hair, hung down over the window slit. Dark eyes glared at them - hot, avid, predatory.

"Tari! Yes!" hissed the face. "Come here!"

Jindabyne and Elena clutched each other. Those hungry eyes! The thing at the window wanted to eat them!

"Who are you? What do you want?" shouted Elena.

"Go away!" cried Jindabyne.

The dark red mouth at the window snarled, "I want it! I need it!" and a hand clawed in through the window slit.

A sudden flash of blue light blinded them and the high pitched shriek of magical wardings screamed out. Elena and Jindabyne cowered back against the other wall of the chamber, hands over their ears. A moment later, the door burst open and Lev shot into the room like an angry hawk. He hovered in the air, glaring round the room. A gesture of his hand stopped the shrieking and made the blue light disappear.

"What happened?" he demanded, landing neatly on the floor before them. "Did someone try to get in here?"

Elena squeezed Jindabyne's hand.

"It was a bird," she cried. "A messenger bird. It must be from my daughter." She threw herself at Lev's chest.

"Find it for me Lev. Please!"

Jindabyne crouched by the wall, judging it best not to speak till she knew what Elena was up to. When Lev turned and asked her brusquely if Elena spoke truth, she agreed.

"Lev please!" pleaded Elena. "Find it for me. I need to know about Alyx." She was still pawing at Lev.

"Be quiet," he ordered and he put his hand on her mouth and suddenly she was still and silent.

"Here!" he snapped, pushing Elena back into Jindabyne's arms.

She was a dead weight, her body limp, her eyes open and frightened. Jindabyne clasped her against her shoulder.

"What have you done?"

"Shut up!"

Lev put his hand against the wall and said something. Shining blue writing appeared all over the walls. He walked along the wall of the chamber, his hand on the blue writing, until he got to the window where they had seen the face. Jindabyne turned her face away. Would the blue writing betray them?

She heard Lev suck in his breath.

"These messenger birds are magical?" he asked.

"Yes," said Jindabyne, not daring to look at him. "I have seen the Mori use them."

Lev clicked his fingers and the spell that held Elena quiet broke. She pushed Jindabyne away.

"You pig!" she screamed, throwing herself at Lev. "Why didn't you go after it? Now I'll never know."

She lifted her hand and slapped Lev ringingly on the face, leaving Lev was so astonished that he didn't even cry out. Elena rushed to the window and reached her hand out of it, calling out something in Mori. Her anguish at losing this non-existent bird was so real that Jindabyne almost believed in it herself.

Lev seized Elena by the arm and hauled her away from the window, shaking her roughly.

"Who do you think you are, striking me like that?"

"Leave her alone," cried Jindabyne, before she remembered that she was supposed to hate Elena.

"Why didn't you go after it?" shouted Elena at Lev. Tears were streaming down her face. "Why, when I asked you? How could you hurt me so?" She beat at Lev's chest with ineffectual girlish fists.

Lev seized Elena, twisted her arms behind her back and bent her over.

"Who is master here?"

"I wanted it," sobbed Elena. "There might have been news from Alyx."

"Who is your master?" thundered Lev, and he kept on asking until at last she seemed to break.

"You are," she whispered weakly. "Oh Lev, my lord, my love. I'm so sorry. I was wrong to strike you. I just wanted that bird so much."

"Get out!" snapped Lev at Jindabyne, who went quickly into the outer chamber, closing the door behind her. She went straight to the door that lead to the corridor and tried it, but it was locked.

All this fuss over a messenger bird, she thought as she sat down at Lev's desk to wait.

Then she stopped.

What bird?

They had seen a face at that window. That Woman's power over people's minds was amazing.

"I'm not sure he believed me," said Elena, later that day when Lev had gone and Jindabyne was let in again.

"Why did you tell him such a lie?"

"If he finds out I was lying, I'll say I was mistaken. But perhaps we have glimpsed an ally through the window. Perhaps we can turn her against him."

"A death mage! She'll just harm us even more."

Elena shrugged. "Any opportunity should be explored. I wonder why she was so interested in us. She was a Mirayan and yet she recognised us for Tari. Don't you think that's interesting?"

Lev was late to return that night. By the time Jindabyne was taken back to her room, it was completely dark.

Despite this she was not given a light, so she shuffled carefully across to her pallet, with only the pale light of the distant flares to guide her. Half way across the room she thought she heard a movement. Here in the dark room with her. She froze, listening.

"Hello," she called out. The silence did not answer and yet her scalp prickled with the conviction that she was not alone. Was that breathing? Outside she could hear the sounds of the compound, but in here, the room was still. Her eyes became accustomed to the dark, but the room remained full of shadows. At length she decided that she must be alone.

She shuffled to her pallet and sat down, feeling the comforting stone wall at her back. She groped in the darkness for the blanket and pulled it around her, more for comfort than warmth, telling herself that everything would look better in the light.

Suddenly someone grabbed her. A hand crammed over her mouth. She struggled, tried to scream. A woman's voice said "Shut up, meat," and Jindabyne's head filled with blue light and terrible pain.

The next thing she knew she was lying face down on her pallet, a sour tasting piece of cloth in her mouth, hands tied behind her back. She didn't remember getting here. She must have fainted or been asleep. She could see nothing in the darkness.

She jumped with shock as a hand stroked her hair.

"That's right," cooed a woman's voice in her ear. "Come back to me." A Mirayan voice. Jindabyne was certain she didn't know it. She tried to move away from the touch.

"Good, good," cooed the voice. "Now hold still, meat."

Hands gripped Jindabyne's skull, there was a pressure and sharp pain as if the fingers had plunged through the bone into her brain and Jindabyne's mind was suddenly full of someone else. She struggled to push the intruder out, struggled to pull away, but there was no way to do it. Somewhere a child's screaming echoed inside her skull. What was happening?

"Show me the good place," hissed the voice. "Show me it. I need it."

The pressure inside Jindabyne's skull became stronger. Spots of white colour danced inside her eyelids.

"Show it to me meat," crooned the voice. "Show me."

Stop, stop! My head is going to explode! Oh life! thought Jindabyne.

The pressure was released and a stinging blow hit her face.

"How can you hide it from me, bitch?" hissed the voice.

Jindabyne could see a dark shape crouched over her, feel the weight of it on her chest. Slap slap, came the hand on Jindabyne's face. She tried to answer but her mouth was full of cloth.

The slapping stopped and there was a sharp intake of breath.

"You've been mindblasted, haven't you?" accused the voice. "Answer me. That's why your good place is so pale."

Unable to speak because of the cloth, Jindabyne nodded. She wasn't sure what the voice meant about a good place, but she had been mindblasted. The voice must have been able to see her in the dark for it said, "You're damaged goods then. Leavings. Tell me - has the beauty upstairs been mindblasted too?" Fingers squeezed Jindabyne's face.

Jindabyne shook her head.

"Good!" said the voice. "I should kill you, useless meat, but I won't. There is some relief to be had from you."

A hand covered her face like a spider and Jindabyne felt the sharp pain of another consciousness pushing through her skull again.

Jindabyne woke to find sunlight in her eyes and the guard standing in the doorway, calling her.

"Get up," he cried. "The Lord is calling for you. Why are you still sleeping?"

Jindabyne looked around. She was not bound or

gagged and the room was empty except for the guard who was now coming over to the pallet. Yet she felt so unclean, so used.

Lev appeared in the doorway. "What's the matter? Are you sick?"

"N-no," said Jindabyne. The terrible nightmare had been so horribly real. She felt her sore cheeks wonderingly.

"Then hurry up, you lazy cow. I've got work to do."

Without giving her time to wash her face or do up her dress properly, he hustled her up into Elena's room and slammed the door behind her.

Elena noticed Jindabyne's distress immediately and gently took her arm and sat her down on the bed.

"What's happened?"

"I don't know," said Jindabyne. "There was someone... Someone in my room last night..."

As she recounted what had happened, Jindabyne found herself weeping. The memory of it... she felt so violated. Elena wiped away Jindabyne's tears and bathed her face with soothing youngflower water. But eventually, when Jindabyne's weeping had ceased, she said, "Now we know that there are no wardings on your room."

"What do you mean?"

"The person in your room last night must have been this new death mage, this Daria Symina. There's no other grown woman here. Who else has that kind of power?"

"Did you expect this?" cried Jindabyne, her anguish turning to anger.

"No!" cried Elena, so intensely that Jindabyne believed her.

"I thought she might try to make contact with you, but I promise I didn't expect her to hurt you."

"She's a death mage. Of course she hurt me," snapped Jindabyne.

"How was I to know that? I had hoped she might have been an ally!" Elena sighed and pressed her hands to her eyes. "Listen! You must find out what she wants. Perhaps you can barter it for freedom."

"I know what she wants. She wants to mindsearch me.

And you, if she can. Why should she barter anything? She can just take it. I'll tell Lev. He'll..."

She wasn't sure what Lev would do.

"Don't tell Lev. You know he won't do anything good."

"You could speak for me," said Jindabyne desperately. "What if she's there again tonight? I... I can't do it again."

Elena lifted Jindabyne's face and looked deep into Jindabyne's eyes. Jindabyne had the chance to make a powerful ally, she told her. Daria wanted something from her. That put Jindabyne in a position of power.

At first Jindabyne pushed Elena away, turning from those beautiful powerful eyes, but she was already beginning to see the sense of Elena's plan.

"She was so rough," she protested weakly. "Mindsearches can damage the mind."

"Perhaps she was rough because you resisted," counselled Elena. "Sometimes it helps if you just give way. If she comes to you tonight, talk to her gently. Be willing and giving. That's the way to find out what she is and what she wants. Be brave. With luck and good management we may be able to use this creature to get freedom, for you at least! Then you can warn somebody."

At least this day Lev came back earlier and Jindabyne was sent back to her room while it was still light and was able to check that she was alone in the room. As darkness fell, the sickly courage she had felt when talking to Elena, deserted her. As darkness fell, she lay down on her pallet with the blanket over her and tried to be invisible.

When Daria came, she made no more than the faintest scrabbling sound, a sound like leaves blow in the wind.

"Jindabyne! Jindabyne!" wheedled the voice, as if it were calling a cat. "Where are you my little slave? My little food."

Jindabyne clutched the blanket round her. Her spine turned to ice.

"Jindabyne!" hissed the voice, close at first, then away on the other side of the room.

She was playing with her, Jindabyne realised with a sudden rush of anger. This creature was a mage. She could find her any time she wanted. She sat up.

"Who are you? What do you want?"

The voice gave a high tinkly laugh. "Oh so brave!"

"Show me who you are. At least show me your face."

A light flared in the darkness. The pale white face of a ghost hovered over Jindabyne. Eyes shone like black wells and a halo of spiky black hair flared out from the head. The only colour was the mouth, the full red lips.

"Tari!" hissed the woman hungrily, clawing out a hand. The light went out as she leant forward to seize Jindabyne by the throat.

This time Jindabyne did not lose consciousness. She lay still and felt it all, the pressure, the pain, the lost child wailing in an empty room.

I must get up and see to it, she kept thinking. She had a nightmare vision of herself running through dark rooms, unable to find the child, afraid it was Olga. When the screaming stopped, she became aware of her body again and felt a head lying at her breast as Wolf had sometimes lain. Greasy smelling hair pressed against her face.

The stranger was weeping.

"Oh Ermora, why did you leave me?" she whispered, in a voice that ached with longing. "There's no satisfaction without you."

"Hush! Hush!" said Jindabyne automatically, still half-dazed. The person on her chest froze, then pushed away from her roughly.

"You're not Ermora."

Jindabyne was confused.

"How can I be Ermora? Ermora's a place."

A slap hit Jindabyne's face.

"Ermora is my beloved," hissed the woman. "Do not say her name, you pathetic slave."

Jindabyne lay still and silent, completely woken by the blow and wondering what it was that this woman looking for.

"Tell me of this Ermora," she asked carefully. "Perhaps I can help you find it."

"You?" said the voice contemptuously. "Ermora is only a shadow in you. I want the other one. How do I reach her? Tell me."

"She is Lord Lev's treasure," said Jindabyne. "You will never reach her. But I can take you to Ermora. I know where it is."

"So do I," sobbed the voice woefully. "There are many Tari here. But they're all underground and Malov won't let me at them."

She is quite mad, thought Jindabyne

"The other Tari? Aren't they in the bottom of this tower any more?"

"They're in a hole in the ground," said Daria. "He will not let me go there. Ermora. I want it! I need it!"

"I can show you Ermora," said Jindabyne. She had a very brief memory of the place. "But it's elsewhere."

The voice was not listening. Hands gripped Jindabyne round the throat and head.

"I want it! I need it!" hissed the voice, as a bony body climbed on top of her.

Daria was relentless. Over the next few days she came every night to Jindabyne's room, shoving her mind into Jindabyne's several times a night. She was a creature of erratic mood swings, purring, weeping and sobbing unpredictably. Occasionally she was pleased with Jindabyne, but mostly she was contemptuous. She wanted Ermora and Jindabyne was not it.

How could Daria have got a taste for mindsearching Tari? Neither Jindabyne nor Elena had ever heard of such a taste before.

"If you could only persuade her that she could have all the Tari minds she wanted if she took you to Ermora," said Elena. "A powerful mage like her would easily be able to get you out of this fortress."

Jindabyne wished Elena would be quiet and let her catch up on some sleep, which was all she did all day now.

"I *have* told her I can show her the way to Ermora, but she doesn't listen. She's convinced that it is a person, not a place."

"Then you must keep telling her," snapped Elena. She had already primed Jindabyne and drawn her a map on a piece of cloth using blood from her own finger so that when Daria finally decided she wanted to see Ermora, Jindabyne could lead her there.

"Last night she told me that Ermora was closed to all outsiders, that she could see this in my mind. I can keep nothing secret from her. I can't fool her into helping me escape from here with false promises."

"From what my sister's friends told me, the Tari forbid outsiders to enter, but Ermora is not the Tari. It's a concentration of the life force. You should be able to enter just by being one of our race. And you should be able to take Daria with you. And surely the advent of such a creature as Daria in Ermora will wake the Tari out of their apathy. Have you asked her what Lev is up to here?"

"She doesn't answer in any way that makes sense. She says he's wounding the earth. Why don't you ask Lev again? You're supposed to have so much power over him."

"I do ask him," said Elena coldly. "I ask him every day." She stared out at the forest beyond the window. "All I know is that he is digging for something. Have you ever thought - the Gen Mountains - if you dug to the centre of them you would be directly under Ermora. Perhaps there is something there... The Tari must be warned!"

"Daria wants to see you," said Jindabyne. She could not keep a waspish note out of her voice. "She won't leave without it."

Elena's delicate skin flushed. Suddenly she picked up a cup and smashed it on the ground.

"Damn!" she screamed. She flung herself round the room shouting curses, upending the sewing table, the wash basin, the wooden box full of trinkets, throwing pillows and quilts from the bed, pounding clenched fists on the wall. At last she was quiet, leaning her forehead against the wall, panting.

Jindabyne stood frozen to the spot. She willed herself to say something, anything, but Elena spoke before she could find the words.

"Well then," she said in a coldly determined voice, "let us see how we can accommodate her. You will tell this Daria that I am curious to meet her. Bored, lonely and in need of new company. And tell her that the room is not warded against women. Only men and magic."

Jindabyne passed this information on to Daria, but the response was so muddled that she had no idea if it struck home. Yet the very next morning, Jindabyne had barely laid her head down to rest on Elena's pillow, when Elena was at the bedside again.

"Get up! He's come back," she hissed. Even as she spoke Jindabyne heard the door being unbolted. She sprang off the bed to stand obediently upright by the loom.

The door swung open, but it wasn't Lev who stood at the door brandishing a key.

"No wardings against women!" cried Daria triumphantly. Then her eye fell on Elena and her face changed.

"You're not Ermora," she said softly.

"How did you get a key?" cried Elena. Jindabyne felt a certain mean satisfaction at her astonishment. But as Daria moved toward Elena and her intent became clear, Jindabyne found herself moving to shield her companion.

"Don't," she cried but Daria grabbed her by the hair and thrust her out into the outer room. The door slammed shut behind her and there was the sound of a piece of furniture being dragged over it.

The door was very thick and Jindabyne could hear nothing through it, so she sat at the table waiting, wondering where Daria had got a key from until she fell asleep with her head pillowed on the table.

"Go now. You must go!" said a voice. "He'll be back soon."

Jindabyne woke up to see Elena pushing Daria out of

the room. Daria was smiling a dreamy satiated smile, but her face changed when she saw Jindabyne.

"Get in there," she ordered and she waited until Elena and Jindabyne were safely bolted into the inner room, before she unlocked the outer door. The moment the door was bolted behind them, Elena went over to the wash basin and began to wash herself all over.

"Are you harmed?" asked Jindabyne.

Elena began to sob.

Jindabyne went over and touched her arm.

"I didn't think it was possible to feel more violated than I already do," Elena choked between harsh shuddering sobs. "But this Mirayan witch... It was almost worse than Alexus Scarvan." She turned her tear-soaked face to Jindabyne.

"I'm sorry," she whispered. "I didn't realise what it was like for you. I didn't... I would never have urged you on had I known."

"We must tell Lev."

Elena took a deep breath, making a visible effort to still her sobs.

"No!" she choked.

"We must. This is no good."

"No!" said Elena, more calmly now. She returned to washing herself, going over and over her skin as if she wanted to wash it all away. "There's hope here. She has a key. She may be willing to take us away from here."

She let out one more sob and then she straightened herself up.

"Get me a clean dress," she said.

"Elena, I really don't think this is..."

"Yes! It will work. Trust me. Do not tell Lev."

Jindabyne got a clean dress out of the linen chest and helped Elena into it. Shortly after Lev was at the door and Jindabyne went away saying nothing. But she was mistaken when she thought she was going to have a peaceful night after this.

She was woken sometime after midnight by a whispering voice saying, "I want it. I need it," and the sensation of something hard and sharp being pushed through her skull. Afterwards the pounding in her head left her wide awake.

"We must run away from here," she whispered to Daria who lay dozing beside her. "You can't keep this up. Lev will find out and he will not tolerate you using Elena so."

"How will he find out?"

"We might tell him."

"You won't. You hope I'll free you. I've seen it in both your minds."

Jindabyne waited to hear if she would free them or not, but Daria only laughed and rolled over.

"Lev will notice his key missing."

"Do you think I'm a fool?" said Daria. "I haven't taken his key. Neevus made a copy for me."

"Neevus made a key? Why?"

"Shut up!" said Daria and would say no more.

The next morning when Daria came to Elena's room, Jindabyne went immediately into the other room, deciding that Elena could deal with the situation. When the door closed, she put her head on Lev's table and went straight to sleep.

The sound of a door opening woke her up, but it was not the door to the inner chamber that opened, but the outer door.

"What are you doing here?" Lev snarled, his face red with fury. Without waiting for an answer, he stalked over to the other door. There was a spark of magic and the sound of furniture sliding away in the room behind and the door flew open.

Following hard at his heels, Jindabyne saw that the room beyond was dark. Elena must have drawn the curtains. At first she couldn't see anyone in the dim light, then she saw movement on the bed. Two figures lying entwined.

"Lev!" cried someone and sat up. "Oh Lev, help me!"

Then there were two women sitting up on the bed.

"You!" shouted Lev. "How dare you!"

Screaming like an animal, Daria leapt up and threw a ball of blue fire at Lev. Jindabyne ducked out of the doorway to avoid being hit. Lev stood firm, hardly blinking as the blue fire hit him, streamed around him and disappeared. Then he lunged into the room, throwing his own magical blow.

Furniture and pottery smashed and the rooms shook under the exchange of magic. Jindabyne peered carefully in at the doorway. The flare of magical light showed Elena huddled on the bed, while Lev, who seemed to be winning, moved closer and closer to where Daria, a dark shadow, crouched, snarling, against the furthest wall. Suddenly she let out a shriek of fury, leapt up and threw herself at the window slit. As she hit it, her body shrunk. Blinding blue light filled the room. The wardings screamed like manic seagulls. Daria must have passed through them to the outside of the tower.

Jindabyne ran to Elena, but Lev was there before her.

"Did she hurt you?" he snarled furiously.

"No!" sobbed Elena against his chest. "She mindsearched me. She... It was obscene Lev. She broke into my very soul."

"You won't see her again," snarled Lev. "This fortress is closed to her now." He turned on Jindabyne. "Why didn't you protect your mistress? Why didn't you call out for help?"

"They overcame me together," cried Elena. "She betrayed me, Lev. I tried to call out, but..."

"I didn't," cried Jindabyne. "Elena, how could you?"

Men were banging on the door outside calling for Lev, asking if he was safe, asking what was wrong. Jindabyne thought she heard the voice of Neevus among them. With a face like thunder, Lev dragged Jindabyne from the room.

"Don't leave me, Lev!" cried Elena, as he slammed her door shut and bolted it. He opened the outer door and flung Jindabyne into the arms of his guards.

"Take her and lock her in the dungeon," he snarled, and slamming the door behind him, he went back into the inner room.

"So! He has blamed you." said Neevus, as he locked the cell door behind Jindabyne. "This Elena *is* powerful."

"Neevus, please! I know you helped Daria. Set me free!"

Neevus snorted with amusement. "I never helped Daria. I only sought to help Lord Lev by getting rid of The Woman. He procrastinates in his plan now because of Her. I'll have to find another way."

How cold his eyes were. His slightly comical appearance had blinded her to it before. "You'll go down to the Abyss with the rest of your kind and so will she. So should all whores."

He watched calmly as the guards locked the door behind Jindabyne.

"Come, little one," he said, yanking the little girl's chain. As he led her away, she stared back at Jindabyne with the wide expressionless eyes of someone who has already seen the worst.

There was no one else down in the dungeons now. No sound except a faint rustling of straw in drafts from the window. Though the weather had been hot, it was chill down here. No torches were lit and when darkness fell, it was very dark. In the depths of the night a niggling fear that Lev would just leave her down here alone, starving and forgotten, played on Jindabyne's mind. She got up and paced the cell just to chase it away.

But someone remembered her. She heard the sound of leaves skittering on the stone floor a moment before someone caught her round the throat and pulled her against the bars.

"I want it. I need it," whispered a voice.

Daria could get in here. Lev had said the fortress was closed to Daria, but he couldn't really do that. Those kind of wardings took weeks and dozens of mages and Lev seemed to be concentrating on protecting Elena. But he'd probably ward Daria out of these dungeons or put Jindabyne down underground with the other Tari if he knew Daria could get in. He was vindictive enough for that. Jindabyne had to make sure that Daria understood that she would soon be unavailable to her – that the only chance she had to feed on real Tari now, was Ermora and that only Jindabyne could get her in there.

With sudden clarity, she saw why Elena had betrayed her.

Chapter 23

Around dusk Kulde woke up and crawled shakily over to where Alyx was sitting. Alyx offered him food, but all he wanted were some herbs, which he dug out of his pack and chewed.

"Yundi is giving me bad dreams," he said in an exhausted voice. "I didn't want him to wake up and be afraid that I've gone, but the Abyss surrounds the poor little rabbit. I don't know why..."

"It's the red fish," said Alyx. "They make people sick in spirit especially those with Tari blood."

"Are we close to them here? Is that the smell?"

"They're in the pool below this cave," said Serge.

"Poor Yundi," said Kulde again, shaking his head at his sleeping brother. "He seems very independent but he's actually quite frail. Dreamers often are. Visions eat into their strength. It makes him a handful to take care of, let me tell you."

"What happened to your parents?" asked Alyx.

Kulde sighed. "I guess you have to know sometime. About five years ago a kind of plague descended on Ermora."

"Something even the Tari couldn't cure?"

"Not a physical sickness. But the adults started to suffer from despair. Many found it hard to leave their beds. Some slept all day. Some did not sleep at all. Our mother was a nectar dreamer and she used to cry all the time and talk of demon fire and hopelessness. Our father took her to the spirit cave so that she could find some peace with the life spirit. He tried to carry on after that... But he got so sad. Finally I told him to go to the spirit cave himself. He left us in Kintora's care and he's been in the spirit cave ever since. He comes out sometimes, but never for very long. He's well enough for a couple of days, sometimes even a week. Then the staring into space begins again and soon he can do nothing else, not even sleep. Sometimes I wish he wouldn't try to come back to us. It breaks Yundi's heart... But it's wrong of me to say that. Most of the others never even try - have not been out of the spirit sleep for years."

"Don't they die from lack of food and water?" asked Serge.

Kulde shrugged.

"They're Tari. The life spirit sustains them in spirit sleep."

"But Jerandine told me the cave was closed. She showed me a crystal," cried Alyx.

Kulde laughed weakly. "Jerandine and some of the others thought if they blocked the mouth of the cave it would discourage people from going in. They think that people should face up to their problems. But the spirit cave isn't really closed. Any mage can reopen it for you."

"So that's where everyone is!" murmured Serge.

"All the nectar dreamers. Most of the others. Some didn't go. Like Kintora. And people like Jerandine who just live for pleasure. And those who were too young like me and Yundi. Though over time a lot of them have sickened also. I do have melancholy days, but I've escaped the worst so far. Yundi is always good at cheering me up. And I like to cook. Jerandine and some of the others took charge and we muddle along as best we can. Keep the barriers intact around Ermora. Though Ermora really protects itself. When we are all sleeping in the spirit cave, it will still carry on. An empty, forgotten place."

Just as people were unnecessary to the rest of the world. A smothering gloom fell on Alyx.

"Hey! Cheer up!" cried Serge. "We just killed two death angels and we'll kill more tomorrow. We should be triumphant. Now smile or I'll sing a song. And then you'll be sorry."

Kulde grinned weakly. Alyx looked away. Idiot Mirayan! Why did he always have to be so damnably cheerful? Worst of all, the insensitive brute was right.

"Do you want to go back to Ermora?" said Serge, suddenly serious again.

"I'd like to send Yundi back," said Kulde. "But the situation out here with the death angels and these fish attacking the very life spirit." His gentle face hardened. "It must be dealt with."

When Kulde woke the following day, he was still white and shaky and when he tried to examine the red fish, he collapsed into helpless retching. Meanwhile Yundi continued to lie at the back of the cave, tossing and muttering, his eyes fluttering open now and again but always unseeing. In the end they decided it would be best for him and everyone else to move campsites.

Serge had to carry the still delirious Yundi on his back so they left two of the packs in the cave to be picked up later. As it turned out they should have left three packs behind, because although Kulde shouldered his pack without complaining, they had only gone a short distance from the cave when he fainted. Alyx took up his pack with her own and, after Kulde had recovered, they continued slowly onward, reaching the new campsite just before dark.

The campsite was a covered platform high up in a wide spreading tree. A couple of big chests lashed to the trunk held stores of acorn flour, dried meat and fruit, and hard cheese. Some sleeping furs were protected by waxed skins. Alyx collected water from a nearby spring and by the time she got back Kulde had opened some of the stores and was sampling them with great interest. Since most Tari refused to take animal life, they were practically vegetarians although in Alyx's experience they did eat meat when it was offered to them. Kulde had never seen dried meat which he looked at in revulsion, nor had he slept in furs.

He was polite about the tree-house, but Alyx could tell he thought it very crude and uncomfortable. As she helped him make a small smokeless fire in the clearing below so that he could brew a healing drink for Yundi, Alyx found herself feeling regret for Ermora's luxuries. Though the thing she remembered most clearly about Ermora was Serge and... No, she wasn't going to think about it.

That evening Yundeman's delirium left him and he was able to speak and eat something. Kulde, still very pale, hovered over him, trying to tempt him with little titbits. Yundeman only took a few mouthfuls before he turned his face to the wall.

"Tell me about your dreams, Yundi. Come on, it'll make you feel better."

"I saw a red plain all soft and damp like the inside of a mouth," whispered Yundi. "Blue flying creatures like that one we saw in Penterong were burrowing into the red plain's flesh. All claws and teeth and bloated like ticks. Blood. Someone was crying. Crying and crying like there would be no happiness ever again."

His visions were so like the ones that Alyx had had when she had been wounded that she couldn't help shuddering.

"You looked into the Abyss," said Kulde softly. "I saw such sights when I fought the death angels. Here drink this healing drink and rest without dreams for a time. I'll watch over you and chase any nightmares away."

Serge seemed to have been avoiding Alyx all day. Was he thinking that she had trapped him, that he had done something stupid while drugged, that he was embarrassed? Well he had no need to worry about her, because she wasn't going to act as if more existed between them than there was. Even though she had never made love before, she knew better than to think it meant anything. She lay down on the other side of the tree-house from him with Yundi and Kulde in between, but found herself lying awake listening to Serge's breathing, trying not to think about what had happened only two nights ago in Ermora.

In the morning she was annoyed to discover that Serge had gone off alone, but since Kulde had seen him sneaking away, she was not overly worried about him. As she sat at the edge of the platform scanning the sky for death angels which were mercifully absent and trying not to think about Serge, Kulde came and sat down beside her. He was still very pale and weak, but he seemed determined not to let that stop him.

"When Serge comes back, we'll have to discuss what to do next," he said. "I want to go back to the pool and see if anything can be done about these red fish. Can you tell me anything about them?"

Kulde was such a pleasant person that after Alyx had told him everything she knew about the red fish, they drifted into chatting about other things. Though in the past Kulde had doubted his brother's gift of foretelling, Alyx's arrival had finally convinced him and now he believed in him wholeheartedly.

"He described you so well. Your Tari features and your dark hair. And that pretty green feather you were wearing."

At that moment Serge's head popped over the edge of the platform.

"Shouldn't you be watching out instead of gossiping?" he snarled. "Anyone could have been climbing up here."

He slung two packs up on the platform before him. No wonder he'd been gone so long. He'd been back to the waterfall.

Alyx blushed. She should have noticed him coming but she and Kulde were speaking Tari and, since it wasn't her best language, she'd been concentrating on that.

"What were you talking about anyway?" snapped Serge.

Alyx scowled at him. "Prophecy. Nothing you need worry about."

"I'll keep watch now," said Serge looking, curse him,

as if he'd caught her doing something rude.

He thought she was a slut, damn him! That was what was wrong with him. All Mirayans thought native women were sluts. Well to hell with him!

"Good," she snapped. "Then I'll have my turn at wandering around wasting time."

"Alyx, we should discuss..." cried Kulde.

"We can do it tonight," retorted Alyx as she swung down onto the ladder. "Since his lordly Mirayaness has been gone all the morning, there's not much we can usefully do today, is there? I'll get some water."

"I already did that!" Serge shouted angrily after her and he had indeed filled the leather water buckets and set them round the bottom of the tree. She was so furious she almost kicked one over, but a Mori never wasted water. Instead she ran out into the forest and after she'd run the edge off her anger, she gathered some early adra berries, some leafy greens and some late lily bulbs. Hadn't Serge helped her gather lilies earlier? He'd seemed so kind and gentle then, not like a real Mirayan.

When she got back it was mid-afternoon. Serge scowled at her and she ignored him. Kulde wanted to try all the food she had gathered and was especially delighted about the greens which he said they didn't have in Ermora and which he wrapped around the hard cheese to eat. After they had eaten, there was still some time till nightfall. Yundi and Kulde put on their shoes and Yundi started to climb down the ladder.

"I'll take Yundi off till dusk," said Kulde in a low voice.

"What? Why?" cried Alyx. It was one thing for Serge to leave the party and quite another for inexperienced people like Kulde and Yundi to do it.

"I think we should keep together," said Serge.

"But you two can't make love with Yundi and me here," said Kulde simply, as he took hold of the top of the ladder.

Alyx felt as if all the breath had left her body. Kulde was half off the platform before she was able to say,

"You really don't need to go. We weren't going to..."

"No?" said Kulde, smiling at her, obviously not believing a word she said. "Well lovers need time alone for whatever reason."

"But we're not... We could never be..."

Kulde put his hand to his mouth. "Oh have I said the wrong thing? Now I think of it, Kintora told me outlanders were shy about love sport. I'm sorry. I didn't meant to embarrass you."

"No!" cried Alyx, fiery red and horribly conscious of Serge. "It just that we're not... I could never... Ermora was a mistake. We were drugged. Otherwise I would never have. I mean it's just not possible."

"Enough," shouted Serge with sudden stunning violence. "Yes it was a mistake, but will you stop going on about it all the time!"

Alyx turned pale. "I didn't mean..." she spluttered.

"I didn't mean it either," snarled Serge, "but it happened. I can't help being a Mirayan. I didn't have any say in it."

"I never said anything about being a Mirayan."

"But you were about to. You always use it as if it's an insult. Well it's not. I'm proud to be a Mirayan and I don't think I deserve any of the accusations you've made at me."

"You don't have to yell. How can you be proud to be a Mirayan! Always yelling and pushing people round and..."

She stopped, unable to think of more insults and deeply aware that Serge wasn't like that at all.

"Sweet life!" cried Kulde. "I'm so sorry. I didn't mean..."

Serge wasn't listening. "Why'd you stop?" he snarled at Alyx. "Go on, say it. Forcing yourself on women. That's what you meant, wasn't it? I've been waiting for you to say it. You can say what you want but it doesn't change things. You came to me entirely willingly."

"So what if I did? It was the drugs. I'd never have... Anyway you did everything..."

"I don't have to stay around here and listen to this," shouted Serge, swinging over the edge of the platform.

So in the end, Serge took Yundi for a long forest walk and Kulde stayed with Alyx.

He asked such sympathetic questions, that even though she told him it was none of his business, she soon found herself trying to explain why things were impossible between her and Serge.

But when she told Kulde how awful Mirayans were, Kulde simply said "But Serge isn't like that. Have you known a lot of Mirayans then?"

The whole sordid story about her mother and Serge's father came out then. Kulde was silent. She thought he was shocked, but then he said, "You can't really blame Serge for having such an awful father."

"Why are you taking his side?" she shouted. "Just mind your own business! I don't like him. I could never like him. Can't you leave it at that?"

With a quiet dignity he said, "It's been my observation that when people fight like you two, it's often because they really like each other and are trying to hide it. That's all."

He turned his back on her and they ignored each other until Serge and Yundi returned.

The following day Kulde insisted that he was well enough to go back to the red fish pool. To everyone's dismay, Yundi refused to stay behind. But halfway through the return journey, when they had come close enough to the river to smell faint snatches of its stink on the wind, Yundi terrified everyone by crying out that he could see black ticks sucking the trees ahead. Only after they had all scampered into the undergrowth, did they realise that he was hallucinating.

"We'd best split up," said Serge decisively. "I'll take Kulde to the river and you go back to the tree-house with Yundi."

His assumption of leadership irritated Alyx.

"Why should it be me to go back to the tree-house?" she snapped.

"Why should you go to the river with Kulde?" snapped Serge back. "We can find the way from here easily. You said this path goes right there."

They glared at each other.

"I will go to the river with Serge," said Kulde gently. "We'll stay there the night and meet you back at the tree-house, Alyx. Serge has no Tari blood. It'll be easier on him."

Alyx felt ganged up on. Men always stuck together!

"Very well!" she snapped. She dragged the dazed and muttering Yundi away. Later when they had almost reached the tree-house and Yundi had suddenly come to back himself and begun asking after Kulde, she felt ashamed of how she had behaved. Kulde had been right about the river, though she did not think Serge had any thoughts about her welfare when he so briskly seized control. She shouldn't be letting personalities get in the way of their important mission to destroy the red fish. Serge Madraga was not setting much of an example in that respect though.

"What's happening between you and Serge?" asked Yundi as they climbed back up to the tree-house.

"Don't you start!" she told him sharply.

Kulde had decided to spend the day examining the red fish to see if he could find any weaknesses. After nightfall when the danger of death angels was lessened, he planned to use magic to try and kill them as he had killed the death angels. Alyx and Serge had warned him about the blood beasts, but they all felt confident that he and Serge would be safe from them in the cave.

As they told Alyx later, they followed this plan to the letter, even though the task of examination made them both physically ill. Kulde quickly discovered that there were just too many red fish for his magic to overwhelm. By the time the blood beasts came charging into the clearing to devour the source of the magic, he had abandoned the idea. He and Serge spent a depressing night in the cave, dozing fitfully and listening to the blood beasts searching around the pool, fighting each other and finally slaughtering some poor animal they found in the forest. They set out for the tree-house first thing in the morning. Rain had fallen during the night and Kulde dawdled, delighted by the beauty of the sun on the drops of water that bejewelled the forest plants.

Suddenly he yelped and jumped backwards almost tripping over Serge. A Mirayan woman had just stepped out of the forest in front of them.

Her short dark hair fell in wild tangles around her shoulders and her red dress was torn and filthy. She had no veil though she tried hide her face with her sleeve. She was beautiful with a strong hawk-like Mirayan face, dark eyes and full red lips.

"Please! Help me!" she cried to the two astonished young men. Even though he couldn't understand the woman's speech, Kulde melted immediately and stepped forward his hand outstretched. Serge fearing a trap, caught his arm and urged him to use his magic to check that the woman was really alone.

But Kulde already knew she was alone. He shook Serge off and responding to the woman's look of hunger, unslung his pack and offered her food and water. As they sat under the cover of the trees watching her eat and drink, Serge questioned her in Mirayan.

The woman had been travelling to a place under the Gen Mountains with her husband and some other countrymen when they'd been set upon by terrible winged death minions. Her husband had hidden her under some leaves and when things became quiet she'd crawled out and found herself alone. Piles of ash were all that remained of the others. She'd been wandering the forest for two days since, hiding from the minions, trying to find help.

"Who was your husband going to see?" asked Serge.

"I don't know," said the woman shyly. "My husband never spoke of such things to me. I think it was an ally of his."

"Lev Madraga? Guilius Appius?" asked Serge.

The woman shrank back against Kulde as if frightened by Serge's intensity.

"I'm not sure. Can you take me back to civilisation? My family will reward you well."

Kulde admonished Serge for scaring the poor woman,

and sighing, Serge gave up the questioning. It was quite normal for a Mirayan woman to have no idea of her husband's business. When Kulde suggested they take the woman back to the tree-house with them, Serge agreed. She seemed harmless enough. Her name was Daria.

Chapter 24

As they waited out the afternoon at the tree house Alyx heard Yundi snuffling and suspected he was crying. She could accept this in a little boy of eleven and did her best to take his mind off things by asking him questions about prophecy. In doing so she learn many things. Apparently when Jindabyne had delivered her mother to Wolf Madraga, she had been carrying out the orders of her uncle Jagamar who had believed that Elena and Wolf would bear the Melded Child that would bring peace between the Mirayans and the people of the Archipelago. She was shocked by such a flagrant misuse of prophecy, for her mother had told her again and again that you must never try to bring about what was foretold.

She also learned that Jindabyne had turned on Jagamar (as well she might) and mindblasted him and in doing so had mindblasted herself as well. This was why she remembered nothing of what had happened. Jagamar now slept in the spirit cave with the others. They had both suffered far less for their crimes than Alyx and her mother had. Yundi claimed that Jagamar's crimes had occurred because he had not communed in the spirit cave and that regular communion prevented such excesses. Alyx was not sure she believed that it was so simple to prevent human evil but she did wonder if the reason the Tari were so now self-absorbed and peculiar was that they no longer went to the spirit cave.

She let Yundi have first watch that night, but her mind was so full of thoughts of Serge, of her aunts and mother and of the prophecy that once again she could not sleep. This was lucky because after a time she heard Yundi snoring. He was just a lad, new to this dangerous world and exhausted by his visions so she suppressed her anger at the unforgivable act of falling asleep on watch, helped him into his blankets, reassured him when he called out his brother's name and moved her blankets across to the ladder so that anyone who tried to enter would wake her. After that she fell into a restless doze, broken up by her awareness of blood beasts prowling round on the ground beneath their tree.

Just after dawn she was startled out of a deeper sleep by Yundi screaming. She drew her sword as she rolled out of her blankets and almost stabbed Yundi as he threw himself at her.

"Kulde!" he cried. "He's in danger. I saw it."

Alyx was so frightened by the near miss that she shouted at Yundi, but he ignored her and kept shouting at her that Kulde was in danger.

"A red leech has latched onto him," he cried, pushing past her and climbing into the ladder. "She holds him captive. We must go and set him free."

If Kulde was in danger, what about Serge?

Since Alyx had grown up among Tari, who all had a tendency towards prophetic dreams, she had no problem believing in Yundi, but she saw immediately that if she was going to set out to rescue Kulde, Yundi would be more of a hindrance than a help to her. After a heated argument she managed to persuade Yundi to stay behind and throwing water and food into a pack, she set out alone for the waterfall, adopting the mixture of running and walking that the Mori used to travel quickly through the forest. She halted only once. The trail climbed up into the foothills of

Gen Mountains and at a certain point you could see down across the forest below. Alyx had already smelt smoke on the wind and now she stopped to see where the fire was. A line of smoke streamed out of the trees away to the south of her. A forest fire? The smoke was much blacker than usual, a thin trail travelling west against the wind which was easterly. That meant magical fire. The Mirayans again? They must be using many mages to make such a long fire. She said a prayer to the forest gods for her mother, wondering where she was and how this magical fire was affecting her and her warriors.

Dark shapes that could only be death angels swirled above the smoke trail like ash rising up a chimney. Because of the way they moved in and out of the smoke, it was impossible to count them exactly. No more than ten, no fewer than six. Was this fire some new devilry of Lev Madraga's? Was this why they had seen so little of the death angels since Kulde had killed the two at the waterfall? She pushed on faster.

Closer to the waterfall she slowed, searching for tracks. She almost stopped breathing when she came upon strands of what looked like Kulde's hair and some spots of blood spattered on the ground. Yundi had been right!

Keeping rigidly calm, she kept searching, finding tracks, the signs of someone being dragged, red threads caught in one of the bushes. It had all happened earlier that morning, probably around the time she had been leaving the tree house. Someone wearing red had attacked Kulde. A red leech. What did that chilling image mean? The footprint seemed to belong to a small man or a woman. Mori, Seagani or Mirayan? There was no sign of Kulde's footprints, but she followed the attacker's footprints and they had companion. She let out a gasp of relief. The companion was Serge - it had to be Serge. His footprints were so deep he must heavily laden. The burden could be Kulde. Since Kulde was a mage and such a powerful one, it was logical that the attacker would have had to knock him unconscious. But how had a lone person made Serge... She could be a mage! Hell and Abyss!

Moving very carefully now, Alyx followed the tracks back towards the waterfall. A short time later, she came upon the tracks of only one person, the attacker, facing towards her and diverting away up the mountain. The footprints showed that now she or he was heavy laden.

Alyx's spine turned to ice. Serge was no longer with them! No longer bothering to track, she plunged down the path through the scrub. No sign of anyone by the pool. Spending far too little time checking for danger, she ran over to the cliff, climbed up to the cave, pulled aside the curtain of moss and charged inside. Nobody there. A sickening vision of Serge's hurt blue eyes came back to Alyx and she felt as if her heart had died in her chest. She leaned against the cold wall of the cave, panic making it difficult to for her to breathe. What if Serge was...?

Calm yourself. Stop crying. There is no body. If there is no body, he may still be alive.

As she left the cave, her eye fell on the pool of red fish seething below. You could push someone in there and there'd be nothing left to find.

Carrying that thought like a dead-weight on her chest, she forced herself to climb up the rock face to wide flat cliff top. The moment she came over the edge, she saw the bundle of cloth. Oh life! Serge! Lying there still as death! For a moment she couldn't move and then, without a second thought, she ran forward crying his name.

The body twitched and turned its head. He was alive! Oh thank life! Thank Labwa and Nezrhus and the Lady of the Animals! She cast herself on him and seized him squeezing him tight and kissed his face all over.

Through her frenzy of joy, she noticed his hands and feet were bound and he was gagged. It didn't stop him nuzzling her as if trying to kiss her and when she pulled the gag and the sodden piece of cloth stuffed into his mouth away, he actually did kiss her.

Then he ruined the effect by complaining of the bad taste in his mouth and spitting out bits of the red cloth gag.

"We have to get under cover," he cried urgently, bringing Alyx back to sensible thought. She quickly undid his bonds, but the blood had gone out of his feet and she had to support him as he staggered off the rock and back into the bushes. As he collapsed on the ground, she knelt down beside him and started massaging his feet.

"I think we'll be safe," she said. "There's something big happening away to the south and the death angels are drawn to it."

For a moment Serge didn't say anything. Then he whispered "Alyx!" and leant forwards. His arm went round her shoulders and without even thinking Alyx lifted her face to meet his.

They kissed - soft tender searching kisses.

"You do like me after all," he said.

She was blushing.

"I shouldn't," she said in a small voice. Sweet life! Why had this happened? She was horrified to find tears in her eyes.

"Oh Alyx," said Serge, brushing her tears away with his fingers. "Is it so bad to l.... like a Mirayan?"

"Your father. My mother," she muttered, suddenly too choked to speak.

"I know. But that was a long time ago and has nothing to do with us."

He pulled her against him and pressed his face against her hair and her body seemed to move naturally into the curve of his chest and shoulder.

"I thought I was done for," he said. "That woman put me out there for the death angels to take."

"Serge!" Alyx smacked him on the arm, annoyed at both of them for getting distracted. "What woman? What happened? Where's Kulde? Quickly, tell me what happened! We can't dilly-dally here. Can you walk?"

As they followed the woman's trail, Serge told her of how they had met Daria and offered to bring her back to the campsite. They had not gone far before Serge heard the sound of a blow and spun round to see Kulde crumpled on the ground and the woman standing above him with a rock in her fist. Her face had changed from gentleness to complete savagery and before Serge could protest, his will had been overcome with magic.

"Didn't you consider that she might be a mage when you met her?"

"Mirayan woman mages wear neck manacles."

"Why?"

Serge found himself blushing. "Um..."

"It's so they can't do anything against their menfolk, isn't it? Do you know what that does to mages over time? It's barbaric."

"Yes, I know you opinion of Mirayans. Mir knows I've heard it often enough," snapped Serge.

There was a difficult silence.

"I'm sorry. Tell me the rest," said Alyx, in her mildest voice.

"She must have used magic on Kulde too because he stayed unconscious even though he didn't seem badly hurt. She made me carry him. I didn't want to, but I couldn't resist her will. Then she tied me up and left me."

"All this magic. Wasn't she worried about death angels?"

"She called them her little friends. When she left she said her little friends would clean me up. Up till then she had been keeping them away. She had some words she said, every time they came. She must have been a death mage!"

Daria's tracks were easy to follow and she had moved slowly, stopping several times to put Kulde down and rest. Marshalling her power, Serge suggested. Non-Tari mages only had limited amounts of magical strength to draw on.

Her trail lead up towards the Gen Mountains over the now empty grasslands to where tumbled boulders lined the towering mountain cliffs. Even over the rocks Alyx was still able to follow Daria's trail from the broken twigs and scraped stones along the way.

"She's close," she whispered at last. Serge squeezed her hand and she smiled at him, unable to feel as worried as she knew she should feel. Keeping under cover, they crept forward, testing each step on the loose rocks and peering carefully around every new boulder.

It was now mid-afternoon. From up here they could see the line of smoke travelling through the forest south of them and the death angels circling over it. The thing that caused it must be moving fast, because it was much further west than Alyx remembered and closer too.

Daria was making no attempt to stay quiet and they heard her well before they sighted her. From behind the cover of some boulders, they watched her dragging a woman's body out of a crevice in the side of the cliff. It was not one of the Mori's camping places, but its narrow opening would make it a handy place to hide from blood beasts and death angels.

"Where's Kulde?" mouthed Alyx at Serge. He shrugged.

With a contemptuous look Daria dumped the body on the rock as if it were dirty laundry. She looked about to kick it. Then her face changed and she looked at the smoke in the forest away to the south. She turned, reached into the crevice behind her and pulled someone out by the wrist.

Kulde! Alyx breathed a sigh of relief. From the way the woman stroked his face, she wasn't likely to kill him in the near future. He was pale and he flinched from the woman's touch as if she were unclean. Witch manacles were fixed round his neck and wrists and a bandage had been bound carefully around his head.

Smiling, Daria pinched Kulde's cheek. She took a couple of strips of cloth and stuffed them into his ears. When he touched them, she held up her finger and shook her head admonishingly at him. She took out another couple of pieces of cloth and stuffed them in her own ears, before reaching into her bodice and bringing out a pale white flute which she put to her lips.

Kulde chose this moment to run. Daria must have been expecting it, for she thrust out a foot and he tripped and fell flat on his face. Calmly she sat down cross-legged on his back so that he could not get up. Alyx could not see Kulde's face, but the way he put his head in his hands expressed a world of despair.

Daria blew into the pipe and suddenly Alyx wanted to throw up. She could not hear a sound but she could feel the note ringing vilely throughout her body. She clapped her hands over her ears, and she leaned back into Serge's body until the nausea passed. A moment later Serge pushed her down against the rock in front of them. Daria came clattering past them, dragging Kulde by the wrist. Neither she nor Kulde saw them crouched in the shadow between two boulders, though they might easily have done so had they turned their heads. But Daria was intent on getting away as fast as possible and she was plunging straight down toward the cover of the forest.

Serge was in a hurry too. Daria had not yet gone out of sight when he hissed "Come on!" and darted out of their cover. Alyx saw the need for haste. Two of the death angels had left the trail of smoke and were winging towards them.

Serge was bent over the body on the ground.

"Sweet Mir!" he cried softly. Alyx, assuming the woman was dead, looked round for cover. "Here!" She hissed at Serge, making for the crevice.

"Help me! She's still alive," he whispered, picking the body up. Alyx squeezed backwards into the crevice and put out her arms to take the weight of the body that Serge was pushing towards her. With a shock, she recognised the unconscious woman as Jindabyne, Serge's stepmother.

"Come on! Come on!" cried Serge.

Through the opening of the crevice, Alyx could see the death angels shooting towards them like arrows with intent. Every fibre in her being tingling with fright, she pulled the woman against her as hard as she could. She could see the angels' leathery wings, their blank toothy faces, their claws.

"Serge!" she screamed pulling so hard on the woman that she lost her balance and toppled backwards. The woman fell on top of her and Serge hopped in on top of them both, stepping on Alyx's leg in the process and...

Bang.

The death angels hit the rock outside with a thud that made everything shudder. Trickles of sand came down the crevice.

Serge was manoeuvring the woman's unconscious body upright. Banging both elbows against the rocks on either side, Alyx scrambled backwards along the crevice till she was wedged into the narrow space at the back of it. Serge thrust the unconscious woman at her and she held her hard against her side. She could see the faces of the death angels peering in at them. They were struggling with each other, each trying to get in first. Screaming like an insane parrot, one turned and bit the other.

Alyx couldn't seem to tear her eyes away from them. One managed to push the other aside and charge forward. There was a thud as its shoulders and hips caught in the crevice opening.

Thank life! It was too big. But its arm snaked in through the opening, claws grasping at Serge. Alyx cringed backward trying to make room for Serge to get in further, but she had gone as far as she could. She tried to pull Serge closer, but the moment she let go of Jindabyne, the unconscious woman started to slide to the ground.

"It can't reach me," hissed Serge. His fingers squeezed her wrist. Sulphurous air swished against her as the angel grabbed for Serge again and again. She held onto his hand tightly, expected at any moment to hear him yell and see him dragged away from her.

The angels let out an ear-splitting scream of rage and frustration and after a scuffle outside the crevice, the other angel began reaching through, its grey hand feeling along the wall towards Serge, swiping at him, missing and swiping again.

For hours after that, Alyx and Serge stayed pressed up against the end of the crevice, their legs and muscles cramping with tension, as the death angels tried to reach them. Alyx remembered as a child trying to get beetles out of thin necked storage jars. Now she knew how those beetles had felt. She hoped the angels wouldn't think about using sticks as she and the other children had, but they seemed to be too busy snarling at each other and fighting over the opening. Sometimes they disappeared completely and there came a sound like a gigantic cat fight from outside. Mostly they just hurled themselves against the opening of the crevice as if trying to break it. But earth was a strong element and though the rocks shuddered, they held firm.

The worst thing about the death angels was the miasma of gloom that they carried. Alyx's thoughts turned to her mistakes and the hopelessness of her life, to the death of Didier, to her failure to keep her followers alive. Why was she trying to escape these creatures? They would destroy her in the end. But Serge's warm strong hand on hers brought a flicker of joy to cut through that misery.

As the day wore on and it became clear that Alyx was not going to get back to the tree-house, she started to worry about Yundi. Would he do something stupid when they didn't turn up?

"I wish there was some way we could get a message to him."

"One of your birds?" whispered Serge. The angels outside had fallen quiet.

She sighed. "I can't call one from here."

"Perhaps the angels have gone."

"No! I can still feel them around."

As if it had heard them, one of the death angels let out a cry. A shower of dust trickled down on them from above and Alyx saw a blue grey hand and arm creeping like a spider through the gap in the rocks above. Much too far away, but she couldn't help cringing away from it. As she did, the other angel appeared at the opening of the crevice and snatched at Serge, making him yelp with fright.

The death angels stayed outside groping in at each opening to the crevice until the light failed and suddenly, with a flapping of leather wings, they were gone. Alyx felt the heavy weight of them lifting off her spirit. She didn't even pause for a sigh of relief.

"We have to get away from here," she hissed. "The blood beasts may come and trap us in here and I can't take another day of this."

As if to support her words, a howl rose eerily up the

forest.

Together they pulled Jindabyne out of the crevice and out onto the open rock. Alyx picked up the pack that she had thrown down outside. The death angels hadn't even noticed it. She pulled out the water skin and slaked the thirst that had been troubling her all day, then passed the skin to Serge.

"Why doesn't she wake up?" muttered Serge. "What did that creature do to her?"

He bathed and patted Jindabyne's face, while Alyx, sword drawn, watched and listened to the howling of the blood beasts in the forest below. The moon had risen by the time Jindabyne began to awaken.

The sleeping drug Daria had given Jindabyne had made her very sick. She began to vomit and she could not see.

"Don't worry!" she gasped. "I'm free. I can heal myself."

"Don't!" cried Serge and Alyx as one.

"You'll draw the blood beasts to us," explained Serge.

"We'll have to get somewhere safe before we do any magic," said Alyx.

"And not here," said Serge. "The Death Angels may remember us and come back in the morning."

"What's happened?" choked Jindabyne, between paroxysms of vomiting. "Where's Daria?"

"She left you for the death angels to take. She took one of our friend's prisoner."

Jindabyne shivered, but she didn't seem surprised.

"It was a Tari, wasn't it? She feeds on us."

A blood beast howled nearby.

"Let's see if we can get to the waterfall cave," said Alyx. "It's not far away and we'll be safe. You'll be able to heal yourself there."

Helping a sightless Jindabyne across the expanse of rocks proved too difficult. At least the vomiting had subsided.

"You're so thin!" cried Serge as he lifted her onto his back.

"Be glad my boy! You are the one taking my weight."

She sighed. "Sweet life, my blood is full of poison. Yet I feel the life spirit too. Like the sweetest freshest water in the world. Have you seen anything of Olga? Is she safe?"

"Safe and well in Ermora," said Serge. "Where have *you* been?"

"Hush you two!" hissed Alyx. "They'll hear us."

Under the trees it was so dark that Alyx could barely see the path and several times she blundered into the scrub. Meanwhile blood beasts howled and seemed to be coming closer and as far as she could tell in the darkness, they were between them and the waterfall cave.

"Let's find a tree," suggested Serge. "If we get high enough maybe Jindabyne can heal herself."

Alyx picked a suitable tree and shinned up smooth trunk to the lowest branches.

She dropped back to the ground.

"It's too tall. The lowest branches are further than my rope will stretch."

A beast howled nearby.

"Foolish child," said Jindabyne lightly. "You don't need a rope. I'm a mage. Tell me where to go and I'll fly."

Alyx climbed the tree again and Serge followed, much more slowly for he didn't have the knack of climbing a smooth tree. When Alyx reached the place where the tree forked, she called to Jindabyne and kept calling.

In the darkness she saw a pale shape floating up along the tree trunk towards her. Not a moment too soon. A blood beast burst out of the bushes with a howl and threw itself at the tree.

"Hang on" Alyx cried to Serge, who was still scrabbling upwards. She reached out and managed to catch Jindabyne by the arm and guide her onto a branch in front of them. She was as light as thistledown.

"I can feel the life spirit," Jindabyne cried joyfully, seeming oblivious to the blood beast throwing itself at the tree trunk below. "I can feel...eew!" Suddenly she leaned over and vomited.

"Jindabyne!" cried Serge below and there was a sudden sound of scrabbling and then slipping.

"Serge!" screamed Alyx.

"I'm fine," said Serge below her. "She didn't hit me. Is she all right?"

"All's well," choked Jindabyne. "Just the poison in my blood. I'll drive it out now."

"For life's sake Serge, concentrate on climbing," snapped Alyx, upset by her own fear.

"Yes mother!" retorted Serge but he was laughing. Always laughing. How did he do it? He was still chuckling when he climbed into the fork of the tree.

"This is cosy," he said.

"I'm glad you're comfortable," said Alyx tartly. She was holding Jindabyne round the waist, while the Tari lay along the huge branch in front of her, vomiting.

"You want to change places."

"Stay where you are," snapped Alyx.

Serge leaned close to her so that his mouth was against his ear.

"You're so sweet when you're worried," he whispered, and kissed her lightly on the cheek.

"Stop that!" snapped Alyx, but laughter started welling up inside her.

Jindabyne's self-cleansing seemed to require a lot of vomiting and since she was using magic, blood beasts began to collect round the tree, growling and fighting amongst themselves just as the death angels had.

As Alyx sat there with her hands at Jindabyne's waist feeling her muscles clench as she retched, she felt the familiar gloom that surrounded death minions settle on her. The night was warm, but they would be cold before dawn.

Probably the gloom was affecting Jindabyne too, for between retching bouts she groaned, "Sweet life when will this end!"

"It's just the blood beasts," Alyx whispered to her.

Suddenly Serge began to sing a very silly song about a donkey who wanted to be a hopping mouse. Even though the snarling of the blood beasts below drowned out some of the words, Alyx found herself smiling and humming along. When he finished that song, he launched into another song about a woman and man out courting. Alyx's Mirayan wasn't good enough for her to understand all of it, but it was clearly as full of double entendres as such songs always were.

"You missed one of the verses," said Jindabyne as he finished.

"I'm not sure you should even know of the existence of that verse," mocked Serge primly.

"I... Oh noo!" Jindabyne retched again.

"You know this all has a very homey feel to me," confided Serge. "Just like all those nights out carousing with Alain." He stroked Alyx's hair. "The company of dear friends. The night. Singing to pass the time while someone else throws up. My father's court mage never could hold his ale. The only problem is that most of the songs we used to sing are not suitable for the delicate ears of ladies."

"Don't spare us," smiled Alyx. She rubbed Serge's ankle. "If we're hardy enough to bear your voice, we're strong enough for any song you know."

"I'm wounded," laughed Serge. "I'll have you know my voice is much admired by people who want favours from my father."

"Toad," groaned Jindabyne. "Don't make me laugh when I'm being sick."

"My dear Lady, I apologise. I'll try and think of something suitable for the occasion."

And he kept on singing songs, some of them very beautiful and some of them extremely rude. In between he told stories of nights out with his friends in Lamartaine which all seemed to involve much drunken "borrowing" of horses, balancing on seawalls and bantering with bar maids.

At length Jindabyne stopped vomiting, lay back against Alyx, relaxed and had some food and water. By now Alyx was glad of her warmth. They swapped tales of what had happened since they had last met. Serge's story carefully skirted round what had happened between them in Ermora. Alyx was torn between distress at her mother's imprisonment and relief that she was alive, and Jindabyne in her turn was troubled by the name of Olga's guardian.

"Kintora is the only person I remember from Ermora," she said. "She hated me. Is she good to Olga?"

"She thinks Olga is some kind of saviour for Ermora," said Serge. "Was I wrong to leave Olga there?"

"I'm glad she is not with us now," said Jindabyne. "But I would like to take her from Ermora as soon as I can."

And she told them of Elena's fears about Lev.

"Why would he tunnel into the Gen mountains?"

"Surely Ermora is strong enough to resist him," said Alyx. She could hear a lack of conviction in her own voice.

"You tell me," said Jindabyne.

Alyx wasn't sure how an Ermora with most of its population sleeping in the spirit cave and the rest wallowing in pleasure could resist an attack by Lev Madraga. Hope began to drain away.

Suddenly Serge said, "Damn blood beasts!" and began to sing again even though his voice was hoarse.

Finally after a forever night, dawn came and the blood beasts slouched away into the undergrowth.

"I wonder where they go," said Serge.

"Wherever it is, they're well and truly gone," said Alyx. "I can't feel them any more."

"Do you feel strong enough to take on this Daria, Lady?" asked Serge.

"Yes," snapped Jindabyne, her eyes narrowed into a scowl.

After a moment or two of staggering round on the ground, getting their night stiffened muscles to work, they searched out Daria's trail. Her path was easy to find. She'd gone crashing down through the forest towards the waterfall.

"Makes sense for her to spend the night there," said Alyx.

"Or perhaps she saw the circle of stones in Kulde's head," suggested Jindabyne. "If so, they could already be in Ermora."

"There's only one way to find out," said Serge.

Just then a scream rang out through the forest ahead.

Jindabyne, who was not as fit as Serge and Alyx and had been lagging behind, suddenly broke into a headlong run. Luckily Alyx had the presence of mind to grab her arm as she passed her.

"Let go!" hissed Jindabyne.

"Let's see what we're up against before we go rushing in," hissed Alyx keeping hold of her arm. Even so by the time they reached the stone circle, Jindabyne was dragging Alyx along and Alyx had to pull her back again to prevent her charging into the circle.

Daria and Kulde were struggling among the stones. Daria slapping at Kulde's face, but Kulde was holding her arm away from him.

"Tell me how to get there," shouted Daria. "I know you can do it."

"Tell me the secret of the red fish first! If you made them, you must know how to kill them."

Daria kicked Kulde, knocking him over and Alyx found herself holding thin air as Jindabyne leapt into the stone circle. A gesture from Jindabyne made Daria slump into sleep. To Alyx's horror she stalked over to Daria's sleeping form, her jaw clenched with anger and kicked her hard in the ribs. Tari didn't act like that!

"Come on!" cried Serge, dashing towards Jindabyne. Kulde was sitting with his face in his hands and Alyx pulled him to his feet. "Death Angels. We've used magic. We have to get away."

As Alyx dragged Kulde out of the circle, he turned back.

"Daria!" he cried. "We have to take her with us. We need her. She knows..."

"I've got her!" shouted Serge, who had already slung Daria over his shoulder. "Let's go!"

They dodged through the scrubby bushes. Half way down to the waterfall cave, they saw two dark shapes streaking across the sky towards them and took cover. The moment Serge put Daria down, she sat up opening, her mouth to cry out. In a flash, Jindabyne hit her with a piece of wood.

"Mir! Jindabyne!" hissed Serge. He took the piece of wood out of her hands. "Calm down! We need her alive."

After checking that Daria was still alive, Alyx started hunting in her belt pouch for a key.

"We have to put the witch manacles on her. We can't have her waking up... Here it is!"

"Down," hissed Serge. They all lay still as the death angels passed overhead and landed with a thud on the slope above. Once they were out of sight below the tree line, Alyx leaned over to Kulde and undid his manacles. As the angels screeched at each other and crashed around in the trees on the hillside above, she wriggled back to Daria and put the manacles on her. Before she had finished, the angels, shrieking with insane laughter, took off again, forcing everyone to flatten themselves down among the undergrowth again.

"Not much of a search!" said Serge.

"You complaining?" said Alyx.

Serge grinned at her.

"I guess they're more concerned with what's happening down south," she continued and told the others about the line of smoke.

"Oh life! Another thing!" groaned Kulde.

Jindabyne had pulled a strip of cloth off one of her petticoats, and pouring water on it, was applying it to Kulde's face. His lip was cut, his nose bleeding and one of his eyes was closing.

Alyx winced. "Sweet life! She made a mess out of you."

"I'm a really crap fighter," muttered Kulde miserably.

Serge squatted down and clapped him on the shoulder. "I have to agree with you, my friend. But thanks to you, we'll soon know how to destroy the red fish."

Kulde's smile made Alyx smile too. How like Serge to know exactly the right thing to say.

"Where's Yundi?" asked Kulde, his face changing.

"He's fine. He's back at the camp," said Alyx.

"We'd better get back to him," said Serge. "Let's see if we can wake Daria up. I don't want to have to carry her."

While Serge worked to bring Daria back to consciousness, Alyx searched her, coming up with several coloured vials containing some kind of powder and the bone flute which Daria had called up the angels with.

"Is this all you travelled with? What did you eat?"

"Daria called birds and animals to her and killed them," said Jindabyne. "She is utterly, utterly ruthless."

Since no one else could bear to touch it, Serge put the flute in his belt pouch. Even he felt squeamish, knowing that it must almost certainly be human bone, yet it was too valuable and dangerous to leave behind.

"Some of these vials are the sleeping drug she gave me," said Jindabyne. "The others energise you. I'm not sure which is which."

Although Daria stirred, she appeared to be concussed and Serge had to carry her on his back anyway.

"If only you'd just put her to sleep," he grumbled.

"If I'd used a sleep spell, the angels would have found our traces. Just be glad I made her wash a couple of days ago. Usually she stinks."

Daria was too dazed by the blow to the head to be a difficult passenger, but when she started to weep, her tears dribbled down Serge's neck. Though both he and Alyx asked her about the red fish, all she did was snivel about Ermora.

"Stop it! Or I'll give you something to cry about," snapped Jindabyne, pure hatred in her voice. After that Daria wept silently, refusing to answer any questions. Soon enough they were all too tired to talk more. Except for Kulde, they had been awake all night. They plodded on longing for the rest and safety of the tree house. Though Kulde was dazed from the beating, he set a fast pace, walking strongly and refusing rest stops, anxious about his brother. He noticed immediately when Alyx stopped short in horror.

"What is it?"

The tree which had held the tree-house had fallen and was sprawled over the ground - a chaos of broken branches and smashed wood.

Chapter 25

The huge cracked branches and shattered pieces of tree-house were covered in blackened marks - the footprints of death angels. The stench of sulphur tainted the smell of crushed mangiri leaves.

Screaming, Kulde rushed forward, getting caught up in the tangled mass of branches where the tree had bought down several smaller trees in its fall. Alyx went after him, chopping away the thinner branches with her sword so that she made quicker progress towards the part of the tree where the tree-house had nestled. Jindabyne began searching through the curtains of leaves hanging around the crown of the fallen tree. Fortunately Serge kept his head. When Alyx looked back at him, he was standing guard over Daria and calling out Yundi's name.

Alyx could find no sign of the boy among the collapsed house at the tree's centre nor, to her relief, any blood or piles of ash.

"Either he wasn't here or he was thrown free," she shouted to the others.

"Yundi!" shouted Kulde in a despairing voice, thrashing around in the branches nearby. Then Serge let out a surprised yelp followed by the shrill scream of a child.

When Alyx broke free of the fallen branches, she found Serge struggling to hold a small Mori boy, who was shrieking with terror.

"Gibadgee! Gibadgee!"

"Don't be afraid," cried Alyx in Mori. She knelt down and looked into the boy's face. "Come now, you know me, don't you? Alyx Verdey the Forest Child. And your name is Sebie, isn't it?"

Recognising her, the child stopped screaming.

"Lady, what are you doing with these Gibadgee and who are...?" He caught sight of Kulde. "Are there more Tari? Have they truly come back to help us?"

"You've seen other Tari?" cried Kulde, clutching at the boy.

"Yes! A Tari boy came to our camp yesterday. I was coming here to get you when I saw the Gibadgee and got scared."

"Yundi!" cried Kulde, hugging the boy. "Thank you, Sweet Life!"

His happy cries were interrupted by a scuffle between Jindabyne and Daria, who had managed to slip free of Serge's grip in the excitement.

"No you don't! We haven't finished with you yet," snarled Jindabyne, smacking Daria hard around the face.

"Stop!" shouted Serge.

"Why do you have to be so rough with her?" cried Alyx.

"Don't blame her!" said Kulde. He took Jindabyne's arm and said softly, "Remember you are Tari. Don't lower yourself to her level."

"I... She...," Jindabyne's face crumpled and she burst into tears. Serge put his arm round her and drew her face against his shoulder. Alyx, feeling uncomfortable with this emotional scene, seized firm hold of Daria's neck manacle and turned towards the wide-eyed boy.

"So," she said. "Take us to this young Tari then."

As they trudged through the forest after Sebie, several more Mori children appeared out of the undergrowth. Alyx recognised them as part of the group who had left her mother's camp when the Mirayans attacked. Later in the day, after what seemed like hours of walking, a group of old people and children appeared out of the bushes, carrying wreaths of flowers which they hung joyfully around Kulde and Jindabyne's necks or pressed into their hands. An ancient woman held up her hand for silence.

"The Tari have finally answered our prayers!" she cried. "We welcome the Tari Lords!" Wild cheers rang out all round.

Kulde paid no attention to the welcome.

"Yundi?" he asked.

"The Tari Lord fears for his brother," explained Alyx and the old woman bowed and gestured for them to go forward. Shortly after they entered a clearing full of people. In the middle sat the small figure of Yundi, cheerfully eating nuts from a bowl.

Sometime after Alyx had left, Yundi told them, he had fallen into red visions of flying things and, frightened, had crawled into a basket to hide. There had been insane laughter and things had started to crash and then the basket was falling. It had bounced down into some springy branches and Yundi, unhurt, but terrified, had crawled through the tumbled branches and the bracken and hidden under a fallen log. Outside his hiding place, the world had seemed full of laughing death angels, shrivelling the bracken under their heavy feet. He could not tell what was real and what was a vision, so he stayed still until the visions had lessened. Later as he was wandering through an untidy forest, full of fallen logs and prickly bushes in the wrong place and still troubled by intermittent visions of three-winged birds and huge black ticks, he came upon some Mori children collecting nuts. At first he hadn't known if they were real or not, but the children had brought him back to their camp and treated him as an honoured guest and a healing woman had given him a herbal drink that had cleared his head wonderfully.

"You must get the recipe for it, Kulde."

"You horrible little rabbit!" cried Kulde, shaking and

hugging his brother at the same time. "Weren't you even worried?"

"I knew you'd come today," said Yundi cheerfully. "I saw it in a dream last week. Have some nuts!"

The trees surrounding the clearing were full of temporary tree-houses, and as night fell the Mori retired up into them and treated the party to a feast, untroubled by the blood beasts prowling below.

These Mori were those who could not fight, mostly the very old and the very young, but they were hard at work gathering as much food as they could to send south to feed the warriors. They also had news of the Mori's battle with the Mirayans. The Mirayans had seemed invincible in the early summer, but after they'd conquered all the forest up to the first river, the red fish had proved as much of a barrier to them as the Mori - more so, for they didn't know where to find alternative sources of water. At first, the Mirayans seemed to be contenting themselves clearing the forest they had conquered, while the Mori constantly harassed them, but now, due to the clever actions of Queen Elena, the Mirayans' alliance had fallen apart and they'd completely stopped their clearing. There were rumours that the Seagani were harassing them too.

"What's the line of smoke to the south?" asked Alyx.

"A terrible thing," said an old man. "A few days ago the Gibadgee passed by with a new mage. He is Mirayan but as powerful as a Tari and he's been desecrating the trees to make a wide path for the Mirayan army to cross the forest. May Labwa forgive us but we haven't the strength to stop them. Any Mori they catch they kill, even if it is a child. Otherwise they have no interest in us. They are heading as fast as they can for Eabri where the death angels and blood beasts come from and the dark lord has his keep. It's he the Gibadgee have fallen out with. There are Mori warriors following them but they have not engaged them. Let the Gibadgee kill each other and save our arrows."

There was much to consider here but full of food and exhausted from two long days without sleep, Alyx could no longer keep her eyes open. One of the Mori showed her to a platform loaded with clean skins and she snuggled down among them and was instantly asleep.

Alyx's first priority the next morning was to find out the secret of the red fish from Daria. This was surprisingly easy. The Mori had fed, bandaged and washed her, but none of these things mattered to Daria.

"Show me Ermora," she wailed as soon as she laid eyes on Alyx and her companions. Her face was pale, her eyes haunted and she was scratching compulsively at the backs of her hands till they bled. Jindabyne struck a deal with her. She would let her mindsearch her, if she told her the secret of the red fish. Daria gave in almost immediately and told them what they wanted to know.

Salt, simple salt killed the red fish.

"Fools! Haven't you noticed that they didn't spread into the sea?"

Angry at Daria's sneering, Jindabyne got up to walk away, but Kulde stopped her.

"We must keep our bargain," he said. "If you cannot face it, I'll do it."

Jindabyne flushed and looked at the ground. "No I'll do it. You're too young."

They stayed two days with the Mori so that Kulde might recover from the beating Daria had given him. At night when the death angels were gone and they were safe from the blood beasts in the tree houses, he used healing magic on himself. By the third day the bruising on his face had gone. He still cringed every time he heard Daria's voice, but he'd began to show an interest in Mori cooking, which Alyx counted as a sign of recovery.

Alyx spent the two days of rest with Serge. On that first morning she had woken up, seen him lying asleep in the skins nearby and been overwhelmed by all the problems that her feelings for him would cause. Already she had noticed how uneasy the other Mori were at Serge's presence though Alyx sensed that they were unwilling to voice their disapproval to her face.

But when Serge opened his eyes and smiled at her that morning, suddenly the problems didn't seem important. Over the next two rest days, Alyx always found herself near him even when she'd had no intention of seeking him out. If she sat separately, their eyes kept meeting and when she was away from him, she thought about him the whole time. How did anyone do anything useful or sensible in this state?

Together they helped gather berries, fetch water and dig plants and roots to be sent to those fighting the Mirayans. The Mori were giving little thought to the winter and with the lack of water, the depredations of the blood beasts on the game round about and this heavy demand on the food stocks, famine would be inevitable if this situation were allowed to go on much longer.

"We cannot even heal the river," she said to Serge while they gathered adra berries. "Jindabyne and Kulde are full of good ideas for destroying the red fish but they need to use magic. If we do that, the death angels or blood beasts will attack us in such great numbers we'll be overwhelmed."

"I'll have to go to this Eabri place and destroy Lev," muttered Serge, his jaw clenched.

"And I cannot hide here while my mother remains his captive," said Alyx.

Serge squeezed her arm and she was suddenly aware that their companions had moved away and they were alone in the adra thicket. This was the first time they'd really been alone since they'd kissed at the waterfall, but after Serge squeezed her hand, he moved away to another branch. And they were off to Eabri tomorrow and who knew when they would have the chance to sort things out?

"Serge!" she cried.

He swung round.

"What's the matter?"

"Can't you... Haven't you got anything to say to me?"

He met her eyes and flushed. Thank life, he knew what she meant.

"Um yes I do but... I didn't want to press you. I know

I'm a problem for you."

"Oh!" said Alyx, suddenly feeling mean. She'd been worried that Serge was uninterested, when he was actually being considerate.

They both stared at the ground. Alyx found her voice.

"Are we um... courting or...?"

Courting. How could she have said such a stupid word!

"Do you want us to be courting? I'm happy with whatever you want. I just like being with you."

Dismay filled Alyx.

"Oh Serge!" she wailed. "Oh I'm sorry. This is hopeless."

"What's the matter?" cried Serge. He put down his basket and stepped anxiously towards her.

"What do you want from me?" she wailed.

"We can be courting if that's what you want. What does that mean exactly? I mean, what am I supposed to do?"

Alyx looked at her feet. Mori courting couples slept together just like she and Serge had in Ermora. She felt herself flushing.

"Can courting couples kiss each other?" murmured Serge

"Yes," whispered Alyx, suddenly too shy to look at him.

"Right," said Serge. "That's good then."

They stood there for a moment.

Maybe he doesn't want to kiss me, thought Alyx.

She lifted her head to see what he was doing, just as he was lowering his head and her cheek banged him on the jaw.

"Ow!"

"Oh no! I'm sorry."

"No it doesn't matter."

"Are you hurt?"

She leaned anxiously towards him. Serge took his hand off his jaw, took her firmly by the shoulders and kissed her on the lips.

A thrill went through Alyx. Her arms seemed to go

round him of their own volition. He felt so hard and strong. They kissed and kissed, holding each other closer and wanting to get closer still.

Later as they lay under a fern, Serge traced the shadow of the fern fronds along her naked belly.

"I was afraid that it was only the drug," he murmured.

"Me too," said Alyx.

"It wouldn't have mattered if you didn't want to again," he said softly. "I, um... I really like you, Alyx."

"Me too," whispered Alyx, kissing him.

That night as they sat round the glowing red brazier in their tree-house, they put the proposition of going to Eabri to the others.

"But you don't need to go," said Serge to Jindabyne. "You should stay here. Put on some weight."

Jindabyne shook her head.

"I can't rest while these death minions pollute our island. I'm strong. Don't be afraid I'll slow you down."

"Well I'm definitely coming," said Kulde. "I wonder if the Mori will let us take some of those really good dried berries they make. But you should definitely go back to Ermora," he said, turning to where his brother was curled up on some furs looking dreamily into the glowing coals. "You can't keep wandering round lost in visions."

"I'm coming with you," cried Yundi. "My dreams tell me that my destiny is in Eabri. And I have this potion to control my visions now. I haven't had any problem with the blood beasts down here, have I?"

"But you're half asleep all the time," retorted Kulde.

"If you leave me behind I will just set off alone after you," insisted Yundi, and there was no answer to that.

At least they would be free of Daria. After much persuasion from Alyx, their hosts agreed to look after her. Unless she was drugged, the death mage wailed and screamed all day.

"It would be better if we killed her," said Alyx ruefully, feeling guilty at laying such a burden on her people.

"Can you do it?" asked Serge.

"You know I cannot. I can't even bring myself to ask the Mori to do it."

"I can't either," said Serge. "I pity her, poor mad creature. Ironic, isn't it? She wouldn't hesitate to kill us."

The following midday, they set off with full packs and the blessings of their Mori hosts. Alyx led, Yundi, Kulde and Jindabyne came in the middle and Serge took up the rear. For the next couple of days they travelled north-east along the line of the Gen Mountains stopping at Mori tree platforms. The month in Ermora had softened Alyx, so that at the end of every day she ached all over. Yet every afternoon after they had stopped, Serge would smile at her and she would go with him into the forest. The delight they found together made every day seem bright.

Only Jindabyne remarked upon them. Serge told Alyx that his step-mother had drawn him aside and warned him that Alyx's family would hate their liaison.

"I know," Serge had replied, "but that's a long way in the future."

Although they were not used to travelling so far by foot, Kulde and Yundi did their best not to slow the group down and they made good time towards Eabri. On the fourth day they came to a place where the forest suddenly stopped and became a desolate corridor of ashy ground scattered with odd bits of burnt tree. The opposite edge of the forest was more than a bow shot away.

Alyx felt a physical pain in her chest at the sight of the destruction.

"Labwa!" she gasped, knowing that this must be the road made by the powerful mage the Mori had told them of. "Why kill so many trees?"

"Removing cover for archers," muttered Serge. "Look out!" A patrol of Mirayan soldiers appeared at a bend in the road, loading their bows. She and Serge hustled the speechless Tari into the trees and dragged them under the refuge of some ferns. As they crouched there, watching through the fronds for pursuers, Alyx found tears were running down her face. Serge put his arms around her.

"I know," he whispered softly. "They are evil men."

No one came after them. The soldiers obviously had no taste for chasing people through the forest.

"Someone did that with magic," said Jindabyne when they regrouped. "Surely only Tari have such power."

"A Tari would never do such a thing," cried Kulde.

"The Mori said a Mirayan mage," said Serge. "But with such power? This can only be death magic."

No one said anything for a couple of minutes. The sense of horror among the group was palpable.

"Come on. We achieve nothing here. Let's get going," said Alyx at last.

For the rest of the day they walked north near the edge of the cleared area. Their pace was slow for death angels regularly flew above the new road and they had to keep under cover.

The road angled closer and closer to the edge of the Gen Mountains which rose in craggy grey cliffs above the forest. The only break in these cliffs were the ravines which been had eroded back into the mountainsides. Alyx knew from experience that most of them ended in a wasteland of rubble and more sheer cliffs, but a few cut deeply back into the mountains.

"Eabri is such a ravine," she told the others. "And near it is another one, Wirrawee which goes almost as far back. You can get over into Eabri from the end of Wirrawee, but I imagine your Uncle's well aware of that."

"How did you get out of Eabri, Jindabyne?" asked Serge.

"Daria killed some guards and we went out through the gate," said Jindabyne. "The fortress was only defended against the outside. There's a limit to how much Lev can do alone, even when he draws on demon power. He concentrated most of his wardings on Alyx's mother."

The group reached the opening of the Wirrawee ravine in the mid-afternoon. Just before the ravine opening, the burnt road reached the bottom of the cliffs and continued along just under them. They decided to spend the night in a cave Alyx knew and to spend the following day tracking down the Mori warriors they knew must be shadowing the troop of Mirayans.

They walked back along the cliff, until Alyx found the right fold in the rock.

"Doesn't seem big enough to hide a cave," said Serge, peering upwards.

"We need to get up to that ledge. You stay here under those bushes. I'll go up. There should be supplies inside and likely a rope too."

With the help of a dead branch, Alyx climbed easily up to the ledge only to find that Serge had followed her.

"I don't think you should go alone," he explained. "The Mirayans may have found that cave."

"I know that," retorted Alyx, scowling at him, tempted to bite his head off. He'd become very protective in the last few days and she wasn't sure she liked it.

"I'd follow anyone up here," he said, smiling apologetically so that she smiled back before she realised what she'd done.

"I wonder," she retorted, turning to move along the uneven ledge. "I'm not one of your delicate Mirayan women, you know."

"I know, I know."

In the fold of the rock was an opening so small it seemed nothing more than a shadow on the cliff face.

"Are we going to fit in?" hissed Serge. "Let me go first!"

Alyx ignored this silly suggestion. Entering this cave always gave her a queasy feeling, but this was no reason to let Serge take the risk.

"It's bigger than it looks. You turn your body left immediately you wriggle through. I know where some torches are." She passed her tinder box to Serge. "You light some tinder and I'll pass the torches out to you."

She pushed her shoulders through the hole, enduring the brief squeeze and pulled herself out into the cave mouth on the other side. With the fear of the thick blackness of the cave nibbling at her, she groped for the hollow near the tunnel where the torches were kept.

By the time she had found them, Serge was leaning into the cave opening with the burning tinder. She pushed the torch into the tinder and it sprang easily into flame. She stepped back twirling around to light up the cave...

Someone grabbed her. She managed to let out a squeak as a hand came down over her mouth, then she was pulled away from the opening. She heard Serge shout and a scuffle behind her. Someone lifted up the torch she had dropped and held it up. She saw Serge and the shadowy form of a man behind holding him in a firm grip with a hand over Serge's mouth.

"Well, well! A fine young Mirayan," said a Mori voice, a voice Alyx thought she recognised. A knife came up to Serge's throat.

What if they killed Serge out of hand without even asking questions? Desperately she struggled to free her mouth from her captor's hand.

Then suddenly a voice cut through the darkness.

"Alyx? Alyx, is that you! Let her go!"

A familiar voice! The figure that came plunging out of the darkness familiar too.

"Yani!" shouted Alyx. "Don't kill him!"

Yani and a group of twenty Mori warriors had been hiding in the cave waiting for dark. When their sentry had seen two strangers climbing up to the ledge, they had prepared an ambush.

"Nobody knew where you were," cried Yani.

"I've been in Ermora."

"Ermora! Did you get any joy there?"

Alyx avoided Serge's eye and said, "Two Tari agreed to come out with us. Only one mage."

"Tari!" cried Yani, hugging Alyx. "You have a Tari mage with you? Blessings of life. Alyx, you lifesaver! This is going to make everything so much easier. Bring them up immediately."

While Serge and a couple of the warriors lowered a rope down to bring the Tari up, Alyx and Yani shared news. Yani had lost weight and her face was etched with new lines. Alyx understood why when she heard of the fate of Marigoth and of how Yani had followed her sister's captor here from Miraya.

"Malov Symina used her magic to make all this damned road through the forest," said Yani dully. "She would be better off dead."

Alyx could not speak for the lump in her throat. Then Serge, calling through the opening, chased all sad thoughts away.

"Alyx. They've lost Yundi."

"How could they? What's happened?"

"He went off for a piss and didn't come back."

Down on the ground outside the cave, Alyx picked up Yundi's trail easily. Soon she found the slightly trampled ground where someone had seized him.

"Someone wearing red," she said, holding up a couple of threads.

"Daria!" cried Kulde and Serge together.

"Daria?" cried Yani. "A dark haired death mage who likes to mindsearch Tari? She's here? Hell and the Abyss! That's Malov's sister."

By now the setting sun was lengthening the shadows. Yani and a couple of the Mori warriors joined Alyx, Serge and Kulde in following Daria's trail. She had made no attempt to cover her tracks but the gathering dusk made them difficult to see. At last Kulde stopped them.

"I smell magic," he said, and even as he spoke, the howls of two blood beasts cut through the dusk. "She's left a magical trail for them! I can see it in the dark." Kulde turned around. "She's doubled back behind us."

"Curse it! We'd better get back to the cave, otherwise we'll be spending the night in trees."

"We've got to find Yundi," cried Kulde. "You don't know what that woman's like."

"Believe me, I do!" said Yani, grabbing his arm and pulling him along firmly along behind her. "But she won't really hurt him. Come on."

"No!" shouted Kulde. Yani gave a cry of pain as he

used magic to break from her grip and a moment later he was gone. They heard him crying out Yundi's name as he ran away in the darkening forest.

"Abyss!" cursed Yani. "We were going to go up into Wirrawee tonight." The howling of at least three blood beasts drowned her out. They sounded horribly near.

"Come on! Find a tree!" shouted Yani, grabbing the trunk of the nearest.

"This one," cried Alyx, dragging Serge towards a tall mangiri. "Come on, up with you!"

"You first!"

"Don't be stupid!"

Somehow they got into the tree before the blood beasts came crashing through the scrub and clung to the shuddering branches for what seemed like ages, while blood beasts threw themselves at the tree trunk. Between the yowling, they could hear Kulde shouting Yundi's name in the distance and at last the blood beasts went crashing away in the direction of his voice.

Alyx and Serge took the opportunity to climb higher into the tree where they found a forked branch wide enough for both of them. Alyx stuffed her cloak into the fork to make a comfortable seat and she and Serge sat astride it - Serge's back against the tree, Alyx back's against him, Serge's cloak round both of them.

"Another wonderful night up a tree," muttered Alyx.

"Any night is wonderful with you," said Serge, nuzzling her neck.

"Sshh. Not so loud. Yani'll hear."

She felt him tense and knew she'd said the wrong thing.

"That's your aunt Yani, isn't it? The leader of the Guardians."

"Yes," said Alyx tensely. The future had caught up with them sooner than either had expected. Alyx felt a moment of regret that they had met up with her aunt, and cursed herself for even thinking that.

"Maybe I should leave," Serge muttered. "She'll hate me."

"Of course not! You mustn't... Yani's always very fair. Really. It'll be all right. When she knows you're my friend."

"We are more than friends," said Serge softly. "How's she going to like that?"

Alyx sighed and leaned back against Serge, pulling his arms tighter around her.

"I don't know. I just don't know."

There was little to do in the darkness, but worry about why Kulde's voice had gone silent and listen to the distant howling of the blood beasts. At least the creatures didn't come back. Alyx and Serge dozed in their tree nest and woke at last in the grey dawn, covered in chilly dew. As Alyx stretched her stiff muscles and Serge smiled at her, her eye caught sight of something lying on the ground beneath them.

"Mir! That's Kulde!" she shouted, almost falling out of the tree in her astonishment.

They swung down from the tree as fast as their stiff morning limbs would let them. Kulde was curled up on a nest of crushed bracken. He had a gash on his forehead where someone had hit him, but he seemed to be sleeping rather than unconscious. Except that they could not seem to waken him. Nor could Yani when she joined them.

"I am holding him asleep," said a voice behind them. "Till we have finished our parley."

Daria stood in the nearby scrub holding Yundi by the hand. His eyes were unfocused and he swayed from side to side and muttered. The death mage was as pale as mist except for her deep red lips.

"What have you done to the boy? What have we got to parley about?" demanded Yani.

"I don't want these two little boys," said Daria. "I want you, Ermora."

As she spoke she pointed at Yani. Yani bit her lip and her thin face seemed to become hollower.

"What will you give me in return?" she said at length.

"In return?" Apparently Daria had not considered this

aspect of a deal.

"You will aid us against Lev Madraga," said Yani firmly. "You can be useful."

Daria's face softened. "Then you will...?"

"If you help us!"

"Oh yes!" whispered Daria. She held out her hand beseechingly. "Come to me Ermora! Please!"

Yani turned to the others. "Take the boys. Go back to the cave. I'll see you there."

"Yani! You can't..."

"She won't hurt me. If I'm not back by noon you can come and find me." She dropped her voice. "Everything will be fine," she hissed. "Go now!" She walked towards Daria.

The death mage let go of Yundi and moved forward, with both arms outstretched and her skull-like face suffused with joy.

"Ermora!" she moaned softly. "It's been so long."

As Yani reached her, Daria put her arms round her and laid her head on Yani's shoulder before drawing her away into the bushes.

"Yani!" whispered Alyx, remembering how last night she had wished her away.

Yundi took a few steps forward and tripped over. "Birds! Why have they got three wings?" he wailed despairingly. Serge ran over and scooped him up.

"Come on," he said to Alyx. "We should get these two back to safety." He touched her shoulder. "I'm sorry Alyx. But we'd best do as Yani says."

Chapter 26

Malov gave up wearing his imperial purple robes and exchanged them for a serviceable black. On every night of the long journey over the sea to the archipelago and the island of Yarmar, he would vow, "I'm going to kill Lev Madraga, no matter how much it harms me."

Then he would cast himself on his bed and Ezratah would watch him toss and mutter all night. Even drugs did not grant him quiet sleep.

Marigoth remained a pale sleep walker, her bones becoming sharper and sharper under her skin. Sometimes Ezratah would awaken in the early morning light to see her sitting in her cage on the other side of the cabin from him, watching intently while Malov tossed and muttered in his sleep.

"Is he changing?" he hissed at her once.

"This is what the Raven promised," she said and her eyes glowed as she said it. This brief sight of the old Marigoth filled him with happiness but he did not see it often.

Malov hadn't changed all that much. He still hit and

kicked Ezratah and the slaves who tended him with casual brutality, and Ezratah feared what he might do to Duke Wolf and his family when they arrived. Yet when the ship slowed and stopped, and he first smelt the scent of mangiri trees that told him they were in Yarmar, he could not help being glad to be home.

Huddled in his cage in the dark cabin, he heard the sound of a brief magical battle on the deck above. When Malov came below shortly afterwards, Ezratah could not resist asking him what had happened, but Malov merely snickered nastily as he unlocked Ezratah's cage and dragged him out by his neck manacle. This was the first time in almost a month that Ezratah had been out of the cage, and even though he had carefully stretched himself every day, his muscles were so weak that he fell over.

"Get up useless slave!" Malov kicked Ezratah in the ribs. "The villain in charge of this rancid little hole speaks such foul Mirayan I need you to translate." He pushed his face into Ezratah's. "And don't try and fool me. I intend to take the meanings straight out of your mind."

Could Malov be speaking of the Duke? But as the death mage settled himself on his throne with Ezratah and Marigoth seated at his feet as if they were pet dogs, Ezratah saw that things had changed in Lamartaine. The graceful towers no longer flew the dragon flag of the Madraga's, but the banner of the mercenary captain, Guilius Appius and it was a delegation of mercenaries, clad in a mixture of dirty silk and rags, who slouched up onto the deck.

They were disposed to be friendly to Malov, telling him that their lord Guilius Appius had been allied with Lev Madraga, but that now they were bitter enemies. Madraga was a death mage and must be put down. They give no hint that they saw that the same criticism could be applied to Malov.

"I have a score to settle with Lev Madraga," Malov told them. "Tell your master I'm willing to aid him in any way possible."

The mercenaries' spokesman, a slightly cleaner looking individual who spoke a southern peasant dialect of

Mirayan, replied that their master was away attempting to subdue an unruly forest tribe who were blocking their route to Lev's hiding place, but that when he heard of Malov's offer of aid, he was certain to come galloping back to accept it.

Ezratah took the opportunity to ask after the Madraga family and learned of the death of Duke Wolf and his sons.

"Lord Lev accused the wife and youngest son of the murder, which no one believes now but it's too late, ain't it?" said the spokesman. "Disappeared, ain't they, and the little daughter too, even though the local Seagani have rose up in their support. Like as not the evil bastard killed 'em all."

A few days later Guilius Appius came calling, just as his henchman had said he would, and Malov seated himself in state to receive him with Marigoth and Ezratah crouching at his feet again. The mercenary captain didn't seem to recognise the skinny man with the white-streaked beard and long tangled hair crouched at Malov's feet, as Ezratah, the Mirayan he had once called traitor, but he clearly recognised Marigoth and smiled thinly at her.

"You have one of the Guardians captive," he said. "I'm impressed."

"Such is my power. And now I can draw on hers as well."

This was a clear admission of being a death mage, yet Appius' only reaction was the raising of an eyebrow. He had lost weight and a strange intensity burned in his eyes. His throat was bandaged, his left arm moved stiffly and he looked scruffy, where he had always been well-groomed before.

"Let us get to business then," he said, as if Malov had said nothing wrong. "I need help to get through the forest to where Lev Madraga is holed up in those mountains over there. Will you help me in return for a share when we defeat him?"

"Gladly," said Malov simply.

"There is only one condition. I must have all captives taken."

"Fair enough," said Malov. "All I desire is Madraga's death."

At the mention of captives, Ezratah sensed a lifting of Marigoth's listlessness. Later when they were shut up in their cages in the dark cabin while Malov drank wine up on the deck with Appius, Marigoth said, "I sense Elena behind this. Madraga must have her captive. He and Appius have fallen out over her."

"What makes you think that?"

"He looks as men always look when they have seen Elena. Eaten alive by desire."

Two days later they rode out, Ezratah tied onto the saddle of a horse and Marigoth riding up before Malov as she always did. What a terrible journey that was! For after they had crossed a terrible poisoned river which had once been water and was now red slime, Malov used Marigoth's power to cut a swathe through the forest beyond. With a wave of his hands, huge trees were tossed aside, ripped out by their roots like grass, and their bodies burned to form a pathway of ash. The destruction churned up huge clouds of dust and leaves and seeing the beautiful forest destroyed so callously, filled Ezratah with grinding misery and made tears well up in Marigoth's expressionless eyes and seep down her cheeks. Ezratah's only consolation was that Malov looked more ill than usual.

"They're only trees!" Malov muttered in his sleep at night. "Only trees."

Malov kept himself, Appius and their immediate entourage free of the dust and smoke, but at the end of each day when the army came together, Ezratah saw that the ordinary soldiers were covered in dust and ash and coughing up black phlegm.

On the second day they were attacked from the rear by a large number of Mori, but Malov simply threw them aside as he threw aside the trees and the soldiers slaughtered those they could catch. After that they saw little of the Mori, though Ezratah sensed them watching them from the forest beyond the ash road. A couple of days later death angels came winging out from the mountains ahead of them. Even as dark dots in the sky, they made Marigoth whimper and cover her head and caused the soldiers to flee into the trees.

Unconcerned, Malov held up his hand as if holding up the sky and began to shout in a bitter language that sounded exactly like the language he'd used when he'd summoned demons to speak with him. The death angels didn't attack, but simply circled overhead and Malov went calmly back to his work of destruction. After a time the soldiers crept out from under the trees and followed them.

The death angels came every day after that and hung around as long as the daylight lasted, circling, dipping and rising with a kind of infernal playfulness through the smoke from the burning trees. When the death angels had gone for the night, blood beasts appeared and howled and scuffled around their camp throughout the dark hours. They too were kept away by some bitter words from Malov, but the soldiers built small barricades out of the fallen brush anyway. They won't have kept the blood beasts out, but they made everyone feel safer.

Ezratah heard the troops wonder how anyone, even someone with tame Tari, could defeat a man who could create so many of creatures of the Abyss. He heard other mutterings as well. Mercenaries might be bad men, but even they wondered how Appius could ally himself with Malov, who was so clearly a death mage.

Ezratah hoped they might mutiny, but his hope proved vain. The miserable journey towards the cliffs of the Gen Mountains ground forward, until on the twelfth day their party suddenly broke through the line of trees into a place where the forest had already been long cleared. Before them rose tall cliffs and a huge thick wall and a moat built across the mouth of a ravine. A small keep was built onto the wall - the lair of Lev Madraga, usurper and death mage. An extremely defensible position to build a fortress, for on two sides the mountains were impassable and the front could easily be defended by someone who had winged death minions at his command.

That evening as the army settled tensely into a camp under the shelter of the trees, a mercenary rode out from the fortress. He strode up to the tent where Malov was seated on his throne with Ezratah and Marigoth at his feet and Appius sitting beside him and said bluntly,

"Lord Malov, my master offers you a duel to the death. Your power against his."

"No!" cried Appius.

Malov, pale but perfectly steady, replied, "Tell your scum master that I will meet him with pleasure and when I defeat him, I will desecrate his filthy betraying hide with even more pleasure."

The messenger shrugged, clearly unimpressed, and was gone. Appius protested, but Malov argued him round. "I draw upon the strength of the Tari. Even a death mage cannot defeat that!"

Was he right?

Only Ezratah and Marigoth knew how Malov paced the tent sleeplessly that night. His fear affected Ezratah.

"Let us flee from here," he urged Malov, afraid for Marigoth. "If you lose, it'll all be for nothing. You'll simply be handing Marigoth and her power to Lev Madraga."

"Be quiet!" cried Marigoth. She turned to Malov. "Think of how Lev Madraga used me to trap you, to make you impotent, a half-man. Only his death can make up for that. You cannot let him live to triumph over you."

All night she urged Malov on with fierce words and Ezratah realised how wrong he had been to advise flight. If Malov defeated Lev, Ermora would be saved. Malov was a mere shadow of the death mage he had once been and could no longer destroy mountains or kill people without conscience. And with his access to Marigoth's power, surely Malov must win.

The contest was held on the cleared dirt before the fortress. The ground was dotted with the newly killed stumps of trees and now only rank grass grew sparsely between scuffed patches of clay. Lev had demanded that

Appius' army move out of missile range so that no one could distract him by attempting to assassinate him, but he did say that each mage might have an honour guard of two to accompany them.

Two thrones were set up facing each other and when the time came, the tall fortress gates swung open and Lev came through surrounded by a contingent of guards. He was tall and golden haired and his impeccably clean robes billowed magnificently around him as he strode confidently out towards them. Malov looked small in comparison and the way his hands picked at his robe betrayed his nervousness.

Each mage mounted his throne, and except for two guards who stayed beside Lev, and Ezratah and Marigoth, who were as usual chained up at Malov's feet, everyone withdrew and the duel began. At first Malov threw sleep spells at Lev, but he lacked the detachment to make his spells pass through Lev's considerable defences and Lev made him even madder by laughing at him and not bothering to attack back.

"Smite him," shouted Marigoth suddenly. "Smite him with all your power. Go on, do it."

Malov shook himself and smiled.

"Of course," he said. "The old methods are the best."

He pulled himself up and threw a huge blast of killing power at Lev and it might have worked had Lev merely relied on a conventional magical defence. But, quick as lightening, Lev used his magic to pick up one of his guards and throw him into the killing blast. Most of the blast was absorbed by the unfortunate soldier who, with horrible shrieks, was burned alive, and Lev was able to dodge underneath the rest. By the time Lev had picked himself up off the ground, Malov was writhing and screaming in pain, helplessly sharing the soldier's death throes, while Marigoth crouched shivering at his side. Clearly Lev knew exactly how Tari magic had affected Malov and had planned the whole thing. With a laugh he swaggered forward and lifted his arm to deliver the killing blast.

"No!" shouted Ezratah, leaping up with his arms

spread, and flinging himself between Lev and Malov. "Don't kill him. If you spare him, I'll serve you faithfully. And Marigoth can be useful to you."

For a moment Lev wavered, obviously tempted to kill. Then he grinned and looked more closely at Ezratah.

"Is that you, Ezratah Karanus? Well, well. You've changed."

With a flick of his fingers he sent a fireball towards Appius' troops who fled further into the forest. Then he motioned his own troops to come out of the fortress' gate.

"Very well," he said to Ezratah. He bowed and gestured as if he were inviting them into his private chambers for wine and cakes. "You and your precious Tari are welcome to the hospitality of my fortress, such as it is. And bring your little master."

As Lev's soldiers scooped up Marigoth and Malov, Lev strolled casually back towards the fortress. Meanwhile Guilius Appius had recovered from the shock of seeing Malov so comprehensively defeated.

Ezratah heard him shouting at his men to fire and ducked as he heard the swish of arrows. Lev did not even bother to turn round. He simply waved his hand and Ezratah saw most of the arrows turned in mid-flight and shoot back at the army. To the sound of screaming men, Lev sauntered back through the fortress gates, with Ezratah and the rest of his entourage scampering along with him, and with a wave of his hands he slammed and bolted the heavy doors shut behind them.

Ezratah felt chill shadows passed over him as eight death angels flew out over the wall to attack the army.

"Yet another prison!" thought Ezratah grimly.

The cells beneath the fortress were new, the stone still fresh, but in his cell someone had already scratched the Tari symbol, four circles bisected by a cross, in the wall. He put Malov down on the floor where he continued writhing and screaming with pain and terror. Ezratah could not help feeling smug that he experiencing the fate he had inflicted on so many people, but Marigoth had been locked in a separate cell and Ezratah was more worried about her. In the intervals when Malov was quiet, he called out her name and after a time she answered and Ezratah realised that she must be just in the next cell. She told him in her expressionless voice that she was well enough though feeling some of Malov's distress.

"Why did you save us?" she asked.

"I love you," said Ezratah. "Forgive me!"

She didn't reply to this or to anything else he said.

The muffled shouts, screams, clash of metal and the occasional detonation of magic that told of the death angels attack on Appius' troops, faded away quickly. At least two phalanxes of mages were needed to overwhelm even a single death angel and Guilius Appius did not have that many mages among his troops. His army would be forced to flee.

How easily Lev Madraga had won!

As night fell, guards came and took Ezratah from his cell. To his astonishment he was taken to a bathhouse where a barber cut most of his hair off and showed him to a bath full of medicinal herbs designed to rid him of any vermin he might have picked up. Then he was given worn but clean mage's robes and lead to a small chamber at the top of the keep. Lev was waiting for him, seated by a table set for dinner.

So I am the dinnertime entertainment, thought Ezratah with a sinking heart. He was amazed when he was offered the seat opposite Lev and a servant placed a bowl of steaming stew and a platter of bread in front of him. Though the scent of the food made him drool with hunger, mindful of the effects of starvation, Ezratah ate as slowly as he could manage and pushed the bowl away as soon as he was full, which was much too quickly.

"My poor Ezratah," crooned Lev mockingly. "You're just a shadow of your former self."

"What are you playing at?" said Ezratah bluntly.

"I'm longing to hear about your adventures with Malov and I thought I might as well be civilised about it."

"And if I refuse to co-operate?" said Ezratah, irritated

by Lev's courtier's manners.

"Oh don't be like that! I can take it out of your mind. I can even kill your little Marigoth. She's really not that important to me. I've got lots of Tari prisoners. All of the Tari who live outside Ermora languish in my custody."

"I'm not sure I believe that," said Ezratah. "Tari are such powerful mages."

"Mages are still 'human'. They can be tricked or drugged or even just hit on the head. That's how I captured all mine. Tell me how Malov captured you."

There seemed no point in resisting Lev, so Ezratah recounted his adventures in Miraya, just as actors and fools had always paid for the hospitality of great men.

When he was returned to his cell afterwards, he found Malov lying unconscious in a puddle of his own urine. Reminding himself that this was Marigoth he was caring for, not the horrible man who had destroyed her life, Ezratah mopped him up with some fresh straw and covered him with a blanket so that he wouldn't catch a chill. In the morning Malov's death throes had ceased and he lay there alternatively whimpering and singing to himself, clearly driven insane by his experience.

Ezratah was feeding Malov a little bread soaked in water when the guards came for him the following evening. Once again there was food and conversation. Ezratah could almost imagine he was back at Lamartaine visiting Lev in his chamber in the days before Wolf Madraga had married Jindabyne Tari and Lev had become impossible to bear. Back in the days when Ezratah had looked on Lev as a friend.

"I've been without civilised company for some time," Lev told him. "Here it's all natives and mercenaries. And one would-be death mage who likes to fuck children. Hard to work out who is actually the more despicable."

Suspecting that Lev needed an audience to admire his cleverness, Ezratah was as agreeable as he could be without appearing false and his plan paid off. Lev told him everything.

He described how, disgusted by his brother's marriage

to a native and determined to end the endless humiliations the Tari were inflicting on the Mirayans, he had returned to Miraya to see if he could find a solution. There he had rapidly decided that death magic was the only way.

"After all Tari are life mages, the demons call them so, and we all know that death extinguishes life. So I became one of a college of death mages. They welcomed someone with my natural power with open arms, but what an uninspired dregs, bogged down in obedience, demon worship and sadism. Too many of them pursued violence as an end in itself. So inefficient. No wonder they've never achieved greatness.

During his researches Lev stumbled upon Malov Symina.

"He was more like me, interested in demon magic not for itself, but for its ends. An arrogant young sprig of a decadent family but very cunning and clever at choosing wise advisers. He was a weak mage - all his magical power came from his sister, but he used what he had to study the awesome power of earth's fire. In the time I knew him - worked with him - sat admiringly at his feet - me who was far more a mage than he would ever be - he used that power to dominate his part of Miraya.

"What most interested me was his manipulation of volcanoes. I knew that the volcano of Mount Koriot, at the centre of the Gen Mountains, must be under the Tari homeland of Ermora and that surely even the Tari would not be able to survive a catastrophic volcanic explosion. Of course, Malov, the cunning little shit, knew how to exact a price for his knowledge. He used my magic to help him and withheld the final secrets as long as he could. But I learned despite him and in return I used his weakness, his desire to have true power of his own, to destroy him."

"How did you learn how to do that?"

"My dear fellow, you gave me the first hint when you told me how the Tari are affected by killing other peoples. Oh, I'm so sorry." Lev smiled silkily at the look on Ezratah's face. "But I'm afraid you did. My demon advisors confirmed what would happen if Malov tapped a

Tari. It had to be done. I didn't want him coming out here and making trouble for me. Five long years it took me to learn what was needed for my plan and another two to set it in motion, but now the world will soon be rid of the Tari and I will be master of Yarmar. You, my friend, are here just in time to witness the fruition of it. A pity for you. But perhaps I'll save you with my other favourites. You always were amusing."

Still sickened at the thought he had played a part in Lev's plan, Ezratah could not resist needling him.

"So you have a plan to release death power into the volcano here. Clever, but I doubt mere force will subdue the Tari."

"Oh no! When I first came here, that was what I intended. The secret of exploding a volcano is to work with it. They build up pressure beneath the earth and a well-calculated explosion can be more powerful than a hundred thousand fireballs. But once again I found myself up against those interfering Tari. When the miners first broke through into the lava tunnels, they proved to be lousy with Tari runes and we discovered that the lava chamber was only half full. It seems the Tari regularly release the lava from the chamber to reduce the pressure. Imagine, the creatures make a festival of it. No chance of an explosion there! So another plan was needed. From my Tari captives - Tari are so weak in facing the torture of others - I learnt that the magical protections at the top of Mount Koriot are weak. They have to be to enable the foolish creatures to let lava out. A demon could easily break through such protections and once through..."

Ezratah so far forgot his intention of being calm and urbane, that he grabbed Lev's arm.

"You are going to let a demon out? Into this world! That's insane! You can't. It'd suck the life out of everything."

Lev laughed in his face.

"I can," he said. "And I'm going to."

"But no one has ever been able to control a demon. In the end they always break free."

"No one else!" said Lev smugly. "But this is me we're talking about. I've studied the mistakes of the past, the pacts, the spells. And I've taken a leaf out of young Daria Symina's book too. The demon I extract will be destroyed by seawater. It'll be unable to leave this island."

"But you'll kill everyone in Yarmar!"

"I should care! A nice clean sweep. No more tedious natives preventing Mirayan civilisation. And there are always more mercenaries."

"This will end in disaster. Calling up demons always does."

"Have a little faith," said Lev languidly. "Look at everything I have achieved so far. The overthrow of my brother. The tunnelling into Mount Koriot. The poisoning of the Mori rivers and with it the Mori. I have summoned death angels and created blood beasts without ill effects. After all that, a demon is a small matter."

"Lev! I beg of you..."

"Oh shut up! You're becoming boring. Guards take this fellow away."

Chapter 27

Alyx was looking out for Yani and ran out to meet her when she came back to the cave around noon, carrying Daria on her back. The death mage's cheek was pressed against Yani's shoulder, her face shone with a secretive smile and she stroked Yani's face and hair as if she were a beloved cat. Even though she got down from Yani's back so that they could get up into the cave, she would not let go of her. Yani met the questioning eyes of the warriors with a defiant face and leading Daria to the back of the cave, she settled her to sleep on a mat. Even in sleep Daria kept hold Yani's wrist, forcing Yani to sit beside her. Yani beckoned the rest of the party to come over.

"As you know, our difficulty has been to get up into the back of Eabri," she whispered. "Wirrawee ravine is so full of Madraga's devil dogs that we had thought to risk the death angels by climbing it in day light. But Daria here can control those dogs."

"She's a death mage!" hissed one of the Mori, drawing his blade. Yani seized his wrist.

"I am the Raven. If I choose to ally with a death mage in order to protect the life spirit then that is my right. If any of you can think of a better plan, I will gladly hear it."

The Mori warriors glared at her, and she glared back

till one by one they dropped their gazes.

"Don't worry!" she said, once she had regained their submission. "Daria is a death mage who can no longer kill. The life spirit has broken in and illuminated her darkness making her living proof of the power of our cause." She looked at the sleeping woman and Alyx was surprised to see a certain tenderness cross her face. "When this is done, and if, life spirit willing, I am still alive, then I shall take her to the Tari and see what they can do to heal her."

She turned to Alyx. "Daria told me that one of you took a bone flute from her. Do you still have it?"

"I do," said Serge.

"When she wakes give it back to her," replied Yani. "Now we should all rest." Her face was pale and strained and she kept squeezing her eyes shut as if her head hurt.

"Eat!" Jindabyne urged Yani, handing her food and water. "If Daria feeds on you, you'll need to keep up your strength. Do you want something for your head?"

"No. Daria's mind searches are much gentler than they used to be."

"Sweet life!" exclaimed Jindabyne. "What must they have been like in the beginning?"

Yani looked questioningly up at her.

"Daria has fed off me too," explained Jindabyne.

"How can that be? You're from Ermora. Has Daria already been...?"

"I'm not from Ermora," said Jindabyne, kneeling down beside Yani. "I thought you might know me. I'm Jindabyne. Jindabyne Madraga."

"Jindabyne... The Duchess of Lamartaine. Abyss! What are you doing here?"

"She's been helping us," said Alyx quickly. "She escaped from Eabri. She's seen Mother."

"And the lad with you?" Yani nodded at Serge. "Who's he?"

"I am Serge Madraga."

Yani regarded Serge with narrowed eyes before giving an ironic laugh.

"So. How do we know we can trust you Madragas?"

"Because Lev Madraga killed my father and brothers!" growled Serge.

"And I am Tari before I'm a Madraga," said Jindabyne. "These death minions. The fish in the rivers. With all my heart I wish these things cleansed. You can trust us both to help you to the top of our powers."

Yani laughed a soft ironic laugh.

"Sweet life! Misfortune makes strange bed fellows." She shook Jindabyne and Serge's hands. "I won't waste my time making threats to you. All help in this business is most welcome, no matter why it comes. Tonight we plan to climb Wirrawee and the following night to get into Eabri. Our ultimate aim is to find the captive Tari and set them free. This'll give us some power to combat Lev. This is a dangerous mission with a strong chance of death. Are you with us?"

"We are!"

Before Alyx had time to talk this initial meeting over with Serge, Kulde was plucking at her sleeve.

"Your aunt. What did she call herself? Did she say she was a raven?"

"Yes."

"With the shape shifting and the markings and everything? Sweet life!" He shook his head in awe. *'The Warbird flies at their command to reign in the people of the dragon.'* Who are the people of the dragon?"

"The Mirayans," said Alyx. "I understood that part of the prophecy the minute I heard it. It's the rest that's mysterious."

"The truth of prophecy!" Kulde shuddered and smiled at the same time. "It makes my flesh crawl. But what about the demon fire? That's bad for Ermora!"

"And good," said Yundi, who had come back to himself and was sitting beside Kulde staring at Daria in horrified fascination.

"True. But we can't just expect it to come true. One of these death mages must be the source of the demon fire. We did very well to come out of Ermora, Yundi."

"Do you think we could come back to the real world?" said Serge brusquely. "I want to find out exactly what our plan of action is."

Kulde and Yundi looked at him thoughtfully.

"You don't believe in prophecy, do you?"

"I can't say I do."

"Tari can...!" started Yundi but Kulde stopped him.

"Everybody is different," he said. "But for myself I feel very reassured. If one part of the prophecy can come true, than the demon fire will yield!"

The Mori remained uneasy about Yani's adoption of Daria, but Alyx was more worried about how drawn and exhausted Yani looked especially after her aunt had told her what she and Marigoth had been through in Miraya. Could Yani cope with the added demands of Daria?

A small struggle between the two delayed their departure that night.

"I need it," Daria was moaning.

"You can't!" said Yani firmly. "It exhausts me. We're going into Wirrawee and I need my strength. Don't you understand? Lev Madraga will kill me, kill us all if he can. Then who will you feed on?"

"I won't let him kill you, Ermora."

"How will you stop him? He's more powerful than you," retorted Yani. "Once we have traversed the ravine you may visit the place and only then."

"I could make you give it to me," said Daria sullenly.

"The mages here are also more powerful than you," snarled Yani. "They'll stop you and then I won't let you any more. Is that what you want?"

"Bitch!" snarled Daria.

"Daria!" Yani held out the pipe. "Do this for us." She put her hand on Daria's cheek. "Please. Don't let me be killed by the blood beasts. Otherwise you'll have no one."

Daria snatched up the pipe angrily.

"Let us get it over with then."

The night was chill with bright stars, but no moon. A

couple of the Mori carried small lamps which gave off a dim light and helped them to find the mouth of the Wirrawee ravine in the darkness. Blood beasts howled in the forest nearby, but none attacked. Fallen trees and stones had been placed over the mouth of Wirrawee by Lev's forces, leaving only a small gap for the blood beasts to go through.

Once they had squeezed through the gap, the lamp light played sinisterly on the steep ravine walls, giving the impression of movement where there was none. The air was thick with the stench of sulphur and rotting flesh and as they picked their way among the torn up animals that lay scattered over the ground, there came a howl and the first blood beast came pounding down the ravine towards them. Tensely the warriors drew their weapons.

"Cover your ears," cried Yani, as Daria calmly lifted the bone flute to her lips and blew into it. Even though Alyx could not hear the sound, her nerves cringed and several of the warriors, who had been too curious to cover their ears, vomited.

But the blood beast instantly sat down on its haunches with its head on its paws, for all the world as if it were a tame dog, and closing its eyes, went to sleep. Every single blood beast they met as they walked up the ravine that night responded in the same way.

"We cleverly make them thus so that they can be trained," boasted Daria.

Later the ravine began to slope upward. By now they were close to the towering cliffs of the Gen Mountains and their shadows blocked out what light there was. The Mori lit more of their small lamps and by their light Alyx saw the walls of the ravine - completely sheer on one side, but overhanging on the other. At last they come out onto the smooth rock ridge at the top of the ravine and saw the dark bulk of the Gen Mountains looming against the star-speckled sky.

According to Daria, the blood beasts would not come beyond the top of the ravine. She traced out the magical wardings made to keep them away - dark red shapes that were difficult for even the mages to see but which gave off heat when touched. Feeling that it was safe, Yani sent some scouts off to try and find the way down into Eabri. The rest of the party turned back and took shelter under the overhanging wall of the ravine.

"Find a place where you are well covered from the sky," ordered Yani. "We will rest here the day."

At this Daria let out a squeak of delight, seized Yani round the shoulders and dragged her away into the shadows.

Exhausted Alyx wrapped herself in her cloak and fell asleep. Her sleep was troubled by dreams of death angels, but when she awoke with a start, she found it was midday. The day was hot and the sun beat down on the ravine, making the air stifling. Serge and Kulde were sitting beside her whispering together.

"Ssh! Don't say that out loud," hissed Serge.

"But it is hopeless. This handful of people against eight death angels. Someone should tell them, it's hope..."

Serge clapped his hand over Kulde's mouth.

"Shut up. You never say that before a fight. Warriors fight better with hopeful hearts."

Kulde made a strangled noise of protest, but Serge kept his hand over his mouth. "No! Calm down and listen to me! I'm sure they know the danger. These people have been fighting death angels for over a month now. And they've been doing it without magic. Do you understand?"

Kulde nodded and Serge took his hand from his mouth.

"But... But why then? I mean there are only two of us mages. I don't think... Someone should explain..."

"Listen! It must be done. How else are they to heal the river and get rid of the death minions? And anyway it's not hopeless. It's not as if they're making a frontal assault. They may never even see the death angels. They seldom fly at night. They don't see well in the dark."

Kulde shook his head. After a moment he said, "I guess I'm just scared. But it's my duty to go and I have powers... some chance of survival. These others... Such courage. Such care for the life spirit. The Tari always believed outlanders to be barbarians, but they show great courage."

"Hey!" hissed Alyx. She was going to object that they were not barbarians, but as they turned to face her and Kulde's face flushed with guilty embarrassment, she decided against it

"I need a drink," she muttered.

"Here," said Serge. He put his arm round her and helped her up.

She opened her mouth to protest this tender treatment, but as he moved, she was suddenly exposed to the full heat of the sun streaming in under the overhang. She groaned as she took a sip from the water skin.

"We should move out of this sun."

"It's the same all the way down the overhang. And we can't move. Angels keep flying over," said Serge.

"I felt them in my dreams," sighed Alyx.

"So did Yundi," said Kulde. "The little beast kicked out so hard that I woke up covered in bruises. The worst of it is that he's slept through the whole thing. I'll go and see how he is." He got up and crept away down the ravine wall, stepping carefully over recumbent bodies.

Alyx lay back down again.

"You make a nice bit of shade!" she told Serge. "Why are you sitting there?"

Serge blushed.

"Are you sheltering me?" asked Alyx.

"Well I was awake and the sun was getting in your eyes."

"Serge!" She laughed, at once touched and embarrassed. "You really are..." She couldn't find the word.

"Gallant?" suggested Serge. "Thoughtful? Kind? A wonderful person?"

"Crazy!" laughed Alyx. "Maybe those other things as well."

Serge grinned. Then he yawned.

"Lie down and rest, why don't you?" said Alyx. Serge shrugged.

"I like watching you sleep," he confided disarmingly.

"You look so sweet."

Alyx rolled her eyes.

"An illusion! I'm not the slightest bit sweet."

He stretched out beside her, smiling.

"Oh, I don't know," he said.

His smile went straight to the centre of her. She reached out and, her heart filled with the wonder of him, she drew him down and kissed his lips.

"Alyx!" cried a voice behind them.

Yani stood above them, her face white with shock.

"Madraga!" she blurted out, backing away down the overhang.

"Yani!" cried Alyx.

"Shh!" hissed Yani angrily. "For life's sake they'll hear you." She turned on her heel and, picking her away down the overhang till she reached her place, sat down with her back to them and her head on her knees.

Alyx got up and made her way down to her, trying not to step on sleeping warriors.

"Yani, I...!"

"Don't talk to me!" snapped Yani, turning on Alyx. "He's the son of your father's murderer. Did you forget that?"

"No! I haven't forgotten," hissed Alyx, suddenly very angry. "But he didn't have anything to do with it. Did you think of that?"

Nearby Daria stirred, flinging out a pale hand.

"Ermora!" She moaned. "Where is Ermora?"

Yani groaned. She leaned over to Daria and whispered, "Hush! I'm here!"

"Yani. Please, understand..." begged Alyx.

"Leave me alone," snapped Yani. "I've got enough to bear without you..." She turned and saw Alyx's stricken face and her own changed. "Just go away, will you? We'll talk later. Please! I can't take this now."

When Alyx crept back down the overhang later she found Yani lying in an exhausted sleep beside Daria and knew it would be wrong to wake her.

"Don't be a baby!" she told herself. "You don't have to

have her approval!" But Yani had always been on her side before.

When darkness fell, there was no time for private talk. The group gathered at the end of the overhang to discuss their plan of action. The scouts, who had been away all day, described how they'd crept down along the Eabri ravine. The tumbled rocks at the upper end of it gave plenty of cover, but further down the area along the top of the ravine had been swept clear of rocks and they had had to crawl to keep under cover. They would have to do so after dark as well for at night the ravine was illuminated with huge magical flares.

Where the ravine curved around the side of Mount Koriot, a huge tunnel had been dug and men came in and out of it carrying baskets which were loaded with earth. Huge piles of dumped earth ran along the ravine's sides, some reaching almost to the top showing that this digging had been going on for a long time. Further down the ravine were the filthy pens where the miners, who were clearly slaves, were kept.

"The Seaganis keep their pigs better than those men are kept," muttered one of the scouts.

The stench of the pens was almost overwhelming, even from where the scouts were crouched on the cliff top. Tattered canvas sails hanging over one end of each pen were probably drawn over them to keep out the rain. They counted about forty men, many of them Seagani, but some of them Mori in each of the pens. There were several other pens which were empty, but looked as if they had been used at some point. "Lev may well have killed most of his slaves," suggested Yani. "So many death minions must require much sacrifice."

"Such an ugly thing," murmured one of the Mori. "We must succeed in this venture."

In the evening the men were marched out of the pens and down into the mine and another group were marched out of the mine and locked into different pens. At dawn the process was reversed.

"What's he mining for?" asked Alyx.

"We don't think he's mining. We think he's looking for a weakness in the Gen Mountains so that he can exploit it to destroy Ermora."

"How could he do that?" cried Alyx.

"When I was in Miraya," said Yani. "I met the man who taught Lev how to destroy mountains."

"My brother Malov," said Daria suddenly. "I wonder where he is. Perhaps Lev has killed him by now. Am I glad if he is dead? I don't know. But I'm glad I can be with you, Ermora." She took Yani's hand and smiled at her. Alyx felt Kulde shudder, but Yani simply patted Daria's hand.

"When a mountain has fire in its heart, careful application of magic can cause it to explode," Yani continued. "I saw Malov blow the tops off such mountains."

"Could he destroy Ermora so?" Alyx asked Kulde.

"I don't know. Ermora is founded on layers of magic. But even if it didn't harm Ermora, blowing up the highest mountain on Yarmar must damage the rest of the island."

"I saw terrible destruction wrought in Miraya when Malov released power into the roots of mountains," said Yani. "Vast areas reduced to plains of ash and rock. Enough destruction to cover the whole of Yarmar."

"Lev plans to release a demon," said Daria dreamily. "He wants to be a demon master. The fool's in love with the idea."

Her words caused an outcry and Daria, obviously pleased by the attention, continued, "Oh yes. But Madraga is deceiving himself. Demons are far too clever. And such deceivers. They always ask for a far greater sacrifice than they need so that they have the power to get free. Then they can do whatever they wish. That's why Malov never used them."

Alyx looked at Serge. She knew so little about death magic.

"How bad *is* this?" she whispered.

"Insanely bad!" replied Serge. "Demons act like quicksand, sucking up all life."

"Why didn't you tell me about this before?" cried Yani to Daria, who shrugged unconcernedly.

"Surely a demon couldn't get into Ermora," said Alyx.

"Maybe not. Surely not. But demons are a piece of the Abyss," said Serge. "It would be like wiping a sponge over the island of Yarmar and mopping up all the living things. It might even destroy other islands in the Archipelago."

"We need to get going," said Kulde urgently. He clearly thought the demon was a danger.

"Plans first," said Yani. "Releasing our captive Tari friends is still the best answer. With them on our side we will have more magical power than Lev Madraga can ever hope to muster. The scouts have found a place where it should be safe to lower ourselves down onto the spoil heaps. From there we should be able to move down behind the heaps till we come close to the opening of the cave. Now we have you two," she nodded at Jindabyne and Kulde, "it should be easy for us to get down into the mine using Tari sleep magic."

The sliver of moon that night gave enough light to make it possible to see where you were putting your feet and once they were over the ridge and crawling along the top of the cliff, the way was clearly illuminated by the stark white of the flares down inside the Eabri ravine. They crawled past the mouth of the mine below and down along the cliff top. Then, as Yani held up her hand for the party to gather round ready to drop ropes down onto the spoil heaps below the cliffs, Alyx felt a cold flutter in her belly.

Kulde who was crawling in front of her, stopped and peered round anxiously.

"Minions," he hissed. "There must be blood beasts..."

A huge winged man-shape crossed the moon and they heard the beating of leathery wings. Death Angels!

Eight winged shadows were coming straight at them.

"Is that someone riding on the back of one?" cried Serge.

"Shut up and get down," cried Alyx, as she dragged him down beside her.

The death angels swooped low over them, their wings

bringing the scent of sulphur. Alyx, lying face down with her arms over her head, hoped desperately that they might just be passing over, but then she felt the rock beneath her shudder under their heavy landing and dread fell upon her, stifling and heavy. Nearby someone screamed, "Kulde!"

She turned her head to see a figure jump up and throw his arms round one of the angels. A second angel turned and seized the figure round the shoulders, and it disappeared in the darkness of their shapes. Another figure rose from the ground and seized the nearest angel round the waist.

The sight of Kulde, such a gentle soul, doing battle with the angels shamed Alyx into action. She rolled and drew her sword, struggling to get to her feet. Even as she did, she could hear Didier's voice in her head, shouting, "Wrong order of movement Forest Child!" And just as he had always warned, her feet got tangled in her cloak, her sword got in the way of her steadying herself and she tripped and fell.

She managed to fall correctly, but dropped her sword. The rock sloped away and she kept on rolling towards the sheer edge of the ravine, scrabbling desperately. She kept rolling and kept rolling and then suddenly there was no more slope and she fell. A horrified cry of No! filled every fibre of her being. Was she going to die so stupidly?

Then with a thud, she hit a loose yielding surface and started to slide. A spoil heap! She was rolling, sliding down the heap of loose earth. The wall of the ravine slid up towards her and thrusting out arms and legs to protect herself, she slammed against it with a bone-shuddering jolt.

For a horrible moment Alyx was too stunned to move anything and lay there helplessly, listening to the screaming up above. Just as she was getting her breath back and her limbs were starting to respond to her brain's urgings, she heard the soft thump of something landing on the slag heap behind her.

The death angels must have seen her fall. She rolled over to face it and, as she did, heard Serge's voice give a stifled yelp of pain. He slid down the slope and hit the ravine wall nearby.

"Serge!" Alyx hissed, not daring to touch his still form. Was he hurt? Dead even? Her heart dropped like a stone and with shaking hands she touched his shoulder.

Serge. Oh Life, Serge! Please be all right. Please!

Serge let out a groan and rolled slowly over.

"Alyx," he groaned. He grabbed her and squeezed her hard. "You're alive."

Her relief was so great, she started laughing.

Cackling rang out above them. Alyx's laughter died in her throat and she and Serge hunkered down against the wall of the ravine, burrowing into their cloaks, trying to look like shadows. How much noise had they been making?

With harsh predatory shrieks five dark shapes flew off the cliff above them. Alyx saw bodies dangling in front of them. They had taken captives? How many? Who? And who had been killed?

Surely there had been three more angels. Shaking with tension, Alyx and Serge waited. But the five did not return and there was no sign of any more angels. Nor was there any sign of movement from above. Calm settled on the ravine. Sounds of earth being dumped came from the opening of the mine. The bleak white light of the nearby flares made the place where they huddled seem even darker.

"They can't have noticed us," whispered Serge.

"A miracle!" whispered Alyx.

"That was my uncle on top of one of those things," said Serge. "I recognised his voice. I went to attack him, but he was too far away, and then you fell and I tried to catch you and fell myself. Curse it."

The fate of the others lay like a black cloud over them, too big to forget about, too dark to speak of. Just like Didier and the others, thought Alyx. Did she bring bad luck to everyone? And Yani! The last words they had spoken had been angry ones. Perhaps the angels had taken her captive. Dared she hope for that?

"What do we do now?" asked Serge at last.

Alyx didn't trust her voice enough to reply and Serge

answered his own question.

"We've still got weapons. I guess we should try and carry out the mission. The only way out is forward."

"Yes!" said Alyx bleakly. Since they had no mages, they would have to find some other way of getting into the mine. The task seemed overwhelming.

Serge put his arm round her waist. For a moment they squeezed each other tightly and the strength of his arms comforted her, put the strength back into her.

"Any ideas?" she asked.

"Do you think the slaves might help us? They're Yarmarians. If nothing else, we might be able to get into the mine with them, when they change shifts."

"Good idea. Let's go have a look at them."

Keeping in the shadows, they skirted carefully around the side of the slag heaps. Each step caused a noisy shifting of dirt and gravel, forcing them to move very slowly.

Beyond the slag heaps, Madraga's keep was a dark finger against a lightening sky. Dawn was coming - another problem.

Light shone from one of the keep's upper windows and Alyx spared a thought for her mother. Was she there in the keep or down in the mine with the other Tari?

Chapter 28

Ezratah was woken by the sound of Marigoth calling him.

"Something's happening!" she cried. As sleep left him, Ezratah recognised a vague nausea.

"The death angels are nearby. That's all."

"No it's...."

At that moment guards charged in, opened Ezratah's cell and hustled him up the stairs into a room where Lev paced, his face like thunder. His friend Neevus hovered in the shadows wringing his hands anxiously and two shivering figures crouched fearfully on the floor before them. Two Tari! Ezratah was even more astonished to realise that he only recognised one of them.

"Lady Jindabyne," he cried involuntarily.

"Lady Jindabyne indeed," said Lev. "I never thought to see her alive again. But who's her little friend? I thought I knew all the Tari outside Ermora."

"Just a lad we found living in the forest," cried Jindabyne. "We enlisted him to our cause."

"Do you think I'm stupid?" snarled Lev. He turned Ezratah. "Do you know this one?"

"No, but the lady could be telling the truth. There

are..."

"Could she just?" hissed Lev. Without warning he seized Ezratah's head in his hands and, like a knife, his mind went into his. "I can see you don't believe her."

His mind pulled back out of Ezratah's so fast that Ezratah staggered.

"You think this one comes from Ermora. So do I. And he knows how to kill death angels."

Lev seized Jindabyne's arm and twisted it behind her back so sharply that Jindabyne screamed.

"You're from Ermora," shouted Lev at the boy. "Tell the truth or she will suffer."

The boy, he looked only fifteen, clamped his lips together, but when Lev called over one of the guards and told him to cut Jindabyne's face with his sword, he spoke out.

"Yes, I am from Ermora," he shouted defiantly. "And if you harm us, the Tari will come down on you like an avalanche. Then they'll find out what you're doing and they'll stop you."

Neevus glided up beside Lev. "Your woman said Jindabyne would never be allowed back into Ermora. She said she was an outcast. She lied to us!"

Lev scowled so savagely that Neevus stepped back.

"Or maybe she was just mistaken," he added in a small voice.

With a roar of fury Lev flung Jindabyne away from him so that she landed on the boy and they both tumbled over.

"Take these Tari away to the cells," he shouted to the guards.

The moment they left the room, he went over to his work table and overturned it.

"Damn, damn, damn her! Corrupting bitch. They are all corrupting... filthy... evil... She's made me blind. And now! Now they know! Perhaps it's even too late."

He smashed a bowl onto the floor and stood staring down at the pieces, breathing heavily. The he laughed hollowly.

"Lev! You stupid fool! This is how she got you last time."

"My lord, there's no need to give up hope," purred Neevus. "We're almost ready to do the ceremony. We can do it tomorrow night before moon rise."

"Yes," said Lev. "And we will. Begin the preparations. I'll join you shortly. First I have some business with that woman upstairs."

As Neevus scurried from the room, Lev turned to Ezratah.

"Do I have to threaten to torture Marigoth or will you mindsearch a Tari for me without being threatened?"

"Whether you actually harm her or not, the threat is there," said Ezratah with dignity.

"Good! You understand me!" Lev grinned wolfishly, but his eyes remained cold. "You've already been corrupted by the Tari so searching Elena's mind shouldn't change you. And after that I can search your mind and see what you have found out. Perhaps if I can be truly certain that she's a lying bitch, I can be free of her."

As the sun rose, guards came to rouse the slaves in the pens. They distributed food and harried the men out of the pen with shouts and blows. Shortly after the slaves had gone, another group of slaves came rushing eagerly into the pen towards baskets of food that had been placed in the centre. This whole noisy business provided enough cover for Alyx and Serge to move quickly forward till they were behind the slag heap that backed onto the pen. The scouts had been right. The stench of the pens was eye-watering.

Most of the men were from other parts of the Archipelago, but there were a handful of Mori slaves as well. Alyx decided that she was the obvious person to creep up to the pen and talk to the slaves - she could speak with one of the Mori and be assured of their support. Serge objected that he should go, though he seemed to have no logical reason for it. They still were hissing protests at each other when a push cart surrounded by a troop of guards came out of the bottom of the fortress and marched up the ravine. In the push cart sat Jindabyne, Kulde and another unknown Mirayan man with witch manacles around their drooping necks. Walking dully behind them were two other people that made Alyx gasp.

"That's my aunt Marigoth," she hissed to Serge.

"And Ambassador Ezratah!" whispered Serge back. "I'm sure of it. I wonder who the Mirayan is."

A dispirited murmur passed among the slaves as they watched the push cart go past.

Exactly how I feel, thought Alyx.

"Where's Yani?" she wondered aloud.

"Perhaps she got away," said Serge.

"Do you think they've got Yundi too?"

"Don't forget Daria."

Alyx snorted. "She's probably gone over to Lev. Maybe he let her keep Yundi as a pet. I'm going to go talk to those slaves. We have to do it this way and you know it."

Serge sighed. "Just be careful. I'll do that bird call you Mori use if there is danger."

His words gave Alyx an idea. "Let's do the bird call now," she hissed.

"What?"

"It's a forest bird. This is the wrong environment for such a bird. Any Mori who hears it will know it's a person calling and they'll be expecting to see us."

They each made ten bird calls, carefully spaced out. One of the slaves in the pen sat up and looked around in surprise, but the rest just lay there, seemingly asleep.

Serge caught Alyx's arm and kissed her quickly on the mouth. His lips were gritty and hers must have been too, for as they pulled apart, they both surreptitiously wiped grit from their mouths and catching each other's eyes, couldn't help grinning.

"You be careful too," she said, creeping away.

The pens were man-height and consisted of rows of wooden planks nailed onto a framework which was driven into the ground. Not a very strong prison, but then it wouldn't be easy to get out of this ravine if you escaped from the pen. The slag heap had slid down against the edge of the pen, but there was a small distance where she could be seen by the guards. Fortunately they seemed to be having a game of dice on the ground in front of the pen and Alyx was able to creep her way along the pen wall peering in through the planks. Halfway along the wall, a couple of men were lying within earshot and as she was trying to decide if she should speak to them, one of them hissed in Mori, "Who are you and what do you want?"

Alyx recognised the voice as Jacquot, a friend from childhood. He was so thin and dirty she wouldn't have known him. The other man was Mori too, although he was not familiar, and the three of them spoke together for some time. The men were careful to make it seem as if they were talking to each other and the guards did not even lift their eyes from their game.

When Alyx returned to Serge, she was full of good news.

"They'll gladly help us! After darkness the shift will change and as they go into the cave, the cry of wild dogs will be the signal for them to start a brawl. We should be able to get inside the cave mouth while the guards are busy with that. Inside there are others who will help us."

"The others, are they trustworthy?"

"The non-Mori you mean. Jacquot says so. They hate the Mir... the guards as much as the Mori do." She paused. "You know, he said a funny thing. Some of the older men, those who've mined before, say that Lev Madraga finished all the mining he needs to do a while ago. That what they are doing now is just busy work. Why do you think...?"

"Who can say? I hardly knew my uncle. I don't understand how he could kill my father, let alone what makes him do this."

"If what they say is true, he could have carried out his plan anytime this last month."

"Perhaps he needed more life spirit to sacrifice," suggested Serge. "And he has it now he has our group captive."

"Then it's a good thing we're going into that mine tonight."

Chapter 29

All through the rest of the day, Alyx and Serge crept along step by step behind the slag heaps back towards the mouth of the mine. By the time the shadows had broadened into late afternoon, they were hidden close to the mine entrance. Just after the sun dropped behind the ravine wall, covering their hiding place with dark shadows, they heard a whispered voice.

"Alyx, Serge! Is that you?"

Blood turned to ice. Serge's hand went for his sword while Alyx seized a rock.

"It's me, Yani!"

Alyx wanted to shout for joy. Her aunt's voice came from the deep shadows under the ravine wall and the moment she hugged her, Alyx knew why she had not come closer.

"Quick, take off your tunic," she hissed back at Serge.

""Why?" asked Serge.

"Yani needs clothes. She always loses them when she changes shape."

Serge made an embarrassed noise and drew away.

"Are you well?" asked Alyx

"As well as I can be after seeing all my comrades slaughtered."

"Are they all dead then?"

"As far as I can tell. Good warriors every one."

They were silent for a moment, before Yani continued, "I turned into the Raven of course and when daylight came I flew back here. I've been watching you all day from up there." She nodded at the cliff face above the cave. "I'm proud of you, Alyx. You've found a way in without magic, haven't you?"

"Here," hissed Serge behind them. With his face turned away, he tossed the tunic to them. "I'm sorry it's not very clean," he said.

"At least it covers me," said Yani. "Now what's this plan?"

As darkness fell, the flares sprang into life and the harsh white light banished all the shadows around the cave. A horn blew and slaves came filing out of the mine, putting their tools and baskets in a pile by the entrance. Shortly afterward the new shift of slaves came filing up the ravine. As they entered the cave, the howling of wild dogs began.

"What the hell?" yelled the closest guard as, with the sound of clanking chains, the line of slaves erupted into fighting. The guards sprinted away from the cave mouth to stop it and as soon as the last one passed their hiding place, the party slipped across the bright white space and into the cave.

A group of slaves had gathered at the cave opening looking at what was happening outside. The men stared at Alyx and the others, showing only astonishment in their faces, before one of them darted forward whispering, "This way! Quickly, they're coming!"

Another, it was Jacquot, carrying a torch, grasped Alyx by the arm and started to pull her down the tunnel. The five of them ran down the dark sloping passage.

"Stay here," hissed Jacquot, pushing them into a side tunnel. "The lift is round the corner, but there are guards. When you hear the sound of fighting, come down, but watch out."

Then he was gone leaving them in total darkness.

"Hell!" hissed Serge. Alyx found herself squeezing his hand and told herself it was only to comfort him.

A short time later they saw torches and slaves began filing down past them, flanked by guards. Each slave had a big basket on his back. A few carried tools. A couple of the slaves and one of the guards bore the marks of fighting. The Mori among the slaves made the sign of Labwa as they filed past the end of the tunnel where Alyx's group were hiding, and a couple of the others furtively glanced their way. A short time after that the sound of shouting and blows echoed up from below. Two guards ran past, pushing through the slaves and yelling "Stop that, you scum!"

The closest prisoners lunged into the side tunnel, seized Alyx and the others and hustled them down round the corner into a small, flat, well-lit space. Several tunnels led steeply off it and a dark downwards shaft lay directly ahead of them. Over the shaft hung a huge wooden platform surrounded by wickerwork walls, large enough to hold twenty men. The platform dangled by thick ropes from a pulley.

The prisoners hustled them onto the platform, told them to lie down on the floor and started piling empty baskets and tools down around them.

"Thank Mir, we don't have to climb," whispered Serge.

"What happens?" asked Alyx. Neither she nor Yani had ever seen such a contraption before.

Suddenly a voice rang out nearby.

"Careful! Don't mess them up, you fools."

"That's all, Lord," said another voice. The platform creaked as Jacquot and another man got onto it.

"Right," said the guard. "Ready. One, two heave!" The lift shuddered and began to drop slowly down the tunnel, the ropes creaking as it fell.

Alyx held tight as they were lowered down into that black hole. Soon they were lying in total blackness and only the shuddering of the lift told her that they were still descending.

The wooden platform seemed to descend for ever. Several times they passed dimly lit openings in the rocky shaft. Alyx had expected it to be chill down here, but as the lift dropped, the air grew hotter and hotter until it was so humid, it was hard to breath. Beads of sweat ran down her face.

"Will this never end?" muttered Serge, putting Alyx's feelings into words.

"The centre of the mountain is very deep," whispered Jacquot, their guide. "But we're near the bottom now."

"What's that sound?" asked Yani.

Alyx could hear it too - a roaring that sounded like a fire in the chimney.

"There's a huge lake of burning stone down here," said Jacquot. "Be quiet now. There are also guards. I'll distract them while you get out the other side."

With a thump, the platform settled on the ground at the bottom of the shaft. Jacquot swung open the wicker work gate at the front of the lift.

There was only one guard down here and almost immediately he began berating Jacquot.

"We don't need baskets, you stupid sod. Only tools. Get the tools out."

"But the lords up top insisted on baskets, sir," protested Jacquot. "I must unload them."

"Do as you're told," shouted the guard, swishing at him with a whip. Jacquot ducked away from him and the resulting shouting and chase was enough of a diversion for Alyx and the others to slip out of the back gate of the lift, where there was enough room between the lift and the wall behind for it, for them to squeeze along to where another lift sat in the space beside the first and take cover there.

As they waited, Yani tapped Alyx's shoulder and pointed at the wall behind them. The rock here was very smooth, almost as if it had been glazed, except for a line of runes that ran along it. Tari runes, four concentric circles bisected by a cross.

The argument ended and Jacquot, who now had a whip cut on his arm and face, finished his unloading, climbed into the lift and pulled a rope. The platform creaked away up the shaft above.

Once it was gone, the guard stuck his whip in his belt, picked up a couple of picks and shovels in each hand and stumped off away down a tunnel towards a pinpoint of reddish yellow light that seemed to be a distant opening. Torches burned along the walls, but at such a wide distance apart that the light was very dim. Alyx and the others were able to stay in shadow as they followed the guard at what they hoped was a safe distance. Here too, Tari runes were carved at regular intervals. The Tari must have built these tunnels back in the past as they had built so much on Yarmar.

The heat was stifling and the guard obviously felt it as much as those following him, for he trudged forward doggedly without once turning around. The tunnel was extremely long, its floor sloping downwards all the way. By the time they reached the pinprick of light, it had turned into a huge opening. The guard passed through into the brightly lit chamber beyond and Yani, Serge and Alyx stopped just outside and peered carefully round into the opening behind him.

Beyond was an immense space filled with torch light. A roaring like the sound of a furnace filled the room and the air was as hot as the breath of a furnace too. There was no need to be quiet.

"We must be close to the volcanic lake at the heart of the mountain," murmured Yani. "Mount Koroit is said to be honey combed with tunnels and chambers where the lava collects."

"There's something terrible there!" whispered Alyx. Her eyes had been drawn as if by some compulsion to a sort of pinnacle that reared up to a point in the centre of the cavern. Torch light sparkled on its dark glass surface.

Though the surface of the glass was smooth, it was

knobbly as well. Something was wrong about those lumps -
looking at them felt like looking at weeping sores on the
skin of a loved one. Yani shuddered.

"What are those horrible lumps?" she muttered.

"They're faces," whispered Serge, and Alyx realised
that each lump was indeed a little head with a gaping
mouth. Such a wave of horror overcame her that she
huddled back against the wall so that the faces couldn't see
her, arms wrapped around herself, eyes tight shut,
struggling with a rising sense of panic. Serge's arms came
round her and they clung to each other.

"It's part of the Abyss, isn't it?" whispered Alyx in his
ear.

"I think it's a demon altar."

"Come on you two!" hissed Yani. "Seize your courage!
We always knew that Lev Mad..."

A voice shrieked from within the chamber. Three
figures came into view, two dragging a violently resisting
third across the cavern toward the altar.

"It's Diyar! Thank life, he's still alive after all this
time," said Yani wonderingly.

The Tari mage, who had been captured in Ishtak with
Yani, was a stick figure clad in rags, but despite that he
kicked and fought so hard that he broke free of the black-
clad guards. Another guard appeared and knocked him
unconscious before he could reach the opening of the
cavern and the first guards picked him up, dragged his limp
body over to the obsidian pinnacle, dumped him down
against it and chained him to it.

"Oh Mir!" whispered Serge. "They're going to have
some kind of ceremony."

"We'd better move quickly then," said Yani

"Right! No way to go except forward," said Alyx. She
unslung her bow, strung it and nocked an arrow into it.
Serge drew his sword and Yani, pulling a face, hefted a
large rock in her hand.

Ignoring the obsidian pinnacle and Serge's hissed
objection, Alyx slid through the opening and into the
shadows beside it. At one side of the cavern were large

cages. Shadowy figures sat hunched inside them, but it was so dim back there that she couldn't be certain of their numbers.

She counted five guards. Three of them were busy getting another Tari out of the cages - one holding the door, the other two struggling with the figure inside. The two who should have been guarding the rest of the cavern were watching and laughing, clearly certain of being safe here.

That's about to change, thought Alyx grimly. She beckoned the other two, holding up five fingers for the number of guards as they slid up beside her.

"A frontal assault then," whispered Yani. Serge nodded, lifting his sword.

"Just give me a moment to soften them up," murmured Alyx, as she drew back her bow.

Such was the noise in the cavern, that the guard she shot in the back had fallen to the ground before any of the others realised they were under attack. Alyx's next arrow knocked the guard beside him down as he turned to look.

Then Serge and Yani were off, racing across the stone floor to where the other three guards had leapt out of the cage and were drawing their swords. Alyx ran after them.

Yani reached the cages first, but as she stopped to pull a sword from the belt of the fallen guard, Serge overtook her and the guards charged, both of them swinging at Serge. Alyx raised her bow to shoot but hesitated. Even at this close range she was afraid of hitting Serge by accident. Serge fought well with impressive grace and control, parrying one guard while dodging the other. As he dodged, Alyx saw an opening and let her arrow fly. It pierced the man right through the neck.

A searing pain cut through Alyx's own neck and her vision went red. She screamed out and fell to her knees. It only seemed a moment later that Serge was shaking her and calling out her name. Everything was numb. Why were they waking her up? It had been so peaceful.

"Oh Mir, Alyx! I thought you were dead," whispered Serge.

"It's just the Tari death taboo," said Yani, lifting Alyx

up. "And, thank life, only a mild reaction too."

Alyx felt so cold. The heat, the infernal roaring, the sense of darkness beyond the torchlight seemed distant and unreal, but her feelings of loss were very real. For a moment the life spirit had abandoned her and still it seemed far away.

"This is a bad problem to have in battle," muttered Serge.

"You'll be fine," said Yani, clapping her on the shoulder. "The life spirit will return to you. You're lucky you're only half-Tari. Take a break, but don't make it too long. We need to keep moving." She sprang up, striding away toward the cages. "I'll let them out."

Yani fell over so suddenly that for a moment Alyx and Serge thought she had simply tripped. Then a voice spoke, turning their blood to ice.

"Well, well! Well done, young Serge! You're the last person I expected to see here."

Lev Madraga stood in the doorway, clapping his hands in slow ironic applause, surrounded by a large number of guards who were in the process of drawing their swords.

Chapter 30

Alyx had never seen Lev Madraga before and, oddly, the main thing that stuck her was how very handsome he was - all square jaw, crisp golden hair and blue eyes.

Very cold blue eyes.

"More damned Tari," he spat. "Always popping up where they're not wanted. Is there no end to them? They're supposed to be safely in their kingdom in the mountains, yet here they are. Meddling again."

The guards were on Serge and Alyx now, swords pressed to their throats, pushing them flat on to the ground.

Lev stalked over to where Yani lay on the stone floor and rolled her over.

"Yani Tari. I might have known," he snarled, kicking her hard in the ribs.

"No!" screamed Alyx, leaping up and taking her guard by surprise. He caught her arm as she flung herself at Lev, pulled her back and threw her down on the floor.

"Alyx!" Serge caught her. Alyx's neck stung where the guard's sword must have cut her in passing. She put her hand to her throat and it came away bloody, but the wound didn't feel deep.

"Stupid!" hissed Serge. "Is it bad?"

"It's nothing,"

Cold fear filled her gut as Lev Madraga hunkered down beside them.

"So who's this then?" he sneered, pulling Alyx's head back by the hair and looking down into her face. "Some Mori half-breed?"

He clicked his fingers at a man in scholar's robes. "Give me a knife, Neevus!"

Serge tried to get between Lev and Alyx.

"No!" cried a voice behind them. A veiled woman started forward from among the guards.

"Mother!" cried Alyx, recognising the voice.

Lev looked at the woman through narrowed eyes, then back at Alyx. He reached out and turned Alyx's face to him, his hand lingering on her cheek.

"Yes!" he said softly. "You do have the look of your mother."

"Leave her!" Serge slapped Lev's hand away.

Lev laughed and stood up.

"Ah Sergie! Is this your special friend?" He tutted. "Not that I blame you, my boy. The Tari are far too charming for we mere mortals. But never dip your wick in polluted oil. I learned that the hard way."

"Tie them!" he shouted curtly to the guards. "And that creature there too!" He pointed to Yani on the ground. "Put them all round the altar!"

His gaze swept round the room, over the fallen guards. "Look at this mess. But it's not going to stop me, do you hear?" He was suddenly shouting. "Ermora is done for and so are all your people."

"You shall destroy yourself, Lev Madraga!" shouted one of the shadowy Tari in the cages.

"Fuck you!" snarled Lev, striding towards the voice. "Now who wants to help open the gate? And who wants to feed the demon when it's newly arrived? What, no volunteers?"

The word demon sent a further chill through Alyx. Daria had been right. She wondered where the death mage was and if Lev had killed her, before her attention was drawn back to the horrible present.

Lev was pointing to a couple of cages. "You, you and you can go on the altar."

"And your nephew, lord?" asked one of the men worriedly.

"Especially him. Serge my lad, you're going to have a much more exciting end than your father."

"Traitor. How could you kill him? He was a far better man than you!"

"Yes, probably. But weak. He let the natives tell him what to do. Natives instructing Mirayans! And he let those filthy beasts pollute our blood when he married this animal here," he said, waving at Jindabyne, who was being pulled out of a cage. "It had to end. The Tari had their hooks in him. Just like they almost had them in me."

Neevus was leading the veiled woman over to the altar. Lev seized her arm as she passed.

"Aren't you going to plead? Aren't you going to beg for your life? Tell me that you love me as you have so many times before?"

"I will plead for my daughter's life," The woman's arms were bound behind her back, but she pressed her cloth covered head into Lev's shoulder as a lover might. "Spare her and I will always be grateful. In time it could happen for us. There's no reason why not."

"Would you?" said Lev. He touched the woman's cheek through the veil. Then his face changed.

"I've seen the truth of it. You would smother me with a pillow the first chance you got. Neevus is right. Your death is the only way to free myself from your power."

Yet as the scholar led her away from him, Lev stopped him.

"No! Not on the altar!"

"Lord?"

"Flesh and blood can only bear so much. Put her in one of the cages."

The guards were dragging two more struggling Tari, Kulde and Mathaman, from their cages. Marigoth followed docilely behind them. "My dear," she said, and nodded to Alyx as if they were meeting on the road to market somewhere.

"Marigoth! What's happened to you?"

"Maybe she just doesn't like you," taunted Lev. Alyx kicked out at him. Laughing, he ducked back and one of the guards came at her with a raised fist. She heard Serge shout as the fist came towards her and a flash of light and darkness.

When the world swam painfully back into view, Alyx found her feet as well as her arms tied and a strand of rope round her waist tethering her to the altar. The lumpy obsidian felt unclean against her skin and she pulled away from it. The rope did not have enough give for her get free of the touch of the altar. Serge was tethered too and so were the others; Diyar, Mathaman, Kulde, Jindabyne and Yani.

Surely this couldn't really be happening! Alyx's head throbbed. She dropped her chin on her chest and breathed in deeply to still the rising panic. The altar behind her felt like a gaping hole.

Lev had donned a red robe and was inspecting the sharpness of a tray of knives that the scholar Neevus was holding out for him.

"Hurry up, you men!" he shouted. Looking over her shoulder, Alyx noticed that the guards were opening up a rough-looking section of the wall very close to where the altar stood, strewing rocks and mortar all over the floor.

"What's taking so long?" snarled Lev.

"It's hard, Lord," said one of the guards. "The Tari must have drawn the lava up this month. It's coated with obsidian on the inside wall."

"Typical," muttered Lev. "Cursed Tari!"

He strode over to the wall, pushing the soldiers aside.

"Get going! You need to be up above and inside the circle of protection by the time I've killed the fifth sacrifice," he told them. The guards scuttled out of the cavern more quickly than was dignified.

Lev put his hands on the shiny rock and leant his head against it, whispering some words. A crack broke through the wall and a blast of hot air seared through the chamber, blowing out several torches and replacing them with a red-gold light. The roaring sound of fire had increased fivefold. Suddenly Alyx could taste the acrid scent of the gases on her tongue.

Lev stepped back as the crack widened and sections of the wall began to fall back into the roaring void beyond.

He turned and looked at the cages for a moment. Then he took a deep breath and strode towards them, Neevus trotting behind him carrying the tray of knives. With a curt nod of his head, Lev dismissed the scholar, who placed the tray on a stool nearby and scurried out of the cavern even quicker than the guards had.

Lev bent over the tray of knives and picked one up. Stepping close to the altar he spoke some words over it. Then he cut his arm. Loudly intoning words in a language which Alyx did not understand, but which was full of horrible sounds, Lev dripped his blood on the stone above Yani and a sound like the opening of a very creaky door came from within. Throughout the cavern, the Tari let out a scream.

"What is it?" cried Alyx. The altar behind her felt like it had become a huge sucking mouth drawing her to it.

"He's calling the Abyss into the stone," cried Mathaman. "Now the demons will come."

Even as he spoke, the altar became warm, soft, and slightly sticky as if it had turned to flesh. Alyx found herself leaning harder into the rope around her waist in an effort to get as far from it as possible not caring at the way the rope dug into her belly and left her breathless

"Don't get any blood on it," cried Serge, from beside her.

Lev looked over those tied to the altar as if he were choosing cake from a tray. Then he shrugged, leaned over and seizing Yani by the hair, pulled her head sideways to expose the artery in her neck. Yani, who was conscious again, glared unflinchingly up at him.

This couldn't be happening!

"If you only knew how long I've wanted to do this!" Alyx heard Lev shouting as he lifted the knife up.

"No!" screamed Alyx, "No! Don't!"

Suddenly an even louder scream rang out and a flash of blue fire hit the knife making it spin out of Lev's hand.

"Ermora! You shall not harm her! Ermora, I'll save you!"

A black stick figure stood at the door of the cavern, arms outstretched. It was Daria, eyes staring, spiky hair standing out all over her head.

"Arrgh! Does it never end?" yelled Lev.

He let go of Yani's hair and swept round to throw a blast of magic fire at Daria. But Daria had ducked away before the blast hit her and even as the fiery magic poured over the place where she'd been, she was up and racing towards Lev. With a scream like broken glass, she launched herself at him and before he could throw another fire bolt, she had him by the collar, beating at his face with a rock and biting and kicking at him. The rock didn't seem to bother Lev. He threw a bolt of power at her, but she must been too close or have had magical defences, for it ricocheted off and hit the wall with a flash of blue light. He seized another sacrificial knife from the tray beside him and slashed blindly at the frenzied Daria. She yelped as the knife cut her shoulder, but she kept on smashing at him.

Alyx felt a tug on the rope round her waist. A small figure was sawing away at it with a sword. Yundi! He was straining at the blade but the task of cutting the rope was obviously too great for his strength.

"Here let me," shouted Alyx, reaching out as far as she could with her hands tied behind her back.

Together she and Yundi pressed down on the sword. The pressure of the rope round Alyx's waist felt as if it was going to cut her in half and then the rope went limp. Alyx staggered forward falling to her knees. Quickly Yundi cut the rope at her wrists and ankles and the moment she was free, she seized the sword from him and started feverishly sawing away at Serge's bonds. Yundi darted away around the altar. He seemed to have an arm full of swords.

A roar of fury came from Lev as he realised what was happening. His face, bloodied from Daria's blows, glared wildly at Alyx and he thrust his bloodied hands out towards her. Instinctively she ducked away from the altar, dragging Serge after her.

At that moment Daria, seeing he was distracted, threw herself at him at the same time as she threw a blast of magical force. The magical force was thrown off Lev's defences but Daria herself caught him by surprise. As her body hit his, he lost his balance and staggering backwards both he and Daria fell against the glowing altar.

There was a loud sucking noise and Lev's bloodied hand seemed to become stuck to the glowing rock. Desperately he dragged it, while Daria, who paid no attention to the fact the blood seemed to be running down from her shoulder, kept scratching and biting at him.

An obscene slurping sound came from the altar and the blood from Daria's shoulder wound began to gush out over it. Only now did she realise her danger. Screaming, each death mage tried to use the other as a lever as they pulled away from the altar, struggling together in an ecstasy of terror. Even as they did so, their bodies began to pale as if some vital spirit was being sucked out of them. So did the body of the last Tari, the unconscious Diyar, who was leaning against the altar. Alyx ran towards him, but Serge pulled her back. Another Tari, Ginna, had seized Diyar and was now caught. She struggled to free herself for a moment and then buried her head in Diyar's shoulder, unable to struggle any longer as the altar drained her life spirit. The bodies of all four mages lay limply against the obsidian.

The altar screeched with the mad parrot scream of death angels magnified a thousand times. As the screeching rose to an unbearable pitch, it gave a resounding crack and lurched.

The whole chamber shook. Horror and nausea filled Alyx and yet she couldn't tear her eyes from the altar. A dark spilt had formed down it, a thin split not much wider than a crack, and yet it seemed to fill her mind like an enormous chasm. It drew her as the ground draws someone from high up - only much more strongly. Had Alyx been at the top of a cliff at that moment she would have fallen to her death - such was the cold pulling despair of that split in the altar. She tried to take a step towards it but Serge was still holding onto her.

"What are you doing?" he cried. Then, "Mir! What's that?"

Something the grey-blue colour of dead veins was oozing out from the split along the altar and creeping slowly across the floor towards them.

"Hell! That can't be good!" muttered Serge. Alyx agreed, but was too heavy with despair to move her lips. All around the altar, the other Tari stood, eyes wide and hopeless watching as the ooze slid out across the obsidian floor like a slug. Except it was not alive and could never be. It was the same colour as the skin of a death angel and like a death angel it was sucking the life spirit out of the very rock it touched, eating it away, and filling the world with a terrible stench of rot and death. Everything was hopeless. There was no point in being alive.

"Alyx!" shouted Serge, shaking her. "What's the matter with you? Wake up!"

He squeezed her tightly and, turning her to face him, kissed her hard on the mouth. At the feel of his warm lips, Alyx's horrible dream receded. She flung her arms around Serge and the warmth of his familiar body lit a flicker of hope in her.

"Alyx, everyone's just standing around and that stuff is eating into the floor!"

"They're all mages!" cried Alyx. "Mage's or Tari. They feel it too strongly! Quickly! Help me! And don't look at it!"

She ran to Yani who was the nearest person.

"Don't look! Don't look!" she cried, dragging Yani's limp body around to face her, shaking her and lightly slapping her face.

With a shake of effort, Yani came back to herself.

"I have to free the others," she cried, running away towards the cages.

Together Alyx and Serge ran around the cavern, turning the Tari away from the altar, trying to shake them out of their stupor. The mages were hardest to rouse for they felt the despair most strongly, and wearing witch manacles were unable to defend themselves from it. Yundi, who had succumbed to one of his visions, and Marigoth, who barely seemed to be breathing could not be roused at all.

Despite Alyx's advice, Serge kept looking at the oozing matter as they ran and suddenly he shouted, "It's going through the wall! What's going to happen when it contacts the lava?"

At that moment, the sound of the lava chamber below increased tenfold followed by an explosion from below. The whole mountain shook.

Several Tari came running past Alyx. The caged Tari were free not only of the cages, but of their witch manacles! Even though their faces were serious, there was a brightness about them and now they were setting the others free. They seemed to be shouting, but Alyx could hear nothing over the roaring of the fire and the explosions below. Arms caught Alyx round the waist and squeezed her tight. Her mother! Alyx turned and hugged her back, kissing her through her veil.

A moment later, Jindabyne appeared at their shoulders, tugging Alyx, her mother and Serge towards the hole that Lev had opened in the side of the chamber. Yani and some of the other Tari, Mathaman, Syndal and Murran, were leaning out of the hole in the wall, pointing upwards. There was a long dark vent there, obviously the place where the lava escaped from the mountain. The hot air stank of gases, sulphur among them.

So hard to breath. Alyx's lungs felt burnt with every breath she drew.

The lava below looked like a red-gold cauldron of boiling stew and the heat coming of it was so intense that even looking at it sideways made Alyx's eyes weep. Yet she could not drag her eyes from a blackness that had battened onto the lake's orange heart, causing great waves of molten rock to rise up as if trying to escape from it.

An almighty scream broke through the chamber and Marigoth, with Ezratah clutching at her, raced at the hole in the wall. Somehow Alyx knew that she wanted to throw herself into the lava below. Two of the other Tari threw themselves on her, caught her in time and made her sleep. Ezratah scooped up her unconscious body, and Mathaman picked them both up. He carried them to the hole in the wall, leapt through it and flew up the vent above the lava as lightly as ash flies up a chimney.

A storm was breaking out in the lava below. The dark matter had sunk beneath the surface of the lake and great gouts of fire burst forth. Explosions rocked the mountain so hard that rocks fell from the ceiling of the cavern behind them. The floor of the cavern shook making walking as difficult as staggering along a very unsteady canoe.

Jindabyne nodded at Yani and seized Serge and Alyx round the waist. "Hold on!" she shouted in Alyx's ear.

"Mother!" cried Alyx. But even as she shouted, she saw Murran seize Elena round the waist and follow Mathaman through the hole in the wall.

"Go! Go!" shouted Yani, and Jindabyne leapt upwards. The sides of the holes flickered past and for a brief terrifying moment, they hung over the lava lake before flying upward. The vent was dark and suffocatingly hot and the roar of the lava below was deafening. Drawing breath was a burden and Alyx's mouth tasted of metal. She clung to Serge with all her might. The volcanic glass walls of the tube glistened with the sullen glare of the lake below. The glass was cracking and, as the mountain shuddered around them, great splinters of it fell back behind them.

Tari runes glowed warning red on the vent's walls.

Up, up, Jindabyne hurtled, with such speed that the stifling air whistled past them. Alyx looked down. She saw others coming behind them, some holding mage lights, some with their arms around others. And beneath that, a circle of hot orange yellow light, the lave lake glowing like the beady eye of the living volcano.

Then they were at the top and most of the mage lights went out. Jindabyne rested her back against the rock wall, steadying herself with her feet so that Alyx and Serge were sitting on her knees. She was holding them tightly and Alyx had no sense that she would fall. She put out her hand and felt the rock above them. It was an ordinary jagged, gritty rock, with no coating of obsidian glass. This must be the plug at the top of the volcano. Alyx had only the haziest memory of an enormous rock being pushed into the volcano's mouth during the lava festival. The plug must have been at least two man lengths wide to cover the mouth of the vent.

How heavy would it be?

Grit was streaming down beside the rock plug as the mountain shuddered and Mathaman and one of the other mages beat at it.

Oh life! Alyx couldn't feel it moving. Were they trapped? She felt Serge's sweat slicked hand gripping her shoulder.

"Why is there no way of getting in?" she cried.

"People aren't supposed to come in this way," shouted Kulde, who had appeared beside them with Yundi in his arms. "Here, can you take Yundi? I'll help them push it out."

Alyx took Yundi and felt Jindabyne tense as she supported the extra weight of the boy with her magic. Yundi was still shivering and muttering, but he looked at Alyx as if he knew her, doing his best to stay conscious. Alyx leaned against Jindabyne, her face turned towards the top of the shaft, trying not to think of falling, of burning, of the boiling air searing the inside of her lungs.

Jindabyne sounded exhausted, her breath coming in gasps, but then the heat up here was making everyone gasp and sweat was pouring off them all. Alyx's eyes streamed from the acrid fumes. Most of the mages were now gathered under the plug, feet pressed against the wall, faces grimacing with effort as they pushed upwards with muscles and magic. Even Yani, who was riding on someone's back was helping. Alyx pushed the rock with her free arm. Such useless force, but she did it without even thinking. Why didn't the cursed thing move?

The mage light had dimmed even further as all magic was channelled into the effort.

"It's moving!" cried someone joyfully.

"Oh shit!" cried Serge, who was looking down. Beneath them the beady eye of the furnace was growing bigger and bigger, bursting into a seething mass of fiery light and molten rock that roared up the black vent toward them. Alyx could hear nothing above its roaring and it was only when Jindabyne leapt upwards that she realised that the volcanic plug was gone. Still carrying them, the mage shot out of the volcano mouth with a swish and a plunge to the left. As the ground leapt up at them, Jindabyne swerved but she was flying too fast. They landed hard and tumbled over and over in a mass of arms and legs, hard joints and hard ground hitting soft flesh and.

Through the frenzy of landing, Alyx heard a mighty blasting roar and she looked up to see a geyser of fiery rock was streaming out of the volcano's cone, spurting up into the blue sky above.

Three Tari, a man and two women all dressed in silken robes were standing nearby, a broken jug of wine fallen at their feet. They staggered as the mountain shuddered and rumbled, but they were laughing and clapping their hands with delight at the geyser of molten rock.

"Idiots! What the hell are you doing?" Alyx shouted picking herself up and leaping at the laughing Tari. She caught hold of the man who was the closest and as she shook him, she recognised him as the Tari who had almost killed Serge.

Wiping tears of laughter out of his eyes, he shouted at her. "Isn't it magnificent?" he seemed to be saying.

"It's a demon!" she screamed.

"What?"

"A demon!"

He grinned and shook his head, pointing at the volcano behind her, indicating that it was impossible to hear her against all this noise. Alyx looked round. All over the edge of Mount Koroit were small groups of Tari in night dress or festival clothing, watching with great enjoyment as the volcano spewed smoke and hot ash into the air. A couple of them waved their arms using magic to protect themselves from falling rocks or to redirect the rivulets of lava that were seeping over the side of the crater.

"How can they!" cried Alyx. No one could hear her over the roaring, but Serge was up now and Yundi and Jindabyne too. They shared her bemusement - except for Yundi who seized Alyx's arm and began to pull her away down the slope.

Suddenly the roaring of the volcano stopped leaving a strange silence punctuated only be the pattering of small hot stones on the ground.

Then the whole mountain gave a deafening crack and a lurch as if it had jumped to one side. Alyx was pitched forward into the dirt again. Serge and Yundi tumbled down on top of her.

Silence.

So quiet was it that Alyx could hear birds twittering in the forest at the bottom of the mountain. So quiet was it that she could hear, with perfect clarity, a soft crackling that sounded like sea-foam dissolving.

She looked up and saw thick grey-blue slime oozing out of a crack in the side of the crater. It looked like the finger of something huge and formless, a dark jelly-like mass that was rearing up out of the broken mountain. It seemed to be melting the rock beneath it.

Smothering despair came down on Alyx just as it had in the cavern when the demon had first appeared. She and Serge gripped each other and gaining strength from the contact, shook themselves and struggled, panting, to their feet. All around the Ermora Tari were standing still, all laughter frozen on their lips as they stared hollow-faced at the slime.

Others were moving. Yani and the other Tari were running away down the slope.

Serge tried to pull Alyx after them, but she shook him off.

"No!" she cried. "We have to fight!"

Her own voice sounded unconvincing, but she knew what had to be done even though it felt hopeless. She reached down to a Tari, a young male mage who was sprawled on the ground, head raised, staring forward at the horrible thing in the mountain.

"Please!" she begged, shaking him. "You have to get up. You have to fight it. Please!"

"Leave him!" shouted Yundi, heading off up the slope. "We have to tell the others."

"There's nothing we can do," shouted Serge, catching Yundi's arm.

"We have to tell them!" Yundi's face held absolute conviction. "Quickly. They're already doing it wrong."

The gap in the mountain side was becoming wider and wider as the thing inside it reared upwards. Its smooth slick surfaced was like leech's and like a leech, its giant head quested the air. Alyx could see Jindabyne, Syndal and the other Tari mages from the cavern throwing bolts of magic at the creature. Green fire crackled as the bolt hit the slick blue-grey mound, but there was no sign that it had done any damage.

"They're making it stronger," screamed Yundi. "We can't use magic on it. We have to tell them. I've seen it. We have to dig. We have to surround it. Starve it. I've seen it."

Serge held hard to Yundi's arm, stopping him from running back up the slope, clearly not sure whether he believed him or not. Alyx had no such doubts. The energy of hope infused her.

"Come on then," she cried, pulling Yundi away from Serge.

They ran up the now broken slope, ducking behind Tari staring upwards in horror and jumping over others who lay still on the ground, many of them curled into foetal balls. Serge came pounding along behind them.

The thing oozing from the mountain appeared to be twisting round, turning in the direction of the magic.

Alyx and Serge screamed at the mages to stop, but Yundi wisely saved his breath for running until he saw his brother. As he reached him, Kulde turned, lowering his head and listening to what Yundi had to say. Then Kulde and Yundi racing towards the other mages shouting instructions.

"We have to surround it! We have to contain it."

The things shadow fell over them. It was rearing up, higher and higher, like a huge wave rearing up out of the sea. It's mass filled the whole crack behind it - a crack that was widening, the crater's sides dissolving against the thing's slimy flesh.

"Sweet life," cried Diyar. "How are we going to surround that? We need help. We have to wake some of the others."

A movement caught Alyx's eye.

"Look!" she cried.

At the bottom of the mountain, a line of people were stumbling out of the forest, moving stiffly and looking dazed. They wore long white robes and the hair of many of them was white with age.

Alyx knew immediately where they must have come from.

"The spirit cave! The sleepers are awake!"

"Look out!" shouted Diyar. "It's going to fall! Run!"

Alyx and Serge took to their heels. The ground shook as something crashed down behind them. A mass of grey-blue jelly, as tall as a house and as wide as two, wobbled on the ground. Another mass was looming wavelike up out of the earth behind it. The crackling sound of foam bursting was deafening now and Alyx realised that it was the sound of the earth beneath the Abyssal creature dissolving. Through the dark mass of jelly, she could see the bodies of Tari who had been transfixed by the thing and had been engulfed as it fell. They were dissolving too, flesh falling apart as chicken boiled in soup falls apart, only much more quickly.

But hundreds of figures in white were running up the slope past them. These newly awoken Tari knew exactly what to do. Later Alyx learned that they had dreamed of this moment again and again as they lay asleep in the spirit cave. When they awoke they were immune to the horror of the Abyssal for in their dreams they had already felt and overcome the despair it caused.

Thus had the life spirit moved to save itself.

493

They swarmed around the Abyssal mass, using magic to blast out large trenches, cutting runes into the earth banks, casting defensive barriers over the top of the thing and drawing those Tari still overwhelmed by horror down the mountain side. Watching them, Alyx felt a heavy burden finally lifting from her shoulders.

Chapter 31

From the opening to the spirit cave Ezratah watched Marigoth sleeping. He remembered the time he had lain here and how the golden light of the life spirit had burned away painful memories and bad deeds, bringing peace and cleansing. Marigoth looked peaceful - pain lines smoothed away from her face.

Not so Malov who lay nearby writhing and muttering. As the golden light cleansed you, you were forced to face every past wrong you had ever committed against the life spirit and to experience it as if that wrong had been done to you. Which would mean a world of pain for Malov. Ezratah almost felt sorry for the little bastard. Almost.

"And they will be truly separated after this is finished," he asked of the mage who stood by the cave door.

"Yes!" said the mage emphatically. "Nothing of the Abyss can survive light of the Life Spirit. The white and gold robes of a Spirit Cave Guardian hung on her skeletal body. She had clearly lost weight during her own long sleep in the spirit cave. Now her eyes shone in her lively face. Hard to believe that she had once been too depressed to bear the world outside the cave.

"That's the third time you've asked that question," said

Mathaman, nudging Ezratah.

"Perhaps it's time you came away and stopped pestering the Guardians," said Syndal, taking his arm. "There's nothing you can do here until she wakes up."

"Unless you're going to join her in spirit sleep," added Mathaman.

"Oh no!" said Ezratah. "Once was quite enough, thank you. Spirit sleep is too rich for my small Mirayan mind."

Gently but inexorably, Syndal drew him out of the cave. He knew he should go with her. He took one last look at his beautiful Marigoth.

"Do you think she will be the same Marigoth?" he asked wistfully.

"After what she went through I don't see how she can be." Mathaman frowned.

Ezratah sighed. "If only she doesn't become serious and responsible."

Syndal laughed. "Life forbid that that should happen!"

"We can only wait," said Mathaman. "At least she won't want to kill herself any more."

Ezratah nodded. "That would be more than enough."

"Trust to the life spirit's healing," said Syndal. "It will do more for her than you can. Come and join the others! Rest! Have some food!"

Yani was arguing with another woman outside the spirit cave.

"But he's Wolf Madraga's son. I can't bear it." It sounded as if the strange woman was crying.

"It's Alyx's life."

"How could she?"

"But it was never Serge's fault. And he's a nice boy. I know it's difficult, but..."

Yani's voice faded as the woman turned on her heel as if to storm away and came face to face with Ezratah. Ezratah had never seen her before. With alarm, he realised he was looking at Elena Mori, the fatal beauty, the woman whose looks had destroyed Mirayan dominance years ago. Even though he'd read her mind for Lev Madraga he'd never seen her face before.

He and Elena stared at each other wide-eyed. She was very good-looking but he didn't feel any surge of feeling at the sight of her.

"Ah shit!" sighed Yani. "Marigoth's going to kill us."

"No," said Elena, looking searchingly into his eyes. "He's not affected. Maybe it's because we're in Ermora. No one seems to notice me here." She sniffed, straightened herself up, wiped the tears from her eyes and was suddenly every inch a Queen.

"How is my sister, Ambassador Karanus?"

"The cave Guardians are very hopeful."

"Thank you Ambassador." She turned and strode away.

"Elena," called Yani.

"No! Leave me alone! I need to think about this!" She disappeared among the trees.

"Is something wrong?" asked Ezratah.

Yani had put her hand over her eyes. She shook her head.

"No. Just some... unexpected news. Thank you Ezratah."

"Come on!" said Syndal, taking Ezratah's hand.

As he let her draw him away through the sweetly-scented forest toward the volcano, he was astonished to discover that it was morning. When had that happened?

"It used to be a wonderful mountain," said Mathaman sadly as the trees thinned.

The tall volcanic cone had gone. Now the earth sloped down into a wide caldera filled with a seething grey-blue whirlpool. Had the whirlpool been formed of water, sun would have glinted on it, but the slug-slick surface of the Abyssal did not glint. It absorbed light, consuming it just as it would have consumed everything else in the living world had it not been contained within the caldera by Tari magic.

Great waves rose from the whirlpool's centre and, as Ezratah watched, a geyser of dark liquid shot up.

"Look out!"

But the liquid crashed against an invisible barrier above it, was stopped by it and ran down the inside, showing the barrier's domed shape.

"We've put defensive spells over it and below it now," said Syndal. "The thing is entirely contained. We could never have defeated it, but stuck in there, its own hungers will consume it. Rather an elegant solution, don't you think?"

"Yes!" said Ezratah, feeling guilty. "I should have helped you instead of fussing so much about Marigoth. I put my individual happiness above the greater good. That's not serving the life spirit," he said sadly.

"On the contrary, the greater good is made up of individual happiness," said Mathaman. "If you examine the life spirit within you, you'll see that it's so."

"Any way there were enough of us that we could spare you," laughed Syndal. "Stop being miserable and look at us all!"

All around to edge of the caldera sat hundreds of Tari, watching with set faces as the Abyssal churned like thick soup inside the wide depression. A low humming rose for their ranks, just two notes up and down and up again. They swayed back and forth.

The sight made Ezratah shiver.

"They look like they're willing it to die. Like vultures."

"Well, so we are," said Syndal. "The effort to keep it contained takes most of Ermora's strength. It's a powerful creature."

"We're the righteous in this," protested Mathaman. "We have contained the Abyssal which that fiend set free and stopped it consuming this island and maybe even the world beyond."

"How could one ordinary mage, with the sacrifice of a mere four life spirits, even if two of them were powerful Tari life spirits, have let such a powerful thing out of the Abyss?" marvelled Ezratah.

"I wondered that too. Lev Madraga thought he would have to give them ten Tari lives with all the life spirit that contained. That was how much they told him to pay.

"But I was always told that demons are great deceivers. And their hunger knows no bounds. I think this one just asked for as much as it thought it could get, when in reality a much smaller blood sacrifice was all that was needed for it to break into our world. The wonder of it is that with the Tari's attention elsewhere, no one has let such a creature through before."

"This is a fortunate day," cried Syndal. "No, Mathaman, hear me out! I know Mount Koroit has been destroyed and that abomination has been let loose on the world, but today as we strove to contain it, I realised that this was what we Tari were made for. I think all the Tari, both Guardians and Ermora Tari, did. When this thing consumes itself with its own hungers and is gone, I'm certain the Ermora Tari will come out of their seclusion."

Mathaman smiled at her. "Perhaps," he said. "Working for good is no easy task. There's much discouragement. Will our Tari be able to resist that?"

He pointed to a place under the trees.

"Here are the others! Sit with them, Ezratah and promise you'll eat something. I have a mind to join the singers."

Close by sat Jindabyne with Olga cradled in her arms, surrounded by all the other Outlander Tari. The outlander Tari had joined the swaying and humming, but Jindabyne was simply rocking Olga back and forth, both of them with eyes peacefully closed.

Behind her sat Serge, Alyx and those two odd young Tari brothers, Kulde and Yundeman. They were completely focused by an animated discussion.

Ezratah sat down nearby, and suddenly finding himself ravenous, took a piece of bread from the basket in the centre of the group. As he ate he listened to the young people.

"But surely it must be able to escape further down," said Serge. "It might get into the earth's very core and eat it out."

"It's contained below too," said Yundeman, the funny little lad who seemed to know all about it. He was standing and waving his hands, as if giving a lecture on Abyssal masses in ruined volcanic cones.

"Those runes that were carved all over the inside of the

mountain, that's what they were for. This afternoon the sleepers drew on them to trap the Abyssal in the cup of the mountain."

"But they were carved hundreds of years ago," cried Alyx.

"I know. But the life spirit - it sees everything, past, present and future. Our ancestors put those runes there as foundations for Ermora *and* to protect it from the Abyss and today they have served both their purposes."

"Hard to believe they could have had such forethought," marvelled Serge.

"Ermora is a centre of the life spirit. The Abyss seeks to consume life. It is a logical target for creatures of the Abyss. Prophecy has told us this again and again."

Serge shrugged. "I just can't bring myself to believe in prophecy."

"That doesn't matter," shrugged Kulde.

"But you must believe," cried Yundi. "How can you not? Look at all we've seen! Hasn't the Warbird reined in the people of the dragon and hasn't a demon fire burned towards Ermora?"

"Hardly a fire," said Serge. "More like a disgusting demon sludge." He pulled a face as he looked over his shoulder at the muck raging round inside the caldera.

"It started with fire," insisted Yundi.

"And the last bit," said Kulde. "Little Olga over there will become a great queen of the Mirayans and bring peace to both the Seaganis and the dragon people on Yarmar. That seems pretty obvious."

Ezratah shook his head. He could see no way such a thing could come true. Mirayans would never follow a woman.

"That's not what the last bit means," cried Yundi. "Alyx is the melded child and she and Serge, who are both heirs to thrones, are going to get married and live happily ever after and breed more melded children between them. Thus bringing peace in clasped hands. Obviously a marriage."

Ezratah dropped his bread in astonishment and stared

at Serge and Alyx. What was this?

Serge put his hands over his face and groaned.

"You don't have to!" snapped Alyx angrily.

"No!" cried Serge. "It's not that at all. It would be a delightful fate." He put his hand out and took Alyx's. "I can think of nothing I would like more. Truly."

Alyx smiled and looked away, confused and overwhelmed.

"But I'm not heir to any throne," said Serge. "The Dukedom of Lamartaine is in ruins and chances are the Seagani will want a Seagani leader now. I have nothing to offer but myself and that's hardly enough for the Forest Queen."

Alyx turned to him. "That's more than enough for me!" she said softly, shyly.

Serge kissed her hand.

For the second time that morning Ezratah stared wide-eyed at someone. Now he understood what Elena and Yani had been arguing about. Alyx couldn't possibly... Not with Wolf Madraga's son. The son of the man who killed her father and forcibly married her mother.

He remembered Yani's words. There was no way the past was Serge's fault. But poor Elena. How would she bear it? And yet... The diplomat in Ezratah came to life. Without the history between the two families, it would have been a logical match. A sensible peace-bringing match between Mori and Mirayan, which brought both personal and political happiness at the same time. And they were both fine young people and should have a chance at happiness.

"The Seagani have always been a contentious people, said Ezratah. "Chances are that they will still need an outsider to adjudicate amongst them and Serge may still get his Dukedom back."

They all turned and looked at him and he saw the anxiety in Alyx's face. She must be aware of how this would affect her mother. Ezratah smiled at her reassuringly at her, already thinking of ways to smooth the way to the match.

"Chances?" cried Yundi. "Who knows how the prophecy will come to pass? But I am certain that Alyx and Serge will marry. I have seen it! And I am a Dreamer!"

The End

ABOUT THE AUTHOR

Jane Routley was born and lives in Melbourne, Her first three books – Mage Heart, Fire Angels and Aramaya were first published by Harper Collins. They have since been reprinted in ebook format by Clan Destine Press and in paperback by Ticonderoga Publications as The Dion Chronicles. Fire Angels and Aramaya both won Aurealis awards for Best Fantasy Novel.

As Rebecca Locksley, she published The Three Sisters which concerns the Miracle Sisters. It has been reissued by Clan Destine Press in Ebook. .